The Nemesis Crystals

Book One of the Blade Files

The Nemesis Crystals

Book One of the Blade Files

by

Daniel Allen Butler
and
C. Scott Bragg

Dan's Dedication

This one's for you, Mo –
against my better judgment, mind you,
but I like to live dangerously....

Scott's Dedication

To you, the readers.
Without you, I'd still be doing this,
but it'd be one hell of a lonely road to travel.

A Note from the Authors

When the original edition of *The Nemesis Crystals – Book One of The Blade Files* was released in 2016, the authors had planned to follow up in a timely manner with additional novels in the series. However, circumstances, both personal and professional, made it impossible to do so. As a result, some of the "world building" that was foundational to the original story was rendered obsolete by events in the real world, and required that the story be adjusted to accommodate them. The authors are now pleased to present this new edition as the definitive version of *The Nemesis Crystals* and hope that you, the reader, enjoy following this story of Blade, Hobbes, Spazz, Raven, Compton, Radome *et al* as much as we enjoyed creating it.

The Nemesis Crystals

Prologue

The match scratched noisily across the matte-black tabletop, the noise unnaturally loud in the small, quiet room where two men sat facing each other across that same table. It sputtered then flared, and the hand holding it lifted the flame to the tip of a long, dark cigar. Bridelow's gaze moved past the cigar to the face of the man lighting it. *Odd*, he thought, *there's nothing particularly unusual about that face.* Even, regular, but unremarkable features, a strong jaw, hazel eyes that gave off a disinterested, almost distracted look – a person had to be extremely perceptive to be able to tell the left one was not the eye the man had been born with. A full head of short, dark brown hair, a neat, closely-trimmed beard and mustache that were peppered with bit of salt. An almost *ordinary* face, one that most people would never look at twice. It was hard to believe that its owner was one of the most dangerous men in the world.

Which, of course, was why, at that moment, Brian Bridelow was absolutely terrified.

"Right then, one more time from the beginning." The man's voice was surprisingly deep, given that he was barely above medium height; despite a somewhat stocky build, he was not a particularly big man. The Scottish burr was unmistakable. "When exactly were Chastain and Chamblee killed, and who killed them?"

"The DisCom goons. They caught us while we were still in the data centre."

"Caught ye? Took ye by surprise, you mean? Ye hadn't posted a guard, somebody to watch your back?"

"We got in clean, we were still clean, we were getting ready to leave – nobody knew we were there!"

"Obviously somebody did, now, didn't they?"

"Well, yeah."

"What happened next? Tell me again."

"It was a running firefight getting out of the underground complex. DisCom didn't seem to know how we got in, so they didn't know how to block our way out – they just pursued us."

"Did ye lose anybody else on the way out?"

"No, we got out of the park, onto the freeway, and made it to Herndon. Once we got out of the tunnels, the DisCom goons had lost us completely."

"No pursuit?"

"None."

"Really?" Inwardly Bridelow cringed at the sarcasm dripping from that single word. His eyes flicked downward briefly to the HSc automatic lying beside the ashtray the other man was using; Blade had gently, wordlessly, placed it there when they sat down, an unspoken message in its presence. Slowly, Bridelow brought his gaze back to his interrogator's face. He held up his hands, palms out, in a sort of conciliatory gesture.

"Hey, aside from that run-in with the security people, everything went like clockwork. We got in, got the data crystals, got out. Yeah, the shit hit the fan at the data centre, but by the time we hit I-4, it seemed like it had all blown off. The only things that weren't part of the plan were finding Red in the data centre when we got there, and leaving Chastain and Chamblee behind. When we left, Red said she was coming with us. She held together pretty well in the firefight, so I decided, why not?"

The other man cocked an eyebrow, and Bridelow began to sweat as he continued. "I know what you're thinking. But when we got to the van, I did a complete RF scan on her, and it came back negative. And the van was shielded. Even Radome gave her a clean bill of health – and if she says someone or something is clean, it's *clean*. So even if Red was a plant, there's no way DisCom was tracking her. I know my job, MacLaren!"

At the tightening around the eyes of the other man – MacLaren – Bridelow realized he'd just made a tactical error. "Sorry. I meant 'Mister MacLaren.' Or should it be 'Major'?"

"Just go on. I can't say I'm enjoying this, but I am finding it extremely entertaining. Ye reached Herndon and...."

"And that's when things blew up, literally. The AV6 was on the apron, Ang had the engines fired up, and just as we cleared the terminal, it blew. I don't know what it was – I didn't hear any shots, didn't see any rocket exhaust, no laser flicker. It just blew. Then the DisCom goons opened up on us."

MacLaren drew heavily on his cigar. "Ye're sure they were DisCom?"

"No mistake. The black uniforms, you know – the Big Black Rat's Little Black Rats. They tried shooting the hell out of the van, but they were using pretty lightweight stuff – whatever they did know about us, I'm guessing they didn't know that the van had been combat-prepped. Polymer appliques, solid tires, armour around the engine, the works."

Bridelow took a long pull from the water bottle he had brought with him, then continued. "We busted ass out of Herndon, got on the East-West Expressway, hit the Turnpike and then I-75. We had about eight Rat-vans follow us onto the 75, I don't know where they came from, but at least one of them had some serious firepower. A .50-cal or larger – we took three rounds that were through-and-throughs, back to front, even with the polymer. One of them went through Esposito on its way. So then it was just the six of us – me, Compton, Radome, Hadley, Houston, and Red. The Rats didn't give up until we were past Gainesville – then they just went away."

"Any police pursuit? There was a lot of lead flying about."

"Are you freaking kidding me? In Florida? DisCom has at least half the law enforcement in the state on its books. If DisCom doesn't want somebody pursued, they don't get pursued."

"So the 'Rats,' as ye call them, apparently gave up and the police left ye alone as well?" Bridelow nodded. "Doesn't that strike ye as rather odd?"

"Mr. MacLaren, with all due respect, is there anything about this entire charlie-fox that *doesn't* strike you as 'rather odd'?"

MacLaren nodded an acknowledgment. "A point. Definitely a point. Go on. Were there any other...incidents before ye got to Atlanta?"

"None." Bridelow began to relax a bit, as MacLaren had taken some of the edge off his voice. "We crossed the Georgia line and dropped back to a sane speed – about 80. We'd been doing almost 130 up I-75 in Florida, but decided that whatever arrangement DisCom had with Florida police, we didn't want to attract the attention of the Georgia State Patrol, especially with a dead body aboard, so we did our best imitation of a van full of normal people."

"That must have been quite the challenge."

Bridelow bit his lip at the barb: the last thing he wanted to do was piss off this man. Nonetheless, he mustered sufficient courage to get a bit of his own back. "We managed it well enough to get all the way into Underground Atlanta without attracting unwanted attention from anyone."

"Tell me about that."

Bridelow closed his eyes and slumped in his chair, his head falling back on the headrest. "Everything was already arranged. We were supposed to meet Calvin here, at Bits – he owns the place. We left the van at Five Points and headed straight for the intersection of Upper Alabama and Pryor Streets."

"Ye left Esposito's body in the van?"

"Hey, it's kind of tough to be inconspicuous when you're carrying around a dead body, you know? What else could we do?"

"Nothing, really. But it does mean one more loose end I'll have to tie up eventually. Go on."

"We got about halfway there when about a dozen Rats closed in on us from behind. They were pretty blatant about it, too, they wanted to make sure we knew they were there. It didn't take long to figure out that they were the 'beaters' driving us toward something or somebody."

"That makes sense. Ye were boxed in inside an underground mall, with a very limited number of exits, only two directions in which ye could go. It's what I would have done. Go on."

"Well, they sprang the trap about fifty yards short of Bits. Another squad of DisCom goons came strolling around the corner at Pryor, right ahead of us and right in front of the club. You didn't need to be a rocket scientist to realize a fresh load of fecal matter was about to strike the rotary ventilator. If we could have turned it into a firefight, it would have been no problem, we were all packing and loaded for bear...."

"But...?"

"But there were too many civilians around, enough that some of them would have been caught in the crossfire, and that would have drawn too much attention. If it had been just us and the Rats we could have made it look like a gang brawl – APD would have just stood to one side to wait for the smoke to clear. But when civilians get involved in something like that, APD gets real twitchy. Seemed like the Rats knew that, too, because nobody drew down on anybody. They just closed in like they were looking for good, old-fashioned rumble."

MacLaren said nothing for few moments, just puffed on his cigar, seeming to stare off into the distance at something only could see. Finally, he turned back to Bridelow.

"Tell me about it."

"The Rats made a mistake. I think they're too used to busting the heads of teen-age hackers and strong-arming writers and animators to know how to really fight hand-to-hand. All five of us, Compton, Radome, Houston, Hadley, and me, are pretty well-trained and have a lot of experience – especially Compton."

"I know about Compton. Go on."

"You do? But how – " Bridelow began to ask, then stopped abruptly when he saw the other man's eyes narrow dangerously. Hurrying on, he said, "But it was Red who surprised the hell out of us."

Both of MacLaren's eyebrows shot up. "Oh?"

"For one thing, she definitely knows *savate*, and I think those shoes she's wearing have been modified for that. Plus she pulled this spring-loaded ASP baton out of her handbag, and then she just went to town on the Rats. Fractured skulls, broken arms and legs, a couple of busted kneecaps. God, is she *fast*! Let me put it this way, Mr. MacLaren, there's obviously a lot about that woman we don't know, but I do know I was glad she was on our side. The DisCom goons had us outnumbered about five-to-one, but it wasn't long before they were ones pulling back."

"I take it that events followed the same pattern as they had previously in this little escapade: just when ye thought ye were clear, something else went wrong." The edge was back in MacLaren's voice, but this time Bridelow didn't notice.

"We almost made it, dammit! Most of the civilians had scattered by then, and we were about to unload our hardware on the Rats when somebody somewhere opened up full auto on the entire corridor – they didn't care who they were shooting at. Us, the Rats, civilians, it was 'spray and pray.' About thirty, maybe forty, of Arasaka's *reisen*, it turned out. How they got there, how they knew we were coming, I have no idea. It was like they materialized out of thin air."

"And ye did what?"

"We ran for it. Hell, it was a twenty yard sprint to the front door of Bits. Compton had the security codes and got the doors open, the Rats and the Arasaka tried to rush us, but we got inside before they could get to us. Well, most of us did. Hadley went down right in front of the club. It was bad, it was pretty obvious that there wasn't anything we could do for him, so we left him there."

"Ye're rather good at that, aren't ye?" MacLaren asked coldly, and inwardly Bridelow cringed at the barely suppressed fury in the other man's voice. Wisely he said nothing in return but just took another long drink from his water bottle before he continued.

"Anyway, that's it in a nutshell. We've been holed up here, in these three safe rooms Calvin had built into the club, for just over eleven hours now. DisCom's storm troopers took over the club, the Arasakas set up a perimeter around them, and according to the newsfeeds APD has sealed off all access to the Underground and brought in SWAT teams. Nobody has gotten in or out – well, except for you."

"Except me. And if ye were watching the video feeds, you know that I left the Swatties alone, but there aren't nearly as many storm troopers and Arasaka out there as there were before I arrived."

Bridelow frowned, puzzled. "Yeah, well, that raises a question, doesn't it? Just how the hell did you pull off that trick? Getting in here, I mean."

"Let's just say it was messy, because none of the DisCom people or the Arasakas were really professionals, at least not in my book, and leave it at that."

"All right. But then how do we get out of here? I mean, you do plan on getting out of here, right?"

MacLaren leaned back in his chair, closed his eyes, and appeared to be lost in thought for several moments. Finally, he sighed, brought himself forward and looked intently at Bridelow.

"Yes, I do have a plan, and no, I haven't any intention of telling ye what it is, so don't ask."

"What do you mean you won't tell me? I'm the one running this op!"

"Brian, you stopped being the HMFIC the moment I walked through that door. Hobbes called me in to debrief ye, to learn what went wrong, where, and why, and then take over. And I've done just that. I've been in this line of work in one form or another for fifteen years, and as it happens, I have never – *never* – met anyone who could bollocks up by the numbers the way you do – if that's what ye really did! On the face of it, ye're a bloody walking catastrophe. It so happens that I know a bit more about what took place in Florida and here in the Underground that ye realize I do. I also know quite a bit about *you*. To all appearances, ye don't plan for contingencies, ye don't anticipate, ye just react. Ye don't think, ye *think* ye think. If there is a single thing ye did right in that entire extraction op, I don't know what it was. God help ye, ye could find a way to shoot yerself seven times with a six-shot revolver!"

Bridelow began to come out of his chair. "Now just a goddamn minute, MacLaren! I ran a good op! You know damn' well that sometimes none of the breaks go the way you want them to!"

"Sit down!" For the first time, MacLaren raised his voice, and the two words were as sharp and harsh as a pair of pistol shots. Daunted, Bridelow quickly settled back into his seat.

"It's possible that on a really bad day, the Keystone Kops coulda done a worse job of running an op than you did, but I wouldn't bet money on it. Ye didn't post an overwatch on the corridor outside the data centre at DisCom, so ye had no warning when the Rats arrived, which meant Chamblee and Chastain had their backs to the door when the bullets started flying. Ye brought out an unknown – Red, ye call her – when ye left the data centre, and assumed that because Radome said she was clean and that the van was a rolling Faraday cage she was harmless. Ye had no overwatch at Herndon, so ye hadn't a clue ye were walking into an ambush there. It never seemed to cross yer mind that there was a reason why DisCom stopped pursuing ye long before ye got out o' Florida, so ye merrily drove straight to Underground Atlanta, where upon arrival ye promptly swanned your way into yet another trap – the third such by my counting. There's an old saw of which you Americans are very fond: 'Once is happenstance. Twice is coincidence. Three times is enemy action.' That's what we have here. Ye're not incompetent, Bridelow, ye're a liar, a Judas, and ye tried to stab Hobbes in the back."

"That's enough, you son of a bitch!" Bridelow sprang up again, lunging toward the table. "I don't care who you are, I'm not going to let you accuse – "

The impending torrent of words was cut off abruptly as MacLaren's left hand swept up the HSc and leveled it at a spot between Bridelow's eyes. Bridelow froze in place, staring at the muzzle of the automatic: it never wavered, never quivered, never *moved*, and seemed to grow in size with each passing second. Very slowly and carefully he moved his hands away from his body, palms out, and raised them to shoulder level. MacLaren resumed speaking, his voice calm, almost conversational.

"I don't like people who betray their friends or their employers, especially when they betray both. I don't have the time – actually, *you* don't have the time – for me to explain why, so just take my word for it. But even worse than being a Judas, Brian, is the fact that ye aren't even very good at it. And I hate incompetence. To me, ye're the worst thing of all: an amateur."

The HSc fired twice in less than a second, and two holes appeared in Bridelow's forehead, the first at the bridge of his nose, the second a half-inch above the first. He collapsed like a marionette whose strings had been cut.

Barely two seconds later, Compton burst into the room, pistol at the ready. He found MacLaren standing behind the table, the still-smoking semi-automatic in his hand, staring down at Bridelow's corpse. Compton followed MacLaren's gaze and lowered his pistol, muttering as he did so, "Aw, shit, there goes my paycheck."

Part One

A Fistful of Crystals

Chapter I

"Blade, I need your help. I just killed my wife."

That got his attention. *Really* got it.

He hadn't wanted to take the call when Sandy, his major domo, announced that it had come through. At that moment, he was lying on his back, replacing the right rear trunnion of a 1972 Triumph Spitfire, one of the quartet of venerable British sportscars he owned. It was just on seven o'clock in the evening and he wanted to finish the job tonight so he could take the little two-seater out for a jaunt along the roads and lanes of the Highlands in the morning. Dawn comes very early to Scotland in mid-August, and he wanted to be on the road by sunrise. But when Sandy informed him that the call came from a "Mr. Hobbes," Blade thought the better of telling him to call back. Pushing his way out from underneath the rear of the Spitfire, he got to his feet, quickly wiped the worst of the grime from his hands, and took the receiver from Sandy, who stood patiently by, holding the cradle – the telephones in Mont Creag House were all antiques.

"What?"

"Blade, I need your help. I just killed my wife."

Blade was momentarily non-plussed: for of all the reasons Hobbes might have to contact him, this was the one he never expected to hear.

"I think ye better explain that to me," he said slowly, "in a wee bit more detail, Hobbes."

"I didn't murder Kim, if that's what you're thinking. She's technically not dead, at least her body isn't, but her mind is gone – she's in an incredibly deep coma. And I think it's because of a mistake I made." Blade quietly noted the air of desperation in Hobbes' voice in that last sentence. He sat silent for a moment or two, perplexed, wondering just Hobbes though he could do about the situation.

"You still there, Blade?"

"I am, though I confess I have no idea how ye expect me to be able to help ye."

"I want you to get her mind back for me."

At this Blade took the receiver away from his ear and looked at it in disbelief, certain that either he had badly misunderstood what Hobbes had said, or else the other man, perhaps unhinged with grief, had done his nut. It would be best for Hobbes, he decided, if he were let down gently.

"Hobbes, I really don't think I've got the skills or the qualifications for that. Do ye think ye might –"

"Blade – David – you are precisely the person I need. I'm sending you a data packet right now that will explain everything to you. It's both a lot simpler and a lot more complicated than you think it is, but believe me, there's nobody else who can do what I need done – I mean it. You'll see why when you read through the packet. Help me, Blade, you're my only hope."

----------------xxxxx----------------

"– you're my only hope." With that, Calvin Coleridge, whom Blade had somewhat cryptically nicknamed "Hobbes" when they first met years before, broke the connection and sat back in his chair with a sigh. *That was well done*, he mused, *I dangled the bait, and once Blade reads what's in the data packet, the hook will be set. Now, if he just doesn't get too curious....*

Everything Calvin told Blade was true, but there was a rather large difference between telling the truth and telling the *whole* truth. Yes, Calvin's wife Kim was clinically brain dead, and yes, it was due to a mistake Calvin had made, and yes, Blade was probably the only person in the world who could help him at this moment in his efforts to recover from that mistake. And the entire content of the data packet was true – as far as it went. But...there were things Blade didn't need to know and, if Calvin had anything say in the matter, would never learn. The Scot had a highly-developed – sometimes over-developed, Calvin thought – sense of ethics and morality, and he could get rather prickly when he found himself in circumstances where either were engaged. There was no doubt in Calvin's mind that Blade would be considerably less than enthusiastic about the work Calvin and Kim had been doing, should he learn of it, and Calvin had once witnessed the consequences of Blade's...disapproval.

Calvin liked to think of himself as more...flexible in his thinking, embracing the idea that rules were put in place to be strictly followed so that when the time came to break them, one could recognize the moment. It was a concept that had a certain efficiency to commend it, save for the fact that as time passed he became increasingly convinced that he alone possessed the required intelligence and insight to know when such a moment had arrived, and so imposed a rigid system of protocols and procedures in his company's research facilities. It was an attitude which Kim, who was easily his intellectual equal, found increasingly restrictive and chafing; still, her rebellions were always relatively minor, though pointed, and usually verbal, and it amused Calvin to imagine that he was exercising his "flexibility" when he allowed Kim the occasional small victory against his otherwise inflexible guidelines. Then Calvin broke two of his own rules – by omission rather than commission – and suddenly his "flexible" thinking didn't appear to be so attractive after all.

Dammit all! Dammit to hell! Why didn't I make that copy of the baseline scan when I had the chance? he chided himself bitterly for perhaps the thousandth time in the past ten days. *Why didn't I lock out the scanner in the first place, so Kim couldn't use it by herself? Shit....*

Nearly losing Kim forever was bad enough, but when he thought he had the situation in hand, accident had piled on mistake which in turn combined with misfortune to produce a near-disaster. Calvin stood on the brink of a catastrophe, not merely a business calamity, but a personal cataclysm as well. Kim was more than just his wife and colleague: she had been his perfect opposite, the even to his odd, the yin to his yang. For Calvin she had brought a balance to a brilliant but seriously unbalanced life, one that was for the first time in a decade threatening to again spin out of control. Blade truly was his only hope: of all the people he knew, only that extraordinarily dangerous Scotsman possessed the skills, the ruthlessness and the discretion Calvin needed to recover from the consequences of his own folly. If Blade succeeded – and he had to succeed! – Calvin would owe him a huge debt. And that created its own set of problems, because he hated being indebted to anyone for any reason.

----------------XXXXX----------------

Once Hobbes broke the connection, Blade thrust the receiver at

Sandy, then began idly pacing, cleaning the remaining grime and grease from his hands with a shop cloth, lost in thought for several moments. Finally he stopped, tossed the cloth into a dustbin, and said simply, "I'll be in my study."

That study was a fairly expansive room, lined on three walls by tall bookshelves, mostly filled with the thousands of books Blade had collected – and, more importantly, read – over the years, though a handful of shelves held the model ships and armour that he loved to build, lavishing on them untold amounts of time, effort, and attention to detail. Settling himself in at the large, oversized flat-topped desk that sat in the centre of the room, he quickly accessed his email server and found the communication from Hobbes. The decryption was swift and Blade was soon poring over the information sent by his friend in America, idly stroking the fur of his cat, Wellington, who was comfortably sprawled across the desktop. The email was, Blade thought, fascinating reading, as much for what it didn't say as what it did.

Blade spent an equal amount of time reading between the lines as he did assimilating the information itself in the data packet. As Hobbes recounted it, Kim had somehow been reduced to a vegetative state – clinically brain dead – although he was noticeably sparing of the details of exactly what had happened and how. According to Hobbes, there were prototype AR and VI programs he'd written that, theoretically at least, had the potential to revive Kim. The problem was that the only existing copies of those programs had been stored on a set of memory crystals – which were stolen just days after Kim's accident.

According to Hobbes, he was certain as to who was responsible for the theft, as well as where the crystals were taken, and had sent what he fondly termed an "extraction team" to recover them. That particular stunt had, however, gone rather spectacularly south and now the extraction team itself needed to be extracted from a rapidly-deteriorating situation. Blade blew a gust of air past his lips as he pondered the details that Hobbes had provided – as well as those he hadn't.

DisCom.... All right, I can see that their involvement makes sense. But Arasaka as well? Blade sighed quietly. The more thought he gave it, the more unsettling he found Arasaka's presence in the mix. *There's a deeper game here than just a brain-dead wife and some missing property.... Hobbes damned well knows what buttons to push, doesn't he?*

It so happened that Blade knew things, as well: for example, he knew that the financial resources of Hobbes' company, Cogito Orbis, were being stretched to their limits by Hobbes' near-obsessive adherence to protocols and procedures. His relentless pursuit of perfection was the reason why Cogito Orbis hadn't released new software or hardware in over three years – Hobbes still hadn't truly learned that perfect is the enemy of good. It also happened that Blade knew Kim well enough to understand that in her professional relationship with Hobbes, she was by far the more dynamic partner, and that she openly chafed under her husband's devotion to what she once described as "endlessly crossing imaginary t's and dotting non-existent i's." The short form was that Hobbes preferred to think, while Kim preferred to do. Blade was fairly confident that what had happened to her – whatever it was that Hobbes very carefully didn't explain – was the consequence of her doing something impulsive. That was ominous, for in Blade's world, "impulsive" meant "careless," "careless" meant "stupid," and "stupid" meant "dead."

"Blade," more correctly known as Major Sir David Ian Andrew MacLaren, KT, KCVO, DSO, MC (Bar), Retired, formerly of the re-established Royal Highland Regiment (Black Watch), strongly disapproved of anything which resulted in someone becoming needlessly dead. He was particularly put out by people whom he deemed "amateurs" – possibly the most devastating pejorative in his vocabulary – those who were unable to discern the difference between a "rash act" and a "calculated risk." In that sense, Kim had sometimes been numbered among the rankest of amateurs – most recently, to all appearances, in this latest incident.

What caught and held Blade's attention was finding Arasaka to be a player in this particular fracas. On the face of it, there was nothing there to draw Arasaka's attention: the giant Japanese manufacturer was producer for light, medium, and heavy industry, and also had a highly profitable branch that made small arms used by law enforcement and private security agencies around the world. The company also ran its own security service, which was just short of a private army, and that was what perturbed Blade the most: if the tactical situation was in fact as Hobbes described it, then time was running out for the handful of men and women inside the safe rooms at Bits.

For over a decade the policy of Arasaka security was, when faced with a standoff situation where the opposition was trapped and outnumbered, to give its opponents twelve hours in which to decide whether to honourably surrender, which usually led to their execution, or honourably commit suicide. Once the deadline had passed, Arasaka would go in fast and hard, and there were never any survivors; it had become customary for local law enforcement to cooperate with them, the better to keep such incidents contained and avoid widening the potential for violence. It was a tradition with Arasaka, Blade never learned where or how it had come about, but the results were always the same. In the case of Hobbes''s "extraction team," the countdown had begun

"Right then, Hobbes," Blade murmured to himself, "let's run through this one more time and see if there's anything else ye can tell me that ye didn't mean to." Raising his voice slightly, he called out, "Alistair?"

"Yes, Sirr?" a disembodied voice with a strong Glasgow accent answered.

"Run the contents of this packet from Hobbes through the Bombe and Colossus, will ye? See if there is anything buried inside it – anything – that I should know about, any additional data, that is, along with anything that shouldnae be there."

"Right, Sir. Will nae take me but a jiffy." Hardly a second passed before Alistair spoke again. "The wee bugger's clean, sir. There's nae onything embedded in it onywhere, and no parasites. It's been shunted all over the bloody world aboot three hundred times, mind ye, as if yer Mister Hobbes did nae want onyone tae know where it was goin' or frae where it came. He used that one-time comm address cypher ye gave him a while back – the one Miss Raven cobbled up for ye – so it's as clean as a whistle and as safe as hooses."

Blade smiled to himself. It was sometimes difficult to remember that Alistair wasn't human, he was a Virtual Intelligence, or "VI". While computer science's breakthrough to non-organic intelligence still eluded humanity, for weal or woe, the number of constructs like Alistair was constantly increasing. What made VI's possible was their incredibly complex logic- and decision- trees – and Alistair's core program was the most sophisticated such system yet created. Oddly enough – or perhaps not oddly at all – Sandy and Alistair got along like a house afire. Sandy Young, as Blade's major domo, was responsible for supervising the staff of Mont Creag as well as maintaining the security of the house and grounds of the estate; he was also Blade's personal armourer. Alistair was, as Blade liked to think of him, the concierge of Mont Creag. Sandy, the crusty retired CSM of the Black Watch, and Alistair, the disembodied voice created by a collection of electrons in some computer core, had slipped effortlessly into harness together almost from the beginning of their mutual tenure. Blade shook his head in wonder. *We live in a very strange world indeed.*

"Thank you, Alistair."

"Ye're welcome, Sirr."

Blade stood, went to a sideboard where a quartet of glasses and a half-empty bottle of Clyburn single malt stood waiting, poured himself two fingers of the light amber whisky, and took a healthy swallow before returning to his desk. *So the five survivors of the extraction team Hobbes dispatched to recover the data crystals are now trapped in, of all places, a nightclub in Atlanta Underground – a nightclub Hobbes owns. Because of who are the players in this little comedy of errors, the clock is ticking; in fact, just over three hours have already been run off. I wonder why Hobbes took so long to comm? This is going to be tight: if I'm to arrive to help them before time runs out and everybody in there who isn't an Arasaka goon gets killed , I'd best start moving* now.

"Sandy?"

"Sir!"

"Call the airfield, have them start preflighting the Bombardier. Tell Hamish to file a flight plan for Atlanta-Hartsfield. And get the F-1 stowed aboard. I want to be wheels-up in thirty minutes. I've got a job to do."

---------------XXXXX---------------

"So, do you think he's on his way yet, Mike?"

"Let me see, Calvin." There was briefest of pauses, more of an affectation that Mike – short for Mycroft, Calvin'sVI– had unexpectedly adopted once upon a time than a necessity. "Mycroft" and "Alistair" were akin in that they were both actually AP's – Artificial Personas, interfaces created to make the interactions between humans and VI's more efficient and intuitive – and like all

AP's, over time they had developed what could only be described as distinct personalities that bordered on actual identity.

"Yes, yes he is. According to Scotland's Air Traffic Control net, his Bombardier left British airspace twelve minutes ago, on a heading of 232 at an altitude of 8,000 meters – that would be 26,000 feet to you – and climbing. Airspeed was 517 knots."

"What's his ETA, then?"

"Assuming the weather forecasts are correct, he should be touching down at Hartsfield at approximately 11:06 PM."

"By the time he clears Customs, that'll give him less than two hours before the deadline expires."

"That is correct, Calvin."

"I don't like the idea of cutting it that close."

"I seem to recall that it was your idea to put off contacting him until it was almost too late." There was just the slightest hint of reproach in Mycroft's cool, cultured, Oxbridge-accented tenor.

"Meaning just what exactly?"

"Meaning that had the decision been mine to make, I would not have allowed personal fears and prejudices to inhibit me in making what is such an important, clear-cut, and, under the circumstances, ultimately inevitable decision."

"Sometimes, Mike, you talk too damn much like a machine!"

"And sometimes you think too much like a human."

Hobbes never really wanted to have Blade involved in the first place – in fact he had studiously avoided the idea. When Bridelow commed him to report on how the op went down, and told him that the five survivors were trapped at Bits with zero chances of escape or evasion, Calvin knew immediately that he needed the services of a top-flight solo. The list of those men or women who Calvin believed were capable rescuing his extraction team – at this point it was useless to pretend that the situation called for anything other than an out-and-out rescue – was short, and those who Calvin was able to contact were reluctant to the point of outright refusal to get involved. With on virtual eye on the virtual clock, Mycroft decided there was no more time for Calvin's dithering.

"You might as well stop beating around the bush, Calvin – we both know who it is that you really need."

"Who? *Him*?"

"Yes, him."

"God help us, because if I do, it's gonna get messy – and expensive."

"True, but with Arasaka now in the equation, the situation is very close to getting completely out of hand anyway. I know that you usually use Bridelow for this sort of thing, but since he's one of the five people trapped inside Bits, using him is... problematic, shall we say? And we both know that Bridelow isn't a quarter the operative that Blade is."

"Mycroft, you know as well as I do that bringing in that damn Scottish solo will add complications we really don't need. The man has too damn many connections, he's too damn smart, and he's too damn good at asking awkward questions. And if he somehow finds out about Bowman...."

"I was under the impression that he was also your friend – part of an ever-dwindling species, as I recall."

"He is, that's the problem. There are friends and then there are friends, and some of them get to know you too well. I know damn well that Blade can pull off this stunt, even if no one else in the world could. The reason I don't want him involved – why I've contacted damn near ever other top-shelf solo in the world *but* him – is because I can't be certain that if he starts asking the wrong questions, he'll back off if I tell him to. And if he doesn't back off, and gets that damn 'moral integrity' of his involved, I'm going to have even bigger problems."

"Calvin, have you forgotten that the clock is still ticking? Clearly no one else is interested in helping you with this little problem, and if you don't get Blade aboard *now*, he won't be able to get here in time to help you." Mycroft took a moment to allow the implications to sink in. "Should that happen, I don't believe your problems will be big at all – they'll be gigantic." Another pause. "So, what will it be?"

"All right, you win. Set up the call." Less than a minute later, Calvin was saying, "Blade, I need your help. I just killed my wife."

----------------xxxxx----------------

The Bombardier G7500 was just west of Ireland when Blade turned to his copilot, Hamish MacCollough, and said, "You have the aircraft."

Hamish immediately put both hands on the control yoke, gave it a quick, firm shake, and replied, "I have the aircraft." Blade nodded his thanks, unbuckled his harness, and stepped out of the cockpit and into the forward cabin. Immediately to his left – that is, on the right side of the cabin – was a small computer suite that doubled as a wireless communications link. Settling in front of it, he entered a comm number from memory and sat back to wait for a response.

It was not long in coming. On the monitor there appeared a heart-shaped face with a pair of huge, luminous, dark-brown eyes, framed by hair that fell about it in a mass of even darker, almost black, soft waves. A dimpled smile appeared below a straight, pert nose as the woman recognized her caller. There was the usual sharp but mercifully brief pang of regret he always felt upon seeing that face, and for perhaps the millionth time in his life, Blade was again reminded of the uncanny resemblance his friend Ligeia Parrish had to the actress Vivien Leigh.

"Hello, David! I see you're still keeping peculiar business hours."

"Ye would know as well as anyone, Ligeia, that my line of work doesn't allow for regular office hours."

"So you're working right now." This was a statement rather than a question.

"That I am. At the moment I'm somewhere over the Atlantic Ocean, assuming, of course, that Hamish hasn't gotten us hopelessly lost – "

"I heard that, Sir!" Hamish called back from the cockpit.

"– and I could use a bit of yer expertise, if ye have the time." Blade continued as if the interruption had never occurred, but Raven saw his momentary grin. "Our old friend Hobbes called me today asking for my help in a rather sticky situation he's in, and I was hoping ye might be able to tease out a bit more detail than I have from the data packet he sent me."

Ligeia Parrish's username was "Raven," her screen-name, "Sphinx." A generation earlier, she would have been, had she allowed such a thing to happen, recognized as one of the premier computer hackers in the world. Now of days, every would-be geek who cracked a security code or deciphered a password imagined himself to be a "hacker," so that the true meaning of the word *hacker*, with all of its subtexts and implications, not mention perverse prestige, had become hopelessly diluted.   In short, *hacker* had become hackneyed.

Instead, Raven was pre-eminent among what were known as *cyberghosts*, materializing and dematerializing effortlessly, gracefully, silently, but above all *invisibly* into, through, around and about computer systems in ways that would have seemed impossible to the casual observer. Five years previously, she and Blade had been involved in passionate romance, one that all of their friends were convinced would eventually lead to a marriage. But the romance had suddenly faltered then died for reasons that neither ever spoke of to anyone; today, they were the best of friends, and, as they still made a formidable team, frequently worked together.

"I'm assuming that you've already had Alistair go over the packet with a fine-tooth comb?"

"Indeed I have. Electronically, he found nothing that shouldn't be there."

"So what you want from me is more deep background and any dirt I can find clinging to this little incident?"

"Got it in one go, ye did."

"Then I'd best get started."

Blade sat back and watched Raven's fingers fly across her keyboards, at times swiftly shifting to her mouse or raising a wand to another screen he couldn't see. In less than thirty seconds, Raven announced, "Eureka!" and sat back with a satisfied smile on her face.

"Ye have something, I take it?"

"Yes...yes...here it is. It's in bits and pieces all over the place, though. Everybody is, for some reason, keeping this whole story very close to the chest. It hasn't made the national screamsheets, the state and local newsies are completely mum on the subject, and there's damned little about it on the Grid – even the government networks. FBI, Secret Service, US Marshals Office...." She made a face as if having just bitten into something sour. "Are their security programs this bad because they *want* us to see what's inside them, or are they just so stupid they don't know any better? Anyway, it looks as if somebody decided to suppress any news about it."

"'It' being exactly what?"

"At approximately 2:00 AM local time, there was an armed break-in at the DisCom Data Centre – their primary cybernetic R &

D facility, despite its name. There was an exchange of gunfire, there were fatalities, the perps – Calvin's 'extraction team,' obviously – were able to compromise DisCom security systems long enough to escape DisCom property.... Let's see.... An incident an hour later at a local airport...a civilian AV destroyed on the ground there, a vehicle identified as the one used by the team was spotted leaving the scene. An extended high-speed chase up the turnpike and I-75. Then the trail goes cold for a few hours, until a firefight breaks out inside Underground Atlanta at around 10:30 AM local time. Facial recognition software in the CCTV system identifies the extraction team. It takes a couple of hours to get everything settled down and sorted out, but by 1:30 PM the situation was this: the team was holed up in safe rooms inside Bits, a handful of DisCom security types had occupied the rest of the night club, and a small horde of Arasaka goons effectively took over the rest of the mall.

"Here's where it starts to get really interesting, though. At 1:30 PM local, Underground Atlanta was officially locked down tighter than a drum, on the orders of Atlanta PD. Anyone who was anywhere inside the mall is essentially trapped there. It has *not* been declared a hostage situation, however. *Arasaka* has set up its own security perimeter around the mall, with APD establishing a cordon of its own outside of that. Arasaka – and no one, apparently, is supposed to know about this – informed Atlanta Police at exactly the same time APD announced the lockdown that it was issuing a twelve-hour deadline to Calvin's team inside Bits, effective as of 1:30 PM local. Apparently they plan to go with their SOP once the deadline expires." She looked briefly offscreen. "That means you'll have about two hours' grace when you arrive at Hartsfield International."

Blade grimaced. "I don't like cutting things that close. Makes it dramatic as all hell, mind ye, but it doesn't leave a lot of room for error. That idjit Hobbes waited too long to call me in." He shook his head in exasperation. "Right then, what else have ye found? Can ye tell me anything about what happened to Kim? And have ye got anything on the extraction team?"

"Way ahead of you, David. According to hospital records – some of which are harder to crack into than most government databases – Kimberly Lynn Coleridge was very quietly checked into Emory University Hospital six days ago, her condition critical, diagnosis incipient brain death from unknown causes, prognosis poor. That much at least of what Calvin told you is true." For some reason, Raven never called Calvin "Hobbes," while Blade rarely called him anything but. "Calvin tried to keep it a secret, but a hospital still has to have records, and their security is rather pathetic. They ought to hire Calvin to write a new security suite for them – they can't afford me."

Raven scanned her information displays. "Toxicology was negative, there were no visible injuries of any kind, not even small contusions, apart from some minor hemorrhaging clearly associated with whatever mental trauma she experienced, so foul play has been ruled out by the Atlanta DA's office. Aside from her current vegetative state, all of her vital signs and organ functions are currently nominal." Raven fell silent for a moment, then murmured, "That's odd."

"You found something?"

"According to the hospital's monitoring systems, her EEG has completely flatlined, and yet her autonomic functions are still working. By every measure, Kim's not just brain dead, she should be clinically dead – but she's not.... What happened to this woman?" That last bit came out in a still, small voice, as if Raven was talking to herself.

"I'll have to come back to that later. Something tells me that it's important, but what and why eludes me at the moment. What you need to know about Kim right now is that her condition has begun to deteriorate: her autonomous systems – respiration, heartbeat, renal function – have begun slowing down. In a few days, she'll reach a point of no return. Even if they hook her up to a cardio-pulmonary bypass and dialysis, the damage already done to her systems will not only be irreversible, but they'll cause an eventual systemic collapse, and she'll physically die, whatever has happened to her brain. So while I can't understand why Calvin thinks you can help him, this makes his urgency a lot more understandable. I'm wondering if he's beginning to panic a little bit....

"Turning our attention for now to the 'extraction team' Calvin sent down to Florida, they're what you might call much of a muchness. This Compton fellow is an interesting chap – I'll send you his file, it makes for entertaining reading. Short version is that he's ex-U.S. Air Force Special Operations, has a lot of street experience, he's a pretty good solo, he's as honest as the day is long, and he keeps some really...remarkable company."

"'Remarkable' how?"

"He seems to have some sort of 'in' with every major urban gang east of the Mississippi River – he's got connections to almost all of them. But get this: he doesn't have a police record! Anywhere, under any name. It looks as though he manages to run with the hares and hunt with the hounds, as it were. He's been wired up with some rather serious cyberware, so he's probably an incipient head case. Keep an eye on him, in case he goes cyber-psycho. If he ever starts singing 'I'm a Little Teapot' or some such, you'll know he's finally cracked."

"I'll make a note of it. Do ye have anything on the rest of them?"

"It would appear that Chamblee and Chastain were little more than hired muscle. They had worked with Bridelow before, Chastain five times, Chamblee three. That's interesting...." Raven's voice trailed off and Blade could hear the sound of more keystrokes. "There are at least three instances, all in the last eight years, where Chamblee and Chastain went completely off the grid – I mean there is *no* record of them anywhere at any time – for long periods. I'm talking ten to fifteen months. And they did it simultaneously. There's no way of knowing if they were together when they did, although I wouldn't bet against it. I'll have to dig deeper there."

"Is that it?"

"Oh, no, I'm just getting warmed up. Esposito was a born wrench – if something broke he could fix it. Ha! Get this – he was actually a Scotsman, James Carlisle, but he used the streetname 'Esposito' as some sort of cover. Oh, I see why...he spent a few years as His Majesty's guest at Barlinnie. He tried to combine his mechanical skills with a set of sticky fingers and got caught. Anyway, it's not hard to see why he was part of Calvin's extraction team – a good handyman can be quite useful to have around."

"Well, if a Scot canna fix it, it's nae broke, lass...."

"Stifle yourself. Hadley – real name Paul Jacoby – is more hired muscle. Well, well, well, surprise, surprise – not! He was off the grid at the same times as Chamblee and Chastain."

"At my age, I don't believe in Santa Claus, the Easter Bunny, the Tooth Fairy – or coincidences like that."

"David, I'm five years younger than you, remember, and *I* don't believe in any of them either. More homework for me."

"What about Radome, Houston, and Red?"

"Radome – I know her by the way, although she doesn't know I do – is one of those birds who can build a death ray out of a pack of cigarettes, an LED, some chewing gum wrappers, a length of wire and a 'C' cell battery. She's the team's electronics and communications specialist. Her real name is Trish Crabtree. I think she's clean, at least she looks to be, but I'll make certain of it before I certify her as 100% fresh." There was a somewhat lengthy pause as Raven's eyes flicked back and forth between multiple screens.

"Houston – real name Elliot Ross – is something of the joker in the deck. He's a fairly accomplished solo in his own right, mainly works the southwest United States, the son of a Texas Ranger. Reading between the lines of the files I've been able to bring up on short notice, it appears that he tends to be more cooperative with American law enforcement than your typical solo." She lapsed into silence and Blade watched as she rhythmically tapped the nail of one forefinger against her front teeth – her "tell" that she was concentrating intensely. "I'm going to have to dig deeper into this, because it doesn't make sense for him to be there – everything that the 'extraction team' was doing was soooooo illegal that it's almost out of character for him to be part of it. Curiouser and curiouser...."

"Agreed. And Red?"

Raven frowned. "On Red, I've got nothing. And I mean *nothing*. Nada. Zero, zip, zilch. I can't match her to anybody in any database I can access anywhere. It's like she doesn't exist."

"Except that clearly she does."

"Except that clearly she does." She was back to tapping her teeth again, and a minute went by before she spoke again.

"There are one of two possibilities here. First, that she has undergone an incredible amount of body-sculpting to change everything about her that could be used as a physical identifier. Not impossible, but very, very expensive and time consuming. Second, that she – or someone, at least – has managed to erase every trace of her from every database on the planet. While I won't say that's completely impossible, I don't know of anyone, person or organization, that has the skills and resources to do that. Not even governments can do that, David."

Blade pursed his lips and let out a long, low whistle.

"Whichever it turns out to be, she or someone she's associated with or working for has expended a great deal of effort to conceal her real identity. As you say, curiouser and curiouser...."

"Which brings us to Bridelow. And he's a real piece of work, David. He's a solo-for-hire, just shy of being top-tier. This extraction op should have been a piece of cake for him – instead everything that could have gone wrong did go wrong. It could very well be that Demon Murphy showed up in the tunnels under DisCom and threw an enormous spanner into the works, but I doubt it. You see, Bridelow has worked for DisCom in the past, something I doubt Calvin knew about, and you know that as far as they're concerned, once a member of the Rat Pack, even by association, always a member of the Rat Pack. Plus, two of the times that Chastain, Chamblee and Esposito went off the grid, he did, too. You were just saying about Santa Clauses, Easter Bunnies, and Tooth Fairies?"

"So the person Hobbes put in charge of his little extraction operation may have been playing both sides of the fence?"

"If you truly believe it went down any other way, I understand the Americans have a bridge in Brooklyn they would like to sell to you."

"Ligeia, it looks as though I owe ye one – again. What'll it be this time? Dinner at Churchill's in the West End?"

"Make it a picnic in the Lake District and you have a deal. Bring the Healey."

"Consider it done. Can ye send me copies of everything ye've got so far?"

"It's on the way right now." Raven's tone suddenly grew very serious, as did her expression. She leaned forward and peered at the monitor earnestly. "Just one thing, David. Be careful – I mean *really* careful. DisCom or Arasaka alone are bad enough, but working in tandem, that's scary – it means a lot of firepower being brought to bear, maybe even Nakajima. But that's not what worries me. There's something about all of this that is making me very, very twitchy, as if I've just had a 'blink' moment. There are wheels within wheels within wheels in this that I haven't discovered yet. Calvin hasn't told you everything, or even the majority of it, but I don't think it's because he doesn't trust you. I think he's scared – of what I don't know, at least not yet. The stress analysis I ran on his voice nearly went off-scale in some places. And something tells me there are other players in this affair that even *he* doesn't know about. I can't tell you why I think that, call it a hunch, but you'd best watch your back. I've got a bad feeling about this, David."

As it happened, Mycroft's estimate of Blade's arrival time was off by only seven minutes, the Bombardier touching down at Atlanta-Hartsfield at 11:13. Hamish carefully taxied the aircraft over to Concourse F as Blade prepared to deplane. Once the jetway was in place and the cabin door opened, Blade strode straight through the terminal to Customs, where he was waved through in fairly short order, courtesy of a diplomatic passport, one of the consequences of that meeting with C several years earlier. Hobbes was waiting, alone, just outside Customs.

Blade saw immediately that his friend wasn't aging well. Short, rotund, he'd put on weight in the last several years, and he didn't wear it as well as once he might have done. He was going bald, and there was a pallor to his skin, with a scattering of unhealthy-looking red blotches here and there. Deep creases ran from his nostrils to the corners of his mouth, and his beard, which had always been immaculately trimmed, was now straggly and shot through with gray. But it was Hobbes' eyes that held Blade's attention, at once fascinating and disturbing. Wide, the pupils so dilated that the gray irises were almost invisible, they were haunted, filled with the look of a man being pursued by demons of his own making, but that he couldn't recognize. The physical changes Blade knew he could attribute to the passing years – Hobbes had never had a particularly robust constitution – but the fear in his eyes was something very recent. And something about it told Blade that it wasn't all because of Kim's accident.

"Well, Hobbes, ye look like hell – but then, ye never looked all that good to begin with."

"I suppose you're still wearing one of those Scottish skirts of yours and chasing sheep."

"Nice to know that some things never change, isn't it? Still, it's good to see ye, ye great lump." At that they shook hands.

"Is there someplace we can get a drink while I wait for Hamish to get my bags through Customs?"

"Not really, Blade, everything on this concourse closes at 11:00 or earlier. But never fear, I have a bottle of Clyburn waiting in the back of my limo – you can have one of your 'wee drams' there before you collect your car. I assume you brought the F-1?"

"I never leave home without it."

"Good, because you'll need it if you're going to get to Underground Atlanta before the deadline expires."

Blade glanced at his watch. "I've got just on two hours before that happens."

"Yes, you do, but I seriously doubt you're about to go swanning right up to Underground Atlanta in that Batmobile of yours."

"Ye know damned well the F1 was a production car."

"Yeah, they produced how many, a hundred?"

"I never said 'high-volume production car.'"

"Whatever. Anyway, the Blade I used to know would park that beast a few blocks away and take the time to look around, get a feel for the situation before he unleashed his own personal brand of mayhem."

Blade nodded in mock-sage agreement.   "Under the circumstances, I think that would be a wise thing to do."

"So do I. There's too much at stake, especially for me."

"I need a situation report, Hobbes. Knowing what happened in Florida yesterday and how yer team got caught in that nightclub doesn't do anything to help me get them out. I need to know what the situation is right now, the best tactical information ye have. First of all, are there any new players?"

"According to Bridelow, as of five minutes ago, nothing has changed since I commed you at Mont Creag House. Everyone, my people, the DisCom Rats, the Arasaka operators, even Atlanta PD, are sitting tight."

"And precisely who has these crystals ye want back so desperately"?

"Bridelow says that Red has them."

Blade cocked an eyebrow at Hobbes, who nodded in confirmation.

"She has them, Bridelow says she was the one who actually took them out of their docking station at DisCom, and she hasn't given them up. He says that after seeing her in action, he's not too enthusiastic about trying to take them from her."

"All right, at least we know *somebody* in there still has them. Now, tell me, just what *are* those crystals?"

"They're standard-design lattice-network memory crystals, 16 petabytes each."

"And they do what?"

"I think it best you don't know, Blade."

At that the Scot drew himself up, looked Hobbes squarely in the eye, and said, "In that case, I'll have Hamish file a flight plan for an immediate return to Glasgow – and ye'll get a bill for my time that ye wasted tonight."

"You wouldn't dare."

"Try me." There was a pause. "I came here as a favor to ye, Hobbes, but I'm not goin' into what amounts to a free-fire zone without knowing what's really at stake before I even reconnoiter the site. I'm not one of yer corporate flunkies ye can whistle up on a whim and say 'Bring me this trifle, this least of things.' Now, what'll it be – truth, or consequences?"

Hobbes tugged at his beard, as he was wont to do when anxious or upset, and thought hard for several moments. "You win. What's in them is a virtual world builder – a program that can interface directly with the brain and allow you to create virtual realities – whole virtual worlds – just by thinking them up."

"'Cogito Orbis' indeed."

"You never imagined that name was an accident did you?" Hobbes gave Blade a tart look. "Nothing I do is ever by accident. Anyway, it's still in the development stage, a prototype if you will, but I think it can help me unlock Kim's brain."

"Unlock –"

"Despite what the doctors are saying, I don't believe for a minute that, apart from autonomous functions, Kim is brain dead. I'm convinced – and there's some current research to back me up on this – that somewhere inside the human brain is the neural equivalent of a safe room, a 'panic room,' if you will, where the intellect and identity go when facing an overwhelming trauma, and that's where Kim's mind has gone. In theory, if we can create a virtual reality outside that safe room, one that doesn't in any way resemble whatever it was that drove her in there in the first place, then maybe she'll come out, and we can begin reintegrating her with her actual brain before her physical condition gets any worse."

"God knows I know next to nothing about neuroscience, but it sounds plausible. And it explains why yer so anxious to get those crystals back. Speaking of safe rooms, are yer people still in those safe rooms at yer nightclub?"

"Yeah, and DisCom's stormtroopers are still holed up in the club itself. The Arasaka goons are still holding a perimeter around the club and the mall itself. There are still a handful of civilians who got caught down there, trapped in some of the shops and bars. APD's cordon around the whole of Underground Atlanta is sitting tight – nobody's getting in or out. Bridelow thinks that everybody is waiting for the deadline to expire before anyone makes a move."

"Why did you wait so long to call me?"

"I had my reasons."

Blade looked at Hobbes expectantly, but the other man just shook his head.

"Have it your way, Hobbes." A pause. "Right then, I've got two hours to get in there before the balloon goes up. And if I don't...."

"Then Arasaka will jump first, and it'll get ugly. My people won't stand a chance in hell."

"And if you lose them, you lose the crystals."

"And if I lose the crystals, I lose Kim."

"Then I'd best go get them out of there."

Chapter 2

"Goddamned Americans."

The exclamation forced its way past the man's lips almost against his will. A big man, tall for a Japanese – he topped out right at six feet in height – he was powerfully built but moved with surprising grace. At this moment, his looming posture perfectly communicated the frustration he was feeling at having to wait to take action. He hadn't wanted this mission, considered it hasty and ill-conceived, and the likelihood of failure was, in his considered opinion, unacceptably high. But he was Hideki Nakajima, *Bumon rida* of Arasaka Corporation's *Keisatsu tai*, so the task had fallen to him and him alone, as would the consequences.

The outburst started his assistant, whose head popped up over the holo display of his computer deck. "Is there something wrong, Nakajima-sama?"

"No, Umori-rin, nothing is wrong – or at least, there's nothing *else* wrong that hasn't already been wrong for the past day and a half."

Saburo Umori, Nakajima's executive assistant, peered owlishly at his superior, his big dark eyes looking out through large, round, black-framed spectacles. Appropriately enough, as the shock of unruly black hair sitting above the spectacles and a tightly-pursed mouth perched below them created an uncanny image of a pensive owl, so much so that Nakajima had nicknamed Umori "*Fukuro*" – "Owl"– within days of the man coming to work for him.

"You still haven't reconciled yourself to this mission, have you?"

"No, and I doubt I will, even after it's over. I *despise* having to work within the United States, I *despise* having to cooperate with their law enforcement departments, and I *despise* Americans in general. They give ordinary, decent *gaijun* a bad name."

"You rail against the wind and waves, Nakajima-sama, and we both know it."

"That may be so, *Fukuro*, but the railing at least lets me vent my frustration." Grateful for the distraction, he turned away from the panoramic window that made up one entire wall of his top-floor suite in the Centennial Plaza hotel; he had found the view only mildly interesting, accustomed as he was to the garish vistas of Tokyo's nightscapes. "You know that I don't like operating outside of Asia. I don't like governments that won't get out of the way and let businesses do business. I can work in Europe: the Germans give us pretty much a free hand, since the PanEuroEcon is a German puppet, and everyone there but the British kowtows to Berlin. The whole world recognizes that where a Japanese goes, he is protected by the laws of Yamato – posture all they want, other nations know that their laws have no *real* authority over a Japanese national."

"All except the Americans."

"All except the Americans! They don't even realize that they're *gaijun*! They imagine that they are our equals, and demand that we act as such! They expect – they *demand* – that we honour *their* laws! They actually believe that corporate horseshit about the *Jukuko no kikan* being created by us twenty years ago to 'minimize violence in an increasingly turbulent business world.' They have the sheer, unmitigated gall to expect us to abide by our own policies! We wrote them, we can un-write them whenever and however we see fit, and no one should be able to gainsay us when we do! Instead, we're forced to stand idly by while the Americans self-righteously trumpet their platitudes of 'fair play' and 'due process.' What we should have done – what we should have been *allowed* to do – was move hard against Coleridge's people inside that nightclub as soon as we had them isolated there, and say the hell with the body count."

"You know as well as I do, Nakajima-sama, that if we did so, the Americans would retaliate. Not against you, but against Arasaka. The loss of face would be terrible, but even worse would be the practical consequences. The Americans are looking for any excuse to nationalize Arasaka's legitimate operations the same way they did with the Japanese and German automakers a decade ago – this is not news to you, I know."

"True, it isn't, and you're right, they are." Nakajima grimaced in agreement. While his habitual expression was one of bland indifference, his was not the stereotypical "inscrutable Oriental" visage: his face could be as animated as any Westerner's when he so chose. It was not, however, a remarkable face in any way. His regular, if slightly blunt, features, close-cropped black hair and bushy eyebrows rendered him indistinguishable from millions of other Japanese executives and industrial functionaries, a situation which Nakajima found perfectly suitable for his position and responsibilities. Flamboyance was for the *gaijun*, and Westerners' desire to be "noticed" was, in his opinion, far more of a liability than an asset.

"It's a pity that so much manufacturing moved back to the United States after the PRC broke apart," he went on. "They don't *need* us the way they used to."

"True, but then, neither do we really need them they way we used to," Umori reminded his master. "And if – when – this mission succeeds, it will only be a matter of time before they will need us more than they ever did before." He took a quick glance at the small chrono-window on his holo display. "In two hours this will all be over. Patience, Nakajima-sama, patience."

Hideki Nakajima was usually an incredibly patient man – usually. Raised in a culture that demanded self-discipline to a degree most Westerners found nigh incomprehensible, his self-possession was extraordinarily even by Japanese standards. His sixteen-year tenure as the Division Chief of Arasaka's Security Bureau had been marked by a succession of meticulously planned and methodically executed security operations, all of them hallmarked by seamless contingency planning and multi-layered strategies. Nakajima took great pride in watching his missions unfold like an origami puzzle, with an efficiently low profile and a minimum of violence, the results of his patient preparations.

But this newest operation, this *Yanki Jigyo,* or "Yankee Project," to secure the memory crystals so coveted by his corporate masters sitting on Arasaka's board of directors, allowed no opportunity for the sort of finesse and subtlety he favored. It was, in fact, an operational nightmare, one thrown together, as it were, in less than thirty-six hours, with what Nakajima considered woefully inadequate intelligence, and using whatever personnel were available in the United States – including mercenaries – or could be brought into the country on very short notice. There was no time for the careful selection of operatives whose talents and skills neatly dovetailed with the mission's requirements – he had to make do with whatever skills the available personnel had to hand. In short, this was a brute-force operation.

The urgency of the moment imparted to Nakajima by various

members of the board forced him into making these compromises and taking such shortcuts, both of which he abhorred doing. But the window of opportunity was very narrow, the crystals would only be out in the open, so to speak, for a few hours, so the risks had to be taken. Once those crystals were back in Calvin Coleridge's hands, taking them away again would become *very* costly in lives, money, and resources. As a rule, Arasaka was rarely over-concerned with the former, but was famously reluctant to condone the needless expenditure of the latter two. The fact that Arasaka designated its security personnel who were active in the field as *reisen* – "zeroes" – was an open acknowledgment that they were seen as empty ciphers and nothing more.

Compounding Nakajima's problems was his masters' refusal to tell him exactly why those crystals were so vital to them. Had he known their reasons, he might have had the opportunity to work angles or exploit personal weaknesses among Calvin Coleridge's people. Instead what he knew was little enough: nine memory crystals had been stolen from Cogito Orbis' main research facility by someone very senior in the company who had been suborned by DisCom. That person had disappeared less than twenty-four hours after the theft was discovered, and the crystals themselves had been spirited out of Atlanta, only to reappear in central Florida, in DisCom's Advanced Cybernetic Animation centre.

It was there, the corporation's senior executives decided, that Arasaka would make its move to secure the crystals, and ordered Nakajima to put together a *shinden* ("lightning") strike team – long on firepower and short on finesse – to raid DisCom and take the crystals. Nakajima gave the appropriate instructions, and soon his gaggle of mercenaries and *reisen* began descending on Orlando. At almost the last moment he learned that Coleridge's "extraction team" had gotten there first and were now in possession of the crystals; the same source that told him this also informed him that Coleridge's people were on their way to Atlanta, where they would meet Calvin at the nightclub, Bits.

There was barely enough time for Nakajima to recall his underlings and divert them north to the heart of Georgia; some of them were still in transit. A relative handful had arrived in time to be able to confront the extraction team when it arrived in Underground Atlanta: these were the Arasaka operatives who had opened fire during the melee with the DisCom Rats. Nakajima, complying with the terms of a private agreement between Arasaka and the United States government, had then informed the Department of Justice that he was invoking the *Jukuko no kikan*, the "Time of Contemplation," a sort of truce giving Coleridge's people twelve hours to decide whether or not they were prepared to surrender peaceably. The agreement had been an attempt by the Americans to reduce the increasing amount of corporate violence within the United States, much of which had for years been passed off to the American public as domestic terrorism or the actions of the South American drug cartels. It mattered little to Nakajima that the Americans had been quite scrupulous in observing the terms of the agreement when they were invoked. All he recognized was the fury he felt at the sheer scale and finality of the American response whenever *Arasaka* broke the terms of such a truce.

His corporate masters had been explicit in their instructions that there be no such mistakes in this operation: though they refused to explain what the stakes were, they made it crystal clear that those stakes were too high to be put at risk because someone had gotten over-zealous. At the same time, in the classically Japanese manner of exquisite subtlety and indirection, they gave him to understand that consequences of anything short of complete success would go far beyond the mere loss of face. He would be expected to atone for his failure with his life, almost certainly in the traditional Japanese manner of *seppuku*, currently much in fashion with the senior executives who ran Japan's *keiretsu* and imagined themselves the latter-day heirs of the *samurai*. Should it become necessary, Nakajima was prepared to accept this, as he fancied himself cast in the ancient *bushido* mold.

But he was even more determined that such a fate not be necessary, so now he smiled at his assistant and said, "You're quite right, Umori-rin. I will be patient. As you say, there are only two hours to go."

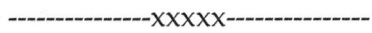

Blade collected his F-1 at Customs, and carefully motored the low-slung sapphire-blue coupe out of Hartsfield Airport then onto I-75, headed north into downtown Atlanta. Following Alistair's instructions, he exited at Edgewood Avenue and turned left, heading west until he reached Courtland, where he took another left. Just past where that street changed its name to Washington sat a three-story pavilion that had once housed a museum dedicated to, of all things, a soft drink. The building was now the centrepiece and stage of a small amphitheatre – Warren Plaza it was called. Because of its proximity to Underground Atlanta, the local police routinely swept it clean of vagrants and hop-heads, so Blade was counting on it being deserted. On the drive in from Hartsfield Airport, he and Alistair had carried on a lively discussion about the lay of the land around the underground shopping complex, and decided that the amphitheatre offered two advantages no other building in the immediate area could provide. First, it was outside the perimeter the Atlanta Police Department had set up; second, it offered an unobstructed view of the three atrium skylights as well as all of the entrances to the subterranean mall.

Underground Atlanta had begun life in the wake of the American Civil War as the city's downtown railroad depot, with hotels, banks, law offices, and saloons being built around the train station. By the turn of the century, bridges and roadways had been built above the depot, turning it into a vast underground complex that was gradually abandoned and all but forgotten as rail travel declined and railroads were rerouted out of downtown Atlanta. In the late 1960s, the original buildings were rediscovered, and their still-pristine marble facades, decorative masonry, granite archways, and gas street lamps were adapted to what was hoped would become the city's epicentre of shopping, entertainment, and nightlife, christened "Underground Atlanta."

In the sixty years that followed, the subterranean complex had gone through several cycles of boom-and-bust. All but abandoned by the end of 2020, it was currently on the rise again, as the surrounding neighborhood was experiencing yet another cycle of "gentrification." Consequently, both levels the underground mall, styled Upper and Lower Alabama and Pryor Streets, were a melange of boutiques, coffee shops, bars, restaurants, and clubs. Hobbes, who had always fancied himself an impresario as well as an entrepreneur, had acquired a nightclub he named "Bits"; it was Hobbes' favorite hangout whenever he was in Atlanta itself and deigned to venture beyond the bounds of his downtown penthouse.

It was also, Blade knew, more than just a bar: it was in many ways the unofficial but very real headquarters for Calvin's occasional venture into "business opportunities" of the sort which might wander into moral, ethical, or legal gray areas.

The plethora of small businesses that filled Underground Atlanta meant that when the complex went into lockdown just after lunchtime the previous day, there was a significant number of civilians who were trapped inside. A handful had been able to find avenues of escape, but most were still there inside those shops. This was the biggest tactical complication for Blade: he was not entirely adverse to accepting collateral damage if it was absolutely necessary to accomplish a mission, but that didn't mean he ever liked having to make that call. He would do his level best to keep civilian casualties to a minimum, even if it meant running personal risks he wouldn't ordinarily take. What gave him cause to worry was the near-certainty that when the balloon went up neither the DisCom goons or the Arasaka *reisen* would be so scrupulous and discerning....

As quietly as possible, Blade drove into the pavilion's parking lot, shut down the F-1. "Alistair, do ye have anything new for me about what I can expect inside?"

"Nae, Sir. Ah'm still getting the video feed from inside the mall, and as near as Ah can tell, nothing has changed there. There's six o' them DisCom Rats in the front o' Bits, and forty-eight o' the Arasaka *reisen* on the upper level o' the mall. It doesnae appear that any of 'em are on the lower level. And that's all Ah can tell ye."

"It is what it is. Time?"

"Ye have fifty-three minutes before the Arasaka deadline expires, Sir."

"Then I believe it's time for me to gear up and have a look around."

Before leaving the airport he had changed into a form-fitting skinsuit made of an antiballistic graphene fabric called Weclar, which covered his entire torso, his arms from shoulder to elbow, his legs from hip to knee. Over this he donned black, flocked battledress – made of fabric designed to actually absorb light – and combat boots. Now he opened up the luggage compartment on the left side of the F-1 and swiftly but methodically collected and readied his weapons and equipment. First came his "holdout," a small, slim

HSc .32 automatic. Slipped into a spring-loaded leather holster, this went inside his waistband at the small of his back. Next came the black webbed utility belt and shoulder harness. Clipped to the belt, sitting on his left hip, was a small black ruck; in it he stowed two full-size flash grenades and a pair of fragmentation grenades, along with three stripper clips each holding ten assorted rounds for what he whimsically termed his "blowgun," a couple of small, flat, rectangular electronic gadgets, and an odd-looking, metallic, vaguely boxlike device. On his right hip, a ten-inch long suppressor – "silencer' in popular, if erroneous, parlance – sat nestled in its own custom-made black leather holster; next to it was a brown canvas bayonet frog, which held a black leather-clad steel sheath, the home of a Wilkinson-made eighteen-inch sword bayonet. That worthy was well over a century old, having first seen action at the Somme on 1 July 1916; it had been issued to Blade's great-grandfather, Sergeant Hamish William MacLaren.

Next, he shrugged his way into a shoulder holster that settled comfortably under his right arm, and into which he slid a .357 caliber SIG-Sauer P226, after first loading a full 15-round magazine and then working the action. He carried no suppressor for the pistol – as far as he was concerned, by the time things were so hot that he was close enough for pistol work, stealth was no longer necessary. Two custom-made ammunition pouches were clipped to the front of the utility belt, the one on the right holding six ten-round rifle magazines, the one on the left carrying four full magazines for the SIG-Sauer. He attached a small transceiver unit to the left shoulder strap of his harness and pushed the earbug into his right ear.

One last piece of equipment remained and then he would be ready. Reaching behind the left seat of the F-1, he drew out a Short Magazine Lee Enfield rifle, .303 calibre, a Number I Mark III, serial 7905, manufactured at Birmingham Small Arms in 1912 and issued, like Blade's bayonet, to his great-grandfather. It was, by any standard, an archaic weapon: certainly it had no appeal to the modern generation of what Blade unkindly termed "gear queers," who were obsessed with automatic and semi-automatic weapons and besotted with the latest gadgets and gizmos which could be attached to their fragile, overpriced, unreliable hardware, and which they fondly, if mistakenly, imagined made them better shooters. Blade was far from a 21st Century Luddite when it came to arms and munitions – indeed, he'd had the barrel of this rifle bored out and fitted with a chrome-molybdenum liner to improve its accuracy and reduce wear, then had the chamber chrome-plated to all but eliminate fouling. But aside from working the locking lugs and guides with a whetstone and gun oil to the point where he could work it with almost blinding speed, he had left the action itself untouched. The Lee-Enfield had, over the course of seven decades of active duty and on a thousand battlefields, earned a reputation for reliability that no other rifle ever made, before or since, could equal, let alone surpass. Which was why, when asked once why such an antique was his preferred weapon of choice, he had replied, "What I demand from any firearm is that it goes 'BANG!' when I *need* it to go 'BANG!' If it can't count on it to do that, however tarted-up it may be, nothing else matters."

After confirming that there were indeed ten rounds in the Enfield's magazine, Blade slung the rifle over his right shoulder and buttoned up the F-1. "Alistair, set the security protocols on the car, please, and if ye have the time, keep an eye on it."

"Right, Sirr. Protocols set. Anyone lays a hand on her is in for a great big bleedin' surprise."

"That's what I wanted to hear." He gave a final shrug to settle his gear in place, then murmured, "Time to be among them."

Blade quickly moved to a service access door on the southeast side of the pavilion. The lock on the door, although long out of date, was still powered, and, more importantly, locked. He raised an eyebrow in surprise, then reached into his ruck and extracted one of the small flat electronic devices. Laying it up against the lock, he pressed a key on the face of the device and a split-second later was rewarded with a very satisfying click as the indicator light on the lock changed from red to green and the bolt inside slid open.

As he'd expected, the door he entered gave access to a stairwell that went all the way to the top of the building. Three minutes after he made his entry, Blade was shouldering open an access hatch and clambering onto the roof. He listening intently for a moment for any change in the ambient noises around him that might indicate that he'd been spotted – at night, hearing often provided more tactical information than eyesight – then moved across the rooftop to the service ladder that gave access to the skylight which stood above a long-dormant decorative fountain. Stepping carefully over to the northwest corner, he took a knee. He was grateful that there were no newsies about: the last thing he needed was one of their roving AV's or drones getting curious as to "Who is that man atop the pavilion in Warren Plaza and what is he doing?" and putting his image live and in colour onto the netfeeds. The absence of newsies was hardly surprising, though: the local media, under pressure from Atlanta PD and the mayor's office, had dismissed with a few brief reports the previous afternoon's short firefight outside Bits as one of the infrequent-but-far-from-unknown incidents of gang-related violence that still occurred in or near Underground Atlanta. It was something that had become so commonplace in America's urban landscape as to no longer garner much attention or coverage in the scream sheets or netfeeds. Which was fine with Blade: he'd had enough dealings with idiot "reporters" in the past few years to last him the rest of his life....

Staring out at the collage of buildings before him, he activated his artificial eye's small but effective magnification function and carefully scanned the area, focusing his senses and attention on the task at hand. APD had set up a typical perimeter, what an out-of-date police procedural manual somewhere probably laid out as "Perimeter, police, standard, Type 1" or some such. Its attention was directed outward, he noted, more intent on preventing anyone from entering Underground Atlanta than exiting the complex; that was hardly surprising, since everyone knew that the Arasakas weren't going anywhere until they got what they wanted from the people inside Bits, and as long as the Arasakas were in position, the people inside Bits weren't going anywhere at all. APD was on-site less to prevent the situation within Underground Atlanta from getting out of hand, more to keep out people who had no reason to be there from getting inside the complex and possibly causing things there to get out of hand.

But Blade *did* have reason to get inside the Underground, and quickly : that his avowed purpose was to *ensure* that things there got out of hand – for Arasaka, that is – was a given. The question was how to get inside without giving the Arasakas any warning he was coming – and at the same time keep the chances of civilian casualties to a minimum. APD had put the underground into lockdown when the firefight broke out the previous afternoon, which meant only those civilians caught in one of the handful of shops, bars, and boutiques that fronted onto the sunken open-air courtyard on the north side of the complex had any chance of escaping. For all of the businesses lacking such frontage, anyone trapped inside when the police sealed off the complex were still there. For Arasaka, such people would be an inconvenience; for Blade they were a responsibility. That meant he couldn't force an entrance through one of the courtyard shops, lest he be seen approaching, or use the service entrances of any of the others, unless he was willing to put civilians in harm's way. He wasn't willing.

A glance at his watch showed that there were forty minutes left before the Arasaka deadline expired. In a matter of minutes, then, it would all begin. Right, then, time to send up the balloon.

"What do ye have for me on the perimeter, Alistair?"

Although Blade liked to describe Alistair as his "concierge," the VI was much, much more than a glorified electronic minder. Constructed specifically for him by Raven, Alistair had begun "life" as a development of "Dennis," or DNIS, the Direct Neuro-Intelligence System, the original Virtual Intelligence program that had been created by, ironically, Hobbes' own Cogito Orbis Corporation. But Raven had turned the program into something special, transforming him from a PDA with delusions of grandeur into a valuable tactical asset, almost an ally, for Blade.

"Quite a bit, Sir! The Atlanta PD's SWAT perimeter is nothin' tae be writin' hame aboot – ye might want tae note that they seem tae have left their NBC gear at hame – but there are six o' those Arasaka *reisen* wi' what look tae be sniper rifles in positions overlookin' the whole Undergroond complex. There're also twa o' them on some sort o' rovin' patrol on the roof o' the mall, but no one else above ground."

"Sounds as though they're being a wee bit careless there."

"Aye, Sir, they are at that."

"Can ye mark the positions of the Swatties for me?"

"Aye, Sir! Will nae be twa jiffies!"

When she was building Alistair, Raven had given him the capability to serve as a highly competent tactical reconnaissance system that linked and processed data from satellite, aerial, and ground level surveillance systems. This gave him to ability to provide Blade with real-time tactical intelligence; it allowed him to cover Blade's "six" as well. She had also thoughtfully provided him with a very comprehensive – and very advanced – package of programs designed to evade or disable all but the most bleeding-edge security software. Thus, tapping into the City of Atlanta's video surveillance system was child's play for him, which was why he was able to provide Blade with such detailed information about the numbers and positions of the opposition.

"Ready when ye are, Sir!"

"Right then, Alistair, light 'em up."

At that, a series of small glowing blue markers appeared in Blade's field of vision, projected into his cybernetic left eye, that marked the positions of the Atlanta SWAT teams forming the protective cordon around the entrances to Underground Atlanta. Selecting one of those positions to be his point of entry, he reached into the ruck attached to his web belt and produced strange boxlike device he'd stowed there moments earlier. At the touch of a button it quickly unfolded into a shoulder-fired, pump-action pneumatic projector – a shotgun-like compressed-gas-operated small-bore mortar that he called his "blowgun." Working by feel alone, he loaded three rounds into the blowgun and brought it up to his shoulder. A quick mental command changed the projection in his left eye, so that now it showed a ranged target reticule that put up red hashtag markers on the spots Alistair calculated –

Pffft – thup! Pffft – thup! Pffft – thup!

Three times Blade worked the action on the projector, launching three plastic cartridges that landed with quiet *plops!* within inches of their aiming points, fracturing on impact and releasing an extremely fast-acting nerve agent that introduced both temporary paralysis and deep sleep. The three pairs of SWATs who had been the targets slumped to the ground in a dreamless, nerveless slumber....

"'SWAT – Special Weapons and Tactics.'" Blade gave a snort of derision. "All that means is they've got bigger guns than the street cops. Doesn't mean they know what they're doin'. Bloody amateurs."

"I ken they'll have some creative explainin' tae do when they awaken, Sirr."

"That they will, Alistair. What I need now is for ye to mark the Arasaka snipers, and while you're at it, tag the two rovers with yellow."

"Way ahead o' ye, Sir! Here ye go!" Instantly eight target icons

– six green and two yellow, the snipers and the rovers – appeared in Blade's field of vision. Moving quickly, he reloaded the projector with two fresh rounds, took aim at what he decided was more-or-less the centre of the *reisen*'s irregular perimeter, fired the first projectile, waited for one second, fired the other, then closed his eyes tightly.

The two small flash grenades went off one second apart, just as Blade had intended, the first catching and drawing the attention of the Arasaka snipers, the second going off and dazzling them before they had the time to figure out what had happened, why, and take measures to prevent being effectively blinded. Blade opened his eyes, swiftly folded up the blowgun and returned it to his ruck, then snatched up the Enfield, chambering a round as he did, and performed a swift tactical scan, prioritizing his targets.

One of the rovers was the first to go down. Less than sixty yards away, he was close enough to be an immediate threat. The Enfield coughed and the man dropped in a sprawl, the old-fashioned .303 caliber Glaser bullet tearing into his forehead and making a puree of his brain. For the next twenty seconds, Blade's right hand was a blur as he worked the Enfield's bolt in between shots. Moving the rifle from target to target, his cybernetic left arm was steady as a rock while lining up the next shot, while the bioprocessor in the optic chiasm in his brain projected the his artificial left eye's sight picture into the "smart" contact lens he wore on his organic right eye, and automatically compensated for parallax as it did so. In frighteningly quick succession first three snipers, then the remaining rover, then the last three snipers all fell victim to violent .303 head trauma.

"Did APD notice anything, Alistair?"

"Nae, Sirr. They heard the flash-bangs go off but since it was inside their perimeter, they ignored then. Almost *studiously* ignored them, ye might say. Worth makin' a note of that, Ah ken. As for yer shooting, they probably thought someone was havin' a wee coughin' fit. Except for those *reisen*, that is."

"Oh?"

"Aye, Sirr. For them it was more of a wee coffin fit."

"Alistair, ye're one cold-hearted bastart."

"With respect, Sirr, ye're wrong on both counts. I dinna have a heart, and 'tis nae my fault ye and Miss Ligeia are nae married."

"Alistair?"

"Yes, Sirr?"

"Shut up."

"Aye, Sirr."

Blade spun the suppressor off the muzzle of the rifle, stowed it in its fitted pouch on his utility belt, changed out the magazine for a fresh one, then slung the Lee-Enfield muzzle-down over his right shoulder. Dashing across the roof, then down the stairs to ground level, he stopped outside of the pavilion and went back into his combat crouch. With his left hand he drew the SIG-Sauer, while with his right he slid the Enfield bayonet from its sheath on his right hip. Once he was comfortable with his grips on both, he nodded to himself.

"Right then, Alistair, take down the lights and start the clock. Time to be among them."

Less than a second later, electric power to every street light with in a six-block radius of Blade's position was shut down: Alistair was equally adept at infiltrating the controls of a power grid as he was at tapping into security video feeds. Backup lighting came on in many places, but far dimmer and more dispersed than the illumination they replaced. Knowing that he had just minutes before the SWATs' night vision adjusted, he gave the command for his artificial eye to shift to infrared, and swiftly advanced across Warren Plaza, keeping to the shadows as best he could, making for the gap in the APD perimeter where his nerve agent had laid low the six SWATs. As he passed by, he noted wryly that two of them were snoring.

"Which entrance, Alistair?"

"Tak' the alley just tae yer left. At the bottom o' the slope there's a service entrance."

"Got it. I'm there." The door was locked, as Blade expected, being the default mode in a power loss. A quick pass with the electronic pick solved that problem and he was inside Underground Atlanta.

Hardly had he stepped through the door than he encountered his first Arasaka. Clad in the dark gray trousers and tunic which was the mark of an Arasaka field operative, the man had his back to the door and was smoking a cigarette, a lapse in discipline a regular *reisen* would never commit, meaning that this one was a mercenary. It mattered little to Blade or the Arasaka, however, as the bayonet plunged into and through the man's throat, severing windpipe and carotid arteries in a single thrust.

Coming through the service door Blade had stepped onto a catwalk that appeared to traverse a fairly large storage area; the room was almost totally dark, with only one small emergency lighting unit. At the far end of the catwalk stood another Arasaka: whether it was some sound Blade made while taking out the first *reisen*, or simply the unexpected movement which caught his attention, this one turned toward Blade and began to bring up his weapon, some sort of large-bore pistol. Blade, though, had already leveled the SIG-Sauer, and he fired two quick shots, both of which took the other man in the forehead.

"Game on," the Scot muttered: there was no way to have concealed the sound of those gunshots, so the rest of the Araskas certainly he was here now.

"What? What was that? What is going on down there?"

The burst of agitated chatter on the comm channel Nakajima used to monitor the *reisen* in Underground Atlanta jolted him out of the near-meditative torpor into which he had forced himself over the past hour. Pressing the "transmit" button on his comm unit, he spoke urgently.

"Nagumo, what is it? Is there a problem?"

"We have a perimeter breach, Nakajima-sama! I don't know who it is, or how many of them there are, but at least two shots were fired in a storeroom where I had one man posted to cover a service entrance. He is not responding to my comms, nor is another one of my *reisen*. I have men reconnoitering now."

"Do whatever you feel necessary to contain the situation, Nagumo. Keep me informed as best you can – I will continue to monitor this channel."

"As you wish, Sir!"

Nakajima turned to briefly look at Umori, but shook his head wordlessly. He was a wise commander, who knew that tactical micro-management was almost always a prescription for disaster. The man on the scene didn't need a superior looming over his shoulder, second-guessing every decision. Nagumo was a very experienced field operative; had he not been, he would not have been placed in charge of the *shinden* operation at Bits. All Nakajima could do at this point was get in the way. He nodded to himself, satisfied he was making the right decision. Yes, best let Nagumo handle it.

Blade opened the storeroom door that led to the main mall of the underground complex, only to find two more gray-clad *reisen* waiting on the other side, about to open the door themselves. Startled, slow to react when the door abruptly swung open, the man never had a chance to defend himself, as Blade gave a wide sweep with his right arm, cutting open his opponent's throat. Stepping past the falling body, he now faced the dying man's partner. She raised a handgun and got off one round – it went wide – before Blade slashed down hard with the barrel of the SIG-Sauer. He heard the satisfying crunch of breaking bones in the woman's forearm, followed by her hollow gasp as he drove the bayonet under her breastbone and up into her lungs. Twisting the blade, he pulled it free, not bothering to watch her collapse, gaping like a landed fish.

A *reisen* jumped from a doorway, lashing out with what appeared to be a *wakizashi*, but Blade parried the move with his bayonet, and the Japanese crashed into him. The two men went down, ending with Blade sprawled atop his assailant, his right arm across the Arasaka's throat. Catching movement in the corner of his eye, Blade looked left to see a fourth *reisen* approaching, gun drawn, firing wildly as he ran forward.

"Would ye mind just soddin' off?" Blade bellowed as he fired two rounds into the gunman's chest. "And ye can bleedin' sod off, too, while yer at it!" he shouted at the *reisen* beneath him as he put a bullet into the man's right eye. Rolling off the body, he scrambled to his feet and began running toward Bits.

Another Arasaka lunged out of a doorway, but Blade spun quickly enough to avoid grappling with him, plunging the bayonet into the man's shoulder while ripping off three shots in quick succession at yet another charging Japanese. The first shot missed, the second and third took the man in the abdomen, and he went down screaming. Turning back to the man writhing with the bayonet in his shoulder, Blade put the muzzle of the SIG-Sauer on his sternum and squeezed the trigger twice. The man went limp.

Something went "ping" to Blade's left and he suddenly felt as if his arm had been whacked with an axe handle. Looking up he saw yet one more *reisen*, this one ten yards away, taking aim in a half-crouching shooting stance. Using his right hand to steady his left, Blade walked three shots up the man's torso, hitting gut, breastbone, and throat. Scooping up his bayonet in his right hand, feeling his left arm reset itself, he continued his weaving run toward the nightclub. Halfway down the mall an Arasaka tried to take up a shooting stance, only to be rewarded by catching a pair of .357 caliber slugs, one through each lung.

---------------XXXXX---------------

"Sir, the situation is not yet out of hand, but we are taking serious casualties here."

Nagumo made his report with a professionalism that Nakajima had to admire, and yet the anxiety in the subordinate's voice was unmistakable. "How many of them are there, Nagumo, and how heavily armed are they?"

"It's one man, Sir, and he appears to be – "

"Wait, 'one man' did you say?"

"Yes, sir, one man. I know it must sound absurd, but he has taken down at least nine of my people – and I have no contact with the snipers I placed in the roofline perimeter!"

"One man!" Spinning to face Umori, Nakajima said tightly, "Get me a video feed right now – I have to see what is going on down there!" Returning his attention to the comm, he spoke quickly. "Nagumo, I'll have reinforcements to you as quickly as I can. But whatever you do, do not let that man get into that nightclub! Do whatever it takes to prevent that!"

"Yes, Sir. Nagumo clear."

"I have that video feed you asked for, Nakajima-sama," Umori announced.

"Put it on the large monitor."

The image was grainy and the focus a bit blurred at times, but Nakajima saw all that he needed to see in a matter of seconds as he watched the lone attacker working his way through the ranks of the Arasakas in Underground Atlanta. *I recognize those moves, those stances, those weapons*, he thought. *How the* hell *did he get here?* Turning back to Umori, he said simply, "The game has changed yet again, Umori-rin. I know that man. That's Blade."

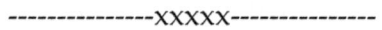

The SIG-Sauer was empty. In a well-practiced move, Blade slid the bayonet back into its sheath with his right hand, while with his left he raised the muzzle of the pistol and thumbed the release catch on the empty magazine. His right hand dove into the left-side ammo pouch, extracted a full magazine and slid it into the butt of the pistol before the spent magazine had hit the floor. Blade thumbed the slide release and he was back in business. The bayonet came back out of the sheath with a flourish, and not a moment too soon.

A pair of Arasakas were converging on him, one to his left, one to his right, both wielding *katanas* in a manner that left no doubt about their ability to use them to good (or, in his case, bad) effect. He allowed them to approach, the man on the right arriving a half-moment before the woman on the left. That split second difference in the timing of their attack was their undoing. As the man raised his sword high for a slashing attack, Blade's right hand was a blur as he shifted his grip on the bayonet, swept it forward in a slashing attack that laid opened the man's bowels, then once more reversing his grip Blade shoved the bayonet through the man's throat. The woman attacking from the left was almost upon him, her sword held at the high quarter, when he thrust forward with the SIG-Sauer, her momentum carrying her right into its muzzle. Two rapid squeezes of the trigger caused two rapidly-spreading red spots to appear on her chest as she tumbled to the floor.

Though his Japanese opponents didn't know it, Blade was using their own culture as a weapon against them. To a Japanese, it was dishonourable to attack from a distance an enemy who was already engaged by another, closer opponent. At the same time there was much face to be gained by killing an enemy in personal combat, whether it was with blades or firearms; hence the repeated attempts to rush him, as well as the attacks that were made with either long- or short-swords rather than pistols or rifles. It all worked in Blade's favor, so if the Arasakas insisted on continuing to play that way, he would happily oblige them.

There were three of them working together this time, rushing forward. He was able to drop the first with three shots, two to the chest, one to the head – he couldn't afford to not make certain of the kill, but then the second attacker was on him, his *katana* at the high guard, the third rushing in on the right. Blade was able to interpose his bayonet at almost the last possible instant, stopping the edge of the Japanese sword just inches from his face, gaining enough time to fire twice at the other *reisen*, hitting him once in the leg and once in the groin. The Arasaka with the sword was bringing all of his strength to bear to shove aside Blade's block, but before he could the Scot brought the SIG-Sauer around and pressed it against his assailant's stomach. Boiling over with a sudden, unexpected anger, Blade jerked the trigger three times, the muzzle blast alone tearing open great gaping wounds, the bullets passing through the Arasaka's body. Stepping back he then fired one clean shot into the man's head, then turned to the wounded attacker and dispatched him the same way.

Alistair was not alone in his ability to tap into the Atlanta CCTV system: Mycroft was equally adept at such details, and now Calvin, ensconced in the comfort of his private office, was watching Blade tear his bloody swath through the Arasaka henchmen.

"How does he fucking do that?"

"I take it, Calvin, that your question is rhetorical? Or would you like a blow-by-blow, shot-by-shot analysis?"

"Just shut the hell up, Mike."

"As you wish."

Calvin watched in silence for a few moments longer. *He's going to make it,* he thought. *Part of me was worried that a friend might be walking into a death trap, and part of me was concerned that he wasn't. God help me if he ever finds out about that.*

"He's got thirty yards to go. Best let our people know he's almost there, Mike – tell them to get ready for a visitor."

"Of course, Calvin."

---------------XXXXX---------------

Blood and gore was splattered across the front of Blade's clothing, and when he dragged his arm across his brow to wipe away the sweat, it left a bloody smear behind. None of it, though, was his.   The SIG-Sauer was almost empty again, so Blade sidestepped to his left, into a doorway, where he rapidly reloaded. Most of the *reisen* had gone to earth, so to speak, finding whatever cover they could, waiting for him to make a break for Bits. It had to be obvious by now to every one of them why he was here – he was clearly not some amateur thrill-seeker hoping to make a name for himself, and there was nothing else in the whole of Underground Atlanta that was worth the attention of someone such as himself apart from whatever was in the possession of those idiots trapped in the nightclub.

"Less than thirty yards to go, lad," he muttered to himself. "Now for the last dash."

"Uh, Sirr, beggin' yer pardon an' all," Alistair's voice came piping into his ears before he could make a move. "Before ye take off on yer 'last dash,' ye might want to take a wee gander to yer left, just aroond the corner o' the doorway, doon by the floor. I think what ye see might interest ye."

Normally Alistair remained silent when Blade in action, the better to not distract him. But when he did speak, Blade listened. Peering around the doorway, looking down, he saw, of all things, what appeared to be the front half of a boot sticking out into the mall: there was an Arasaka standing in the very next doorway not five feet away, one who hadn't realized they were nowhere near as well-concealed as they thought. Had Blade gone dashing out into the mall, whoever was there could have riddled him from behind before he got ten feet. As it was....

"Thank ye, Alistair, ye're a lifesaver, literally. Remind me of that the next time we're discussing raises."

"Sirr, ye dinna pay me a salary noo, so I dinna ken that a raise will be doin' me ony good."

"Alistair, don't quibble with me when I'm feeling generous."

"Aye, Sirr."

The Enfield bayonet was never designed to be a throwing weapon, but at a range of less than five feet, it didn't need to be.

Blade hefted it in his right hand, then turned and heaved it viciously at the exposed boot. The high-pitched, clearly female scream of genuine pain told Blade that this had been no clever decoy, and he burst from his cover, spun, snatched up the bayonet and fired twice into the head of the unfortunate woman who had hoped to bushwhack him, all in one swift, ballet-like movement.

Now he was running for his life. The processor implant that coordinated his left eye and arm worked wonderfully, as another four *reisen* went down, two of them fatally. But there were more targets than opportunities, and Blade was out of time. Ten yards to go, he thought.

"Alistair, if ye're watching, get the door codes ready for Bits, I'll not have time to stop!"

"Aye, Sirr, just hit the door full tilt, I'll have it open for ye!"

Bullets were flying all about him now, one hitting his left shoulder, only to be stopped by his anti-ballistic skinsuit, while another slammed into his ruck, reducing the blowgun to scrap, but aside from momentarily knocking him off stride the hit did no actual damage. A third grazed his left shin, cutting a deep furrow in the skin. Blade cried out in pain as he stumbled at last, but he was there, the double doors of Bits were in front of him, and as he hit them they swung open, then slammed shut again, the locks falling back into place with clearly audible "thunks" as he sprawled on the floor of the nightclub lobby. At first the DisCom Rats inside the club thought he was one of them, misled by his black battledress, but even as they realized their mistake Blade was taking action.

One of the Rats was standing not two feet away, holding a machine pistol – in an odd instant of detachment Blade recognized it as a Mil-Tec MP30 – and was bringing it to bear when Blade dropped him with a leg sweep, then slammed the Rat's head on the floor while putting two shots centre mass in the next closest Rat, who couldn't swing her MP30 around in time. Shoving off from the first Rat, he put a bullet into the back of the man's head, then rolled to his feet and made a dash toward the wall panel that concealed the door to the safe rooms.

Not even trying to aim, firing only in the hope of distracting the four remaining Rats and spoiling *their* aim, he spaced his six remaining shots out to cover the short sprint to the wall panel. Two 9mm slugs hit him in the chest, stopped by his Weclar body armour, but causing him to stumble nonetheless. *I thought these bastarts were supposed to be stormtroopers!* At last he hit the panel, which instantly pivoted 180° on a central pillar then "thunked" securely closed behind him, and he was inside the safe room suite at Bits.

Nakajima's fist slammed against the desktop as he watched the video feed from Atlanta Underground. "Damn it! He got in!"

Calvin's fist thumped the tabletop as he watched the video feed from Underground Atlanta. "Hot damn! He got in!"

Slightly stunned by the impact with the door, winded by the two bullets that had struck his chest, it took Blade a moment to realize that there were four people pointing a variety of firearms at him from a range of less than five feet, some of them with pistols in each hand. For a few tense seconds, no one moved or said a word, then finally a diminutive platinum blonde wearing nondescript light-blue coveralls said, "Oh, so it really *is* you. We had to make sure, you know."

Blade nodded. "It's me all right. Do ye think anyone else would be mad enough to try to get in here like that?" He eased himself up into a sitting position, then gave his somewhat bemused welcoming committee a lopsided grin.

"Right then, now that I'm here, there are three things I need. First, a large single malt. Second, a good cigar. And third, a talk with the stupid bastart who is supposed to be in charge of this buggered-up dog-and-pony show...."

Chapter 3

"'The stupid bastard who's supposed to be in charge of this buggered-up dog-and-pony show'?" a voice asked from the far side of the room. The speaker was a big man, taller than Blade, bulky, with close-cropped brown hair and a neatly trimmed goatee. "That would be me; I'm Bridelow. C'mon, we can talk in the other room."

"Hold on there, laddiebuck," Blade said as he got to his feet, smiling. Had Bridelow been paying attention he would have noticed the smile never reached Blade's eyes. "I said ye were the *third* thing on my list. First, my whisky and my cigar, then ye."

"I would think you'd want a situation report."

"I do, when I'm good and ready. I'm good enough now, I'm just not ready. Ye're time's coming, don't doubt that. Now, where's the bar?"

"I hope you don't mind me pointing this out, Blade, but you're leaking." Radome, the platinum blonde, gestured first to Blade's arm and then to his leg. He looked down and saw the wet stains on his clothing, just a hint of redness showing up on the black fabric.

"Why, yes, yes, I am," he murmured. "I'd best get a bandage on the leg right away – I hate to sound like the modest hero, but it really just is a scratch. Still, it will bleed like a copper-plated bitch if it's not tended to."

"And the arm? Or is that just a 'scratch' too?" This from Compton.

"Oh, not to worry, the nannies will take care of that."

"Nannies?"

"There's a nanotech maintenance unit built into the arm – it'll have the skin there knitted up in a few hours. The arm itself is working fine."

Radome and Compton stared at him; Houston and the red-haired woman standing beside him were expressionless.

"I thought ye knew – seems most people in our line of work do. Eight years ago I was invalided out of the Army – the British Army, obviously – because somebody tried to kill me with a car bomb. I survived, but it cost me my left arm, left eye, and the hearing in both ears: they've all been replaced by cybernetic implants and prosthetics."

It was Radome who recovered her composure first. "In that case, I guess we should see to getting a bandage on your leg, then." She gestured to Compton and Houston. "Help him out of his harness, will you? Be careful with that rifle! Then get him into a chair and get that leg elevated, please." She left the room, returning a moment later with a medium-sized carrying case prominently marked with red crosses. Moving over to where Blade was now sitting, she placed the case on nearby table and opened it, revealing a rather impressively stocked first aid kit. She extracted a pair of scissors and reached for the fabric on Blade's wounded leg. He quickly jerked it out of the way.

"Here now, dinna cut it! Pull off my boot and roll up the trouser leg – these things are too damned expensive to be hacked up like that. It can be mended – just more work for Alistair, that's all."

"Alistair?"

"My...electronic concierge, Radome. He keeps track of all of my bits and pieces and keeps them tidy."

"A VI?"

"And an AP. Custom designed and built."

"Ooooh! Can I talk to him?"

"If he's in the mood for conversation. Ye have a cyberlink?" At that, Radome gave Blade a look that a teacher might give an exceptionally slow child. "Right, foolish question. Alistair?" he asked, apparently addressing thin air.

"Yes, Sirr!" The reply came immediately, although only Blade could hear it.

"Miss Radome here would like to talk to you if ye have a mind for conversation. Do ye have her link address?"

"That I do, and I think I would enjoy talking wi' her. She's got a remarkable reputation fer developin' new uses fer practical app-macros. I might learn a thing or two."

"Well, then, go at it if ye like." He turned back to Radome. "He has some hard and fast security protocols hardwired into him, so if he tells ye he canna talk about something, he truly can't talk about it. Aside from that, I'll leave you two alone. Och, wait, who's going to finish stopping up my leaky leg?"

"I'll do that."

The voice was a soft soprano, the speaker the tall, lithe red-haired woman whom the extraction team had been rather unimaginatively christened "Red." A heart-shaped face with high cheekbones, widely-spaced china-blue eyes, a rosebud mouth, and a slightly retroussé nose, all surrounded by a mass of shoulder-length wavy auburn hair, suddenly held Blade's undivided attention. The woman was, to say the least, striking.

"Ye will?"

"I will. I know a thing or two about bandages and first aid."

Blade opened his mouth to reply, then snapped it shut. Despite his curiosity, this was not the time or the place to be quizzing this woman about who she was and how she came to be here. Instead, after a moment, he said simply, "Then I'll let ye be about yer work." He raised his voice slightly. "And while ye do, can someone see about that whisky and that cigar?"

Compton frowned, then brightened, suddenly very animated – Blade would quickly learn that the young black man with the close-cropped hair was always at least somewhat "animated." "Oh, yeah, right! I'm pretty sure that Calvin keeps a few bottles of the Macallan stashed away under the bar – lemme get it for you!" He rushed over to the bar and began noisily rummaging around.

Houston, tall, lanky, with long white hair and a rather impressive mustache adding extra character to an already well-worn face, gave Blade a wry grin and in a deep-voiced drawl said, "There're times I think somebody must've dropped a handful of ants in that boy's diapers, and after all these years he still ain't got rid of 'em all." Blade smiled back, nodding agreement. "I'll see what I can do about that see-gar, Mr. Blade." And with that he went over to a wall cabinet and opened it wide. "Got some Romeo y Julietas here, Churchills. Will one of them do in a pinch?"

"'Do in a pinch'? That's my cigar of choice! Sir, I am deeply in yer debt!"

"Then here you go." Houston held out a trio of the cigars to Blade. "One fer now, an' a couple fer the road. Need a cutter?"

"No, I always use this." Blade unwrapped one of the Churchills, then produced an old Swiss Army knife, popped out the Phillips-head blade, used it to neatly punch a hole in the end of the cigar. The knife disappeared, to be replaced in his hand by a box of matches. "I'll do the rest of the honours in a moment, when I have my talk with Bridelow."

Compton rushed up, the promised bottle of the Macallan in one hand, a whisky glass in the other. He set them on the table beside Blade. "I was right about Calvin's stash! Do you need any ice for that?"

"Lad, I'll not have ye mucking up perfectly good whisky with ice! Just bring me a small glass of water, please." Blade poured a generous measure of the single malt whisky in the glass – a very generous measure – and when the water appeared, he dipped the tip of his right finger into it, then allowed a single drop to fall into the waiting amber liquid. Looking up at Compton, he said simply, "*That is all the water good whisky ever needs. Remember.*" He then raised the glass to his lips, took a long swallow, closed his eyes and sighed in contentment. From the beatific expression on his face no one would have ever guessed that not five minutes earlier he had been engaged in mortal combat.

Setting his glass down, Blade watched Red work for a few seconds, then looked up at Houston and Compton. "Right then. Would the two of ye mind keeping an eye on the door, as it were? By my reckoning, we've got thirty, maybe forty-five minutes before the Arasaka people get their act together and get permission to come in after us, but I could be wrong...."

"And yor thinkin' a reception committee might be in order if they do decide to arrive early," Houston finished the sentence for him.

"Exactly."

"Just you leave that to young Compton and me, Mr. Blade." The tall, lanky solo jerked his head at the younger man, and together they took up positions behind their makeshift but stout barricade inside the door to the safe suite. Houston hefted into position an impressive-looking rotary-magazine semi-automatic shotgun, and Compton settled in with an H&K assault rifle that he looked quite comfortable with.

By now Red had Blade's boot off and was methodically wrapping gauze around the middle of his calf, having already cleansed the wound and placed a thick gauze pad over it. Her movements were sure and precise, her face utterly expressionless: slight as it was, this was clearly not the first gunshot wound she'd ever seen, nor was it the first time she'd tended to one. *Curiouser and curiouser*, he thought. *This is a most intriguing woman, in a number of ways.*

Taping off the end of the gauze, Red paused for a moment to look at her handiwork, as if evaluating its quality, then said, "All finished here. You can put your boot back on."

"Thank ye, lass. That was good work ye did and I appreciate it." At that she gave him a small smile – it was memorable.

Lacing up his boot, Blade stood and tested the leg: the pain was an annoyance, but bearable. "Right, then. Time we had our little chat, Mr. Bridelow. I take it you want to talk in there?" He indicated the doorway Bridelow had approached earlier.

"That I do."

"Then let's get down to business. The sooner we get this over with, the happier I'll be." This time there was ice in Blade's eyes, and this time Bridelow didn't miss it. He suddenly felt very apprehensive. Something told him he was not going to find the coming conversation at all to his liking.

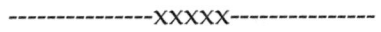

"Sir, I most humbly apologize for my failure." If you will show me how I can atone –"

"Never mind, Nagumo, it isn't your fault. You really never stood a chance of stopping him."

"But, sir, he was only one man."

"No, Nagumo, he was Blade. I should have told you, but I didn't. If I had, maybe you would not have felt compelled to sacrifice so many *reisen*." At the word "Blade," Nagumo suddenly gave out a hiss, sharply drawing his breath between his teeth: for a Japanese it was a sure sign of agitation and anxiety.

"That would explain much, Nakajma-sama."

"How so?"

"I sent a man up to ground level. He just informed me that all eight of the *reisen* who were posted in overwatch are dead, each one killed by a single headshot – it sounds like the work of very efficient sniper."

"Indeed. That he is. Go on."

"During the shootout I personally saw him terminate three of my people who were already incapacitated. Those were not mercy killings, Nakajima-sama."

"No, they wouldn't be. How many did you lose, Nagumo?"

"In addition to the eight on ground level, sixteen down here. I have thirty-two effectives, sir. Blade did not leave any wounded."

"Understood." A pause. "Nagumo, do you still have your heavy weapons?"

"Yes, sir. We hadn't broken them out until now – we never imagined that we would actually need them."

"Well, you do now. Our deadline has expired, and in any event, Blade's actions made it meaningless. Get your people re-armed and re-organized, and be prepared to hit the night club as hard and as fast as possible on my order. I have another thirty-five personnel standing by – they will be joining you within the hour. Once they are in position and I've confirmed with our superiors that we will indeed conclude this mission, you must take possession of those memory crystals, no matter at what cost. Do whatever it takes, Nagumo. Do you understand? Do whatever it takes!"

"I understand, sir. May I ask about our status with the Atlanta police or other *gaijun* law enforcement?"

"That is being dealt with even as we speak, Nagumo-sama. I will comm Tokyo and inform them of what I've done and what I've ordered. I will also inform them that you acted entirely on my authority and at my direction."

"I am grateful, sir," Nagumo replied. Nakajima had a somewhat...flexible sense of honour, often determined more by circumstances rather than firm standards, but he had never embraced the idea of sacrificing subordinates for failing to carry out impossible orders or to cover his own mistakes, and he was not about to begin doing so now. Blade was neither superhuman nor immortal, as Nakajima well knew, but Nagumo and his *reisen* had been completely out of their depth trying to stop Blade without escalating the situation to the point where American law enforcement agencies would feel compelled to get involved.

"You'll hear from me shortly, Nagumo."

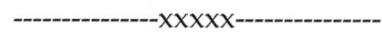

"Aw, shit, there goes my paycheck!"

Blade looked from Bridelow's body to Compton and back again. "Sorry, but I do tend to have a rather short way with turncoats." If there was any emotion in the Scot's voice, Compton couldn't detect it. He shook his head, staring at the corpse at his feet.

"Yeah, all right, OK, I mean, you left the door open and everything, so everybody outside heard everything you guys said...but...damn! Did you really have to shoot him like that? Dead, I mean?"

"I take it ye think there was a better alternative? Or maybe ye imagine ye'd be more...attractive to the ladies with a knife sticking out of the middle of yer back? Because that's the way it would have gone if I'd left him alive."

"Whaddya mean?"

"Have Radome do an RF scan on the body. Pounds to pennies says he's got a transmitter on him somewhere, probably an implant. DisCom, and probably Arasaka as well, was listening in to every word everyone of you said to one another."

"Say what?"

"Ye heard me. Tell me, did Bridelow insist that everyone in yer 'extraction team'" – Compton winced at the sarcasm dripping from those last two words – "use *only* the equipment he supplied – including electronics?"

"Well, yeah, of course. I mean, he told us that the serial numbers had all been filed off the stuff, so to speak, so it would be untraceable in case anything happened to us or something got left behind. 'No loose ends' was how he put it."

"Did Radome stash her kit in here before ye left for DisCom?"

"Yeah, she did."

"Have her run a scan on Bridelow here –" Blade prodded the corpse with his toe "– and see what she picks up. I'll lay odds that when she does, and then checks the scanner he gave her, she'll find that it registers every frequency in the RF band except for the one his implant is set to."

"That goddamn sonuvabitch!" He turned toward the door and shouted, "Radome, can you get in here? And bring your scanner!" Then more quietly, he repeated, "That goddamn sonuvabitch!"

Radome appeared a moment later, RF scanner in hand, and looked inquiringly at Compton. He indicated Bridelow's body. "Blade thinks there's a transmitter implant somewhere on Bridelow – I know, I know, it sounds kinda weird but it makes sense, too, y'know? Better do it quick, too, because –"

"– Because if it's electro-chemical powered, then the current stopped flowing when his heart stopped beating, and those things really don't have much in the way of capacitance. I know my stuff, Compton." Kneeling beside the corpse, she deftly worked the controls of the scanner; it only took a few seconds for Radome to begin nodding her head. "Yep, we've got a signal here. Looks like its coming from somewhere near the base of his throat, just under the skin."

"How hard was he wired, do ye know?"

"He had a neural booster, I know that, and enhanced hearing. I don't think he had anything done to his eyes, and he didn't have any cyberlimbs." She had the grace to blush slightly when she said that. "But I've known him off and on for about five years now, and this is the first I've ever heard about a transmitter." There was concern in her sea-green eyes. "We really were set up, weren't we?"

"Aye, that ye were."

"This is not good."

"No, it isn't."

Seconds passed as the three of them stood in silence, trying to work out all of the implications of Radome's discover. Blade was the first to break it.

"Radome, could you –"

"– go get the first aid kit."

"– go fetch the first aid kit, some –"

"– some bar towels."

"– bar towels and –"

"– and a bowl of warm water. We have surgery to do."

"– and a bowl of warm water. We have –" He stopped and stared at her. "How do you bloody do that?"

"My call sign isn't 'Radome' just for my tech skills and my flowing silver locks, you know." She gave him a cheerful, quirky smile, and with that, she left the room, returning a few moments later with the kit, the towels, and the water. "Here you go."

Blade raised his voice. "Houston, can ye come in here for a minute?"

"On may way."

When he appeared, he took one look at the body on the floor, the med-kit, towels, and water, and said, "Y'all need to get him on the table."

"That's it," Blade nodded. "Can you give us a hand?"

"Sure thing." With some amount of grunting and heaving the three men lifted Bridelow off the floor – he had been a big man, and the flap-limbed posture of death added to the effort. Meanwhile Radome began laying out the instruments she expected Blade would require for the task at hand. Blade looked at Houston inquiringly.

"Red?"

"She took Compton's place when he came in here, and she's holdin' the fort. She snagged one of those MilTecs off'n one of the Rats 'fore we holed up in here, and she's sittin' out there with it and my shotgun behind a couple of those overstuffed chairs, pointin' 'em at the access panel and watchin' the monitors with a gleam in her eye and what looks like Texas murder in her heart."

"Interesting woman."

"You can say that again."

Radome broke in, handing Blade a pair of latex gloves; she was already wearing a pair. "You're going to need these."

Blade nodded his thanks, then took the offered scalpel – it was a very well equipped medkit – then took a deep breath and said, "Right, then, Radome, let's be about it."

Less than three minutes later, Radome was holding up a pair of forceps gripping a sealed electronic package no bigger than the nail on her little finger; two hair-fine electrical leads dangled from one side. Blade nodded approvingly. "There ye are, ye little bastart. Radome, would there be anything we could use to wrap up this wee beastie? Ah, perfect!" He took the proffered glassine bag and held it out as she dropped the chip into it, sealed the bag, and tucked the chip into the right breast pocket of his jacket. "I'm going to have a friend take a closer look at this the first chance I have – I suspect we might learn a thing or two from it."

---------------XXXXX---------------

"That son of a bitch!" Calvin's face was mottled red in outrage as he watched and listened to the video and audio feed from the safe rooms. "That goddamned son of a bitch!"

"I take it you mean Bridelow and not Blade?"

"Of course I mean Bridelow!" Calvin snapped back. "That bastard was playing me! Nobody plays me, Mycroft, nobody!"

"Calvin, I suggest you try to calm yourself. Your biometric readings are spiking. Keep this up and you'll wind up on life-support right next to Kim."

Calvin made a conscious, deliberate effort to bring himself under control, and Mycroft was relieved to see his pulse and blood pressure dropping into less threatening territory. Calvin's anger had not abated one whit, however; it had merely become more focused, and therefore, controllable.

"He tried to sell me down the river to DisCom. DisCom! My worst corporate enemy – and he tried to sell me out to them. If you get right down to it, he's already sold me out." Abruptly, his eyes flew wide open. "Oh, shit!"

"What is it, Calvin?"

"We've got to find out how much Bridelow knew – I mean *really* knew – about those crystals and why they're so damned important to me. If he compromised me, I need to know how bad the damage is. Go find out."

"This may take some time, since thanks to your friend Blade, we can't actually interrogate Bridelow himself."

"I know. Just do the best you can – and do it fast!"

"OK, OK, OK...." Compton's usual staccato delivery was almost manic. "I mean...I...I know we've been sold out – a blind man could see that in a pitch-black room. OK? But – but – but *how*? I mean, it was only Bridelow's team, and...and the boss, and...and...and me who knew about this op. And we were under freakin' em-con from the minute Bridelow began his first briefing! I mean, I know what you told Bridelow and what you think and I heard your 'conversation' so I know you think he was the one who did it, OK? But how? *Why*? I don't freakin' get it!"

"I'm going out to the front room to help Red keep an eye on the rest of the Arasakas," Radome called over her shoulder, working the action on her Malorite rifle as she did.

Blade nodded his thanks to her, then threw a concerned look at Compton. "Best start getting a grip, lad. Bridelow was strictly a freelancer, a 'hired gun,' ye Yanks would call him – and I admit, he was rather good at it." The rolling r's and broad vowels of Blade's

Scottish burr stood in sharp contrast to the other man's rush of words. "But a few years ago, he ran a rather dodgy op for DisCom that crossed over into all sorts of legal gray areas and even strayed now and then into the black. I ran a background check on him – or rather, a friend of mine did so. There seems to have been a very strenuous effort made at deleting any accessible records of that operation – and at burying what couldn't be deleted as deep as possible. I suspect Hobbes took Bridelow at face value because he'd employed him before."

"Kinda sloppy on Calvin's part, wouldn't ya say?" Houston drawled. Blade nodded.

"Ye ken how DisCom operates: once ye work for them, in any capacity, they find a way to sink their hooks into ye, and never really let ye go. They get something on ye that can hold over yer head whenever they need a...favor."

"So it was Bridelow who – it was him – he's the one that ratted us out to the Rat!"

"Precisely. Think about it. A security patrol in DisCom's data centre that had no business being where it was when it was. How did it get there at just the right moment? Someone – presumably DisCom – destroys yer CV-9 and kills the pilot at Herdon Airport just as ye arrive. How did anyone know the extraction team was going to Herndon, and how did they know *that* specific CV-9 was yers?"

"OK...yeah, so...they were expecting us?"

"They had to be, Compton." The scowl on Houston's face was fearsome. "Think about it – it's pretty damn easy to see, at leastways, now it is. After we ran up I-75, the pursuit broke off around Gainesville. Why would they let us make it all the way across the Georgia line when the DisCom goons could've stopped us anytime, anywhere, short of it? They didn't have to worry about undue attention, after all. We were in Florida, son, and you know as well as I do that any time DisCom wants the State of Florida to look the other way, every lawman and newsie in the state goes stone blind."

Compton nodded, slowly at first, then with increasing conviction, the pieces rapidly falling into place now. "Yeah, good point – I mean, why let us get away unless they already knew where we were going, right?"

"Exactly. And the proof of that was...?" Blade cocked an inquiring eyebrow.

"That would be maybe that little reception committee the Rats had waiting for us when we reached the Underground?"

"Right the first time, laddie."

"And they damn near succeeded," Houston said, "They had us outnumbered and outta position, and I honestly can't say we would have made it inside here before they finally overran us, if'n it hadn't been for Arasaka showin' up when it did." He thrust his hands in his pockets looked down as he and scuffed the toe of one boot across the carpet. After a second or so, he looked up at Blade again.

"So how come *I* never noticed any of this?" the Texan asked. He didn't doubt MacLaren, he just hated being duped as much as the next man.

"Probably because at the time ye were rather closely focused on staying alive." The Scot grinned ruefully. "That does tend to have the effect of concentrating a man's mind wonderfully, ye ken."

"Yeah, you could say I was a mite preoccupied," Houston nodded in agreement.

Compton appeared to be centreing himself now. "So Bridelow was tipping off DisCom each step of the way?"

"Most certainly." Blade began rummaging through the late, unlamented Bridelow's kit, looking for spare magazines. Bridelow had carried a Smith & Wesson 99-Gamma, which fired the same .357 caliber round as his own SIG-Sauer: MacLaren had two nearly empty mags that needed to be topped off. "For that matter, he likely handed DisCom the entire plan for the op on a silver platter before yer team left for Orlando. Oh, and ye did notice, didn't ye, that Bridelow was the only person in the extraction team who didn't collect so much as a bruise or a broken nail during your little jaunt?"

"Damn! I missed that."

"It's all right. As I said, there's this bit about being distracted by trying to stay alive. The point is, the Rats almost certainly had specific orders not to harm Bridelow if it could be avoided. He was still an asset to DisCom, and if I hadn't come along, would still be inside Hobbes' confidence."

"OK, OK, OK...." This was Compton again. "Everything adds up, except for one...little...detail."

"Which is...?"

"*Arasaka!* I mean, holy shit, Blade, what the hell are *they* doing here?"

"I think that's kinda obvious, if'n ya ask me," Houston said. "Arasaka's got itself a mole in DisCom's security department. Whatever is stored in those crystals that DisCom wants so badly, Arasaka wants it too. When the Rat got it paws on it, the mole just called his or her masters with the good news. As for showin' up here when they did, I'd say it was probably pure ornery coincidence."

Compton pinched the bridge of his nose between thumb and forefinger. "Oh, man, this is *waaay* above my pay grade! I mean, talk about over-complicating the plumbing! All right. Let me see if I've got it straight now, OK? We have the crystals that Calvin sent us to retrieve from DisCom. They want them back – "

"And you dead into the bargain."

"– And us dead into the bargain. Yeah, right, I could do without that part. OK, OK, OK, so Arasaka has a mole in Ratland that tells them where we are, and the only reason they would be interested in us is the same reason DisCom is interested in us, and they would be just as freakin' happy if we were dead into the bargain, too. How am I doing so far?"

"Full marks, lad, full marks."

"So what I'm wondering is...if DisCom and Arasaka are working together now, how long will it last? There's what, three or four of the Rats still outside in the club itself?" Blade nodded. "I don't think we have to wonder whether or not everybody'll start shooting at *us* again. But when they do, are they gonna start freakin' shooting at each other, too? And when? Sooner? Later? Now?"

"As for how closely they're workin' together, that I canna answer for ye, Compton." Blade smiled mischievously. "I'm reminded of Aragorn's dilemma: 'It is difficult with these evil folk to know when they are in league, and when they are cheating one another.'" Compton threw a sour look at Blade.

"OK, yeah, well, you know, you might have been able to get an answer to that question if you hadn't shot him in the head." He nudged Bridelow's body with his foot.

"Nobody's perfect, lad."

Compton expression turned baleful.

"As for the 'when' of it – " Blade glanced at his watch – "I'd say the balloon is going to go up in exactly...eight minutes."

"'The balloon will...' – what the hell are you talking about?"

Blade made a great show of looking at his wristwatch. "I'm expecting the shooting to begin again exactly eight minutes from...now."

"Wonderful. Just freakin' ducky! You know, I'm starting to think this getting-shot-at-for-a-living shit isn't all it's cracked up to be." Compton took a deep breath, then noisily let it out: he was a much calmer man than he had been just moments before. "Eight minutes, huh? How can you be so sure?"

"Because in eight minutes we're going to give those Arasaka goons the surprise of their lives."

---------------XXXXX---------------

"What the hell is he talking about?"

"I should have thought that would be obvious, even to you, Calvin," Mycroft replied in his most supercilious manner.

"Shut up, Mike, I don't need that right now. If you can tell me, tell me! What the hell is he up to?"

"He was an infantry officer – he still thinks like an infantry officer. He knows that the best time to launch a counter-attack is when his enemy is preparing an attack of their own. Watch and learn, Calvin, watch and learn...."

Mycroft was, of course, right.

---------------XXXXX---------------

"Uh, Blade, just whaddya mean by 'the surprise of their lives'?"

"Unless I'm sadly mistaken, young fella, he means that this is where we grab 'em by the nose and kick 'em the ass," Houston drawled, a hint of a twinkle in his eye. "Seems like a perfect opportunity for it. Leastways, that's how I see it." Cocking his head to one side, he gave Blade a considering look.

The Scot nodded firmly. "Short version, Compton, is this: while we've been sorting out who has been selling out whom in yer little excursion to the Sunshine State, the aether between here and Tokyo has been burning up. Whoever is in charge out there has been waiting for instructions to finish us off, and if he's got the balls to make suggestions of his own, permission to carry them out. Tenacity and thoroughness are mother's milk to a Japanese – thinking for himself isn't. These people are professionals, but they're also hidebound traditionalists."

Compton cocked his head and gave Blade a quizzical look while Houston nodded sagely. "Son, yor basic Japanese don't take a most honourable crap without a plan" – the Texan's drawl was marked by tiny note of derision – "and yor basic Japanese underling won't make a move without first coverin' his honourable ass with his superiors, all the way up the line, 'lessn' somethin' he does causes his boss – or worse, his boss's boss – to lose face. So whatever they're gonna do, it'll be by The Book – whatever 'tradition' says is the way to go. Y'see, son, the Japanese've got a talent for exquisite refinement, but they're not innovators. They don't think 'off the ranch,' so to speak: when they find a solution to a problem, that solution becomes Tradition, and God help any Japanese who bucks Tradition."

Blade picked up the thought. "And in this case, Tradition says they wait for instructions from on high. The Japanese aren't particularly swift when it comes to making a decision: once that decision's been made, though, they tend to get their arses in high gear very quickly."

"How many d'you reckon are still left out there," Houston asked, cocking at eyebrow at Blade.

"Twenty – perhaps twenty-five of them left."

"And they're still goin' t'be shaken up by that ass-whuppin' you gave 'em on yor way in.... Catch 'em off balance, hit 'em hard, get ourselves up to ground level where we've got some room to move and maneuver. Hopefully there'll be some cavalry somewhere who can arrive in time."

Compton cocked his head at that. "Yeah, speaking of cavalry, I've noticed that APD's been doing a whole lotta nuthin' since this whole shitball began. I suppose that means that Arasaka's been leaning hard on APD to leave them alone while they finish us off?"

Blade nodded. "Got it one, lad. Which gives us two choices: we let them come to us and blow us all away with heavy weapons – and they won't need more than a few minutes to do that once they get started – or we take the fight to them and get the hell out of here." Blade looked at Houston. "Well?"

"I'm not much on glorious last stands, Blade. I know it falls somewhere 'tween sacrilege and heresy for a Texan to say so, but I always thought them fellas at the Alamo were a buncha damned idjits."

Blade grinned, then raised his voice to be sure Red and Radome could hear him. "Right then, gear up, everybody! Now!"

"Sirr?" Alistair's voice in Blade's ear was quiet but urgent.

"What is it?"

"All of the internal audio and visual feed aboot yer location has been lost. As near as Ah ken, the loss o' signal is due to the feed lines being disrupted or cut at the main junction inside yon complex."

"Och, hell, Blade's Law Number 22, right on time."

Compton, not privy to MacLaren's conversation with Alistair, did a double. "Say what?"

"One of my Laws of Combat, Compton – 'Communications will fail just when you need something desperately.'" He tapped his earbud. "I just found out that our tactical feed has been cut off. That tells me the Arasakas are close to making their move and don't want us to see them getting ready. Right then, Alistair, give me a display of the last known positions of all the Arasaka personnel inside the mall and above ground."

"Here ye go, Sir." The display was projected into Blade's left eye, and he studied it for a few seconds.

"People, they're moving a bit faster than I expected. From the looks of things on the last images my VI got, they're still getting their shite together, so let's make that work in our favor." He turned to Houston and nodded at the semi-auto shotgun the Texan had retrieved from Red. "Have ye got flash-bangs and smoke for that?"

"I do."

"When I give the word, Alistair will open the door here, and I'll take out the remaining Rats. That will alert the Arasaka goons that we're coming, though, so on your command, Houston, Alistair will open the door leading out to the mall and you open fire."

"Lay down the flash-bangs and the smoke together, two or three of each, alternating?" Houston asked. Blade nodded.

"That should buy us a couple of seconds' worth of confusion. We hit the entrance running: Houston, you take the point, Red, you and Radome follow him. Who has the crystals?"

"I do," said Red, holding up a small, squarish metal security case that looked to be made of titanium.

"Give them to Radome."

"What, you don't think I can take care of them?" The indignation in the woman's voice was almost corrosive. "Or don't you trust me with them?"

Blade sighed. "Radome is the smallest person of the five of us – that means she's also the smallest target. Figure it out, lass."

"Oh." Almost sheepishly Red handed the case to the other woman.

"Alistair, did you copy that? Radome has the crystals."

"Radome has the crystals, aye, Sirr."

Blade looked at each of his four companions in turn as he spoke. "Compton and I will be the rearguard. Once you're through the door, turn left and run like hell down to the corridor to the main stairway. Don't stop for anyone or anything, except the crystals – if they don't get out, everything we've done will have been for shite. Whatever it takes, get up to street level and head toward the pavilion at Warren Plaza."

"Then what?" asked Radome.

"I don't know – I'll worry about that when we get there." Radome gave Blade another of those old-fashioned looks but said nothing more.

"Right, then, people, load and lock. Sound off when you're ready."

"Yo!"

"I'm ready."

"So am I."

"I'm as ready as I'll ever be." This was Compton, and the words were spoken accompanied by a cheeky grin. Blade grinned back, made certain the Enfield had a fresh magazine and a round chambered, then slung it over his shoulder and settled it. He checked that the magazine in the SIG-Sauer was full, then nodded.

"Alistair, open the safe room door."

----------------xxxxx----------------

"He's a madman! He's damned well certifiable!" Hobbes was incredulous, watching Blade lead his four companions out of the nightclub and into the smokescreen Houston had laid down. The microphones inside Bits clearly picked up the cacophony of gunfire erupted, but with no video feed from outside the club available, he had no idea what was actually happening – so naturally he assumed the worst. "He's going to get them all killed, and Arasaka will have the crystals! Once they do, we'll never get them – or Kim – back! Goddamn Scottish bastard!"

"As I said before, Calvin, Blade still thinks and acts like an infantry officer. My suggestion that you watch and learn still holds. Oh, my!" The last two words came out almost as if Mycroft had been startled.

"What is it?"

"Uh, nothing, sir, at least, nothing that changes the advice I just gave you."

The sudden rush out of Bits took everyone outside by surprise. Blade disposed of the four remaining Rats with a quartet of headshots while Houston blew apart the front windows and fired off his smoke and flash-bangs. Caught off-guard and off-balance, the *reisens* scattered, roughly half of them running to the left, toward what was, in fact, a dead end, the rest falling back down the mall toward the main entrance. Confused and disordered, their return fire was, at least initially, scattered, almost desultory.

Radome, Red, and Houston wasted no time, but took the attack to the Arasakas immediately, pressing forward, moving at a half-walk, half-trot as they laid down suppressive fire, picking off a target whenever one presented itself. Radome and Houston were no surprise there, their reputations made it clear they could handle themselves in a firefight; it was Red who was the revelation. She appeared to be every bit as competent as the late, unlamented Bridelow had assured Blade she was. There was a calm, almost detached expression on the face of the long-legged redhead in the crimson dress as she searched for targets that never wavered even for an instant when she fired.

As he and Compton took up the rearguard, Blade noted that, in sharp contrast to the rather excitable demeanor that Compton displayed whenever someone *wasn't* shooting at him, under fire the younger man was tightly focused. He methodically squeezed off controlled three- and four-round bursts of fire, and shifted from target to target with a swift deliberation. *A good man to have at your side or on your six,* Blade mused as he lined up on yet another *reisen*. And the lad was fast – unnaturally so, it seemed – moving from target to target with frightening speed and proficiency. *If we get out of this, I think there are a few questions I'll need to ask him about that,* a corner of Blade's mind thought absently.

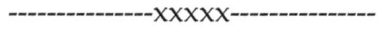

Nakajima was furious. *Goddammit! What the hell is Blade even doing here? I never expected him to show up – and now, for the first time ever, he's actually one step ahead of me!*

Umori looked at his superior and said simply, "Orders, sir?"

Nakajima hesitated, but only for a moment. "Numbers are the only advantage we have at the moment. They are clearly the more skilled fighters, and Blade is a force multiplier in his own right. But that Russian *gaijun*, Stalin, was right: quantity has a quality all its own, and right now our only choice is to make that sort of 'quality' work for us!" He pressed a key on his laptop, then spoke into the comm unit at his throat. "All available personnel move into the attack immediately. It doesn't matter what task you've been assigned, if you have a weapon, move into the mall and press the attack on the *gaijun* trying to break our containment. They cannot be allowed to escape, so, dead or alive, *contain them!*"

The dynamics were shifting, something was changing: the returning fire from the *reisen*, which had been noticeably slacking off, suddenly increased in volume and accuracy. Blade staggered as a small caliber bullet struck his chest, while two more shots narrowly missed his head.

"Alistair, something's happening! What's going on? Have you got anything you can give me as a tactical feed?"

"Nae, Sir, Ah haven't onything for ye. The video feed is still down. Ah'm blund here."

"Do what ye can, Alistair."

"Sir!"

Compton gave a snort and glanced at Blade. "Christ, this is going south so fast I think I can see the red shift. I never expected it to be this bad!"

"Oh, this is no' bad, Compton. In fact, ye haven't *seen* bad, yet," Blade replied. "But if ye just wait a few minutes, it'll be along."

"You coulda spared me that."

"Blade's Law Number 9: 'If you're short of everything except the enemy, you're in combat.' They're definitely getting reinforced from somewhere."

Ahead of them, Red, Houston, and Radome were pressing their own attack. Radome kept up a steady suppressive fire, four- and five-round bursts that kept the Arasakas from getting too adventurous. Houston kept a close eye on where she directed her fire, so that when the *reisen* popped their heads back up, he was ready with a full charge of buckshot. Meanwhile, Red seemed to have a preference for single shots, aimed and cleanly spaced, that took a steady toll on the opposition.

"How you doin', Missy?" Houston called out to Radome.

"I'm OK, but the ammo situation is getting tight. I've got maybe five rounds left in this magazine, and another three full mags in my ruck."

"We'd best git a move on then, get to the stairwell and get the hell outta Dodge!"

"I hear you! Let's hoof it!"

Though he heard none of that conversation, a quick glance over his shoulder a few seconds later told Blade that the trio had picked up their pace considerably, creating a gap between them and Compton and himself.

"C'mon, lad, close it up!"

"Hey, I'm moving my black ass as fast as I can, dude!"

"David!" Raven's voice unexpectedly crackled in Blade's ears, barely audible over the gunfire. "I've got something for you. It's about that implant you took out of Bridelow."

"Not right now, Raven! I'm a bit busy here!"

"But – "

"I love ye, lass, but it'll have to wait." A bullet's impact blew chips off the face of a concrete pillar just inches from Blade's face. "The Arasakas and I are having a wee divergence of opinion at the moment." Raven's reply was drowned out by a long burst of automatic fire from Compton, who swept across a line of advancing *reisen*. They all went down, some permanently, the rest to find what little cover they could in the open mall. But now there were more of them than there had been just moments earlier, and those who dropped to take cover were quicker to get back on their feet.

Calling over his left shoulder, Blade shouted, "Houston, Radome, Red! Get to that concrete kiosk as fast as you can! Wait for us there, then we'll take the stairs together!"

"Y'all got it!" "Roge-o!" "Will do!" all came back to him simultaneously, as the three of them set off at a run for what proclaimed itself to be an information booth. It was that, but it was also a security feature, built of cast concrete, designed and placed to prevent someone from attempting to drive a vehicle down into the mall. It was well suited to serve as a momentary redoubt, and Blade was determined to take advantage of it. As Radome, Red, and Houston charged forward, the remaining *reisen* before them, clearly disorganized and apparently demoralized as well, began retreating up the stairs.

Blade jerked in surprise when a quartet of pistol shots – from the sound of them, from a powerful pistol at that – burst out on his right. Spinning in their direction, bringing his SIG-Sauer to bear on the source, he was astonished to see a slender, very tall, incredibly good-looking blonde holding a classic Isosceles stance, calmly picking targets among the Arasakas and dispatching them one by one.

"Who the hell are ye and what the hell are ye doing here?" he shouted above the din.

The woman never took her eyes off her targets and continued to shoot as she shouted back, "They call me Spazz!" *Bang!* "It's a long story and don't ask!" *Bang! Bang!* "Anyway, I'm here to help – it looks like you could use it!" *Bang! Bang!*

Blade wasn't inclined to argue – "Spazz," whomever she really was, definitely knew how to shoot. Consequently, the added firepower was very welcome: his little band of merry warriors needed all the help it could get. Questions could wait until later – assuming both of them were still around whenever "later" arrived.

---------------xxxxx----------------

Raven stared helplessly at the bank of monitors before her. Alistair had woken her out of a sound sleep to alert her to Blade's situation, but for now she had no idea what he and his companions were actually facing: the video feed from his cybernetic eye had either stopped working or else he had shut it down. But there had been a disturbing undercurrent in Blade's voice, an urgency that Raven had rarely heard before. It took a moment for her to sort it out, and then she knew what it was: fear. Blade, for all of his accomplishments, wasn't superhuman. Raven knew that, in fact, he was sometimes as lucky as he was good – and in her opinion he played on that luck harder and more often than any truly sane human being ever should have done. Now, though, the realization that his luck might be running out and that he just possibly wasn't good enough to get out of this mess had driven itself home.

Yet the fear she was hearing wasn't that of a man in fear for his life. No, what Blade dreaded above all else was failure, to be weighed in the balance and be found wanting. It wasn't vainglory, nor was it ego, nor was it a devotion to some absurd "warrior ethos" concoction. It was duty, pure and simple, self-imposed, but no less binding for that. What Blade feared was failing to do what he understood to be his duty: getting the survivors of the extraction team to safety.

Raven's mind raced as she sought some way she could help the man who had once been her lover and was still her best friend. Her resources were vast, but they were electronic, and what Blade and his people needed right now was raw firepower. Scrolling through a series of displays with a speed that would have left any and all of them a meaningless blur to most anyone else on the planet, she stopped abruptly when her eyes flickered on the display for low-level aerial traffic over downtown Atlanta. There was a *lot* of traffic, far more than would be expected in the predawn hours of a Thursday. Her eyes narrowed as she took note of one particular icon.

"Why, hello there, Mr. NSA drone. Let's see what you can tell me today...." Her fingers flew over her keyboard as she tapped into the video and data feed being sent from the drone to the amateurs at Ft. Meade, Maryland. What she saw in the overhead imagery almost stopped her heart. "Oh, my God," she murmured, then took a quick glance at the other icons in the area, and without an instant's hesitation, she spun up a new com-link.

Spazz, Compton, and Blade slid inside the concrete kiosk, still blazing away at the Arasakas behind them whenever a target presented itself. Houston, Radome, and Red all looked at Spazz, then at Blade.

"Her name is Spazz, I'll explain more later if I can, but for right now, the lady can shoot and she's on our side."

"Good enough fer me," Houston drawled, potting a quick shot at a careless *reisen* atop the main stairway, thirty yards away. "'Specially if'n she can shoot."

"OK by me," Radome chimed in.

"Uh, guys, we've got a problem." This was Red, who gestured toward the top of the stairway. An almost solid phalanx of Arasakas had appeared and began shooting at the kiosk. Blade estimated there were at least twenty of them, a count seconded by Red. "I make at least twenty, maybe twenty-five, half of which are in a position where they can shoot at us." She grinned. "I just love rock 'n' roll!" With that she sent a long burst of automatic fire slamming into the advancing *reisen*. Those who weren't taken down didn't stop, however – they barely slowed down. "Uh, oh."

"Uh, Blade, a little help here?" Compton nudged the Scot in the ribs. "We've got our own problems here on our six." As if to emphasize his point, he emulated Red, firing full auto into the Arasakas coming up the mall, perhaps fifty yards away. "I don't know about you, but I don't have an unlimited supply of ammo, and this 'target-rich environment' shit really sucks!"

It was then that, as if in response to an unheard command, all the Arasakas *really* opened up on the half-dozen people huddled inside the kiosk....

"Yes! We have them now!" Nakajima pumped a fist as he shouted in triumph, a singular demonstration for someone who imagined himself a traditional stolid and stoic Japanese. "You made a stupid mistake, Blade, and now you'll pay the price for your stupidity!" Nakajima gave no further orders to his minions – there were none to give, they all knew what was expected of them now.

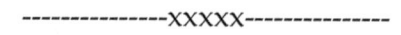

"Goddammit, Blade, I can't get a shot off!" Houston shouted over the din. "There's just too much metal flyin' this way! I know they're mostly sprayin'-and-prayin' but sooner or later they're gonna get lucky! And I'm thinkin' it's gonna be sooner!" Radome, Red, and Spazz had all taken to simply holding their weapons above the countertops of the kiosk, blindly firing toward the Arasakas in the hope of hitting *someone*. Even Compton had given up on trying to achieve anything like accurate fire, but just fired random bursts into the oncoming masses of *reisen*.

Chips and shards of concrete flew everywhere, one of them laying open Blade's left cheek. Three times he'd been struck by spent bullets, once in each shoulder and once in the chest. Spazz's right hand and forearm were bleeding from a half dozen cuts opened up by flying debris, Red's dress was ripped and ragged, there were small bloodstains in Radome's platinum locks. Amazingly, Compton seemed to be unmarked, although it was highly unlikely he would remain so for much longer.

A sudden grunt, a cough, and an "Aw, shit!" sounded to Blade's right, and Houston slumped over on his side. A ricochet had gotten lucky, bouncing off the side of the kiosk and into his side, where it found a gap in his body armour, and retained just enough kinetic energy to penetrate his flesh and force its way into his left lung. Blade had seen enough chest wounds to know that without medical help, Houston had perhaps fifteen minutes to live. It really didn't take all that long for a body to bleed out....

"Right then, that's enough of this shite," Blade murmured to himself, and holstered his nearly-empty SIG-Sauer. "It's about time somebody taught ye little yellow bastarts how to shoot." In a swift, fluid motion, the Lee-Enfield came off his back up to his shoulder, the working of the bolt a series of half-heard clicks as he rose to one knee and sighted over the countertop.

Boom!

Boom!

Boom!

Boom!

And so it went for a series of ten shots, less than two seconds separating each one, and with them ten Arasaka *reisen* died, a single, neat .303 calibre hole appearing in the bridge of each one's nose. Out went the spent magazine, in went a fresh one, and within seconds Blade resumed his deadly fusillade.

As he had hoped it might, the sudden onslaught of incredibly accurate rifle fire caused the Arasakas to hesitate, confounding them with its precision and methodical ruthlessness. Blade was trying to buy his comrades time, time to regroup their thoughts, to reorganize their own methods, a few precious seconds to shift into action rather than mere re-action. It might not be enough – it almost certainly wouldn't be – to let them find a way to survive, but Blade had given his word to Hobbes that he would get these people out of there, and Blade never broke his word: the first time he did so would be the time he died while trying to keep it.

More sensed than seen behind him, Spazz once again was skillfully choosing and capping her targets, and smoothly slid into a position to cover Blade's "six" as he brought the Lee-Enfield into action. Taking advantage of the Arasakas' brief hesitation, Red and Radome brought their rifles to bear and began dispatching their own targets. Compton did likewise, and for a few seconds the little group held their own and gave better than they got. But in the long run, Blade knew, it wouldn't be enough; the thought shamed him, but still he continued to mark his targets, work his rifle's bolt, squeeze the trigger. It would be over soon enough.

----------------xxxxx----------------

Raven watched her monitors with a fevered intensity, not knowing what was going on inside Underground Atlanta, knowing only that Blade was still alive because his comm link was still functional. She saw the mass of Arasakas rushing toward the entrances to the subterranean mall, fumed in impotent rage as the APD stood idly by, and prayed a prayer to any god who might be listening. *Please let me have called him in time, please! Please get there in time, Nathan, please get there in time!*

----------------xxxxx----------------

The grin of triumph on Nakajima's face was almost demonic in its glee, an expression mirrored by Umori. The glee abruptly gave way to surprise, confusion, and then consternation when his communication links were suddenly filled with the intense hiss of pure static, the white noise by product of broad-spectrum jamming.

"What the hell? Where did that come from Umori? Get my comm links back up! I want to watch Blade die!"

----------------xxxxx----------------

Within seconds of each other, all three skylights that illuminated the upper level of Underground Atlanta imploded as the hulls of a trio of AV-10s settled on them, and a score of heavily-armed men and women wearing suits of black Weclar armour rappelled from the bottom hatch of each, firing stunner rounds at the Arasakas. An amplified voice that mixed a central Texas twang with an Ivy League drawl issued forth from a loudspeaker in each vehicle.

"Cease fire! Cease fire immediately! All Arasaka personnel are directed to put down their weapons and offer no further resistance – refusal to comply will be met with deadly force. This is Nathan Gerrard, U.S. Marshal. We'll take it from here, fellas."

Chapter 4

Hardly had the last shards of glass from the shattered skylights settled and the echoes of Nathan Gerrard's announcement died away than Blade and Radome were shouting for medical assistance, while Compton and Spazz did what they could for Houston. Red, meanwhile, was keeping a wary eye on the Arasakas, the muzzle of her rifle pointed up and away, but ready to drop it down and open fire again if provoked. Her expression was a mix of watchfulness and anger, as if she were almost wishing for one of the *reisen* to try something treacherous. Within a minute, a quartet of paramedics carrying a gurney rushed down the main stairway, shoving their way through at least two score of kneeling Arasakas. The Japanese operatives were surprisingly docile, perhaps from the surprise of how quickly the tables had turned against them, perhaps in the knowledge that theirs was a precarious situation that could only be made worse by a meaningless show of resistance. These men and women knew that, under the draconian federal laws passed in the wake of Black Christmas fifteen years earlier, they were technically terrorists, and as such could face the death penalty. Dying a glorious but pointless death for one's overlord – feudal or corporate – was long since a thing of the past for the enforcers of Japan's *keiretsu*.

A smaller VSTOL craft – to Blade it sounded like a Boeing Whirlwind – landed and a moment later a familiar figure began descending the stairs into Underground Atlanta, US Marshal Nathan Gerrard. Impeccably dressed in what looked to be – and almost certainly was – a tailor-made three-piece suit, good-looking in a battered sort of way, Gerrard had a complexion best described as leathery, with deep creases around his mouth, a slightly prominent nose, and a pair Basset hound-like eyes that women found irresistible. At the moment, his expression was grim as he walked over to Blade, who held out his hand in greeting, Gerrard reluctantly taking it.

"Hello, Nathan. Splendid entrance ye made there – I had no idea that ye had such a flair for the dramatic. Not that I'm not glad to see ye, but ye did cut that a bit bloody fine, didn't ye?"

"Don't complain, if it hadn't been your friend Raven, I might not have shown up at all."

"Oh?"

"Yeah. We were keeping an overwatch on the mall here, in case the Arasaka crew got out of hand or broke the APD containment. When we lost the a/v feed from inside here, all we could see was a mass of these *reisen* rushing in. We didn't have any idea why, though. It was Raven who called me and told me what was actually going down in here. Just in time, apparently."

"Damn, I suppose I owe her a weekend at Claridge's now. There'll be no living with her after this."

Gerrard seemed something less than amused. "Dammit, David, what the hell have you gotten your sorry Scotch ass into this time?" Like Houston's, Gerrard's voice was, at the moment, pure distilled Texan.

"Nathan, ye ignorant cowboy, how many times do I have to tell ye, it's not 'Scotch' it's 'Scottish'!"

"No, it's 'Scotch,' because whenever you show up, by the time you leave, I need a bottle of it!" Taking a quick glance around, Gerrard pulled Blade to one side. "Now just what the hell is going on here, David?"

"'What's going one here?' To be honest with ye, Nathan, I'm not all that sure myself."

"Goddammit, Mycroft, get those feeds back up! I have to know what's going on in there! Who has the crystals?"

"Calvin, the video and audio pickups are hardwired – they have no wireless capability, and as I told you a few moments ago, the connections have been physically broken." Mycroft's tone of voice was that of an adult patiently explaining something to an angry child. "There is literally nothing I can do about it."

"Then tap into that NSA drone, see what they're pulling down! Getting my information from the Ignorant News Network isn't going to cut it! I want to know what's happened to those crystals!"

"There is no signal from the US Marshals, Calvin, so there's nothing to tap into from the drone. The NSA is as blind as I am."

"Then think of something else! That's what I built you for! I've got to know who has those crystals!" Calvin's voice grew louder and louder as he went on, so that the last four words were shouted at Mycroft.

"Calvin, ranting about it isn't going to help you or anyone else restore Kim's consciousness – "

"I don't care about Kim right now! *I want those crystals back!*"

"Calvin – "

"Mycroft, my reputation, my life's work, my life are invested in those crystals, and you damned well know it. You also know what's on them. If DisCom or Arasaka – or, God help me, the Feds – get their hands on them, it will ruin me – destroy me! *So find out what has happened to them! NOW!*"

"At the moment, this is what we know: in Atlanta, Georgia, at approximately 3:00 AM this morning, what can best be described as a firefight broke out in the subterranean shopping complex Underground Atlanta." The plasticine-pretty, perfectly coifed, impossibly perky blonde on the television screen, "Courtney Crawford," if the caption at the bottom was to be believed, read from her teleprompter with a well-feigned breathless urgency. "At the time, the Atlanta Police Department stated that the incident was 'gang related,' and in keeping with their standard operating procedure, put the complex into lockdown, with the intention of letting the situation resolve itself before Atlanta Police officers moved in.

"However, INN has since learned that the incident is not gang-related, but instead is a confrontation between this man, Major David MacLaren, an international vigilante popularly known as 'Blade,'" – a photo of the Scot, obviously a stock image, appeared onscreen – "an undetermined number of his associates, and what are alleged to be mercenaries in the employ of the Arasaka Corporation. The confrontation came to a climax a short while ago as US Marshals moved to intervene, and Internet News Network was there to record the action."

The image on the television screen switched to some rather jittery, slightly blurred footage, taken by the INN ground crew, obviously, at the moment of the US Marshals' intervention. For a few seconds, Blade could be clearly seen, as could Spazz and Compton; Red and Radome were completely out of the frame. There was some equally hectic video of Houston being treated by a cluster of paramedics that abruptly ended when a deputy marshal stepped into the picture and rather forcibly shooed the cameraman away.

"Early reports indicate that there may be as many as fifty dead inside Underground Atlanta. How many of those victims were unarmed civilians trapped in the crossfire is unknown, but the number is likely to be high. Meanwhile, speculation is rife as to the cause of this incident, as well as why 'Blade,' a notoriously violent foreign national, has once again been allowed into the United States.

"Again, for those of you just joining us, we have this breaking story from Atlanta, Georgia...." The newsreader droned on, beginning the first of what would be many repetitions, with only the slightest variations, of the same information. Given how much she evidently enjoyed the sound of her own voice, it would be hours before she stopped.

Meanwhile, Umori having composed his expression into one of studied neutrality, very carefully avoided making eye contact with Nakajima, who was pacing about the room like a caged tiger, his face red with suffused rage. The *Bumon rida* was not mercurial, but he *was* unpredictable: it was not unknown for him to resort to an act of physical violence when his temper was stretched to the breaking point, but he almost always made an inanimate object the target of his wrath – almost. The few known incidents where the he turned upon a human being had all been fatal, however, so Umori was not prepared to run the risk of being the next victim.

Having ordered the CCTV system in Underground Atlanta cut off, Nakajima and Umori had continued to monitor the melee in the subterranean mall via direct feeds from the *reisen*, Nagumo in particular. Nakajima had also turned on the hotel suite's flat-screen television, as INN had two news crews on the scene, one on the ground, the other in a VTOL aircraft circling overhead, trying to make head or tails of the chaos. He had been taken aback by the sudden – and unanticipated – arrival of the US Marshals, and the speed with which they had intervened. Within seconds, all contact with any of the Arasakas inside the mall was lost. Now, as INN was replaying the few bits of video the ground crew had managed to record, the faces of Blade, Spazz, and Compton were all clearly visible. As he watched them over and over again, something finally snapped inside Nakajima.

"*Enough!*" he bellowed in red-faced rage. "Is it not sufficient that this man should have been dead ten years ago, but now he thwarts me again? *And who is that woman?* Where did she come from? I will deal with Blade myself, but as for the rest, I want them dead! Do you hear me? Dead! I want their homes burned to the ground so that I can visit them at midnight and defecate on the ashes! All of them! *I want them DEAD!*" At that last word, Nakajima spun on his heel back to face the television monitor, and with a lightning-fast blow drove his right fist into the face of the flat screen and out through the back panel.

In that instant, the rage dissipated and Nakajima reasserted control over himself. Withdrawing his hand from the shattered monitor, he examined it dispassionately, almost fascinated. There was surprisingly little blood, Umori noted, but where the flesh had been lacerated and peeled away, light glinted off exposed metal. After a moment, Nakajima looked at Umori, then at his hand, and said simply, "I suppose I'd best have a repair tech take a look at this...."

----------------xxxxx----------------

"What do you mean, you're not sure? You just turned Underground Atlanta into a shooting gallery, and you don't know why? David, I may have been born at night, but it wasn't last night!"

"I mean it, Nathan. The people I'm working for aren't telling me everything. For that matter, they're not actually telling me a whole hell of a lot at all."

"Hey, don't try to play one of your 'I'm just the hired help' games with me, because we both know – "

"That's just it, I'm not – playing that game, I mean. I really haven't got this all figured out yet." Blade passed a hand across his eyes, drew a deep breath, held it for few seconds, then let it out noisily. "Ye wouldn't happen to have a bottle of water handy, would ye?"

"You actually admit to drinking plain water?"

"Nathan!"

"All right, all right, keep your sporran on." Gerrard turned and gestured to a passing deputy. "Hey, Polaneczky, can we get a couple of bottles of water over here?"

"Sure thing, sir!"

Turning back to Blade, Gerrard said, "You were talking about not knowing a whole hell of a lot?"

"Aye, that's just it, Nathan. I really don't. What I do know doesn't make me particularly happy, though." He went into a concise but detailed summary of everything he knew or suspected, from the moment he took Hobbes' first call. "I can't get away from what Raven said when she reviewed the data Hobbes sent me: 'There are wheels within wheels within wheels here.' I don't know what it was that she saw that made her say that – she never got around to telling me – but when she talks like that, I listen."

"Yeah, well, you should. And it just so happens that I agree with you – and Raven."

"Ye do? There's one for the record books." Deputy Polaneczky returned with a liter bottle of water apiece for Blade and Gerrard. The Scot nodded at him. "Thanks, lad, I'm completely parched!" He then drank deeply for a moment, then continued.

" I truly don't know what's going down with this affair, but I can promise ye this about it: when I do learn what it is, ye'll be the second to know."

"And who's gonna be the first?"

Blade smirked. "Me."

Gerrard rolled his eyes heavenward as if begging for patience, but when his gaze came back to Blade, his eyes were hard. "Look, David, when I said just what the hell is going on here, I wasn't asking what the hell just happened. I already know all of that. The problem is that apparently while Arasaka was leaning real hard on APD to keep their distance, somebody else – somebody with a lot more juice that Arasaka, mind you – was leaning hard on Washington to keep *us* from getting involved as well."

"So what tipped the balance?"

"Rumor in Crystal City has it that your friend, Raven, made a phone call at 2:00 AM to Director Smith. Now, I don't know what she said to him, but the story making the rounds is that five minutes into the conversation Chris was willing to give her anything she asked for." Blade smirked but said nothing. "Anyway, by 3:00 he had me and two complete Tac Teams airborne and on the way down here, violating just about every FAA speed regulation ever written. Not to mention stomping all over a bunch of pissant 'jurisdiction' issues that he's going to get into a lot of hot water over later." Gerrard paused, looked around at several clusters of deputies taking into custody the remaining *reisen* still standing, while here and there paramedics and first-responders worked on those wounded who, in their professional judgment, could still be saved. "Even then we were only on stand-by. It was when Raven commed me personally and told me the shit had completely hit the fan that I decided to give the 'GO' order on my own authority."

"Don't think I don't appreciate that, Nathan – truly I do. But I suspect that ye have a larger point to make?"

"More than one, you thick-headed Scotsman, but the most important to you is this: we've been keeping an eye on this situation almost from the minute that Coleridge's little 'extraction team' – don't look so surprised, we knew all about it! – holed up inside Bits."

"And...?"

"And you're damned lucky Raven called Director Smith. We normally don't get involved in situations that really aren't more than glorified industrial espionage, you know that, but we do like to keep an eye on things when there's foreign nationals involved, especially when they invoke the special provisions of the Pac-Rim Trade Treaty."

"Go on."

"Well, in this case, somebody not only invoked Pac-Rim, they tried to twist its provisions into a legal pretzel to keep us out of the action."

"Right. Now ye're just being cryptic."

"David, somebody on the other side was very careful to make sure that nothing they did would automatically trigger a Federal response. First, there's the question of whether or not the forcible entry into DisCom's R and D centre was actually a crime or an attempt to recover stolen property: the goddamned lawyers could – and would – spend years arguing that one out. So any justification for my department to get involved that way would have been real shaky at best. Second, the DisCom goons following Calvin's people up I-75 broke off the pursuit before they crossed the Georgia state line. Speeding across state lines isn't a federal crime, so my people were left with absolutely no legal grounds there to intervene. Then, there was no way to prove that any of the DisCom people who were waiting here for Calvin's little group to show up had been involved in that clusterfuck in Florida, again leaving me and my department in the same predicament."

"I think I'm beginning to see a pattern here."

"You're damn right you do! Then Arasaka shows up. You'd think that would be enough to bring down the Feds on this little comedy of errors, right? Wrong. Arasaka was busy whispering sweet nothings into the ears of APD, and APD promptly notified us that as far as they were concerned, no Federal laws had been broken, there was no proof that 'foreign nationals employed by the Arasaka Industrial Group had entered the country with criminal intent,' and they weren't going to do anything about the situation but let it play itself out." Gerrard's heavy sigh was a mixture of anger, frustration, and resignation. "This isn't like the old days, when we Feds could just come waltzing in and tell everyone to fuck off. Now most of the time we need permission – permission! – from local and state authorities to come into their jurisdictions and enforce Federal laws. Those assholes in DC may have thought they were untouchable twenty years ago, but the times, they've been a-changin'." Gerrard shook his head ruefully. "It's a sorry goddamned world when foreign nationals show up on American soil, carrying out what meets every legal definition of a terrorist act, and the Federal government can't act to stop them because of how the Feds fucked up twenty years ago."

MacLaren nodded in sympathy. "Nathan, ye're one of the good guys, ye always have been, so in yer case, I feel some of yer pain. But given what the Justice Department was doing twenty years ago, the people in DC were lucky they didn't have a full-on armed revolt on their hands instead of what actually happened. It's their own damned fault nobody trusts them anymore."

"Yeah, I know. That doesn't make it any easier today, though. What's making me really twitch about all this is how well it was put together. It seems like somebody went to a lot of trouble to make sure all the pieces got into the right places at the right time. And *that* makes me wonder if those crystals were really what they wanted after all, or if whoever was pulling the strings had some other target in mind. But there's something else, David."

"And that would be...?"

"On the flight in, before we got the green light, I personally watched a recording of the CCTV feed from down here while you were making your little 'incursion' into the club. Raven gave it to me. And frankly, what I saw made me wonder what the hell is wrong with you, goddammit!"

"What are ye talking about, Nathan?"

"I'm talking about how hard you went in! There were at least five times when you had Arasaka people down, crippled, incapacitated – and you still took them out with head shots! You didn't just take them down, you *executed* them! If it wasn't for the fact that I'm mightily pissed off at illegal Japanese nationals in this country carrying out acts of violence on my turf, diplomatic immunity or not I'd have you up on Murder One charges so fast that even your artificial eye would spin! Why the hell were you doing it, Blade?"

MacLaren's head came up sharply at Gerrard's use of his call sign, the US Marshal's way of accusing him of being unprofessional. "The heat of the moment...tactically it seemed like the best thing to do...I don't know. Why is it so important to ye?"

"Because that's not you! You're more controlled than that – normally. But this wasn't normal, was it? I know you've got a grudge against Arasaka – shit, damn near everybody in this business does! But I understand why yours is more personal. Still, taking out bit players and spear-carriers isn't going to get you any closer to who you really want to take down, and we both know it. And frankly, I don't want to be the one to come after you because you've gone off the deep end and been declared a public menace. So I'm wondering if maybe you shouldn't be rethinking this contract and give it up, go find something less personal."

"This contract will be completed as soon as I get those crystals back into Hobbes' hands, which I will do sometime this morning. There may be repercussions and consequences – hell, we both know there will be, because Arasaka's involved. But I'll deal with those when the time comes. As for Raven's 'wheels within wheels within wheels,' even she couldn't put her finger on exactly what it was. Something kicked her intuition into high gear, and I have a very healthy respect for that woman's hunches, but without something more to work with than some vague suspicion, there's nothing I can do." Blade took a deep breath, held it, then let it out slowly and quietly. "As for how I treat the Arasaka *reisen*...that's between them and me. Leave it at that, Nathan."

Gerrard knew better than to argue. He'd once looked up the definition of "stubborn" in the Oxford Dictionary, and found Blade's photo there. But that didn't mean he had to like what Blade just told him, and he didn't, not one bit.

"All right, David, have it your way. But I gotta tell you one more thing: what went down here in the past fifteen hours was by any definition one hellacious act of terrorism. And like it or not, you were a part of it. Now I know that you came into the country using that diplomatic passport C gave you, but that doesn't mean you can't be PNG'ed in a heartbeat. There's a lotta people in DC trying to reclaim the authority the Fed lost back in 2020, and the way that APD screwed the pooch here is only gonna help them. There's already backchannel talk about police corruption and illegal ties between APD, the City of Atlanta, and Arasaka."

"I shouldn't wonder. There were a lot of cops busily looking the other way when I got here tonight. But what does that have to do with me?"

"Like it or not, David, you're going to be the lightning rod. You're a high-profile figure – and you've got nobody to blame but yourself for that, remember! There's people in Congress, hell, there's Cabinet members, who'll blame you for this whole affair, never mind that it all got started twelve hours before you even arrived in Atlanta. In a couple of hours the screamsheets are going to have four-inch high headers shouting 'International vigilante triggers massive shootout in Atlanta!' And those people in Washington I mentioned are going to be shouting just as loud that between police corruption and having international mercenaries like you running amok it's time to turn the clock back to 2016. You've become the poster boy for everything they say is wrong with the status quo. The way they see it, you're violent, you're unpredictable, you flaunt international borders and jurisdictions whenever and however you feel like it, and the only people you really answer to are yourself and whoever you're working for at the moment."

Blade held out his hands, palms up. "Just what is it ye're trying to tell me, then, Nathan?"

"I'm telling you to watch your back. There's a serious turf war going on over you between APD, the GBI, and about half the departments of the Federal government – FBI, State, DOJ, INS, my bureau, hell, just about everybody but the goddamn EPA. And I have no idea who is going to win. APD wants to lock you up and throw the key away because you embarrassed them so badly on the national 'nets, but I can sit on them for now. The GBI is on the fence – they don't have any egg on their face, at least none that you threw. That bitch Secretary of State wants to fry your ass – mainly because she's one of the power grabbers – but she can't because you've got diplomatic immunity. She's gonna do her damnedest, though, to get it revoked, mark my words. All the enemies you made the last time you were in the country are lining up and sharpening their knives, Blade."

The Scot gave Gerrard a speculative look. "I don't plan on giving them the chance. Right now, Nathan, I'm hoping that I can hand over those crystals to Hobbes, get paid, go home, and be done with it. But ye said yerself that ye agree with Raven that there are more layers to this affair than anyone would think at first glance. And if this isn't over, if this is just the curtain raiser, if it turns out that somebody isn't willing to let me go home...well, if ye're expecting me to just walk away from it, ye're going to be sorely disappointed. So the question is, what do ye intend to do?"

Gerrard gave a heavy sigh, then shrugged. "My jurisdiction technically – technically, mind you! – covers the entire United States of America. Right now, though, in practical terms, my specific authority in this case ends at the municipal limits of Atlanta. Director Smith's orders. Once you're outside the Perimeter, David, you're on your own."

Blade nodded his understanding of the complications Gerrard outlined. As with most of America's law enforcement agencies, the span and scope of the powers exercised by the US Marshals, the Department of Justice were far more restricted than they had once been, one of the consequences of America's social and political upheavals in the summer and autumn of madness in 2020, and the post-election turmoil and violence that for six months had the country teetering on the brink of civil warfare, a period that went into the history books as "The Social War."

When the dust had settled, the fires were extinguished, and the bodies buried, the whole of America's social and political landscape had been irrevocably altered, as had the very nature of law enforcement in the United States. The mayors and city councils who had defunded and restructured their police departments into impotence abruptly found themselves compelled to resort to private-sector security forces in order to avert the cities' total collapse, a reaction that was met with somewhat less than universal approbation; at the same time, the "militarization" of American police forces was sharply curtailed, which no one but power-hungry politicians and bureaucrats regretted.

For the first few years crime spiked in the urban centers – in the suburbs and rural areas, a rough-and-ready form of justice came into existence, one that was often decried as "vigilantism" by the mass media, even as it was for the most part studiously ignored by local law enforcement officials. Overall, the means and methods America used to compensate for and in reaction to the new reality were a far from perfect response, but in time it sorted itself out, especially once the criminals learned that while those carrying out enforcement might have changed, the laws themselves hadn't.

There were, inevitably, unexpected consequences. The most far-reaching was the costly and futile "war on drugs" being phased out of existence within five years – along with the constitutional "irregularities" it had spawned – despite the tooth-and-nail opposition of numerous government officials who had built bureaucratic empires within the long-lived program. The manpower and resources the "war on drugs" had consumed were reallocated and reassigned throughout the various "alphabet agencies" where, it was hoped, they could be put to better use.

For Nathan Gerrard and his colleagues, those consequences translated into new limits imposed on the authority and jurisdiction of federal law enforcement agencies – an effort to curtail the sort of abuses of power that had become all but standard operating procedure for the Justice Department during the terms of the first two American Presidents of the 21st Century. It was also an acknowledged fact that some of those restraints hindered those same agencies when they were called upon to carry out their legitimate duties. Hence the warning to Blade about the limitations under which, fifteen years later, Gerrard was still compelled to operate.

"I get it, Nathan," MacLaren said quietly. "Yer hands are tied. It could be worse. At least now I know whose side ye're on – if ye can't help, I know it isn't because ye're about to stab me in the back."

Gerrard nodded. "I won't come after you, I won't arrest you, whatever you do. But I also can't protect you. Best remember that. Now, you've got one hour to get your goddamn Scotch ass outta here."

"As soon as I get a drink, I'm gone."

"Radome?"

The cool soprano voice coming over her comlink was unfamiliar, and the young techie frowned as she replied. "Yes?"

"This is Raven, Blade's friend. Alistair gave me your combination."

"Ah, OK." Her expression brightened considerably. "What can I do for you?"

"How are you doing right now?"

"I take it the question isn't just cursory?"

"No, it isn't."

Radome took a deep breath, then let it out slowly. "I'm not wounded or injured, if that's what you mean. A little beat up, a few cuts and scratches. But what just happened was intense – really intense. That's the closest I've *ever* come to getting killed. And I just watched the paramedics take my friend Houston away – they *think* he's going to make it. So I won't tell you I'm OK. 'Fine' is probably closer to the truth. You know, 'Fucked-up, Insecure, Neurotic – '"

"'– and *Excitable*.'" Raven finished for her. Both women laughed. "Been there, done that, didn't like the T-shirt so I left it behind. What I'm thinking is that a little work therapy might help you decompress. Do you happen to have your deck handy?"

Radome snorted in amusement. "Do bears bear? Do bees bee? Is the Pope Kenyan?"

"Right, got me. Silly question. But the reason I asked is that David told me that you were carrying the crystals and I'm hoping that you might have a set of UCPs with you. If you do, you might be able to jack into them and then link me so I can get a look at what's inside them."

"I've got the UCPs, and they'll mate with the connectors on the crystals, but I'm not sure if I should be doing that. After all, our job was just to recover them – nobody said anything about looking inside them."

"Alistair, a little help here?"

"Aye, Miss Ligeia." The Highland burr popped into Radome's comlink again, and in spite of herself, she smiled at hearing it.

"Miss Radome, ye ken that this entire kerfuffle is a wee bit more complicated than what ye were first told aboot. Am I richt?"

"I think that's a bit of an understatement, really."

"Well, Sir David is – "

"'*Sir* David'?"

"Aye, Miss. It's a long story and I doubt the Major will be takin' the time tae tell ye aboot it, but ye can ask 'im. Onyway, Sir David has been wonderin' just what it is aboot those crystals that has both Discom and Arasaka so interested in 'em tae the point that people are dyin' because of 'em."

Raven picked up the conversation at this point. "Normally, David doesn't even get involved in this sort of situation – you know his reputation is for 'fixing' other kinds of problems. But he's doing this for a friend – Calvin Coleridge, the man who hired you – and once he found that Arasaka was involved, there was no keeping him out of it. What I'd like to do is see if I can figure out just what it is about those crystals that some people think they're worth killing for. In case they decide to try again."

"Yeah." Radome drew the word out for almost two seconds. "I have to admit that I've had some thoughts along those same lines. It struck me as odd right from the start that the extraction team seemed really heavy on muscle and firepower – lots more than you would think anyone would need for a simple industrial espionage op, even one where Discom was involved."

"And Ah think Ah speak frae the Major when I say that he'll look kindly on anything ye might find that will help him protect his hairless pink bahookie."

"That's it, Alistair! I'm telling David what you just said!"

"Aw, dinna say that, Miss Ligeia – if ye do, well, there goes the raise Ah was promised."

"Alistair, you're a VI. You don't get raises – you don't even get a salary!"

"Aye, Miss, but 'tis the thought that counts, ye ken."

Both women giggled, then Radome said, "We might as well get

started. Give me a second to get everything booted and jacked in. Mind if I watch once you get to work, Raven?"

"Not at all. In fact, having another set of eyes on this is probably a good idea. Alistair, you might as well join us, but stand by in case Blade needs you."

"Aye, that Ah wull, Miss."

The drink that MacLaren had assured Nathan Girrard he would be seeking out was one that the Scot needed...well, "desperately" was perhaps too strong a word, but certainly "urgently" fit the bill. Since the days of the Greek hoplites – and probably earlier – almost the very first act of men who had just survived combat was to seek out *something* alcoholic to drink, whether it be, depending on time and place, rough country wine, cheap rum, the finest Highland malt, or an extraordinary vintage of champagne. It was almost a reflexive ritual that, for those partook of it, through its very mundaneness, affirmed, and in its own way celebrated, that they had survived – if they had time to drink from a bottle, a clay jar, a canteen, or a wineskin, they were out of danger, at least for the moment. True, combat turned the throat of even the most courageous human bricky dry, but that reassurance to the fighter that he or she still lived was every bit as important as slaking his thirst.

It wasn't the effects of the alcohol, then, that Blade craved, nor was it actual thirst that drove him to seek it out – it was the affirmation which taking that drink provided. Less than fifteen minutes earlier he'd been arse-deep in a firefight from which he almost certainly would not have emerged alive, save for the timely – or, more accurately, last minute – arrival of the cavalry in the form of the US Marshals Service. But survived he had, he and – hopefully, as there was no word yet about Houston – all of his little band, and that, without a doubt, was something worth a token celebration at least. And he knew just where he could find a bottle of the Macallan....

As he made his way back to the nightclub, Blade noted the carnage left in the wake of the extraction team's passage. It seemed like there were still-slowly-spreading red puddles covering half the floor of Underground Atlanta. In the middle of each crimson pool was a body, some sprawled awkwardly, others seemingly huddled in on themselves, some lying face-up, others face-down, a few lying on their sides. Blade shook his head, contemplating the slaughter he'd left in his wake. It hadn't been fair, he mused, although he knew full well that "fair" was a concept that only had any validity in board games and amateur athletics.

But in a way, it really hadn't been "fair": those poor dead Arasaka bastards – and the DisCom goons – had been hopelessly overmatched. They had been little better than street fighters, swaggering, posturing toughs more accustomed to intimidating the weak and pliable than confronting men and women who could – and would – fight back. With little real training, minimal fire discipline, and no tactical coordination, most of them had been as good as dead the moment they set foot inside Atlanta Underground. That angered MacLaren, for though his was a profession which all too often relied on violence and death for him to accomplish his mission, this sort of wanton throwing away of human lives flew in the face of every professional precept he embraced. Being that this had been an Arasaka operation, Blade had a very good idea who was behind it, and who bore the ultimate responsibility for the slaughter. That knowledge clouded his mood even further.

Still, there was a bit of a silver lining *Thank God,* he mused, *there weren't any civilians around when I broke in and then we broke out. This is bad enough without there being a few soccer moms or a couple of teen-age kids lying among them. If this truly is your work, Hideki, and I'm certain it is, then you've just compounded the interest you owe on your butcher's bill.* Blade sighed in resignation. *I really do need that drink now.*

---------------xxxxx---------------

Bits was, as to be expected, a wreck. Half the glass in the windows opening on the mall was missing, the mirror behind the bar had been shivered into thousands of pieces, the lighting framework that had been above the dance floor was now lying *on* the dance floor, and almost every other fixture had taken some sort of damage. There were, Blade noted, a few tables and chairs, along with a handful of barstools, left more or less intact, the latter now standing upright before the sadly battered bar. Not all of the barstools were empty: evidently he wasn't the only person for whom an after-action libation was part of the decompression process.

Red was sitting at the far end of the bar when Blade walked in; amazingly, given what she had been doing just minutes earlier and the fact that her knee-length crimson dress was considerably worse for the wear, the woman looked as if she had just stepped off the set of a fashion-magazine shoot. One look at her told Blade that he wasn't ready to tackle that particular enigma – not yet at least. Meanwhile, Spazz had parked herself at the near end, almost as if she had been waiting for him. Her once-white blouse was torn and stained in a couple of places, there was a gunpowder smear on her right cheek, her hair hung around her shoulders in absolute disarray, and if she'd been wearing make-up, it had long since vanished in the action that just concluded. In short, she looked stunning.

Scylla and Charybdis, he thought wryly. *Odysseus, my lad, I'm beginning to feel some sympathy for ye....*

He walked by Spazz, passed up the barstool beside her, and took the next one down. As he sat down, he the thought crossed his mind – not for the first time – that his life was much like a Durrenmatt play. *Not twenty minutes earlier I was fighting for my life; now I'm in what's left of a shot-up bar, about to order a well-deserved whisky, flanked by two drop-dead gorgeous and thoroughly enigmatic females. Whoever said life was strange had a real gift for understatement.*

He nodded to the bartender, whose nametag identified him as simply "Mike", and took note of a rifle and a pistol – a Militec Model 28 and a Sturmer Avenger, respectively – sitting on the counter behind the bar.

"Looks as though ye came back to work prepared," he said conversationally.

"Actually, I never left." Mike half-smirked. He was good-looking, slender, wiry, with brushed-back dark hair, and a mustache that looked as if he trimmed it with a razor in one hand and a micrometer in the other. And he was annoyingly cheerful, almost perky.

"Oh?"

"I was working yesterday when Calvin's people showed up – along with their uninvited guests. There were too many bullets flying around for my taste, so I ducked into my little hidey-hole under the floor of the bar here. Mama Williamsom didn't raise no fool for a son, and besides, Calvin doesn't pay me enough to get involved in a firefight with the likes of DisCom and Arasaka. I stayed there until the marshals gave the all-clear." He laid a proprietary hand on the weapons. "Still, it never hurts to be prepared. Anyway, what can I get you?"

Before Blade could answer, Spazz had slid over to the stool beside him, carefully laying her pistol – a Korth PRS II, he noted – on the bar in front of her. There was a dark liquid in her glass, in which small golden flakes were drifting about.

"What the hell are ye drinking?" he asked her.

"A 'Dead Nazi'."

"A what?"

"It's fifty-fifty Jägermeister and Goldschlager. Want to try one?"

Blade made a face and shook his head. "No, thank ye."

Spazz shrugged. "Or you could settle for just a 'Dead German' – equal parts well-brand herbal and cinnamon schnapps."

Blade shuddered and gestured to Mike. "Did any of The Balvenie survive?"

"It did. We don't leave the good stuff out where the peasants can get at it."

"Then The Balvenie, if you would – ten year-old." He paused briefly, then said, "Best make it a double."

Spazz looked at him carefully, then smiled and purred, "Not going to try to impress me by ordering a vodka martini, shaken not stirred?"

Blade shook his head again. "No way. James drank those. Still does, for that matter, even after his liver transplant."

"He's still around?"

"New face, new identity, goes by the name of Shaw these days, lives in Jamaica with his wife, Heidi. I run into him now and then, when I get down to the Caribbean."

"Amazing, the people you 'run into' in this line of work." The way she said it was layered with meanings.

"Apparently so. Tell me, Miss Spazz, what were ye – what *is* yer real name, by the way?"

"Maureen Collins." She held out her hand. Blade was pleased to find her grip firm, warm, and dry, nothing like the dead fish too many women still offered up in a handshake.

"'Collins.' Irish?"

"A few generations back, yes."

"Just so ye know, on the whole I have somewhat mixed feelings about the Irish."

"Hey, I tried to be born a Swede, but apparently my request got misfiled, so here I am."

"Well, in any case, I can't say I'm not pleased to meet ye – ye handled yourself very well out there." He stopped, frowned, then went on. "That sounded a bit more stilted than I meant it to be. What I meant was, ye did a damned fine job of covering my arse, and I'm grateful to ye for it."

"You're welcome."

"Come to think of it, though, just what were ye doing down in Underground Atlanta at two in the morning? And what in God's name made ye decide to jump into the middle of the firefight when we broke out?"

"I got lucky."

"Come again?"

"You mean you don't know?"

"Don't know what?"

"I watched the whole fucking thing from start to finish when you broke into Bits!" Blade would quickly learn that Spazz's rather liberal use of less-than-elegant expletives came quite as naturally to her as breathing. "I got caught in the coffee shop across the walkway when the whole goddamn mall when into lockdown – APD wasn't letting anybody in or out, even civilians. Ugh!" Her face momentarily screwed up into an expression of disgust. "I suppose it could have been worse – I could have been in a goddamn shoe store when it happened. At least we had food and drinks and a bathroom, but I've had enough turkey-and-swiss sandwiches and double cappuccinos to last me for a year!" Almost in spite of himself Blade laughed aloud.

"But I knew who you were the minute I saw you coming down the mall! I mean, I recognized you right away. You have no idea what an experience it was to be able to watch you in action. And when the five of you busted out of the nightclub, I told myself there was no fucking way I was staying inside that damned coffee shop, not when I could be in a firefight alongside you, though! It was like a dream come true!"

"What the hell are ye talking about?" Blade stared at her as if she were mad.

"For the last five years, I've been following you on the news and the 'Net and the boards and the holos, trying to learn everything about you I could. I've watched every fucking second of every bit of imagery there is of you available, studying your moves, trying to learn how you make your tactical decisions, understand why sometimes you zag instead of zig. There are a lot of people who think you're the best goddamn solo in the world, and I'm one of them. I'm probably you're biggest fan!"

Blade stared at her. This woman was adding entirely new dimensions to the concept "shatterbrained."

"Fan? *Fan?* In case ye hadn't noticed, Miss Collins, my line of work isn't exactly a sporting event."

"Maybe not, but you do have fans. Hell, there's a fucking booster gang back in Philadelphia that call themselves 'The Blades,' dress like you, carry old-fashioned rifles like you do, some of 'em even have those old Scottish swords. And boy, when they clean up a neighborhood, it fucking *stays* cleaned up!"

"I don't believe this. What mental ward did ye say ye escaped from?"

"I'm not a mental case, dammit! I'm a solo-for-hire, just like you." She paused, frowned, then went on. "Well, not just like you – who is? But you know what I mean."

Blade decided to humor her. "Definitely not yer ordinary career path, is it?"

"What's a profession like this doing in a nice girl like me, you mean?"

"Well, if ye want to put it that way, yes."

Maureen let out a short cackle, the sound disturbingly devoid of mirth. "Did you know I have a master's degree in international finance?"

"No, but then, considering that I just me ye, there's a helluva lot about ye I don't know. Obviously."

"True, there is. Anyway, I do have that degree, and I actually started out in international corporate banking. Probably would have been damned good at it, too."

"So what changed yer mind?"

"Bankers and the megacorps. I learned to despise the whole fucking lot of them. Not the industries themselves so much as most of the weasels who work in them. It was a fucking game to too many of them, always trying to one-up each other someway or another, and they kept score with other people's money, the bastards." She had a look on her face of someone who had just bitten into a piece of rotten fruit. "I was pretty fucking good at it myself, and I got myself noticed for it. Part of the problem was that it wasn't always for my work. With this face and this body, I attracted quite a bit of extracurricular attention."

"It would have been odd if ye hadn't."

"Yeah." She grimaced. "There were a lot of them who were cheerfully prepared to 'further my career' – provided that I bent over their desks when and how they asked. And it wasn't just the men, either."

"I take it the brain won out over the beauty."

"That it did. They were spending all their time trying to screw me literally while they screwed each other figuratively. I decided that I would rather be the screwer than the screwee, and have a choice in who I fucked up in the process. Turning solo simplified the process while providing the opportunities."

"The latest champion of the downtrodden and oppressed, eh? And ye've been at it how long?"

"Five years."

"And still in one piece. Impressive. No enhancements?"

"Blade, really?" She cast a quick glance downward at her bustline. "I know I've only got a set of A-cups – a pretty nice set of A-cups, *I* think – but is that really the sort of question a gentleman asks?"

Flustered, Blade stammered, "I – I – that's not what –"

"I know it isn't." Spazz laid a reassuring hand on his forearm. "I just had to yank on your chain a bit. Yeah, I've got a few enhancements – your basic adrenal boost, with a duration limiter. I don't want to shave twenty goddamn years off my life because I burned out my heart and circulatory system from fucking overboosting. I had restructuring done on my right hand and forearm – optimized them for shooting, really – and I had the micro-rez procedure done on my eyes. And that's it."

"I'm glad ye kept yer natural eyes – they're nice eyes."

"Thank you."

As it was, Blade approved of everything Spazz had done. A solo needed every edge he or she could get, both to stay alive and accomplish any given mission, objectives which usually went hand-in-hand. Limited boosting was always a good call, and having the tiny, fractional adjustments to bone and musculature made to improve accuracy and speed was equally prudent. "Micro-rez" was verbal shorthand for "micrometric resolution," an optical process that removed imperfections from the lenses and retinas of a solo's eyes. That Spazz hadn't opted for more radical enhancements spoke well to the fact that she had given long and serious thought about her chosen profession before committing to it: the work she had done was essentially surgical procedures, none of which carried an attending risk of the psychological problems that went with more radical modifications.

Electronic and cybernetic augmentation – "enhancements," in the current parlance – were hardly new: in their crudest form they had begun with the hearing aids of the mid-20th Century. By the beginning of the 21st, prosthetic limbs and organs that effectively mimicked the originals in appearance and function were being developed, and not long after that, some prostheses were beginning to exceed the capabilities of the body parts they were replacing. Dr. Joseph Buckley's breakthrough in applied nanotechnology in 2020 allowed for the creation of true neural interfacing between the human nervous system and prosthetic appliances: a human body could now manipulate its environment with electronic speed and electromechanical strength. Faster reflexes, greater strength and endurance, ultra-refined senses, were all available to anyone able to afford them.

But such "benefits" came with a commensurate cost, it was all too quickly learned, usually first by those who, having more money than functional brain cells, went out in pursuit of achieving some sort of "superman" (or "-woman") status and acquired every enhancement available – new limbs, new eyes, new ears, new circulatory and respiratory systems. What had not been realized as the new prosthetic systems were developed was that in combination they induced a growing sense of detachment on the part of the modified individual from the rest of the human race. In becoming "superhuman," they diminished their empathy for those they now dismissed as "normals" or "mundanes," regarding them as mere objects, tools, or toys, depending on the inclination. In every instance of extreme augmentation and enhancement, the person in question would eventually succumb, always within months, sometimes in weeks, in a few instances within days, to what became known as cyber-psychosis. A full-blown cyber-pyschotic episode was never a pretty thing, as it usually involved multiple homicides of the variety that left hardened coroners retching and shaken.

Even people like Blade, whose non-organic, non-surgical modifications were limited – the left arm, left eye, and both ears in his case – were not entirely immune from some degree of psychosis, which accounted for the apprehension with which the extraction team had first greeted him. While psychotic episodes in someone like Blade were exceedingly rare, they weren't unknown. Blade had been given little choice in his case: his arm and eye were lost to an exploding bomb, which also damaged his hearing beyond conventional repair. He also had a well-established reputation for keeping himself tightly controlled: he had never been known to exhibit the slightest psychotic symptom. On the other hand, the chance, however small, that he *could* crack accounted for Nathan Gerrard's unease over Blade's actions in breaking into Bits....

But in Spazz's case, she had eschewed all of the cyber-limbs and -organs and concentrated on the procedures which enhanced her natural physical abilities without compromising the integrity of her body, which Blade took to be a good sign. Depending on how she came by the user-name "Spazz," she might be perfectly capable of throwing hissy fits or having the odd awkward, graceless moment, but at least she wasn't a potential homicidal maniac waiting to be set off by her own delusions of grandeur. On the other hand, whether it was serendipity at work, or something else entirely, Blade had a sense that the tall, lithe blonde sitting to his right had attached herself to him for reasons that involved more than hero-worship and fan-girl fantasies, and was not about to be easily fobbed off or left behind.

"So why didn't ye decide to 'screw the screwers,' to use yer own idiom, from inside the banking community? I should have thought ye were ideally placed to do just that."

Spazz shook her head, almost violently. "No, I wanted to get out – I *had* to get out. I couldn't play the game any more. I can't say the idea of fucking them over from the inside didn't appeal to me, but I just didn't have it in me to put on the mask and pretend to be one of them while I was doing it. Just being around them made me feel polluted. So I started looking around for some other way to stick it to them."

"And solo work was it?"

"It was easier than you think, Blade. My Daddy and Granddaddy both made sure I knew how to shoot almost before I could ride a bicycle. I've always had good reflexes and exceptional eyesight, and when the other girls in my junior high classes were taking ballet, I was taking *aikido* classes."

"'Ballet'?"

"Yeah, I grew up on the Mainline, so that was pretty much expected of pre-adolescent girls from those sort of families. I quit after my third one, threw a tantrum and my parents decided I needed 'a different sort of outlet for my energy,' as it were. So, *aikido*. A few years after that, I switched to *jeet kun do*."

"Remind me never to piss ye off, lass." He gestured to Mike, who nodded and quickly brought another double Balvenie.

"So ye gave up banking and, suitably outfitted as the Fist of Goodness, you took your crusade to the streets to combat evildoers, right?"

Spazz gave him a withering look much like the one she would direct at some unwanted insect on the wall. "Hardly. At first I was attracted to the solo lifestyle: lots of flash, lots of cash, the good life when I wasn't working, adventure when I was. I imagined it would be one really long, really intense adrenaline rush. I figured I could play it the same way some women run an escort business, except that my stock in trade would be lethality, not sex."

"How did that work out for you?"

"Not bad, for a while. But then it changed, and what really started turning me on was the challenge, planning better, maneuvering better, and ultimately shooting better than the opposition, doing everything about the job better than anyone else, and doing it for life or death stakes – the thrill of pulling off the job and surviving. It turned into more than an adrenaline rush – it was almost like a dopamine addiction, knowing that I'd not only out-fought but out-thought somebody who wanted me or my principle dead."

"But...."

"Yeah, 'but.' After a while I realized that there are a lot of really shitty people out there in general who do really shitty things to other people who don't deserve it. And that pissed me off even more than the goddamn bankers, because for the bankers it was never really personal, but for the really shitty types, it almost always was. So I decided that whenever I could I would do some shitty things to the shitters whenever and wherever I found them."

"Something tells me there's more to the story than just that."

"There is, but that's the Reader's Digest version, and it'll do for now. I'm here to fuck over powerful people who get their kicks out of fucking over the little guys who can't fight back themselves."

"An altruistic solo? What is this world coming to?"

"Don't hand me that crap, Blade, because I know better. You're probably the most altruistic solo out there, and it was you who made me decide to rethink my own motives."

"Me? Altruistic? Hardly." Blade's eyes and voice were equally bleak. "There's a difference between ye and me, Spazz, and that difference means that ye'll never quite be as good a solo as I am – and, ye know, in the end that's actually not a bad thing. Ye chose this life, because deep down ye believe ye can make a difference. For ye, no matter how 'shitty' things get, ye'll always be trying to hold on to some scrap of yer humanity – and ye'll always find a way to succeed at it. Me? This is all I know how to do. Take it away from me, and I'd be shoveling shite in Auchterarder."

"You can't be serious."

"Oh, I am. I'm hardly role model material, Miss Collins. At best, I'm a hired gun with style. At worst, I'm just a hired gun."

"Don't patronize me, Blade! I am not a goddamned amateur!" There was a momentary fury in her eyes and voice, then she quickly composed both. "Look, this isn't some case of hero-worship. I'm a pretty damned good solo myself – my contracts bear that out, plus I think I've already proved this morning that I know my shit. But you're the best in the business, at least by most accounts, so I want to learn from you. I may never be as good as you, but I want to be the only other solo people think to call when you're not available – because if I am, I *will* make a difference, somewhere, someday. So here I am."

Blade looked the woman out of countenance, utterly bemused. After a moment, he collected himself, shrugged, and said, "Well, then, my dear, I submit that it's time for ye to toddle off, now that you've had yer lesson and yer thrill here, and carry on yer crusade elsewhere."

"No way." Spazz's tone matched the set of her eyes: granite hard, implacable.

"And just what makes ye think – "

"Look, Blade, we both know that this – " she made a sweeping gesture with her left arm that took in everything inside and outside of Bits – "whatever the hell 'this' *is* – isn't over." The gushing, slightly shatterbrained blonde of just moments earlier had vanished entirely: now Maureen was speaking in deadly earnest. The shift was so complete that it held Blade's attention almost against his will. "This thing you're involved in is big, that's fucking obvious, otherwise there wouldn't be a bunch of dead DisCom Rats lying around inside Bits. But I think it's even bigger than DisCom suspects – it may even be bigger than the Big Black Rat can handle – because there's even more dead Arasakas lying around outside. Which means that Arasaka wants it, too. Whatever 'it' is...." There was a clear if unspoken invitation in the way her voice drifted off for Blade to explain to her exactly what was the situation here....

Instead he deflected it by asking, "What makes you think this 'thing' is *that* 'big'?"

Maureen shrugged. "Arasaka didn't just get involved, they jumped in with both feet, Blade." Her tone was that of a patient teacher explaining something to a rather slow child. "Look at the fucking risks they ran – are *still* running for that matter: they just carried out what amounts to an act of terrorism on American soil, they brought foreign nationals into the country for illegal purposes – don't tell me you think all those dead Japanese out there were just camera-toting tourists who happened to get caught in the crossfire – and they fired on Federal officers. It was just this sort of shit that got Arasaka run out of the UK eight years ago – you know that better than anyone." She took a sip of her rather unusual drink; he took another look at it, shuddered, and renewed his acquaintance with his Scotch.

"The fact that you and your people are still alive is proof that Arasaka didn't get what it wanted – this time," she went on, her tone almost conversational. "We both know that whenever Arasaka wants something, they keep coming until either one of two things happen. One, they get what they want, or two, they get hit hard enough with a big enough fucking cluestick to make them back off.

You're a damned big cluestick, and they've backed off – for the time being. But whatever it is they're after, I don't think even *you* are big enough to get them to give it up completely. They'll be back."

Blade nodded. "Now that they know I'm involved, ye can go to the bank with that one."

"Which is where I come in. Like it or not, I'm part of this now: Arasaka and anybody else who's involved is going to think I'm working with you, whether I actually am or not. And *you* are going to need someone to watch your goddamned back. Compton over there is good, really good, but he's got enough problems of his own without having to worry about covering your six. I can do that."

"So ye've decided, without so much as a 'by yer leave,' to attach yerself, limpet-like, to me and my op?"

"I did and I have." Suddenly she reached forward, her hand stopping just short of Blade's forearm, then taking it, her gaze and her tone a curious mixture of mischief and earnestness. "Live with it."

Blade looked down at the hand on his forearm, then up into her eyes. *Damn, they really* are *aquamarine!* "Ye're determined to be difficult about this, aren't ye?"

"Damnbetcha!"

Blade frowned, looked at her from under thunderously lowered eyebrows, then gave a sigh of resignation. "*You*, Miss Collins, are going to be a lot of trouble!" He tossed back the remainder of his second Balvenie, then slid off the barstool and turned toward the door. "For now, enjoy your Dead Nazi." He gestured toward his ear bud. "Nathan just commed, apparently he needs to see me about some sort of urgent business."

"Have to meet a man at Marwar Junction?"

Blade turned back to her and, for the first time, smiled at Spazz. "Och, ye're good! Ye're really good!"

"You have no idea," she purred in return.

"So, let's see what we have here, Raven," Radome murmured as she jacked in the first of the seven crystals into her set of Universal Connection Ports. Her deck quickly constructed a detailed schematic of the memory device, creating an abstraction of its design and capacity. Upon seeing it, Radome did a double-take.

"Holy crap! This is optical storage, not solid-state like I was expecting! Wow...."

The same information had appeared on Raven's monitor, and she studied it intently. "It's certainly an impressive piece of engineering, I'll say that for it. I don't recall ever seeing data stored this densely before. This is literally pushing the boundaries of applied physics." She giggled suddenly. "I even see some of my work in here."

"*Your* work?"

"Yep. I don't always publish my papers under my own name. Apparently Calvin has been reading them and didn't know they were mine when he decided to copy the work without permission. What's catching my eye is how these matrices are stacked – the distances between layers are exactly what's outlined in a patent I was awarded about four years ago – they're optimized to prevent covalent instability caused by overlapping interference patterns."

"And the synchronization of the outer shells? Is that your work, too?"

"It sure looks like it. I wonder if Calvin realizes I could burn his arse for patent violation?"

"I want to be there when you tell him."

The seven "crystals" that Raven, Radome, and Alistair were examining were not, in fact, *crystals* in the sense that came to mind for most people when they heard the word. That is, they weren't solid, geometric shapes of ultra-dense, matrixed carbon, quartz, corundum or a silicate-based compound. Rather, they were called "crystals" because inside their smooth, non-reflective carbon-composite housings, were an even dozen of wafer-thin *discs* of ultra-pure quartz, each 25 mm in diameter and two millimeters thick, stacked vertically along a central spindle, the spindle also acting as the guide for the reader heads. While the fundamental design had been around for decades, this iteration brought a degree of refinement to the concept Raven had never before seen outside of prototypes, which these crystals clearly were not. Manifestly, Calvin had been pushing the envelope – and pushing it hard – where storage capacity was concerned: for more than two decades it had been an article of faith that 360 terabytes of storage per disc was the theoretical maximum, but somehow Calvin and his engineers had managed to double that number. Reverse-engineering and then replicating that technology alone would be worth a not-inconsiderable fortune in the short term to anyone who managed to accomplish the feat, but it didn't require someone of Raven's intellect to quickly realize that the most valuable real prize was, of course, what was stored in those crystals.

Raven let out a sigh of frustration. "Damn, I really want to make copies, but we don't have a couple of hours to do it. Oh, well, at least I should be able to construct an index."

After a few moments, Raven sighed again. "I think that's all I'm going to get, for now, at least until I get my hands on the crystals themselves and get them up and running together."

"I don't think that's very likely, considering we were hired to bring these back to Calvin."

"Still, if I can – "

"Pardon me, Miss Radome, Miss Raven," Alistair broke in unexpectedly, "but Ah'm nae so sure that would be...a really good idea."

"Why not?" Radome and Raven spoke in unison, and there was a matching mixture of suspicion and apprehension in their voices.

"Because, ladies, each o' these crystals has a storage capacity of just o'er eight and a half petabytes – a wee bit more than sixty petabytes total. Almost all o' that is in use."

"Meaning...?" This was Radome.

"Meaning that, according to the index I just constructed, the program itself – whatever it is – takes up just under nine petabytes." This was from Raven. "Seventy-eight percent of the remaining storage is taken up by data files, and they're all time-stamped within micro-seconds of each other on the same date – the day that Kim had her 'accident.'"

"Miss Raven?"

"Yes, Alistair?"

"Do ye ken that all o' the headings and subheadings seem tae be labeled fer some specific cerebral, neural, or psycho-neural function?"

Raven began flitting through the index at random, saying nothing. The silence drew out for a full minute, then another; when she finally spoke, her voice was subdued, with an audible quaver in it. "If I hadn't seen it with my own eyes, I would never have believed it...."

"Believed what, Raven?"

Raven went silent again for a few seconds, then when she spoke, her voice was louder, stronger, but still with an edge of apprehension in it.

"Radome, Calvin told Blade that he was certain Kim's mind had gone into some sort of neurological 'safe room' or 'panic room' when she was attacked in her lab That was why it getting these crystals back was so important – they're supposed to contain the only copy of a program that Calvin believes will coax Kim out of it and out of her brain-dead state. But there's no 'panic room' because that's not where Kim went."

Radome's eyes went wide. "Oh, my God. You don't mean to say that she – that's not possible!"

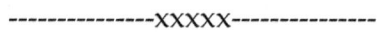

"All right, Nathan, what is it that's so bloody urgent that it had to drag me away from my whisky?" Blade had found the US Marshal sitting on the countertop of the information kiosk where the Scot and his little band had earlier made their last stand. Settling beside him, Blade pulled a small bottle of bore cleaner and packet of patches from his ruck, and tipped a cleaning-rod set out of the butt of his SMLE, having decided that he could clean his rifle while he listened to Gerrard.

The lawman's frown was, if anything, deeper than it had been earlier. "First of all, I thought you'd want to know that your man Houston was just airlifted out. He's gonna make it. He won't be doin' any line dancing for a while, but he'll recover."

"That's good news. I should have asked about him earlier, just damned selfish of me not to."

"You've got a lot on your mind. There's something else, though, that I think you should know. We just got a report from the Milledgeville office of the GBI. Two days ago, some guy who was bass fishing in Lake Oconee snagged a body and dragged it up. GBI Forensics finally made an ID. Her name was Judith Rockley, and she was Calvin Coleridge's senior project manager. She's also the person GBI is certain stole those crystals that are causing everybody so much goddamn trouble."

Blade frowned, perplexed. "I don't see why ye're telling me this. About finding the body, I mean."

"Because from the state of the body, GBI Forensics is pretty certain this Rockley woman had been in the lake for three days before she was found. Which means that she was probably killed the same day that she stole the crystals. Oh, and the body was wrapped in chicken-wire and weighted just enough to sink it. According to Forensics, she was alive when they dumped her in the lake."

"Damn."

"Yeah, damn. This little escapade of yours just took a whole different turn, didn't it?"

Blade nodded wordlessly, pulling the cleaning rod through the barrel of his rifle, replacing the patch, and swabbing the bore again. The implications of Gerrard's revelation were clear. Chicken wire was a good way of insuring that a body dropped into a lake stayed submerged once decomposition began: the gasses that normally buoyed up a body were released when the swelling tissue was lacerated by the wire mesh. Wrapping Judith Rockley in chicken wire and a few weights and then tossing her into Lake Oconee while she was still living, though, was pure sadism: she was meant to know that she was dying. Murder among those who carried out industrial espionage, which technically was what the theft of Hobbes' crystals had been, was rare, but far from unknown. Out-and-out brutality, however, was all but unheard of – it was simply bad for business. People who were prepared to run life-or-death risks in exchange for a potentially huge payoff were rarely willing to chance being placed at the mercy of some psychopath who would find their incremental destruction a source of amusement. There were layered messages in the death of Judith Rockley, the most obvious being *Turn away – you want no part of this.*

After a moment, Blade pursed his lips and blew out a long gust of air. "This is hardly the sort of thing anyone says 'thank you' for, but it's useful information, and for that much, at least, I'm grateful. I suspect, though, since we've recovered the crystals, whatever messages the murder of Ms. Rockley were meant to send are meaningless now." He held up the rifle and peered down the barrel, then went back to work with a fresh patch. "I'm going to hand them over to Calvin this morning, and with any luck, be on my way back to Scotland before noon. Despite what young Miss Collins in there – she's the tall blonde – might think otherwise, this is going to be over and done with today."

"Nothing will make me happier if that turns out to be the case, if only because it'll mean I've been spared all the usual complications that arise whenever you show up. You know – the diplomatic incidents, the large-scale destruction of private property, the pissed-off megacorps, irate politicians hot to fire my ass for something you did...."

"Nice to know I'm loved and that ye miss me when I'm gone."

"Don't kid yourself. You still managed to leave stacks of dead Arasakas for me to deal with."

"Right then, anything else to tell me?"

"Just have a good flight."

"I'll do my best." Blade held out his hand, Gerrard took it. "See ye 'round, Nathan."

"Not if I see you first."

Seeing Compton finish up what had clearly been a long conversation with one of the deputy marshals, Blade waved him over to the kiosk, where he was finishing up his rifle-cleaning chore. The younger man approached with a quizzical look on his face, and Blade came right to the point.

"Compton, telling ye that ye did well out there is something akin to gilding the lily, I suspect, but I'll say it anyway." The young black man looked vaguely pleased at Blade's words. "Still there's something I need to know: just how heavily are ye geared up? Truly."

"Why, do I make you nervous?" Compton's matter-of-fact tone robbed his words of any potential insolence.

"I would be lying if I said ye didn't."

"Yeah, I can understand why. And somehow having the question come from you doesn't offend me. I mean, you of all people know what it's like."

"Aye, that I do." Blade paused. "I know ye were Air Force Special Operations, but yer people never go in for the sort of radical rebuild I suspect ye've had done...." His voice trailed off in an invitation for Compton to elaborate.

"Yeah, OK, OK, you're right. You deserve to know if we're gonna be working together. So here's the rundown. Like you said, I was Special Operations, *not* Special Forces. We didn't hunt gomers in the boonies for months on end, our gigs were finesse and dirty tricks, y'know?" Compton cocked his head at Blade. "You wouldn't happen to have a cigarette on you, would you?"

"No, no gaspers – not my poison of choice." Blade reached inside his tunic and produced one of the Romeo y Julietas. "Will this do? I cadged a couple of extras from Calvin's private stock."

"Better'n nothing." Blade waited while Compton unwrapped the cigar, trying not to wince as the younger man bit off the end, then unwrapped one for himself, punched a hole in the end, then produced a battered trench lighter and struck it. Once they had both lit up, they puffed away in a companionable silence for a moment, then Compton then took up again with his tale.

"Anyway, us and the RAF and the French turned most of the Camel Lot into an FAE test range, right? Everybody wanted a piece of that action, y'know? Not that I really blame them – shit, the only people in the world who weren't looking for payback after Black Christmas were the ones chanting 'Ballyhoo Snackbar!' five times a day. Well, them and maybe the Chinese." He drew on the cigar a few more times, then went on.

"OK, so anyway, there were still some hardcore, hardline holdouts dug in deep in the Camel Lot, y'know. We didn't know if any of 'em had any more Big Booms squirreled away and we *had* to find them,'cuz nobody wanted another Black Christmas. So our job was to spoof the holdouts into the open so our fast movers could drop on them. Otherwise the crunchies had to go in and dig 'em out of their holes." Blade grimaced and nodded at that. "Blowing 'em up was easier – a few tons of fuel-air explosives and you had a whole new recipe for shish kebab, y'know?

"So, our CO was this light colonel, a born A-1 first-class REMF, who had to get his ticket punched in a combat unit so someday he'd be eligible for command of a desk at Fort Fumble."

"I know the type – we called them PONTIs."

"Yeah, I guess nobody's got a monopoly on assholes, right?" Blade grunted an agreement.

"Blade's Law Number 17: 'PONTIs are everywhere.'"

"Ain't that the truth? So anyway, this colonel – Cartman, Cashman, I can't remember his name anymore – not only decided that he wanted to go along with the spoofer team, which was me and my people, on one of our dirty-tricks missions, but when the time came, he wanted to call in the strike. I mean, the dumbass didn't know how to read a map, OK? And he calls down a shit-ton of ordnance on our position. They told me later that I was barely breathing when they medevac-ed us. Arms and legs were write-offs, and I had some spinal damage to go along with a bunch of internal injuries."

"How long did it take to rebuild ye?"

"Eleven months. I was one of the lucky ones, y'know. At least there was enough of me to rebuild, OK? There wasn't much left of Colonel Clusterfuck – I mean, they dumped a buncha body parts they thought *might* have been him into a body bag and tagged it. Served the chickenshit bastard right." Another pause, another long draw on the cigar.

"OK, so I woke up with new arms, new legs, a titanium spine, some vat-grown internal plumbing, and a rewired nervous system, y'know? I also woke up with a deathly fear of going cyber-psycho. I saw what happens with that even before I got rebuilt, OK? I don't *ever* wanna go there. It's one thing to get blown apart and rebuilt – it's a whole different ball game knowing you're gonna get blown apart so that no one *can* rebuild you. So I get my meds and I do my de-stressing routines every day, 'cuz *nothing* is worth *that*. So, satisfied now?"

"I am. I didn't like doing it, but I had to ask."

Compton gave a dismissive shrug. "So now what? You take the crystals and hand them over to Coleridge and we're done, right?"

"Wrong. It so happens that my arrangement with Coleridge is to make certain that someone from the extraction team is able to get those crystals back into his hands. In other words, I'm not here to do yer job for ye, just help ye get it done."

"Right. OK. Meaning...?"

"Meaning that it would be a damned shame if we got this close to the finish line and then buggered it up because we got careless. Tell me, Compton, where's yer motorcycle?"

"My motor – how do *you* know about my motorcycle?"

"Because it's yer trademark – along with those cheap Armani

suits ye've been known to wear."

"Hey, they're not cheap, OK?"

"Well, they certainly aren't Saville Row."

"Whatever. So what do you need my bike for?"

"My friend, I have a little job for ye...."

A few minutes later, Blade strolled into Bits, carrying a metal security case in his right hand. Red was still sitting where he left her, at the far end of the bar. Spazz had moved closer to the other woman, and was cleaning her Korth semi-automatic. Almost in spite of himself, Blade was impressed by the weapon – it had to have cost at least five figures, as it had the look of having been custom made to fit Spazz's long, slender hands. Mike was trying to bring some semblance of order to the bar – which from the look of things was a fifty-fifty proposition at best. All three were engaged in a fairly animated discussion of some sort, which quickly trailed off when they saw him approaching. He held out the case to Red.

"Here. Ye get to carry this now. I want ye to hold on to it as if yer life depends on it – because it does."

The confusion in Red's voice matched that on her face. "I thought that Radome –"

"Change in plan. I've already spoken with her about it. We're going to deliver that directly to Calvin. Are ye ready to go?"

Red picked up the pistol and shoulder rig she'd appropriated from an Arasaka who would no longer be needing it, slipped her arms through the straps and adjusted them. She then took the security case from him, and smiled. "I am now."

The Scot turned to Spazz. "And you?"

The blonde put her cleaning kit away, slapped the Korth together with dazzling, practiced ease, worked the action, then settled it into her handbag in a way that suggested that it was a custom fit. Turning back to MacLaren, she favored him with a smile of her own. "So am I."

"Then I suggest we get moving." Nodding to Mike, he said, "Thanks for the hospitality. Tell Calvin I think yer due for a raise."

"I'll do that – not that he's likely to listen, the cheap bastard." Blade grinned and turned back to the two women.

"Ladies, my car is outside."
"Can I assume it's not an Aston-Martin?"
"No, Spazz, it isn't – and it's not a Mini, either."

----------------xxxxx----------------

"Dear God, that thing must be forty years old!" Spazz blurted out when she saw the F1. "Don't you own *anything* new?"
"Get in. Both of you."

Chapter 5

The F1 was a rather unusual car, as it had seats for three people, rather than the typical two or four passenger arrangements. Once he'd stowed his harness and rifle, Blade slid with a practiced ease into the driver's position in the centre, while Spazz and Red occupied the two passenger seats, one on either side and slightly behind that of the driver, the blonde to Blade's right, the ginger to his left. MacLaren's right hand performed a quick dance atop the right console, inserting the key, hitting the red starter button and locking out the reverse gear in a blur of motion. The engine growled to life, and once he was satisfied both women were comfortably strapped in, he put the car in gear and rolled out of the parking lot of the Warren Pavilion.

He carefully wove his way through the US Marshal's perimeter then that of the Atlanta police, who were, thankfully, keeping spectators and newsies alike at bay. Within three minutes he was turning onto the entrance ramp of northbound I-75, where he methodically worked his way up through the gears, waiting for the transmission to warm up sufficiently for high speed driving. A few moments later the car was hitting 90 miles per hour, the engine bellowing with joy as Blade steadily opened the throttle.

Predictably, Spazz was the first to say something. Leaning forward, she looked at the instrument cluster, noting the engine speed, then at Blade, and asked, "It's not very quiet, is it?"

Blade gave her a sidelong glance as his right thumb flicked to a button on the steering wheel. "Are you going to complain the whole way?"

"Oh, go on, then, eject me. See if I care."

Blade stared at her. "That has to be absolutely the worst 'English' accent I've ever heard in my life."

"Shut up and fucking drive." Spazz lapsed into a petulant silence – briefly: Blade was beginning to think that it was physically impossible for the woman to stop talking for anything more than a few seconds at a time. "Wait a minute, do you know where we're going, because I as sure as hell don't!"

Blade cocked an eyebrow and muttered, "I think between

Alistair, Raven, and my GPS system, I should be able to stumble across our destination rather easily, Miss Collins."

"In that case, where *are* we going?"

"To Hobbes' main R & D facility, a little enclave he has up in the mountains, north of here, that he rather grandly calls 'The Gardens.' We should be there in about ninety minutes. Now, if you don't mind, could you just shut up and let me fucking drive?"

The sudden silence on his right was so frosty, Blade was certain that it would have given a glacier chills. He smiled inwardly and pressed down on the accelerator a little harder.

"Alistair?"

"Sir!"

"Connect with Mycroft, let him know that the crystals are secure and I'm on my way to the Gardens, ETA ninety minutes."

"Very good, Sir!"

Another ninety minutes, Blade thought, *and then I can go home.*

"Listen, Compton, I left some of my gear back in the club, I'm going to go get it. You got everything?"

"Uh, yeah, OK, I think I do, Radome, 'cept I'm low on ammo. And since those Rats back at Bits won't be needing theirs anymore, y'know, I'll go with you and...appropriate some of theirs. I don't think they'll object, do you?" To make his point, he grinned and hefted the MilTech rifle he'd earlier taken from the hands of one of the dead DisComs. "So, lead on!"

Walking into Bits, they found Mike, the bartender, steadily working away in his effort to make some sense of the shambles to which the nightclub had been reduced, moving Black Rat bodies aside, clearing away debris, setting up what few tables, chairs, and barstools remained serviceable. With the departure of Blade and the survivors of the extraction team, there was little else for him to do: at the moment, no one seemed particularly interested in availing themselves of a libation.

"Hey, Mike!" Radome called out as she breezed in.

"Radome! Glad to see that you made it. What's next for you? Come to help me sort out this mess?"

"Nah, I left my jacket and ruck in the back, I'm gonna grab them and be on my way." And with that she ducked into the private suite. Compton, who had trailed into the club in Radome's wake, stopped and surveyed the damage.

"Wow. OK, we really kinda made a mess of your club, didn't we?"

"You might say that," Mike drawled, "but then you did have some help."

"Uh, yeah, we did." Compton then noticed a half-dozen or so MilTec rifles stacked neatly in one corner, along with a handful of assorted pistols. "Say, did you happen to find any spare ammo on those DisCom goons?"

"Nah, didn't check them." A speed-multi-wrench appeared in Mike's hand as if by magic, and he began taking apart the light-grid that had once been suspended above the dance floor. "The Marshals said that people from the coroner's office would be here to take away the bodies, and that they would inventory them when they did. So I left them alone, other than getting them out of my way. If you need ammo and want to go through their pockets to find some, go ahead, I see nothing. Any loose change you find, though, is mine."

"Right, thanks."

After a few minutes Radome reappeared, ruck in one hand, an SMG in the other.

"Ready, Compton?"

"Yeah, I've got four full mags now, plus the one in my rifle. Is that Bridelow's H&K?"

"That it is. I took a cue from you, figured he wouldn't be needing it anymore, and it'll be a lot less awkward than a rifle to keep slung while I'm riding on the back of your bike."

"OK, works for me. Where're the crystals?"

Radome set the SMG on one of the few intact tables, then opened the zip of her ruck, showed Compton the titanium security case, zipped it closed and said, "I think it's time we got moving."

"Then let's make it happen. See ya, Mike!"

"Be careful out there, you two." Compton nodded his thanks, and with that he and Radome walked out of Bits and headed for the main entrance to Underground Atlanta.

"Where's your bike?"

"Parking garage a block north of here."

"Do you think it's still OK?"

"Uh, yeah, I do." There was something very close to a smirk on Compton's face. "I'm pretty sure if anyone tried to screw around with it they've learned the error of their ways, y'know?"

"I guess I'll have to take your word for it. We're going to The Gardens, right?"

"That's where Blade said to go," Compton replied with a shrug.

"And you always do what Blade tells you to do?"

They had just reached the courtyard when Radome posed the question, and Compton stopped dead in his tracks. "I'm not sure what you're getting at, Radome."

"What I'm getting at is that we're working for Calvin Coleridge, *not* David MacLaren. We've been sold out at every turn on this gig, and I'm damned well not going to let that happen again. We're headed to The Gardens on Blade's say-so, but has anyone heard anything from Calvin?"

"No, but then I haven't tried to comm him. Have you?"

"Yeah, I did, while I was in the back room at Bits. I couldn't get through to either him or his VI, Mycroft. Tried everything I could think of to push a comm through, and got nothing. Nada. Zip. Zilch."

"Wait a minute. *You* couldn't push a comm through? I thought you never met a comm combination you couldn't pick!"

"It was like the signals were being blocked just before they reached their destination. As if they were being deliberately bounced. So we're out of touch with Calvin. Now get this: not twenty minutes ago I was having a conversation with Raven, you know, Blade's ex-girlfriend and all-galaxy-class computer weasel? She was making noises about wanting to get her hands on the crystals. And not ten minutes ago, Blade was telling us where to take them. Now do you see why I'm getting twitchy?"

"Oh, man, I don't need this right now, y'know?" Compton pinched the bridge of his nose between thumb and forefinger. "Why would Blade double-cross us? I mean, I could understand it if he'd just waltzed in uninvited-like and announced that he was taking charge, OK? But Calvin's the one who brought him into this mess, right? And he told us Blade was coming, and in case you've forgotten already, it was Blade who, y'know, basically saved our asses from getting blown away about an hour ago. I think that's enough to buy the guy some slack, OK?"

"Yeah, it does, but it still bothers me that we can't get word to Calvin about our plans."

"Yeah, me too, now that you've 'splained it all to me." Compton frowned, thinking fast and furiously. "OK, here's what we'll do – "

"We'll get on your bike – "

"We'll get on my bike – "

"And head to The Gardens – "

"And head to The Gardens – "

"But we won't take a direct route – "

"We won't take a direct route – "

"And run like hell – "

"And run like hell – "

"At the first sign of trouble," they finished in unison.

"Y'know, Radome, sometimes you really creep me out when you do that!"

"Sorry!" Somehow the expression on her face wasn't exactly one of contrition. "I guess it's time we got a move on, isn't it?"

"Yeah."

---------------xxxxx---------------

"Excuse me, Calvin, but Alistair, Blade's VI, just informed me that he, that is, Blade, has secured the crystals and is on his way to The Gardens. His ETA is approximately 86 minutes."

"Thank God." Hobbes let out an explosive sigh as his shoulders slumped in relief. "Now I can get Kim's mind back where it belongs and we can finish this project." For almost a solid minute he said nothing more, just doodled on the scratch pad in front of him, scrawling out the words "Please don't" over and over again. When he spoke again, it was in a distant monotone. "Mike, inform Security that there are visitors on the way."

"Right away, Calvin. Shall I contact Emory University and arrange to have Kim moved to our own medical facility?"

"No, there's no need for that right now – maybe later. Once I have those crystals I'll have everything I need." Calvin's expression was still distracted, but his voice, though still a monotone, was firm. "And start spinning up Gamma lab while you're at it."

"You're leaving Kim at Emory?"

"Yes."

"I don't understand."

"Just do it, dammit."

"I will. I will also point out, though, that the instructions you just gave me are completely at odds with what you'd led me to believe were your intentions. Obviously, it will be impossible to restore Kim's mind if she's still in hospital. Has there been some change in your plans or objectives about which you've chosen not to inform me?"

"I *don't* have to tell you the reason why I make every decision I do."

"No, you don't, but failing to keep me informed of such things, or refusing to do so, can seriously impair my ability to perform my primary function."

"Think, Mycroft, think! Well, all right, so technically you *can't* think – but use the associative capabilities I gave you so that you can wake up and smell the cyber-coffee! This isn't just restoring Kim's mind that we're talking about. Once I have those crystals again, I'll be able to salvage Bowman! You know damned well that's been not just my company's but *my* most important project for the past five years. What happened to Kim is proof not only of how close it is to succeeding, but also just how vulnerable it is in it's incomplete state."

"Which may be all the more reason to back away from it for the time being."

"NO!" Had Mycroft been human, he would have physically recoiled at the vehemence of Calvin's response. "Mycroft, few men have ever had the opportunity to change the world, fewer still to change humanity at the same time. I have that chance almost within my grasp, and nothing is going to divert me from it! Reviving Kim is just going to have to wait. Bowman has to come first. Hell, it's what she would want!"

"You're taking an awful risk here, Calvin. And the consequences, if you're wrong, will go well beyond the personally and professionally catastrophic."

"Mycroft, do I have to remind you again of exactly what your primary function is supposed to be?"

"No, Calvin, you don't. There are times, however, when I feel that there is a distinct difference between how you and I each interpret 'support, promote, advance, and protect the research and financial goals of Calvin Coleridge and Cogito Orbis Corporation'."

"Perhaps there is, but in the end the only interpretation that matters is mine."

"I've never forgotten that for a moment."

Aiko Kurita was a very unhappy woman, and that made Hideki Nakajima a very nervous man.

Petite, with jet-black hair, calm brown eyes, porcelain-like skin and delicate, regular features; there were hints in her countenance that spoke to Korean or possibly Chinese ancestors somewhere in the shaded branches of her family tree, possibly with even a *gaijun* or two tossed into the mix at some point. Her age upward of sixty (no one knew exactly by how much), she was still a remarkably beautiful woman, which somehow accentuated the aura of menace that surrounded her when she was displeased. Like now, for instance....

"I know you well enough to realize that you won't offer me excuses for your failure, Nakajima-san, only reasons. That does not mean there will be no consequences for you, however. Their degree and severity will depend on what you tell me now."

Kurita's face was projected on Umori's monitor, and Nakajima stood before it, squarely in the middle of the visual pick-up's field of vision, assuming a stance not unlike that of a soldier standing at attention.

"I understand, Kurita-sama. I made two mistakes. First, I failed to make certain Nagumo knew to flush out the civilians caught inside Underground Atlanta and drive them into the open once Blade began his break-in. Second, I underestimated Blade himself. He has not slowed at all since our last encounter, despite being older, and his skills have improved. I failed to anticipate that this might be so."

"Indeed." The way Kurita said it, the word was layered with meanings. She pursed her lips and looked into the middle distance, the effect as presented by the monitor being that of looking straight through Nakajima. After several seconds of silence, she spoke again, her contralto voice carrying clearly through the speakers behind the monitor.

"Nagumo cannot be blamed for his actions, I think. Lacking sufficiently clear instructions to the contrary, it appears that he chose to follow what would have been our usual procedures and contain the situation and limit the violence to our intended targets. How could he have known that we wanted it otherwise? Actually, I find this sense of restraint commendable – please tell him I said so, if and when you see him again. Do you know if he lived or died in the second firefight?"

"I believe that he's alive, Kurita-sama, although he is certainly in the custody of the US Marshals by now."

"That's a minor problem at best, then, a mere bagatelle. Loyal subordinates are, as the *gaijun* say, 'a dime a dozen.' Loyal subordinates who also *think* are rare, however; it wouldn't do to lose his services. I shall see to it." Her eyes suddenly bored into Nakajima's. "Your second mistake, however, cannot be so easily dismissed. How can it be that you, of all people, underestimated this man Blade?"

Nakajima knew that he was suddenly walking along the edge of a *katana*. Already, he knew, he would face Aiko Kurita's manifest displeasure when he returned to Japan: a wrong answer here could well mean that when he did so, he would be going to his death. His mind racing at unbelievable speed as he considered the image of the woman before him, Nakajima sought to formulate a response that was at once honest and yet mitigated the degree if not the fact of his failure.

Aiko Kurita was the most powerful woman ever to sit on the board of one of the Japanese *keiretsu*, and at the same time a fearsome figure in the Japanese *yakuza*, a not surprising circumstance considering just how closely intertwined were the two. Her entry into the ranks of the criminal underworld was, in a way, ordained from birth: for almost two hundred years, even before the Meiji Restoration, the eldest male child in each generation of her family had assumed the role of a crime lord, a *Hanzai no bosu*, in Kagoshima Prefecture, becoming ensconced within the ranks of the *yakuza*, Japan's tightly-structured criminal organization which in ruthlessness and dedication made the American *mafioso* look like pikers by comparison.

Having come of age in the 1990's, when many of the customary restrictions on the roles of Japanese women in their society were rapidly eroding, Aiko Kurita decided that the time had come for a change in the familial traditions as well. Not willing to settle for the minor role of *ane-san*, or senior sister, in the family's criminal enterprises, she coveted her elder brother's position as *kumicho*, the family boss; she promptly had him murdered, assumed his position, and then defied anyone to unseat her. After several failed attempts to do so by rival families, more than one of which she personally thwarted in some exceptionally bloody manner, the other *yakuza* family bosses grudgingly accepted her, recognizing a kindred spirit, whatever might be the differences in natural plumbing.

In the four decades which followed, Aiko Kurita worked diligently – and ruthlessly – to expand and consolidate her power base: under her iron hand, *Kurita-ikka*, the Kurita crime family, while not particularly large, had become widely feared, so that the Japanese government designated it *boryokudan*, an especially dangerous *yakuza* family. She also oversaw the expansion of the *Kurita-ikka* into as many diverse, legal enterprises as possible, while letting go of none of the family's more questionable activities. The crowning triumph of her career came when she acquired sufficient stock in Arasaka Corporation to guarantee her a place on the company's board of directors. She took a quiet, not-unbecoming pride in her status and accomplishments, but she had neither the time nor inclination to suffer toadies or lickspittles. Flattery would gain Nakajima nothing, nor would dissembling; in the end, he realized, all he could depend on was his confidence that he was more valuable to Aiko alive than dead.

"Kurita-sama, I would submit that my failure was one of degree, not of kind. Blade is a formidable opponent. While the operation's objectives weren't conflicting, they were, in a way, divergent, dividing our focus and diluting the effort put into each. Circumstances compelled us to use whatever personnel were at hand, most of whom had never before worked together. Blade exploited this – the uncoordinated response by the *reisen* proves it. I underestimated him by not anticipating the sheer ferocity of his response. I expected our man Bridelow to bring his people out of Bits in support of Blade, which would have created an opportunity for Nagumo's *reisen* to enter the nightclub, take possession of the crystals, and then destroy the extraction team. What I did not –

could not – see coming was Blade taking down a third of Nagumo's people by himself. Once he was inside Bits, the only recourse we had was sheer brute force: the rag-tag collection of personnel at Nagumo's disposal left him – and me – no other option."

"Your point about conflicting objectives is well made, Nakajima-san; it hadn't occurred to me until you mentioned it just now. Upon mature consideration, I find I must accept part of the blame for that."

"I would submit, Kurita-sama," Nakajima interjected boldly – and dangerously, "that the overall plan was perhaps too ambitious and thus too complicated."

"Possible. Very, very possible. It *was* Arasaka's intent to first secure the crystals, so that we could obtain and duplicate the technology. Just as important, though, was securing the data they contain. Arasaka could not have done much with that, but if the Rockley woman's information was correct, our employer would have found that data invaluable." Aiko lapsed back into silence again as she closed her eyes. A moment passed, then another, then another. Finally her eyes opened and the spoke again.

"Very well, this is what we shall do. Your original instructions remain unchanged. The tactical situation has been significantly altered, however, so carrying out those instructions will, I realize, become more difficult. That does not concern me. You must know, however, that the price for failure will become very steep indeed." Nakajima bowed his head at this in a short, sharp gesture of acceptance. Aiko nodded briefly in return, then continued.

"You will make certain, by whatever means you require, to take possession of those crystals. You will also ensure that Calvin Coleridge will never be able to duplicate the work done to create them – or the data stored on them. We do not wish him to be killed, however, as his talents might prove useful to us in the future – there is no wisdom in wasting potential assets.

"And finally, you will find a way to draw Blade into an open, armed confrontation under such circumstances that all but ensure a very public bloodbath, one that produces horrifying collateral damage, with numerous civilian casualties. Blade is to be humiliated, his image tarnished to the point of ruin. Aside from INN and MSUBC, who are being quite cooperative, the American media are currently turning him into a folk hero who all but single-handedly defeated a group of foreign terrorists on US soil. This is unacceptable. So, you will create and execute a scenario where he is seen not as some avenging angel, but rather as a psychopath who simply enjoys killing people – the more, the better. But he must not be killed – it is imperative that he be allowed to live in order to face the condemnation, as well as the humiliation which will inevitably follow. That will not only satisfy our employer, but will also have the secondary benefit of removing some of the stigma which is currently attaching itself to Arasaka as a result of this morning's events. See to it personally, Nakajima-san. There must be no one to stop us this time."

"Given all the damage he has done to Arasaka Corporation in the last decade, I would think it preferable to see Blade killed outright, Kurita-sama."

"Is it possible, Hideki" – Nakajima's eyes narrowed warily at the use of his given name: Aiko Kurita was never more dangerous than when she doing her best to appear affable – "that your antipathy toward this man Blade is affecting, or even skewing, your judgment? Are you too close to this operation? Should I give thought to a reassignment, perhaps?"

"I fail to see – "

"Blade will die in due time, when it is deemed proper. He has for too long been...what is that *gaijun* phrase? Ah, yes – a thorn in our flesh. But not now, not yet. Yet you make me wonder, given how determined you are to see this man die, if you've been working for Arasaka for too long, Nakajima-san. Do you forget that you now have another master, as do I?"

"You dishonour me, Kurita-sama, by even implying that my ultimate loyalty is given to anyone other than Hen – "

"No!" Kurita cut him off. "Never use that name openly, no matter how secure you believe this channel to be! For now the shadows are still our most potent ally. You have your instructions – see to them."

Sure enough, when Compton and Radome arrived at the spot where he had parked his motorcycle, a big, garishly painted Ducati ST7, he and Radome found a body, a young man who probably hadn't yet seen his twenty-fifth birthday – and now never would –

lying next to it. Compton knelt and checked for a pulse, a pure formality, he was certain; he found none.

"Poor soul, he was just...too high strung. I'm afraid the strain was more than he could bear." Despite the words, there was little sympathy in his voice.

In contrast, Radome's dismay was quite evident. "This shit is getting real old, real fast. Would you mind explaining what happened here, Compton?" She'd quite evidently had her fill of death and mayhem for the time being.

"Huh? Oh, yeah, sure. My bike is protected by a high-voltage capacitor that will discharge if two or more of the controls – clutch, ignition, brakes, and such – are touched simultaneously. This poor bastard – " he gestured dispassionately to the huddled figure on the concrete – "discovered that the hard way."

Radome gave a shudder that wasn't entirely theatrical, while Compton produced his key fob, thumbed it twice, and the bike gave an almost inaudible "chirp." He then slid his commandeered rifle into a holster set up by the right side of the engine, unlocked a pair of helmets racked on the back, and held one out to his companion. Silver-painted, it was polished to an almost mirror-like sheen.

"Here, you can temporarily change your street name from 'Radome' to 'Chromedome.'"

"Very funny," she growled at him, then, because the grin Compton was giving her was so infectious, she smiled back as she pulled the helmet over her head. Once the chin strap was adjusted, she nodded to him, indicating she was good to go. Compton straddled the bike and hit the starter; with a mechanical cough, the motor caught almost instantly, and when it did, Radome swung into the saddle behind him and tapped the top of his helmet to indicate that she was ready. He clicked the bike into gear and opened the throttle, cruising swiftly out of the parking garage and into the morning Atlanta traffic.

Compton was good, even Blade was acknowledged that, but he wasn't quite good enough to stop and ask himself why the young man he'd found lying dead next to his motorcycle had been there in the first place....

----------------xxxxx----------------

Spazz had settled into a petulant silence, concentrating on her hand-held mini-deck as she read several messages and sent a few. Blade was confident that none of those messages concerned him, and if any of them did, well, Alistair was monitoring them, and there were very few encryption protocols which the VI couldn't crack. If he encountered one, he'd notify Blade and then automatically pass it to Raven, who in turn would work her sorcery on it.

Red, meanwhile, had apparently withdrawn even further into herself, if that was possible. She hadn't said more than a handful of words since she, Spazz, and Blade had left Bits. Blade wondered at that: manifestly, the woman displayed an impressive degree of outward composure, but he was certain that her *sang froid* was a mask. He had not forgotten Raven's bafflement at not being able to find any record anywhere of this woman's existence. Such enigmas were disquieting.

Abruptly, his line of thought lurched in an entirely different direction. Less than two hours previously he had been eyeballs-deep in a firefight with a horde of Arasaka *reisen* – well, it seemed like a horde at the time – certain that his luck had finally run out and that he was going to die at any moment, having failed in his mission. Now he was casually, almost mindlessly driving up I-75 at close to 100 miles per hour, on his way to a meeting with an almost-equally enigmatic, multi-millionaire IT designer and engineer, the same man whose request for Blade's assistance had put the Scot in into the firefight in the first place, all as if it was the most natural thing in the world. It struck him, not for the first time, that this sort of odd situation was his life in microcosm: bursts of furious, usually violent, frequently perilous, action followed by hours, days, or even months of a sort of limbo as the dust settled, figuratively or literally, while the pieces and consequences of his actions sorted themselves out. Later, he knew, he would be left alone with his thoughts – and memories. True, there was always an after-action report to drawn up and studied (and from which hopefully something could be learned), but once that task was accomplished, then his time was his own, and that's when the thinking began....

However, the thinking could wait. For the next hour or so, he could enjoy the simple pleasure of driving through the mountains of north Georgia in the company of two beautiful – and demonstrably lethal – women, neither of whom he had known for more than four hours. As for who and what they really were, well, he would figure that out when the time came to do so.

Keep your friends close, your enemies closer. I don't think I've ever taken that old adage so literally. The thought amused Blade as he silently regarded the blonde on his right and the ginger on his left. *I think I'm going to keep both of ye very close until I'm certain which of the two each of ye are.*

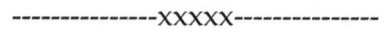

Though she was careful to give no outward sign of it, Red was going through a small, private, and very personal iteration of Hell.

She felt as though sometime in the last twenty-four hours she had stepped into an altered realty, one that shouldn't be hers, and yet it was because she was in it and it was all too tangible. It just wasn't *supposed* to be her reality....

And "Red." "*Red*." She knew from the colour of her dress and the colour of her hair that the tag had been all but inevitable, yet no one in the extraction team had bothered to ask her real name. It was Bridelow who had christened her "Red" and the label simply stuck. Yet the way he had instantly hung the tag on her seemed to imply that there more significance to it than a just being a convenient moniker.

And Bridelow. Why had the only emotion she felt when Blade shot him been not shock, anger, horror, disgust, or even surprise, but rather *relief*? Why, even knowing that he was safely dead (and why "safely" dead and not just dead?), was the mention of his name, or even the thought of him, enough to fill her with apprehension?

And, most unsettling of all, why did the thought that when she, Spazz, and Blade arrived at The Gardens she might find answers to these questions leave her terrified?

Some of her unease must have eventually communicated itself to Blade, for he suddenly gave her a keen, penetrating look that he held for a few seconds before returning his attention to the road. When he looked back again, his expression was a strangely reassuring mixture of curiosity and compassion.

"Feeling a bit unsure of yerself, are ye?"

Red nodded, and Blade gave her a brief smile. "I won't say I'm surprised at that. After all, ye've had more excitement in yer life in the last thirty hours or so than most people have in years – if ever." Quickly, with a minimum of fuss and bother, he slid the F1 two lanes to the right, downshifted and went swooping into the off-ramp for the I-575 spur, dropping his speed to a slightly more sedate eighty-five.

"When we get to The Gardens, and once Hobbes – Calvin – has the crystals back in his possession, this little stunt will be over for me. I'll go back to Scotland, send Hobbes my bill, he'll pay it, and that will be the end of it, right?"

"I suppose so."

"Wrong. My part, my immediate role will be over, true, but there're going to be a lot of ripples in the pond, so to speak, a lot of consequences coming from what went down at DisCom, and what just happened back in Atlanta Underground with Arasaka. Like it or not, ye're going to be part of those consequences, and ye'll have to deal with them when they come. So, what are ye prepared to do?"

"This may sound rude, Mr. MacLaren, but I don't mean for it to do so. Why do you care?"

"Oh, ye're a sharp one, all right." Blade nodded in approval. "Most people would simply open up and treat me like their father confessor at that question. You? Ye're on guard right away, looking for the hidden barb, the trap, wondering what my angle is. Very good."

"Thanks for the pat on the head, but you didn't answer my question."

"The reason I care about what ye might do, Red, is that when I was getting my first briefing on this op, Raven warned me that something about it made her twitchy, that it wasn't as simple and straightforward as it appeared at first glance. I trust Raven, in fact, I've trusted her with my life more than once, and when she says something makes her nervous, I pay attention, because she's almost always right."

"Fair enough, but that still isn't an answer."

"No, but it *is* a preface." He paused, thinking about how to best put what he had to say next.

"Red, ye understand, don't ye, that you're the great enigma in the middle of everything that's happened in the past two days? Ye've clearly had weapons and martial arts training, ye move like a solo, act and react like a solo – and a damned good one at that – *but no one knows who ye are.* And I think that's more important than anything else right now. So why don't we start there. Do ye have a name? A real name, I mean?"

"I can't tell you that."

"Really? Well, perhaps you could tell me how ye came to be in DisCom's R & D centre when Hobbes' extraction team got there?"

"I can't tell you that, either."

Something in her voice set off a tiny warning bell in Blade's head, and what was to be his next question died a'borning. Instead he asked, "*Can't* tell me, or *won't* tell me?"

"Right the first time, Mr. MacLaren. I would tell you if I could, but I *can not* tell you what I don't know." The young woman's face was grim, and there was a mix of real anger, genuine frustration, and not a little fear and desperation in her tone. Blade's reply was gentle but firm.

"I think that, if ye can, ye'd best explain yerself, lass."

"Mr. MacLaren, have you ever had a nightmare where you don't know who you are, but you do know that you aren't who everyone thinks you are?"

"No, I never have, but that *would* be a nightmare indeed."

"Then imagine how much more of a nightmare it would be if it happened to you in real life!"

"Go on."

"That's what's happening to me right now! I didn't always look like this – I didn't have this body, this face, this hair. I know I've been body-sculpted and somebody has done reconstructive surgery on my face – but the terrible part is that, while I know that this isn't the face and body I was born with, I don't remember what my real ones looked like! I have these bits and pieces of memories – or what I think are memories – but I don't know what they mean! I can't remember my real name – as far as I know, I don't have a name at all. I have no memory of a past, a family, friends, pets, anything that would give me an identity. It's not like I'm suffering from amnesia, like I've forgotten who I am. It's more like whoever I was had been erased."

"*Tabula rasa...*" Blade murmured.

"What?"

"*Tabula rasa* – Latin for a 'blank slate.' To someone like Hobbes,

it would be the equivalent of having your memory overwritten."
Silence reigned inside the F1 for some minutes. Spazz had set aside
her mini-deck and was wordlessly following the conversation.

"What's the first thing you remember, Red?"

"Being in the R & D centre at DisCom. The extraction team had
just walked in, and Bridelow said something, but I don't remember
what. The technicians panicked and tried to set off an alarm.
Bridelow blew them away – he used a shotgun, I remember. Then
it jammed on him when he tried to reload it, and he threw it away
because just then all hell broke loose – one of DisCom's internal
security patrols surprised the team. Everybody started shooting, but
nobody had a spare weapon for me, so I just stayed low and out of
the way."

"Good thinking, that."

"When the shooting stopped, all the DisCom guards were dead,
and so were two of people from the extraction team. Bridelow
opened up some sort of electronic vault, grabbed a bunch of small
black cylinders out of it, stuffed them into his ruck and said it was
time for everyone to run like hell. So I grabbed my shoulder bag and
did just that. Ran with them, I mean. Bridelow told you the rest
before you shot him. But that's everything I remember – everything
before Bridelow and the rest of his people walked into the R & D lab
is like a thick, oily gray fog to me."

"And once you'd thrown your lot in with Bridelow and
company, you decided to stay with them?"

"What else could I do? What else *should* I have done? For all I
knew these people had just saved my life. It sure as hell seemed as
if they had. And when the shit hit the fan at Underground Atlanta,
it was like I'd been hit by a thunderbolt. Suddenly I realized I had
all of these skills, lethal skills, all these moves and this muscle
memory, and I just put it to work. And that's something else that
scares me: I don't know where it all came from, but I do know that
it's part of me, the real me. I just don't know why!"

"I have to tell ye, from everything I've seen, ye're pretty scary
when ye're in action – ye held yerself together damned well. It was
rather impressive to watch."

"And why shouldn't I? 'Hold myself together,' I mean? Is it
going to do me or anyone else one damn bit of good if I suddenly
break down in hysterics? That would have been a really excellent

way of getting killed sometime in the last thirty hours or so, wouldn't you say?"

"Oh, I wasn't arguing with ye, lass. Something tells me those skills of yours are going to be very, very important to you in the weeks and months ahead. Meanwhile, I know some people, and know some other people who know other people, who might be able to help ye. I'll contact them as soon as I'm back in Scotland." Turning to Spazz, he gave her his most dazzling smile and said, "Now, Miss Collins, lest you still harbor doubts about my navigational prowess, we just passed through East Ellijay, and this is now officially US Highway 76. It will take us straight into Blairsville and out the other side, and from there lead directly to The Gardens. Satisfied?"

"I will be if you make sure you stop at the next goddamn gas station or fast food joint. I've gotta pee."

Blade sighed theatrically. "You, Miss Collins, are a lot of trouble."

"Holy crap! I'd forgotten how much fun riding a motorcycle can be – once I got past the fanny-pucker stage, that is!" Compton couldn't see the huge grin on Radome's face, but then, he didn't need to, he could hear it in her voice. He laughed.

"Everybody has their own idea as to just what is the most fun you can have with your clothes on, y'know, and this is mine. I mean, the first set of wheels I ever owned was a motorcycle – I've never actually owned a car."

"Where was that? Your first set of wheels, I mean."

"Out in California. I was born there, OK? In Compton, as a matter of fact. That's where my street name comes from, really."

"So what's your real name? I don't think I ever asked."

"Gerry. Gerry Hone. And you're Trish, right?"

"Yeah, I am. Nice to meet you. Do you ever get back there? To Compton, I mean."

"I used to, but I haven't been back since Southern California seceded and got annexed by Mexico in 2023. My family left right afterward and moved to Cleveland, OK? They said it was like an improvement, y'know? I swing through there now and then to say

'Hi!' to the folks. What about you?"

"My parents are long gone, and my only sister hasn't spoken to me in years. Long story, and I really don't want to talk about it."

"OK, fair enough. Enjoy the ride."

Radome had been delighted to discover that Compton had a set of low-power transceivers installed in his helmets, which allowed the two of them to easily converse as they sped northbound on Georgia 400. It had been years since she had ridden a motorbike, and had been correspondingly nervous, holding on for dear life once they left Underground Atlanta and as Compton worked his way through the traffic on I-85. But Compton quickly demonstrated that he was a skillful and considerate driver, and as the miles rolled by, she began to relax more and more until by the time they passed Alpharetta, she was positively enjoying herself.

They had just made the hard left turn at the end of Georgia 400 onto Highway 19 when the trouble began. They were pulling away from the intersection when Radome heard Compton mutter, "Uh-oh."

"What is it?"

"I think we've got company."

"What? Where?"

"Don't look back, OK? The longer they think we haven't spotted them, the better."

"Then you'd better tell me what's going on."

"There's a silver-grey SUV about a half-mile behind us, right? I saw it from time to time on the way up here, but then I would lose sight of it in traffic, so I figured that there was no way it was following us. Well, it just turned onto this road, and it's accelerating, OK? And this isn't a road where you want to be driving a big, clumsy vehicle real fast, unless you've got a real good reason to. I think we're that reason."

"Can you lose it?"

"Not until we get past Dahlonega. But I don't think that'll be a problem – whoever these guys are, I doubt they'll want to try anything where anybody can see them. So they'll wait until we're someplace pretty isolated to make a move, y'know?"

"So what's your next move?"

"Gimme a minute, let me check something." Compton fell silent for a moment, Radome knew he was checking the GPS in the heads-up display in his helmet's visor. "OK, we can go north out of town or head west. If we head west, we can loop back to 400, but that just takes us farther away from The Gardens, y'know?"

"Yeah, probably not a good idea. I don't need a rocket scientist to figure out why somebody is tailing us. So we head north?"

"That keeps us heading in the right direction, at least, plus things start getting deserted outside the town."

"How soon?"

"Well, not for a few miles, but there are some pretty empty stretches, yeah. But that can work two ways – this road starts winding and twisting a lot more once we're north of Dahlonega, OK? Which means more chances to break contact and lose them. Let's just hope there's a paved road there when we need one."

"Why not take one of those back roads? There's no way an SUV could keep up with us on one of them."

"This is a street bike, Radome, not a dirt bike. On a dirt road we really can't go much faster than a four-wheel vehicle. And this suspension can't handle a really rough road at all."

"Oh."

"Don't worry, I'll lose 'em."

"Maybe we can give them the slip in town?"

"No way. Too many people around, y'know? I don't wanna get myself killed, but I'm not real keen on getting some innocent bystander whacked either, OK? Plus, I can't get real enthusiastic about the idea of some pistol-packin', well-intentioned private citizen blowing us off the bike, either. We're not exactly wearing signs that say 'We're the Good Guys!', are we?"

"A point, definitely a point."

Compton slowed the bike a bit as they approached the outskirts of the town. "OK, listen up. Hold on tight and just keep your head pressed against my back. Don't try to lean, don't try to 'help,' OK? Leave the driving to me. I think we're about to make some of the good citizens of Dahlonega a bit unhappy. Are you ready for this, Trish?"

"Go for it, Gerry."

Compton gave a grunt of satisfaction, then downshifted and cranked the big Ducati's throttle wide open. Horns blaring, engine roaring, he tore into the town.

Dahlonega, Georgia was a small college town that was also

popular with tourists exploring the southernmost reaches of the Blue Ridge Mountains. It would have been incorrect to call it "sleepy," but it was most certainly quiet. And it was not the sort of place that ever expected a bellowing Italian street bike, closely pursued by a lurching, tire squealing Ford Endurance, to go streaking through it at seven o'clock on an August Wednesday morning. Fortunately, there were very few pedestrians and almost no vehicular traffic, so no innocent bystanders were endangered when Compton tore into a skittering, tire-screaming right turn in the middle of the town onto the Moore Parkway, followed a few seconds later by the Endurance, which turned so hard so abruptly that it momentarily went up on two wheels .

The Parkway, despite its somewhat grandiose name, was a simple two-lane highway, well-paved and maintained, but offering few opportunities for the pursuing Endurance to overtake and pull alongside the big Ducati. The first six miles were a series of long, sweeping right- and left-hand turns, interrupted by a few short straights, the combination of which allowed Compton to use the bike's superior acceleration and his skill to keep the range open between himself and the pursuit. He swooped into a twisty bit that would have been at home on a Formula One circuit, then opened the throttle wide on a brief straightaway, hoping to put enough distance between him and the SUV to lose sight of each other, giving him the chance to break contact.

For her part, Radome began to anticipate Compton's moves, having become familiar enough with his body language as a driver: she could sense how he was setting up for a turn or a straight by how the muscles in his back and shoulders tensed. This gave her enough confidence to reach behind her back with her right hand and swing the H & K submachine gun to her side, brace the butt against her lower ribs, and rack the bolt handle. She knew better than to try anything so supremely stupid as attempting to shoot back at their pursuers, but if they ever managed to pull up along side her and Compton, she was prepared to give those gumballs a warm un-welcome. Suddenly Compton was speaking to her.

"Radome, decision time coming up, OK? We're coming up on a T in less than a minute, we're outta sight of that SUV, and we finally got a shot at breaking contact. But we've gotta decide what we're gonna do, y'know. We can go left or right, OK? Left'll take us into

Blairsville and then on through to The Gardens, but once we're on that road, basically that's it, there's no way to turn back and pretty much no place to turn off, at least nothing that goes anywhere. Lots of dead ends, y'know? Right'll take us into a little town called Cleveland, and we'll have more options as far as routes, but it'll take us farther away from The Gardens. And I'm kinda hoping the closer we get the more likely the cavalry'll arrive, y'know?"

"I hear you. Take the left – I like the idea of the cavalry arriving sooner. That SUV is the only one we've seen, but something tells me it's not the only out there looking for us."

"Yeah, you've got a point. OK, left it is."

And left it was, as Compton ignored the approaching "STOP" sign completely, and, in fact, barely slowed down as he swung the bike northward. A few hundred yards north of the turn, the roadway curved gently to the right, and by the time the Endurance reached the intersection, Compton and Radome were lost to sight.

Unfortunately, that didn't appear to deter the driver of the Endurance. After sitting at the intersection for a few seconds, the SUV turned left and accelerated, although at a far more leisurely pace than Compton had done.

Meanwhile, Compton, feeling better with each passing second as his rearview mirrors were empty of any sign of the Endurance, guided his bike into what the locals called the Bogg Creek Bend, a long, wavering 180-degree turn that from overhead looked a big, backward "C" drawn by a giant, none-to-steady hand. All he had to do now was keep his speed up – even if that silver SUV *had* turned left back at the intersection, there was no way it could catch up to him now. Another twenty, twenty-five minutes, and he and Radome would be rolling into –

"Oh, shit!"

"What is it?"

"We got company."

"I thought we lost them."

"I mean up ahead, OK?"

Radome snuck a quick glance over Compton's left shoulder, and her heart dropped to where her stomach had been, her stomach having shriveled into a cold, hard knot of fear. Ahead of them were at least three more of the silver-gray SUVs, carefully positioned so that they completely blocked the roadway, with no room to maneuver between them, while the steep ditches to either side of the road precluded any attempt to go around the vehicles. More intimidating were the dozen or so people clearly armed with rifles and submachine guns, all of which were leveled at the approaching motorcycle. Without any warning, they began shooting.

The front of Compton's Ducati exploded in a shower of plastic, composites, and glass as the incoming bullets shredded the wind fairing, windscreen, and lights. At least one projectile punctured the front tire, and it was only Radome's added weight at the rear of the bike that kept it from nosing over. As it was, Compton felt control slipping away from him as he did his best to slow the machine down.

"Get ready to tuck and roll, Trish," he shouted. "The bike's going down – I'm gonna try and lay it on its side!"

"Gerry – !"

Radome felt the motorcycle go over, then suddenly she was on the pavement, skipping and sliding across the road and into a ditch, half on her back, half on her right side. The contact with the road stunned her, and after a particularly hard bounce, her head struck the pavement sharply. The helmet absorbed most of the impact, but it will still enough to knock her unconscious.

Compton, who had spilled bikes before, was better prepared but Fate decided to take a hand, and just as he was about to let go of the machine, the muzzle of the MilTec rifle he had slung in the holster on the right side of the engine dug into the pavement. Instantly, the bike's momentum sent it cartwheeling end-over-end, to crash into the back half of one of the SUVs. Halfway through the first spin Compton and machine parted company, and as he went flying, he found himself thinking "Ooooohhhhh, shhhhiiiiiiiit! This is gonna *hurt!*" Then he managed to twist his body in the split second before impact, so that he landed on his back, trusting his titanium spine to protect him.

Amazingly, he was successful – at least to the point that he was still alive after he landed. That was where the good news ended, however. Stunned, bleeding, with a sharp pain in his side that told him that at least one of his ribs was broken, Compton felt himself slipping away into darkness. The last thing he saw were a half-dozen people advancing in his direction, firearms pointed straight at him. His last thought, just before the blackness took him, was

"God damn it! We were so close...."

----------------XXXXX----------------

The drive into and through Blairsville was uneventful, and all three of the occupants of the F1 were able to be properly appreciative of the frequent picture-postcard-like vistas that would unexpectedly open up before them as they rounded a curve or topped a hill. The only blemish on an otherwise perfect morning was that they seemed to have left the sun behind in Atlanta: gray clouds were gathering not all that far above the tops of the Blue Ridge Mountains, and there seemed to be a hint of approaching rain in the air.

A right turn onto Plottown Road and short drive later, they found a small sign that read simply, "The Gardens," standing beside an unadorned two-lane entrance road. There was no gate, no security guards, nothing to indicate that this was something other than a private drive, "The Gardens" being nothing more than a well-secluded private residence. Certainly no passerby would ever imagine that it lead to one of the most advanced computer hardware and software development facilities in the world. The gently-winding drive followed a small stream that the GPS identified as Yewell Branch for what Blade's odometer said was just over a mile, and then they came upon what was obviously the main parking area. Blade stopped the car, shut down the engine, and sat for a wordless moment, then together, Spazz, Red, and he climbed out of the F1 and gazed in wonder at the scene before them.

Calvin Rowland Coleridge had commissioned some of the finest structural and landscape architects in the world to design the buildings and grounds of "The Gardens," seeking to create the most perfect environment possible for creativity, research, and study. And not just in computer and information technologies and sciences: he also strove to be a patron of the arts, sponsoring the work of dozens of artists, sculptors and writers, all of whom lived and worked at The Gardens amidst their more technically-oriented colleagues. Rolling hills, long stretches of hardwoods and pines, expanses of thick, green grass, meandering roadways and footpaths, half-hidden structures burrowed into hillsides, stone cottages and larger brick buildings, it was what one observer had called "the closest approximation of Tolkien's 'Shire' that has ever existed on Earth." Theme parks might describe themselves as "magical" but The Gardens were simply magic. It was a place of profound and quiet beauty.

Except that it was no longer there.

Part Two

For a Few Crystals More

Chapter 6

"My. God. What happened? Who did this? Who *could* do it?"

It was Spazz who spoke; Red and Blade could only nod in silent agreement.

In the landscape that stretched out before them, no structure of any kind remained standing. The ground was pocked with dozens, scores, maybe hundreds of craters, a few with wisps of smoke rising from them, some holding what appeared to be the remains of buildings. Of human life there was no sign, none at all. About fifty yards where they were standing was an especially large crater that had, apparently, been the reception centre. Now all that could be seen were the broken ends of a few structural beams and a scattering of broken bricks: whatever else remained appeared to have been swallowed whole by the earth beneath it. Blade was reminded of photographs he had seen of the ruins of some French villages once located near the city of Verdun....

Finally, Blade spoke, his voice soft, answering Spazz's very first question.

"Somebody blew it all up. And not all that many minutes ago, either, from the look of it."

"Wait, what? Not that long ago? Then I don't understand why we never heard anything. We should have heard the explosions – felt them, too!"

Blade shook his head. "No, Spazz, we wouldn't have. I recognize this damage pattern. Camouflet."

"Camo-what?"

"Camouflet. It's what happens when an explosive charge goes off deep underground." It was Red who spoke. From somewhere she had produced a pic-stick, a camera no larger than an old-fashioned flash drive, and was methodically taking photographs of the now-destroyed Gardens. Blade and Spazz turned to look at her; MacLaren's gaze was considering, Maureen's one of surprise. "Set off a charge deep enough," she went on, "and it doesn't rupture the surface, it just creates an underground pocket of plasma that expands and then contracts almost instantly, everything above it just collapses into the cavity the plasma leaves behind, and then the earth falls in to cover the wreckage. It's a technique that's sometimes used in construction, but most of its applications are military."

Blade nodded in agreement as he did a slow scan of the landscape. "I think ye've got the right of it, lass. Somebody used Mistletoe here."

"'Mistletoe'? Why do I suddenly think I'm out of my depth here?"

"It's not that you're out of your depth, Miss Collins, just out of your area of expertise." This was Red speaking again. "Mistletoe is the name of a family of 'bunker busters' used by NATO air forces. They're designed to be carried by AV's and helicopters."

Spazz stared at Red. "How – how do you know that?"

Blade held up his hand. "That's a conversation for later, ladies. Raven, are you getting this? If you are, link to all of us – and bring Alistair in, as well."

"I am. And I think you and Red are correct – the damage pattern has all the characteristics of a well-executed military strike against underground installations." Though no one could see her at the moment, she was leaning forward at her desk, tapping a fingernail against her front teeth, intent on the imagery Blade had uploaded to her from his cybernetic eye. "If it wasn't Mistletoe, it was something damned close to it."

"And if whoever it was that did this used standard Mistletoe tactics, they probably demolished the smaller underground spaces outright, and then destroyed the access passages, utility tunnels, and ventilation shafts of the larger ones, then blew out the four corners of those bigger spaces and let the weight of the overburden collapse them. It's faster and more efficient than trying to destroy them outright." Red's face was expressionless, but her voice was grim. "Which means that there's a lot of people trapped down there – in total darkness if the emergency lighting failed – who have no idea what has just happened to them."

"And who can't get out and are slowly running out of air.

What was your estimate of the number of people Calvin had living and working here, Raven?"

"About three hundred, David – there was never a hard figure on the artist colony."

"Damn."

Spazz spoke up at this point. "So...what now?"

"Now? Give me a minute, I'm working on it." An edge of fatigue was creeping into MacLaren's voice, something Maureen might have noted had she not been so tired herself.

Red spoke up. "For what it's worth, I don't think we really want to be here when the local law enforcement shows up – and the longer we hang around, the more likely that is to happen."

"Ye're right. We're not doing anybody any good by hanging about, especially ourselves."

"*What*?" Anger and incredulity suffused Spazz's voice. "So we just leave three hundred people to die?"

Blade whirled on her, anger flashing in his eyes and burning in his voice. "Do ye think I *want* to do that? Do ye think I *like* knowing I *have* to do it? *Do ye think we really have any choice?*" Spazz took an involuntary step back at his fury. "What are we supposed to do, Maureen, dig them out? We'd need heavy machinery for that, and we don't have so much as a shovel! Even if we did, we have no idea where to look, where to start! I don't like it one damned bit more than you do, Spazz. Right now I feel helpless, absolutely helpless – useless – and there's nothing in this world I hate more than that! I hate myself right now, because people are dying out there while I'm standing here talking to you, and there isn't one goddamned thing I can do about it!"

"We can at least call for help!"

"Alistair's already done that – am I right, Alistair?"

"Aye, sir, ye are. Ah began notifyin' the local authorities as soon as ye found out what happened."

"Then we'd best be going. If anyone can help those people down there, it will be the people who are on the way. Not us. Right now we have to – " He froze as Alistair's voice came up in his earbud again.

"Sirr, two things. First of all, Ah've just experienced a total loss o' signal from Mr. Compton and Miss Radome."

"Damn!"

"What is it?" Red and Spazz said in unison.

"Alistair was tracking Radome and Compton – they were supposed to meet us here. He says he's just lost their signal."

"Yeah, like you said, damn." Maureen's lips pressed together in a thin, hard line. "I don't know about you, MacLaren, but I think this whole situation is getting to be about as fucked up as a drag queen's wig!"

"Succinctly if inelegantly put, Miss Collins."

"Far be it from me to appear stupid, but what happened, and how does it affect us?"

The Scot frowned, whether in annoyance or concentration, neither woman could tell. "As to *exactly* what happened, Red, I have no idea, obviously. But Alistair said it was a 'total loss of signal,' which means not only Compton and Radome's comm-links, but their personal transponders, as well. Radome's is in her deck, Compton's is in his neural processor."

"Shutting down the transponder in the deck wouldn't be all that hard, would it?" Red asked. Blade shook his head, and she went on. "But switching off one that's inside a neural processor can't be at all easy."

"It is if you know the right codes to send it."

"Oh."

"Oh, indeed. Ye said 'two things,' Alistair. What's the other?"

"Sirr! Ah have four fast-movers inbound directly fer yer position, thirty-two miles out, makin' 180 knots, flyin' NOE. Ah'm designatin' 'em as Bogeys One through Four. And, Sirr, they are no' – repeat no' – squawkin' *any* ID or transponder codes!"

"Gawd, it never rains but it pours," Blade muttered, then turned to two women. "Ladies, we've got incoming, and they're not friendlies. We need to move, now!"

Red folded the viewfinder back over the body of her pic-stick and tucked it away in a small pocket on the inside of the wide red belt, which matched her dress perfectly, that she wore about her waist. No doubt, Blade mused, that belt was home to other useful bits and pieces as well.

"Got everything ye wanted?" he asked.

"I did. Something tells me having a photographic record of what happened here is going to be useful someday, somehow."

"A hunch?"

"Men have hunches. Women have something far better – a woman's intuition."

"Right, then. This is me *so* not going there. In any case, since we" –

"Can we talk about this later?" Spazz made no effort to hide her impatience. "Red's suggestion a few minutes ago – the part about getting the hell out of Dodge before the locals arrive – suddenly seems like an even better idea now than it did then."

"Ye're right, lass. Blade's Law of Combat Number 32: 'Always know when to get the hell out of Dodge.' We're accomplishing nothing here. Right, Alistair, we're gone! Keep an eye on them, will ye?"

"Consider it done, Sir!"

"Both of ye, in the car. *Now!*"

A movement in the corner of his eye caught Blade's attention and he spotted the all-but-invisible drone hovering over the remains of The Gardens. It was suddenly crystal clear to him how the strike which had devastated the once-beautiful research campus had been guided in with such precision. Equally clear was that whoever was responsible also knew that he, Red, and Spazz were onsite – and were coming back to finish them off. Growling "I've had enough of yer shite," he snatched the SMLE from behind the seats of the F1, drew a quick bead on the drone, and though it was easily three hundred yards distant, shattered it with one shot.

"Won't do any good but at least I got the satisfaction of nailing the bastart!" he muttered, handing the rifle to Red. "Here, ye stow it while I start up."

Slithering into the driver's seat, Blade quickly started the car as Spazz and Red took their places to either side of him. He noticed that rather than put the SMLE in its cradle behind the seats, Red slid it into the left footwell beside her. Blade spun the F1 around, then stopped momentarily while he pressed a switch on the console to his left. The two women heard a trio of metallic clunks come from the rear of the car, but before either could form a question, Blade had engaged first gear and now the low-slung, sapphire-blue coupe was racing up the winding drive back to Plott Town Road.

"Alistair, connect me to Calvin Coleridge." Spazz gave him a very perplexed look but said nothing – for the moment.

"Aye, sir."

"Calvin Coleridge's comm line." The voice that answered was Mycroft's.

"Mycroft, put Hobbes on. Don't argue with me, just do it." There was a brief pause, then, "Hobbes? Blade. Shut everything down, get off The Grid, and stay off The Grid until ye hear otherwise from either me or Raven. Nobody else! Got that?"

"What – why?"

"I don't have time to explain, just do it!"

"And just how am I supposed to hear from you or Raven if all my communications are shut down?"

"Don't worry about that, ye know damned well we have our ways. I'll be there in – " MacLaren glanced at his watch " – ninety minutes. Don't move until I get there!"

"You don't even know where I am!"

"Trust me. Now shut the hell up, hang the hell up, log the hell off and jack the hell out. That's an order. If ye want to stay alive, obey it! Alistair, break it down."

"Aye, sir. Call terminated."

"Wait a minute – your friend Calvin, or Coleridge, or Hobbes, or whatever you call him isn't dead? He wasn't back there buried all that wreckage?"

"No, lass, never was, even for a minute. He's been in his penthouse in downtown Atlanta since he met me at the airport this morning."

"Then why the hell did we come all the way out here?"

"I'll explain later. Right now I need to find a way out of here." He thumbed a button on the steering wheel, and a roadmap of the area was instantly projected on the windscreen in front of him. Spazz gave him a quizzical look and he grinned back at her. "Blade's Law of Combat Number 33: 'Always know *how* to get the hell out of Dodge.'" He scanned the image briefly, stopped for a fraction of a second as the F1 reached the main road, then turned left without hesitation.

"Why this way, Blade?" Spazz asked. When MacLaren looked at her, she quickly followed up. "I'm trying to learn here, dammit, so teach me!"

"Fair enough." He gestured at the heads-up display. "Alistair estimates that our uninvited guests are about eight minutes out. I need to use that eight minutes to put as much distance as possible between us and what's left of The Gardens. I think we've got a fifty-fifty chance of breaking contact."

"And if we don't?"

"Then we wind up playing British bulldogs with a quartet of what are probably AV9s."

"I can't say I'm terribly sanguine about that idea."

"Neither am I, which is why I want to get as far away from here as fast as I can – that will make it harder for them to find us and catch up to us." MacLaren braked hard, downshifted, and drifted through an abrupt 110-degree right, then mashed the throttle and accelerated again. A half-minute later, he brought the F1 to a screeching halt at a stop sign, turned left – Trackrock Gap Road, the sign said – and went roaring southward.

Closed up in a diamond formation, the four "fast-movers," which were indeed AV9s – popularly known as "Shrikes," they were turbine-powered, vectored-thrust lifting-body aircraft designed to do double duty as a small assault shuttle and fire-support platform – came swooping in toward the remains of The Gardens from the north-northeast at an altitude of barely a hundred feet. They were headed directly for the parking area where only eight minutes or so earlier Blade, Red, and Spazz had been standing. The hardpoints under their stubby wings and along the broad undersides of their fuselages were empty, all of their explosive ordnance having been expended on the now-shattered research campus. Still, even a clean AV9 was not to be trifled with: in semi-flexible mountings to either side of and slightly below the cockpit were a pair of 13mm heavy machine guns, while under the cockpit on the Shrike's centreline was a fixed 20mm autocannon. It was well-protected as well, the whole vehicle, save for the pilot's windscreen, being covered by three millimeters of Weclar anti-kinetic armour.

Deprived of the data input from the drone Blade destroyed, the four aerial vehicles were using onboard sensors, along with their pilots' Mk 1 eyeballs, to scan for signs life – primarily movement and infrared signatures – in the pummeled remains of The Gardens; as expected, they found none. As they neared the parking apron, all four pilots noted that it was now empty. None of them, however, caught sight of the trio of battleship-grey cylinders sitting on the tarmac, pointed directly at them. They could hardly have been faulted for failing to do so, given the cylinders' bland colouration and small size – 50mm in diameter and three times that in length – and because the cylinders weren't radiating an EM signature, none of the AV9's sensors detected them either.

But just because they weren't radiating electro-magnetic energy didn't mean that they weren't receiving any. Seconds after MacLaren had released them from underneath the F1, each of the cylinders had sprouted four tiny articulated legs, which promptly set them upright, then, acting on instructions from Alistair, who employed the same satellite link he'd used to spot and track the incoming Shrikes, oriented them in the direction of the approaching aircraft. With the sort of precision only a machine could achieve, Alistair waited until what he judged to be the perfect moment, then sent a signal that set off the propellent charges inside the cylinders.

Two of them went off simultaneously, each throwing a half-pound projectile a hundred feet into the sky, where they promptly detonated. Essentially oversized "flash-bangs" – stun grenades – the projectiles burst in 8-million candle-power flashes just ahead of oncoming AV9s. Their photochromic windscreens went black almost instantly in response, but not before at least a fraction of the light blast filled the cockpits, temporarily dazzling their occupants. The pilot of the first Shrike reacted instinctively, firewalling his throttle and pulling his vehicle into a steep climb, while his wingmen broke left and right, accelerating as they did so.

The fourth AV9 was not so fortunate. The third cylinder, for reasons known only to God and the quirks of the laws of physics, fired a fraction of a second later than its mates, sending its projectile straight into the path of the last Shrike. Their trajectories merged just at the instant the flash-bang detonated, the projectile bursting just inches from the windscreen. The raw energy of the light it emitted overpowered the photochromic capacity of the windscreen, and the pilot was subjected to its near-total intensity.

The result was a sensation of someone driving two oversize spikes straight through his eyes all the way back into his occipital lobe; sensory overload shut down the higher functions of his brain, and muscles of all four limbs began to clench uncontrollably, while his hands locked in a death-grip on the throttle and stick. As his arms convulsed back toward his body, he involuntarily voted on the control column at the same instant that he closed the throttle, sending his AV9 into a stall at the same moment it began rolling sharply to the right. Two seconds later, there was a fresh crater in the remains of The Gardens, while a flame-laced gout of black smoke boiled skyward.

----------------XXXXX----------------

Had he been human, Alistair would have fist-pumped in triumph. As it was, there was something curiously resembling satisfaction in his voice when he reported to Blade: "Sir, one o' those AVs – Bogey Four – has been taken doon by the flash-bangs. It appears that the projectile was in direct contact with the vehicle when it detonated, and the pilot lost control and crashed as a result."

"Really? Well played, Alistair, well played. That's definitely good news."

"What's good news?"

"Eh? Oh, sorry, Spazz, Alistair was just talking to me. I dropped off three flash-bang flares in the car park back there –"

"Those three 'clunks' we heard?"

"Those three 'clunks' ye heard, yes. Apparently one of them took out one of the AVs. Rather permanently."

"So now it's three-to-one instead of four-to-one?"

"Exactly. I was hoping to just create some confusion and a bit of disorganization to buy us some more time to get away, but 'gift horses' and all that...."

"I'm not arguing with it."

"Neither am I." Blade braked and downshifted, dropping the F1's speed to the vicinity of fifty miles per hour. "Now we do our best to blend in with the locals. A car doing ninety will attract attention; one doing forty-five or so is just one of the neighbors out for wee morning drive."

Red looked at MacLaren, rolled her eyes, and said, "I hardly think this car is likely to 'blend in' out here in the north of Georgia, considering that it hardly 'blends in' anywhere."

"Oh, ye of little faith." He eased the F1 over to the centre of the road, straddling the double yellow line, flicked a switch on the left console, and gestured forward at the nose of the car. "*Now* tell me it doesn't blend in."

Both women leaned forward and gasped in unison. Where there had been sapphire-blue bodywork there was now an expanse of dark gray that perfectly matched the tone of the tarmac beneath the coupe, while a double yellow line ran down the centre of the car's nose. As Blade gently rocked the steering wheel from side to side, the yellow line moved in unison, following the apparent movement of the one on the roadway – not quite perfectly and not quite instantaneously, but sufficiently well that at more than a dozen yards the casual observer would never notice the difference.

"RAC – Reactive Adaptive Camouflage," Red murmured. "Pixelated body panels. Maybe we can 'blend in' with the locals after all."

----------------xxxxx----------------

"I take it that you have good news for me, Nakajima-san?"

"Yes, Kurita-sama, I do. One of our field teams was able to intercept two of Coleridge's extraction team, Compton and Radome. They were carrying the case containing the crystals. The case is on its way here, to my location, now."

"Has the field team confirmed that the crystals are, in fact, in that case?"

"They are under strict orders not to open or otherwise tamper with the case under any circumstances, but to deliver it directly to me and me only. However, one of our agents, who was in Underground Atlanta but was not involved in the gunfight there, and so not detained by the US Marshals, informed me that she saw Blade personally hand the case to Radome before he departed. Radome and Compton left shortly thereafter, and we had them under surveillance the entire time."

"And Blade himself? Where is he, and what is he doing?"

"At this moment, Mistress, I cannot say *precisely* where he is." Aiko Kurita's eyes narrowed dangerously, but Nakajima held up a hand in a mollifying gesture. "I do know that he arrived at The Gardens just moments after our airstrike went in – our reconnaissance drone provided a positive ID on him and the women called 'Spazz' and 'Red' on-site."

"In that ridiculous automobile of his, I suppose...."

"Yes, as a matter of fact, he is driving his F1."

"And how is it that you don't know *precisely* where he is now?" Kurita cocked her head as her eyes narrowed slightly, but Nakajima was unfazed.

"He destroyed our drone, shot it down, actually."

"And was this before or after the destruction of The Gardens?"

"After, Kurita-sama. Approximately fifteen minutes after."

Aiko Kurita steepled her fingers and pursed her lips, gazing balefully at Nakajima. After a slightly drawn out silence, her voice was sharp as she asked, "And since you don't know *precisely* where Blade is at the moment, what is you best...estimate of his whereabouts?"

"He is doubtless on his way back to Atlanta, Mistress, where he will certainly meet with Calvin Coleridge, at Coleridge's penthouse in Barnett Tower, to report in person on what has happened."

"And what makes you so sure of that?"

Nakajima spread his hands wide in an un-characteristically un-Japanese fashion, and asked simply, "What else can he do? At the very least, he will leave the two women with Coleridge before he himself returns to Scotland, and Coleridge will undoubtedly want an accounting of everything Blade saw at The Gardens."

Kurita's expression softened, as did her voice. "You're quite right, Hideki. There is nowhere else he would go. One last question, then. Is it in any way possible that Blade knows that we have taken possession of the crystals?"

"No, Mistress, absolutely not. He most assuredly knows that both Compton's and Radome's comm-links are down, meaning that something has happened to them, but he has no way of knowing where or why that happened, nor could he know whether or not they reached The Gardens before the airstrike went in. It's quite likely Blade is convinced that the crystals are buried under tons of earth and rubble."

"Which means that you've accomplished two of the three objectives I set out for you, Nakajima-san: you've secured the crystals themselves, and you've made it impossible for Coleridge to duplicate his work."

"Yes, Mistress. All that remains is to stage and execute the incident with Blade."

"Then I best let you be about it. *Sayonara imanotokoro.*" Nakajima watched as she leaned forward and terminated the contact. For a moment he stood before the blank monitor, wearing a very satisfied expression. He looked over at Umori, who peering intently at his own monitor and industriously pecking away at his keyboard. Umori had a well-developed case of selective hearing: he gave no indication of having noted that in his conversation with Kurita, Nakajima very carefully avoided mentioning that the three surviving AV9s were even now trying to locate Blade, and that when they did, they had orders to kill him and his companions on sight. After all, what Aiko Kurita didn't know couldn't hurt Nakajima....

---------------xxxxx---------------

Traffic on Trackrock Gap Road was lighter than MacLaren had expected or hoped – this was, after all, near the peak of the tourist season here in the mountains of north Georgia, so he'd been anticipating a few more vehicles on the roadways. Driving more or less on autopilot, he smirked at the thought of what must be going through the minds of the drivers of the handful of cars and trucks that had passed in going in the opposite direction: they could hear the F1, but they really couldn't see it as it went by. He could almost see them asking themselves what the hell had made so much noise....

His reverie was interrupted when Alistair's voice came into his ear once more. "Sirr, Ah'm still trackin' those wee AV9s, and it seems that they're no' leavin' the area. Ah'm also pickin' up some ground-scatter that looks an awfu' lot like reflected VADER radiation. If they have VADER and somethin' like Crossbow, they'll be findin' ye soon enough."

"I don't suppose ye have any good news for me, do ye?"

"Sorry, Sirr, but no, Ah don't."

"Right then, I'd best be about it." Glancing left and right, he said, "Ladies, we may have some uninvited company. Just because we're damned-near invisible visually doesn't mean we can't be seen electronically, so I need ye to keep a sharp eye and sing out if ye spot anything. And be sure ye're both properly strapped in – it's likely to be bumpy ride."

Neither Red nor Spazz replied but immediately checked there lapbelts then began carefully scanning the sky. Alistair's concerns were well-founded, for the three surviving AV9s, which were now circling at an altitude of five thousand feet, were each equipped with VADER and radar interpreting systems that in all respects save their lack of serial numbers were identical to the Crossbow technology used by armed forces of several western countries. A bit long in the tooth, VADER – Vehicle And Dismount Exploitation Radar – had been around for three decades, continually upgraded and refined, a centimetric radar that could detect and track moving vehicles and even individuals and large animals on the ground. Crossbow was an image interpretation software package that had kept VADER relevant into the 2030s: using the scans VADER provided, it could identify by make and type any known vehicle, tracked or wheeled, and could differentiate between, say, a sniper in a ghillie suit lying in ambush and a napping brown bear.

For Blade and his two companions this meant there was little to no chance, should the F1 be detected by VADER, that it could pretend to be, say, a Chevrolet Vesper or a Toyota Ultron, innocently tooling along at the speed limit, and so, hopefully, be ignored: if it were able to get a good paint on the coupe, the Crossbow system would immediately identify the car for what it was. This also meant that there would be no need for the AV9 pilots to get eyeballs on the F1 to get make a positive identification before taking any action: its radar signature was small, but distinctive. All of which, Blade knew, meant that it was all but certain that things would get very dicey in very short order. If he, Spazz, and Red were to survive, it would have to be through a combination of guile, footwork – well, roadwork, really – and pure dumb luck. It was that last bit that worried him the most: depending on luck to survive in a tactical situation was as good as an open admission that he'd run out of options.

---------------xxxxx---------------

Fifteen hundred feet overhead, the lead AV9 pilot, Charles Whatley, was considering his own options. Sandy-haired, with dough-boy features and watery blue eyes, pushing the half-century mark and running to fat however much he might deny it, Whatley was an ex-US Air Force major who had spent almost fifteen years flying various V/STOL military aircraft. He had never been able to escape his despised childhood nickname of "Chip," which had quickly evolved into the callsign "Chipmunk" during flight training at Sheppard Air Force Base and followed him throughout the remainder of his career. As fate would have it, that career came to a rather abrupt halt when he was cashiered from the USAF for "conduct unbecoming an officer," a charge he still deeply resented ten years later. Dammit, how was he supposed to know her ID was a fake? His other-than-honourable discharge was a black mark that time and again prevented him from finding respectable employment as a commercial pilot – no airline or airfreight service wanted to hire someone with a demonstrably shady (and shaky) past. It was, perhaps, inevitable then that Chipmunk, in the millennia-old tradition of disgraced fighting men everywhere, became a mercenary. Which was how he found himself this indifferent August morning leading a flight of four – now three – AV9s on a covert airstrike that had evolved into a search-and-destroy operation.

The options available to Whatley were effectively limited by only one factor – time – but it was a harsh and hard limit. The Shrike was known for having "short legs," because, like all vectored-thrust vehicles, it was a fuel hog. He and his wingmen had no more than forty minutes of loiter time before they hit "bingo" fuel and had to return to their base in the mountains of southwest Virginia. Thus whatever it was Chipmunk decided to do, he had to do it in short order.

He looked to either side of his own aircraft, where his two wingmen flew, "Thrasher" to his left and "Shinden" to his right, both roughly a mile distant, spaced to provide the maximum coverage for their VADER systems. The three aircraft were moving in a line abreast towards the south, having already made certain that the vehicle which was their designated target had not taken the eastern or western route away from The Gardens. In Whatley's estimation, if need be they could fly as far as Dahlonega in search of their target before reversing their course to the north, and even then, should they locate their quarry on the return sweep, they would still have enough fuel for at least two or three firing passes. All three pilots kept their radio chatter to a minimum, the better to concentrate on finding their target. After all, they were, in their own ways, each a professional

"Thrasher" wasn't just a callsign, it was also the pilot's surname.

Larry Thrasher shared little in common with Chipmunk Whatley, save that he had been summarily dismissed from the United States Army, in his case for "misappropriation and distribution of Government property," a fancy way of describing a black market operation. His conviction by court-martial was an absolute certainty, but a slick civilian lawyer, of the "don't dazzle 'em with brilliance, baffle 'em with bullshit" variety, had been able to keep Thrasher from spending twenty years in Ft. Leavenworth, making little rocks out of big ones. Instead, Larry was busted from WO3 to E-1, forfeited all pay, privileges, and benefits, handed a dishonourable discharge, and shown the door so rapidly that, in the quaint parlance of the United States Army, "it took a week for his ass to catch up to the rest of him." Like Whatley, Thrasher drifted from odd job to odd job before deciding that the only real career path left to him was that of a glorified, flying hired gun. As luck would have it, the role suited him perfectly, and Thrasher, tall and rangy, with dark brown eyes and dirty blonde hair, looked every bit the part of the flying cowboy. Neither Thrasher nor Whatley particularly liked each other, but each had a marked degree of respect for the other's talents as a pilot.

"Shinden," Tomiyashi Yashida, was very different kettle of fish from either Whatley or Thrasher. He was a civilian through-and-through: he had never served a day in any branch of the Japan Self-Defence Forces, but rather had been an Arasaka man from the day he'd finished secondary school. Short, stocky, round-faced, with dark brown eyes and a mop of spiky black hair, Yashida was almost a caricature of an average Japanese. That was not a handicap: his at-best average flying skills were. Despite his limited talent as a pilot, however, Yashida imagined himself a *samurai* of the air, deadly and invincible, hence his call sign *Shinden* - "Lightning" in Japanese. He was younger than both of the *gaijun* pilots, and regarded them as a pair of overrated fossils – he seemed oblivious to the fact that both Thrasher and Whatley could fly rings around him any day of the week, and that he possessed only a fraction of their situational awareness. In short, he was arrogant, overconfident, and under-qualified. Whatley only tolerated his presence on this mission because he was, in some vague, unspecified way, related to his employer, who happened to be Hideki Nakajima....

It was Thrasher who spotted it first. His VADER system beeped an acquisition alert, the targeting display on his instrument panel indicating that the bogey was to his right, almost directly under Chipmunk Whatley. He gave the Crossbow system a few seconds to firm up its confidence in the ID, then touched the switch that activated his comm.

"Chipmunk, I think I've got something."

"What and where?"

"Almost directly underneath you – right in your blind spot. Crossbow is showing a 94% confidence in its ID, but I'm not getting much of a paint on it – probably just the drivetrain and suspension. Those cars have a lot of carbon fiber in their bodies, right?"

"That they do. Have you got eyeballs on the target, Thrasher?"

"Negative. Crossbow says its there, but I can't actually see anything so far."

"Shinden, get in there and see what you can see."

"Rog-oh! Going in!"

---------------XXXXX---------------

"Sirr, one o' the AVs, Bogey Two, has altered course and is headed fer a direct intercept wi' ye. He's above and behind ye."

"Right, Alistair. Ladies, we've –"

"MacLaren, I think I've got something!" Maureen's voice was controlled, but MacLaren could hear the tension in it.

"What? Where?"

"Coming in on our 5 o'clock, high. He's diving down, looks like he's going to try to tuck in above and behind us."

MacLaren scanned his mirrors and then caught a glimpse of the stubby-winged ovoid coming up on the F1, lining up for a strafing run. At that moment, a warning chime sounded, and an indicator that read "Radar Alert "lit up on the display in front of him – the F1 was being actively painted by the AV9's targeting system. With one hand he tightened his grip on the steering wheel, with the other he grasped the gearshift lever. Taking a long look at the map projected on the windscreen, he made his decision. Downshifting, he mashed the accelerator pedal and the F1 leaped ahead. Hoping like hell he wouldn't meet any oncoming traffic, he sawed the wheel back and forth as the coupe swooped through a series of short left and right curves, all the while accelerating, braking, flitting apparently at random from the right to the left lane and back, trusting the F1's suspension to keep it glued to the roadway. As he'd hoped, the AV9's pilot had closed up even tighter, until he was barely fifty yards behind the speeding coupe. That suited Blade just fine: whoever was driving this bird was an amateur, that much was evident from the way it wallowed and wobbled as it tried to follow. The Shrike, though agile, wasn't particularly nimble, so as the F1 swerved, slid, or changed lanes, the AV could never quite match its movements, continually bolloxing up the pilot's firing solution. This game, Blade knew, he could play all day.

----------------xxxxx----------------

"Gaijun son-of-a-bitch!" Clearly Yashida – Shinden – was furious. No sooner did he have a shot lined up than the F1 would abruptly slide out of the targeting reticule of his sighting computer. All he needed was one clear shot – at this range, it would be impossible for him to miss. But he couldn't get that one clear shot, no matter how he tried!

Here Shinden's inexperience was working against him. His AV9, like those flown by Chipmunk and Thrasher, was equipped with a DarkOwl-4 helmet-mounted display and targeting system. In theory, all he had to do was move his head to place the sighting reticule on the target, wait until the target was in the "acquisition basket" of his fire control system, and fire the Shrike's guns and autocannon to assure a hit. In practice, however, things weren't quite as simple: the 20mm autocannon was fixed, so that to bring it to bear, Shinden had to physically line up the vehicle with the target. And while the cheek-mounted heavy machine guns were somewhat flexible, their mass meant that they couldn't react instantly to the input from *Shinden*'s helmet: there was always some lag in their response as they struggled to keep up as *Shinden* jockeyed the Shrike from side to side while he wagged his head back and forth trying to track the F1. A more seasoned pilot would have backed off two or three hundred yards, where he could minimize both his aircraft's movements and the DarkOwl helmet's input into his fire control, in effect enlarging the acquisition basket and giving his guns a chance to lock onto the target.

Still, even a blind squirrel can find an acorn now and then, and for a fleeting second the F1 settled in Tomiyashi's sight, who promptly mashed the firing stud on his stick. The car was moving to the left even as he fired: the autocannon missed, but Shinden watched with satisfaction as bullets from one of his machine guns stuck home.

The F1 took two hits on the right quarter-panel, and the back end of the car slewed violently to the left. Blade steered into the skid, downshifted, and regained control, at the last instant keeping the left rear tire on the tarmac. He couldn't allow a wheel to bog down in the soft shoulders on either side of the road. A schematic of the car sprang up on right side of the HUD: the quarter-panel was glowing amber.

"Spazz! Tell me what the readout says – I don't dare take my eyes off the road right now!"

"'Pixelation 78%; Armour integrity 93%.'" A pause. "'Armour integrity'?"

"Two millimetres of Weclar on all the body panels and the chassis. The pixel layer is laid down on top of it. It's not bad, but, damn, that's going to be bloody expensive to fix! Aw, shite! Hang on, both of ye!"

MacLaren stood hard on the brakes as Trackrock Gap Road ended abruptly at a T-intersection – watching his HUD, he'd been expecting it. What he hadn't expected was finding an estate wagon sitting at the stop, waiting patiently for approaching traffic to pass before turning left. Pushing the F1's anti-lock system to its limit, he laid on the horn as he ran up on the wagon, hurriedly glanced to the right, hoped as much as estimated that the oncoming lorry on the left was just far enough away to clear, and cut to the left of the wagon, throwing the F1 into a hard-right powered drift. As they roared past, Maureen caught a glimpse of the estate wagon driver staring slack-jawed and bug-eyed at the vague blur that had overtaken her.

Accelerating hard, MacLaren glimpsed a road sign in passing. *Just what the hell is a "Town Creek School Road"? A few seconds ago I passed a "Turkey Trot Lane" and a "Possum Trot Road"...and Americans tell me they think the road names in* Scotland *are daft?*

Shinden couldn't believe his eyes. There was *no way* the F1 could have made that drift without being hit broadside by the oncoming lorry. Shinden had heard all of the stories of Blade's incredible luck, discounted them as exaggerated, but now began to believe: only someone who'd made a pact with the devil could have shot that gap unscathed. As the nearly-invisible coupe accelerated southward, he throttled up, shifted his thrust vector, and spun the Shrike to the right, then nosed down and shot forward, trying to re-acquire his target.

Maureen stared as the AV9 seemed to almost stop in mid-air, then pirouetted gracefully to the right and nosing over into a swooping dive toward the F1. She looked at MacLaren, wide eyed. "I never knew those things were so fucking agile!"

"Ye sound surprised."

"I've never been on the goddamned business end of one before!"

"Best get used to it, because in addition to that soda-heed behind us, there are two more of them out there. And from here on in, it's going to be a race, no more, no less. There won't be all that many opportunities for dancing. Hang on!" Coming up on another T-intersection, Blade threw the F1 into a left-hand drift, accelerating hard all the way through: they were now on Highway 19, the same road, had they known it, where Compton and Radome had come to grief, though they were well north of the spot where that had happened.

Red had never let up from her vigil, her head swiveling back and forth as she searched for the two AV9s still unaccounted-for, while doing her best to keep track of the aircraft coming up behind them. Now she watched that Shrike's stubby wings level out as its pilot lined up for another firing run. "Here he comes, Blade – he's setting up now!"

"He's left it too late." Even as he spoke, MacLaren was braking and downshifting for a sharper-than-usual ninety-degree right-hander, and the pursuing AV9 carried straight ahead, skidding out of sight above the trees as its pilot overshot the curve.

Shinden cursed himself for a fool – he hadn't been paying attention and he'd been duped again. Pulling up into a tight looping climb, he did a wing-over and dived for the roadway. As he did so, he had an unexpected moment of clarity: he knew now what Chipmunk had tried to make him understand, realized how important it was that he knew not only where the target was, but where he was while he was in the air. He realized that Thrasher had spoken the truth when he kept repeating that there was more to flying an AV than just the stick, rudder, and throttle. The enemy was not going to be dazzled by your flying, he'd said, the only way to impress an enemy was to kill him. Very well, then, Yashida decided, he would kill this damned *gaijun*. He leveled out his AV9 right on the deck, wingtips scant feet from the trees lining both sides of the road, closing with the F1 until he was less that fifty yards behind it, and switched off his fire-control computer, automatically locking his guns in position to fire directly forward. He would close up with the dark blue coupe until his Shrike could shove the muzzles up the F1's exhaust pipes.

----------------xxxxx----------------

Damn! This bastart is learning fast. Blades' eyes kept darting to his mirrors as the pursuing Shrike followed the centre-line of Highway 19 as if it were on rails. Its pilot was firing short, controlled bursts of machine-gun fire, which were punctuated by the slower, louder crumps of the 20mm autocannon, and bullets *clang*ed, *thunk*ed, and whined as they hit and ricocheted off the rear armour of the F1. Spazz stayed focused on the damage readout: the entire rear half of the car's display was glowing amber now, a few spots edging toward red where the armour had degraded below 33% effectiveness. None of the coupe's vital systems had been damaged – yet – but should one of those red patches start flashing, signaling total armour degradation, and one of those heavy machine gun bullets strike there, the damage to the complicated gizzards of the F1's engine bay would likely prove critical. A 20mm hit would be catastrophic.

One 20mm shell had already dinged the car. Its trajectory took it just under the car, where it had hit the tarmac, throwing up scores of fragments, including a pair that damaged one of the down-force fans on the F1's undercarriage. MacLaren could feel the coupe's grip on the road grow slightly mushy, although "mushy" was a highly relative term where that particular marque was concerned. Still he had to be careful, because while the coupe was more than equal to the task, the road they were following had never been meant to be traveled at speeds surpassing the century mark. Another 20mm shell glanced off the roof of the car and exploded alongside, causing Red to cry out in surprise, throwing up her hands protectively as the fragments pitted the window beside her.

"Stop blowing holes in my motorcar!" Blade shouted in frustration, then he punched yet another switch on the left console, and a small LED screen popped up beside his right knee -- below it were two small red buttons – and swivelled it to face Red. Jabbing a finger at the image of the pursuing Shrike, surrounded by a green targeting ring, displayed on the screen, he said, "The bastart hasn't taken out the rear camera – yet! Ye've got two shots at this, lass, best make them count. When that worthless piece of shit behind us is centreed in the ring, push one of the buttons. If that doesn't do the job, push the second."

"And if that doesn't work?"

"Best start praying."

Yahsida had no idea why the F1 had suddenly steadied up on the centre-line of the highway, but he wasn't about to look a gift target in the mouth. This was the moment he'd been asking for, waiting for, and he would make the most of it. Reactivating his fire-control computer, he waited for the targeting reticule to settle on the centre of the F1s rear panel before moving his thumb over to the firing stud on his joystick. That was the last mistake Tomiyashi Yashida, call sign "Shinden," would ever make.

Red silently blessed Blade for settling down and holding the F1 steady. Reacting with lightning speed, she anticipated the drift of the AV9 and pressed the first button just as the Shrike slid into the centre of the sighting ring. At the back of the F1, a circular cover popped of a concealed launch tube and a compressed-gas charge kicked out a small missile. A friction igniter lit up the rocket motor as soon as the missile cleared the rear of the car. The motor burned out in less than a tenth of a second, expiring an almost immeasurable instant before the missile impacted on its target.

Yoshida had taken that fraction of a second too long. Had he not bothered with the fire-control computer and simply hosed down the F1 with machine-gun and autocannon fire, he would have destroyed his target. As it was, his thumb was still moving to the firing stud when the light anti-tank rocket – which was what Red had actually launched at him – struck just slightly low and to the left of the centre of the Shrike's nose. The rocket didn't know – and wouldn't have cared if it had – that the target was not an armoured vehicle: the impact crushed its nose and triggered its fuse exactly as designed. The one-pound shaped charge detonated and blew a jet of super-heated plasma that literally vaporized the Weclar armour, then shot down along the AV9's fuselage, burning through the instrument package in the nose and the forward weapons bay, finally expending itself in the internal fuel cells behind the cockpit.   In milliseconds the entire AV9 was engulfed, nose to tail, in white flames – by the time Yoshida might have realized he was being killed, he was already dead. Shedding panels, control surfaces, and other bits of debris, the Shrike slammed down the roadway, tumbling end over end as it did, while the F1 blithely accelerated away and out of sight.

----------------xxxxx----------------

"Well played, Miss Red, well played."   Blade's tone was a curious mixture of satisfaction and relief as, while the F1 entered a broad, sweeping right, he watched Shinden's funeral pyre go careering off the roadway and into an open field. "Thank God that's the last of that bastart."

"Yeah, but there's still two more of the fuckers out there, Blade."

"I know, Spazz, but that guy was the one who really had me worried."

"Wait – what? Why?"

"Because he was clearly an amateur. You can take that old saw that says 'Professionals are predictable, but the world is full of amateurs' only so far, but that doesn't mean there's no truth to it at all."

"Go on."   Maureen's expression was dubious, but her tone was curious.

"At first, back on Trackrock Gap Road, he came in hot and fast in a situation that was stacked against him – he didn't think it through. The trees were too close to the road to let him come in from the side and get a good deflection shot on us. The road was way too twisting to for him to be able to consistently set up firing solutions. His situational awareness wasn't worth spit. He lost track of where we were at least twice, and once he began to get his shit together there toward the end, he failed to remember as he was coming in that just because the target hasn't shot back at you doesn't mean it can't or won't. But he kept coming. *He kept coming!* And what worried me about that was that he wouldn't give up – and the longer he hung around, the better his chances of succeeding through pure dumb luck. Which for us would have been pure dumb *bad* luck."

Spazz nodded in understanding, her expression thoughtful even as she went back to scanning the skies. "And the other two?"

"They're out there, studying their maps, deciding where the best spots will be to wait to ambush us." MacLaren pointed to two places on the Heads-Up Display. "I think it will happen either here, or here."

"Why those two and not somewhere closer to where we are now?" This was from Red, who had been following Blade and Spazz's conversation closely.

"Because the trees are still close enough to the road that we're still getting some cover and concealment from them. That means no deflection shots for them, they won't have enough confidence in their firing solutions. This car isn't invisible to radar, but it doesn't show up all that well either. The pixelation on the rear has gone to crap, but that's about the only quarter where they can really get eyes on us. And if they were monitoring their late, unlamented comrade's demise, they won't want to try coming in that way again."

Red and Spazz both studied the HUD intently, and suddenly Spazz spoke up, pointing at the display. "I get it now: we have to slow down for that twisty bit before we crest the ridge here, which means that they can be waiting on the other side of it, their guns already dialed in."

"Give the lady full marks." Blade grinned at her; Spazz stuck out her tongue at him.

"And here we'd just be coming out of that series of short, tight left and right curves before coming up on that straight, which means we would have slowed down." Red's voice was analytical, detached, almost toneless, the first time MacLaren had heard her speak that way. "If they wait there, they'll have a long firing lane that we'll have to drive into and through. We'd have to come to almost a complete stop to be able to turn around and run away from them, and that would make us sitting ducks."

Blade glanced at her consideringly. "You sound as if you've done this sort of thing before."

She shook her head. "I don't remember, I really don't, but something tells me that I did."

"Indeed. Fascinating."

Chipmunk and Thrasher both saw the roiling gout of smoke rise above the trees to the west and immediately knew what it signified. Whatley noted that Shinden's transponder squawk had stopped, and when he commed Yoshida, there was no response. Thrasher vectored in on Chipmunk's starboard wing and the two pilots exchanged mutual headshakes. Neither felt the slightest bit of regret or remorse at the evident death of Shinden – both felt that Blade had done them a favor by relieving them of the deadweight of that obnoxious civilian upstart. Not that Blade would particularly appreciate how Chipmunk and Thrasher would go about demonstrating their gratitude....

"Check out your road net display, Thrasher. I've indicated two places where I think Blade is going to be the most vulnerable."

"Yeah, I see 'em," Thrasher drawled. "I'm likin' this first spot. Knowing Blade, he'll be pushing that car of his as hard as he can through those tight curves. That means just then he'll be focused on the road more'n on any potential threats."

"Yup, that's pretty much the way I read it." Whatley nodded then looked across at Thrasher. "Wanna flip to see who gets to be the shooter?"

"Nah, you always cheat anyway." A pause. "Look, we can't both take the shot, and I'll be real honest with ya, I want that bonus real bad."

"Hey, no more than I do!"

"Yeah, well...."

"Is it the money, or the rep that you want the most? You know, the whole 'The Man Who Took Down Blade' sort of thing. You gotta admit, your street value would go up real fast if you were."

"Yeah, no shit!"

Their employer had given both men an extra incentive for taking out the F1, along with the man who was driving it – a $250,000 bonus for the man who fired the kill-shot. He'd informed them of the driver's identity when he recalled them from their return leg to Virginia after the strike on The Gardens. Whatley and Thrasher especially relished the opportunity presented to them: like numerous other mercenaries who had acquired reputations for allowing the execution of their duties to carry over into atrocity, each had a price on his head, bounties set by the UN's Commission for Law Enforcement, yet another consequence of the radical shift in the world's political landscape in the wake of Black Christmas. Blade, with his monumental air of self-righteousness, claimed to take personal and professional offense at such conduct, and was never adverse to collecting such a bounty whenever he could.

"You're right, Chipster, I want the rep as well as the money, but don't pretend you don't want the rep, too.... Tell you what, I'm thinking of a number between one and ten –"

Whatley laughed. "And you say *I* cheat? Fuck that shit! Listen, you go take the shot, and when you nail that prick, *you* get the rep and *we* split the bonus from Nakajima. That way we both get something out of it, and I won't have to shoot your ass down afterward and claim it all for myself. Deal?"

Thrasher laughed back, and agreed, though, as he banked away, a corner of his brain was wondering just how serious was the implied threat in Chipmunk's last statement. The man did have a reputation as a backstabbing sonofabitch, after all. He would have to watch his six....

----------------xxxxx----------------

"I'm afraid it's confirmed, Calvin. Our onsite assets are virtually nil, but I've been able to siphon off some imagery from one of the Ikon satellites, and, well, The Gardens isn't – it isn't – well, it just isn't *there* anymore...."

Calvin spun his high-backed chair around to face Mycroft's visual pickup for a moment, then stared blankly at the wall of monitor screens with their slowly scrolling texts, business and research and financial reports that only moments before had been so important to him.   His voice was harsh with fear and incomprehension when he asked, "What do you mean, 'not there'?"

"See for yourself." Mycroft threw a half-dozen overhead images onto the monitors. Without realizing he'd done so, Calvin rose to his feet and slowly advanced until he was bare inches from the screens. Try as he might, though, he couldn't make sense of what he was seeing: instead of the familiar collection of buildings and shallow rises connected by a tracery of pathways, walkways, and lanes, there was only a strangely pocked landscape, not cratered like the surface of a moon, but beaten in, dented, as it were, as if some sand-pounding giant had driven his fist over and over again into the surface of the earth. Here and there small wisps of smoke trailed across the images. Mycroft was right: The Gardens just weren't there any longer.

This newest nightmare had begun thirty minutes earlier, as Calvin was in the middle of what he liked to think of as his "Morning Business Briefing," an update of overnight developments that directly affected Cogito Orbis' worldwide interests. It was then that Mycroft had stopped in mid-sentence, stuttered, then resumed his narrative as if nothing had happened. But something *had* happened, and within seconds Mycroft broke off the briefing to report to Calvin on an unexpected, unexplained, and severe drop in his computing resources.

"Calvin, I've lost connection to at least a third of the nodal infrastructure, including databases. And at the moment, the uplink to The Gardens is completely down. Landline, wireless, ethernet, whisker laser, satellite link, all of them are down. This is not a simple disruption of service, Calvin: the signals *all* terminate at The Gardens."

"Then get them back up! Reestablish the connections! What are you waiting for?"

"Calvin, did you hear what I just said? There is apparently *nothing* at The Gardens to connect *to*!"

"Well, get me something, dammit! What happened, what caused it, and how bad it is! Get your electronic ass moving, Mike, and get me confirmation!"

"That's going to be easier said than done, Calvin." Mycroft's voice was clam and collected, as befitting a computer program which by definition lacked real emotions, yet a careful listener would have sworn there was a note of exasperation in his reply. "Right now, all of the backup servers, programs, files, and system redundancies have spun up, but we've been hurt. None of your network – including me – is operating at one hundred percent. I'll get you as much information as I can, but you'd best not be expecting miracles, because I'm not programmed to produce them."

Thirty minutes later, Calvin had all the confirmation he wanted or needed – and for a fleeting moment he'd felt utterly helpless. But then, he admitted to himself, what did he really know about catastrophes on this scale? Though he was just a child when The Great Server Massacre went down in early 2009, he remembered it and learned from it, taking every conceivable precaution against accidents, stupidity, and natural disasters, as well as trying to anticipate possible sabotage. But never in his most paranoid nightmares had he imagined the sort of calculated, brutal, and malicious use of naked force that had just devastated The Gardens.

As reports came in, Mycroft methodically and dispassionately updated Calvin on casualties and damage. Local police and first responders on the scene, along with survivors from the almost untouched artists' colony, were painting a gloomy picture. There was no question but that the death toll would number in the hundreds – the only uncertainty was just how high it would go. *My God, the people! Where am I going to find people who can take over for the ones who are dead? Some of them worked with me on this project for five years! I can replace the skill sets, but the experience, the inside knowledge of the systems and the architecture can't be duplicated or reconstructed.*

As for the physical destruction, Calvin had to assume that most of the facilities would be totally written off, and replacement would be mind-numbingly expensive. Yet even that was bearable, as long as Gamma Lab survived: Project Bowman was in Gamma Lab, and if – when – it succeeded, it would more than pay for everything. And Gamma Lab was the deepest and best-protected of all of the underground facilities at The Gardens....

"...So now you know almost everything I do about the situation, Calvin. The satellite facilities in Phoenix and Holmdel are untouched, as are all of the offsite servers and data backups. Our core technologies and R & D base are intact. However, rebuilding and replacing the facilities and equipment onsite is going to take the better part of twelve months, assuming you choose to do that and you begin immediately. There will be a significant – and sometimes noticeable – loss in performance of certain systems because the loss of the servers and data storage at The Gardens has all but eliminated our margin of unused resources. It will be days certainly, probably weeks, possibly months, before we can account for everyone who is reported missing at the moment. The whole landscape has been altered so drastically that the people onsite scarcely know where to begin digging to look for survivors and bodies."

"You said 'almost everything.' What haven't you told me, Mike?"

"I'm sorry, Calvin, but I've saved the worst for last. I wanted to be sure you understood the full extent of the other damage before telling you this, because, well, frankly, I don't know how you're going to take this. From what I've been able to gather, special attention was given to Gamma Lab. It's been completely destroyed."

It was as though someone had sucker-punched Calvin. He felt the room slide sideways, as if moving of its own volition, and he fell back into his chair just as his legs gave out. For long seconds he sat there, immobile, slack-jawed, eyes unfocused; had he not been monitoring Calvin's vitals, Mycroft may well have believed he had died from the shock. Slowly, like a man trying to swim in treacle, Calvin began to gather and reorganize his thoughts.

Dear God, I've lost the only live instance of Bowman! The only thing that's even close to a functioning prototype. This sets the whole project back by a year. And if Blade doesn't get those crystals to me – fast! – and I can't reconstruct something close to the live instance, I may lose it all. I may lose everything!

As coherence returned, Calvin's shock morphed into anger, anger into fury, fury into rage. Corporate violence, he knew, wasn't just a 21st Century phenomenon, it was as old as the Industrial Revolution itself. *Hell,* he mused bitterly, *Roman businessmen probably used to rough up competitors from time to time, especially when some plebeian got a little too successful for some patrician's liking.* But what was done to The Gardens went far beyond the limits of corporate intimidation. There were *rules,* dammit, and everybody played by them! Corporate warfare was a losing proposition – that lesson had been driven home in 2021, during the Chinese Corporate War. Too-large a surplus of production capacity, coupled with shrinking foreign markets – a situation brought about by Beijing's notorious role in the COVID Pandemic of 2020 – had Red China's economy teetering on the brink of collapse, a situation the Chinese mega-corporations tried to salvage by attempting to literally blow away their foreign competition. The result had been the bodies of dead executives and management-types, often with their families, all over the world; destroyed manufactories and inventory facilities were to be found in every industrialized nation. The consequence was a mass exodus of what few foreign investors remained in China abandoning the People's Republic altogether, while non-Chinese megacorps cut off all sales of raw materials and boycotted Chinese-made goods *en masse,* and the international banking community called due every loan held by any Chinese national or the Chinese government. The aftermath had riven the People's Republic of China, and the seven successor states of the mainly notional Qin

Confederation – Hong Kong and Macau had outright seceded and were no longer politically bound to Confederation at all, while the Republic of China had carved off a fair-sized chunk of the mainland for itself – were a collection of pygmies compared to the giant that had been the People's Republic.

The costs had been high and the gains little, for when the multi-nationals retaliated in kind, they found themselves paying in blood and treasure for what they would have acquired through natural attrition as China's economy shrank. That lesson was particularly taken to heart by the megacorps, so that while general corporate thuggery remained a fact of business life in 2035 – DisCom in particular was especially adept at employing company goon squads to crack skulls, break heads, or occasionally knee-cap independent CGI artists and animators who refused to be "assimilated" into the DisCom "culture" – out-and-out wholesale attacks on business rivals were mostly a thing of the past. There were a few corporations, like Arasaka, that still played rough, very rough, but they were the exceptions, rather than the rule, and even by Arasaka's standards, the devastation of The Gardens was extreme. As the American gangster Al Capone once observed, "Violence is bad for business."

Which made what happened at The Gardens, then, a personal declaration of war on Calvin Coleridge. This was no corporate rival "sending a message," this was the act of someone who sought to wound Calvin personally, deeply and irreparably, by destroying Cogito Orbis. The ruthlessness and precision of the attack spoke volumes about its purpose, for unmistakably its intent had been the destruction of the Bowman Project – the obliteration of Gamma Lab was sufficient proof. For the past five years, the Bowman Project had absorbed almost all of the company's financial and intellectual resources – it had been three years since Cogito Orbis had released any new hardware, firmware, or software: new investors were increasingly difficult to come by, and those few who still stood by the company were growing impatient with their limited returns. If

Project Bowman failed, Cogito Orbis would collapse, and with it would go Calvin Coleridge's *raison d'etre*; like a certain ring-maker of old, he had invested too much of himself, in every sense of the phrase, to be able to survive his company's dissolution.

As Mycroft looked on, Calvin slowly recollected himself, and his expression morphed from one of stunned incomprehension to the purest distilled hatred. When he finally spoke, it was in a voice that Mycroft had never before heard, a dry, flat, hard monotone which, had Mycroft been human, would have chilled his heart.

"We have enemies, Mike. *I* have enemies. Whoever did this knew exactly where and how to hit us. They knew about the Bowman Project – that's why they hit Gamma Lab so hard. Rockley may have told them about it, or we may still have a mole somewhere in the company. Whichever the case may be, I am going to find out whoever did this, and *hurt* them! And I will *keep on* hurting them! I am going to bring them down – you have the tools to do that and I'm going to turn you loose on them. But I won't just lash out blindly, I want to be certain of my target. I have my suspicions, but I want to be certain. So call the Russian, see what she knows."

"Are you sure you want to do that, Calvin?"

"Absolutely. Call the Russian. Call her now."

"Sirr, Bogey Three is takin' up a position exactly where you expected him tae be – down close tae the deck on the other side of yon ridge crest here." A red icon glowed on Blade's HUD as Alistair marked the location of the waiting Shrike. "From the way he's sashayin' aboot, Ah dinna think he knows ye have a satellite feed. He'll nae be expectin' ye tae be expectin' him."

"Thanks, Alistair. And the other one?"

"Bogey One is three miles to the south o' Bogey Three, flyin' a race-track. Ah'd say he's providin' the tactical feed tae Bogey

Three."

Like any good staff officer, Alistair knew when to speak and when to keep silent. There was little he could have done, apart from breaking MacLaren's concentration, while Bogie Two – Shinden – was hunting down the F1, other than inform Blade if either of the remaining AV9s decided to join in the fracas. But now that the problem of Bogey Two had been solved, he was able to provide MacLaren with critical tactical updates in real time.

"And yer estimate of our time to intercept, Alistair?"

"Assumin' Ah've figured yer cornerin' speeds correctly, ye should be breaking the crest o' that ridge in ninety seconds."

"Got it, Alistair. Keep an eye on Bogey One for me, will ye? Right then, ladies, it's showtime." Spazz watched in fascination as Blade did a quick arpeggio on the right console, and a new display lit up on the dashboard, accompanied by a medium-pitched whine that seemed to emanate from somewhere underneath the car.

"What the hell is that noise?" she asked.

"Just preparing a warm welcome for Bogey Three, Maureen. The fire control is on automatic, it'll shoot as soon as the system ID's the target. Call it the ultimate in fire-and-forget ordnance." His sudden grin had more than a touch of the wolf in it. "That numpty on the other side of the ridge is in for one hell of a surprise."

"Get ready, Thrasher. He's just coming out of the last left-hander right now. He'll be making the right and coming over the ridge in just a few seconds." At Whatley's words, Thrasher's face broke into a wide, toothy smile of anticipation, to which the the slight gleam in his green eyes added an almost feral cast, like a weasel waiting to strike. The impression was further enhanced by the receding chin which emphasized his ferret-like features. *Hello, Blade. Hello and goodbye.*

The F1 roared over the crest. There, no more than two hundred yards distant and perhaps ten feet above the road surface, was Thrasher's Shrike.

It was over in less than a half-second. Alistair had been right: Thrasher had no clue that Blade was already aware of his presence, that Blade was waiting for him as much as he was for Blade. As the F1 crested the ridge, the fire-control computer positively identified the AV9 and the targeting icon on the dashboard went green.

There was the briefest of white flashes at the front of the coupe as a pair of near-blinding white streaks shot forward and into the hovering Shrike. Thrasher's thumb hadn't even begun to move to the firing stud on his joystick when the two streaks – or rather the projectiles leaving those streaks in their wakes – blasted their way through the Shrike's nose, cockpit, pilot, and starboard engine. In the second or so that it took him to die, Thrasher involuntarily pulled the joystick back and to the right, sending the hovering AV9 into a slow climbing roll that ended a moment later when the aircraft stalled, fell onto its back, and crashed into the trees. Blade didn't bother to spare the wreck so much as a glance as the F1 raced past.

Red regarded Blade with an expression of approval, while Spazz's eyes went wide with surprise. "Just what the fuck was *that*?" she demanded.

"A pair of 15mm railguns mounted in a special frame attached to the car's front suspension. That whine you heard earlier? That was the capacitors charging. I told you I had a surprise in store for that idjit."

"If that's your idea of a surprise, remind me never to invite you to any goddamn birthday parties."

"Goddammit!"

The curse was torn from Whatley's lips when Thrasher's comm link went dead and his transponder squawk abruptly ceased. Looking to the north he saw a rising column of smoke and flame, and on his search radar display the icon which tagged Blade's F1 was still racing down Highway 19. An unexpected fury rose up inside him, which he quickly but firmly clamped down. Anger sometimes had its uses in a combat situation – uncontrolled anger, he knew, just got you killed.

He rolled his Shrike hard to the left and accelerated, passing well to the east of the roadway where Blade's car was southbound. This attack had to be perfect: he would have never believed before now that it would take four AV9s to destroy a single automobile, but there it was. Kaminski, he knew, had been just plain unlucky when that flare exploded right in front of him above the car park at The Gardens; luck, good and bad, was always a part of this trade. Shinden had gotten himself killed out of sheer stupidity coupled with inexperience, something the arrogant young prick would have done sooner or later. But somehow Blade had gotten the drop on Thrasher, and that worried Chipmunk: Thrasher had been smart, experienced, and patient, and still Blade had taken him down.

Chipmunk abruptly realized that Blade had to be getting a tactical feed from somewhere, one which had allowed him to not only anticipate Thrasher's ambush, but actually get off his killing shot before Thrasher could fire his own. As neither he nor any of the other pilots had expected the F1 to have anything but passive defences at worst, Chipmunk allowed himself the momentary luxury of being extremely pissed off at Nakajima: he'd informed Whatley and his colleagues as to exactly what type of vehicle Blade was driving, but never said a word about any offensive capability. He and Nakajima were going to have a *very* unpleasant conversation once this was over.

So, Blade, you've got firepower to the front and rear, but do you have anything up top? Whatley reefed the Shrike into a tight left turn, settled into an altitude of one thousand feet, and took up position five hundred yards behind the F1 before beginning a shallow dive toward it. *Let's find out if you do.*

"Blade, I think I see the third one coming in. Six o'clock, high."

"Sir, Bogey One is moving into an attack position on your six, high."

Spazz and Alistair spoke simultaneously, and the "Radar Warning" alert reappeared on the HUD as they did so. Taking note of all three, MacLaren frowned as he considered Bogey One's careful approach, then growled, "Somehow I don't think this bawbag is going to be as stupid as the other two."

Chipmunk swooped down until he was only a few hundred feet above and behind the F1, which was now swerving madly across both traffic lanes as Blade tried to throw off his enemy's aim. It was to no avail. Rather than trying to track and follow the car's movements, which had been Shinden's undoing, he simply started to weave above the roadway and opened fire. He kept up a series of short, irregular bursts from the cannon and machine guns, knowing that some of the bullets and shells would hit the fleeing coupe. It wasn't pretty, it wasn't elegant, but as the sparks and small gouts of flame erupted from the surface of the F1 attested, it was effective. Sooner or later, either a lucky hit or simply the accumulated damage would see to the car's – and Blade's – destruction.

Inside the F1, Blade didn't need to have a diagram drawn for him to understand that the situation was deteriorating rapidly. The car juddered under the repeated impact of large-caliber machine-gun bullets, and it actually bucked each time it was struck by one of the 20mm shells. On the damage control display, most of the machine's rear half was glowing red, with the engine deck and the left quarter-panel flashing red, indicating an immanent failure of the armour. Both side mirrors had been shot off, as well as the taillights, and the left rear tire had been hit twice. The latter was the least of Blade's worries, though, since the F1's tires were all airless – the weakness of the protection on the engine deck was his real worry: another hit there would take out the motor, immobilizing the car and leaving himself, Spazz, and Red little better than sitting ducks.

"What the fuck, Blade? Why aren't you shooting back?"

"Because I don't have anything to shoot back with, Spazz!"

"Just use another one of those goddamn missiles you used on the first one!"

"Can't. It's heat-seeking, and that bastart behind us is too high: I'd be firing off-bore and out of the warhead's acquisition basket – the missile would never even know he's there." The F1 trembled as the AV9's machine guns raked it yet again. Another loud THUMP from a 20mm shell was accompanied by a lurch to the right, followed by a startled yelp from Spazz.

"Dammit, MacLaren, you're going to lose control if this thing doesn't fall apart first!"

Blade gave her an unexpected, cheeky grin. "Don't worry, she'll hold together." Then, *sotto voce*, "Hear me, lass? Hold together!"

Spazz shook her head in exasperation. "Dammit, if you've got railguns on this thing, you've got anti-tank missiles, you've got to have a fucking anti-aircraft missile or machine gun somewhere!"

"Sorry, Spazz, but I don't. Not even a pea-shooter."

"You've got no anti-aircraft capability at all?"

"Lady, I had this car modified for urban confrontations, where the need to shoot at aircraft is pretty damned limited! Not to mention the fact that there are only so many places in this car I can put gadgets. My armourer's name is Sandford, not Boothroyd!"

"Well, shit.... I remember seeing something like this in a movie once."

"Really?"

"Yeah. It...didn't end well."

"Thanks for the encouragement."

While Blade and Spazz were sparring, Red was studying the headliner. When he'd acquired the F1, Blade had both doors redesigned and rebuilt to incorporate an escape hatch in each, the hatches corresponding to the upper-inner sections of the doors that formed part of the coupe's roof. A quartet of simple flip-type latcheson each kept them anchored in place. Now, suddenly and without saying a word, Red reached up and popped all four on the panel above her. Reaching for the central grab handle, she missed and the hatch was pulled away by the slipstream.

"Oops!"

"What the – where's the hatch panel?" Blade had to shout to make himself heard over the wind rushing through the hatchway.

"Somewhere back on the road. I lost my grip on it. Sorry."

"Shit! Do ye know how much – never mind, ye're paying for the replacement! Now would ye mind telling me what the hell you're doing?"

"Saving our collective pink – what's the Scots word for it? – bahookie! Now, shut up and drive!"

Pulling Blade's Lee-Enfield out of the footwell, Red drew first one then both of her legs underneath her and pushed her head and shoulders up into the open hatch. Though MacLaren would have never thought it possible, the long-stemmed redhead twisted herself around until she was facing backwards, her shoulders braced against the frame of the windscreen as she crouched in her seat. As she did so, the hem of her dress kept sliding higher and higher until Blade found himself face-to-thigh with a *lot* of leg. Summoning up all of his self-discipline, he resolutely faced forward and concentrated on keeping the F1 on the road while Red brought the rifle up to the ready, dropped the box magazine from the receiver into the palm of her hand, and peered into it.

"What sort of rounds are in this thing?" She shouted down at Blade.

"Standard soft-nose x-outs."

"Dum-dums? Not good enough! Got any Q-metal?"

Blade rolled his eyes in exasperation, then reached into a small pouch on his utility belt and drew out charger holding five curious-looking, sharply-pointed, silverish bullets, and held it out to her. "Here. Don't waste them!"

Red nodded, flicked five cartridges out of the magazine and slapped it back into place, took the charger from MacLaren and slid it into the loading bridge atop the receiver, then pushed down hard on the top round. The five fresh cartridges slid neatly into the magazine, and Red tossed the charger strip aside, working the bolt to chamber the first Q-metal round. She was just in time, for the pursuing AV began settling in for another strafing run. She lined up her own shot carefully and squeezed the trigger; the recoil was considerably harsher than she expected.

It was a good shot, but not quite good enough: as it was designed to do, the Q-metal bullet punched through the Weclar armour protecting the Shrike's fuselage, then tore along the left side of the cockpit and nicked the main spar before blowing out the top of the fuselage – an impressive performance, and the AV staggered briefly, but the damage was insufficient to drive off the aircraft. Instead, the pilot leveled out again and let loose with another burst from his machine guns, while the autocannon rhythmically "thumped" out shot after shot.

Red simply ignored the incoming fire and lined up her next shot, aiming for the Shrike's port engine intake. The Enfield's "boom" sounded almost as loud as the AV9's 20mm cannon, and Red had the satisfaction of seeing metallic sparks flashing in the intake shroud, followed almost instantly by a gout of flame that spit out the two exhaust nozzles on the side of the Shrike. Her hands working the SMLE's action almost as fast as Blade could have done, she sent two more shots into the port engine, then drew a bead on the helmeted head of the AV9's pilot and squeezed the trigger a fifth time.

Chipmunk Whatley couldn't believe his eyes when he saw panel fly off the roof of the F1, and a red-haired woman raised her head and shoulders out of the car's cockpit. He was even more surprised when she then produced what looked for all the world to be some sort of bolt-action rifle and pointed it at him. He saw the muzzle-flash, heard and felt the bullet pass through his Shrike, and quickly corrected as the AV sagged slightly. A few warning lights began flashing on the panel to his left, but a quick scan of the instruments showed that no serious damage had been done.

All right, you crazy bitch, if you wanna play rough, we'll play rough: my 20mm and a pair of 13s against your little popgun. He laid the sighting reticule square on the woman's forehead and pressed the firing stud on his joystick, raking the F1 yet another time. He saw the yellow-white bloom of another muzzle flash, and suddenly his instruments went crazy as something tore through his port engine. Two more flashes and the engine started tearing itself apart as compressor blades and bits of turbine shredded its inner workings. Whatley had time to see one more flash erupt from the mouth of the old rifle, and then he never saw anything again.

----------------XXXXX----------------

Deprived of Whatley's careful modulation of thrust vectors and flying surfaces, the AV9 immediately stalled, the nose dropped, and the Shrike literally fell out of the sky. An orange and black fireball shot upward, marking the spot where Chipmunk Whatley's charred remains would be found an hour later. Red regarded her handiwork with certain satisfaction, then twisted about again and settled back into her seat, then turned to Blade and cocked an inquiring eyebrow. He frowned in return.

"And just how many rounds did ye use, then?"

"All five."

"All five? Dammit, woman, do ye ken how much each one of those DU rounds costs?"

"Fifty-two pounds, sixteen pence apiece from Purdeys," Maureen chimed in sweetly, "assuming they're still your supplier."

"Be quiet, Spazz, ye're not helping here!"

Red gave Blade a withering look. "I suppose you think *you* could have done better?"

"Aye, I know I could!"

"Fine, then. Next time, you shoot, I'll drive!"

Blade glowered at her for a moment, then shook his head in resignation and returned his attention to the road. Red swiftly and expertly replaced the five rounds she'd removed from the Enfield's magazine, set the safety, and tucked the rifle back into the footwell, then regarded MacLaren with a insufferably smug, self-satisfied look.

"All right, all right," he grumbled. "That was well done. Good shooting. Thank you. Now, strap yourself in again. There's somebody in Atlanta I need to have a heart-to-heart talk with, and I don't intend to waste any more time getting there."

----------------xxxxx----------------

Fifty-nine minutes later, the F1 rolled up the entrance drive to the portico of the Barnett Tower, on the corner of Allen Boulevard and Spring Street. Pulling into the entrance plaza, Blade looked up at the tower's thirty-seven stories of stainless steel and glass and muttered, "Well, I'd say this is just a bit more than a wee butt'n'ben, isn't it?"

"It is that," Spazz agreed. "I take it this is where your friend Hobbes lives when he's at home?"

"Ye take it correctly, Miss Collins." Blade slid the now-considerably-worse-for-the-wear F1 into a parking space marked "Reserved – Violators will be towed" and shut down the engine. "I expect that by now he knows we've arrived and that he's thinking he'll be happy to see us. I don't expect him to be feeling that way for more than a few minutes, however."

Spazz eyed him shrewdly. "So this is going to be what's known in polite company as an 'awkward conversation'?"

"Very awkward indeed. Get your Korth ready."

"*What?*"

"Red –" Blade reached under the dashboard and drew out a SIG-Sauer identical to the one already tucked in his shoulder holster and handed it to her "– you'll want this. "

Red dropped the magazine into her palm, worked the action to clear it, slapped the magazine home, and worked the action again to chamber a round. "I'm guessing that you want to be sure that we have Mr. Coleridge's undivided attention."

"Right the first time, lass," Blade nodded as he slid a fresh magazine into his own pistol. "Let's go."

Red climbed out of the car, snatching up the titanium carrying case as she did so, making no effort whatsoever to conceal the SIG-Sauer. Spazz, now understanding Blade's intentions, quickly racked the slide on her Korth, then alighted from the F1; like Red she made no attempt to disguise the fact that she was armed.

As Blade was closing the door of the F1, a pompous, bustling, over-groomed, and bespectacled little man in an expensive suit, evidently a managerial type of some sort, came trotting toward them, hands waving as he shouted something about the F1 not being permitted to park where it was. Blade turned to him, transfixed him with a withering stare, and growled, "If you've seen even a single newsfeed this morning, you know who I am. I'm in no mood to deal with flunkies, lackeys, or hirelings. I have business with a resident of yer wee hovel here, and I'll be back down within the hour. The car best still be there when I return. Now fuck off, laddiebuck."

Eyes bulging and mouth gaping like a landed trout, the little man backed away; the trio brushed past him without so much as a second look. Unconsciously, Red, Spazz, and Blade fell into step as they crossed the plaza to the entrance to the tower, and Blade felt a moment of dark amusement as people who were in their path suddenly found an urgent need to be elsewhere. The passed across the lobby and stopped in front of a lift marked "Private Access Only," Spazz and Red pirouetting outward in unison, pistols held low but ready, to cover anyone who might be foolish enough to approach them. Blade produced a small oblong device similar in appearance to the one he'd used to access the entrance to Underground Atlanta less than eight hours earlier, and pressed it against the sensor pad next to the lift's call button. The doors opened, and as they did he glanced at Spazz and Red.

"Ready for this?" he asked. They nodded in unison. "Then let's go. We've all got questions, and it's time we all got some answers. So what say ye that we have a wee come-to-Jesus meeting with that fat little bastart Hobbes?"

Chapter 7

"Godammit to hell, Hobbes! What is going on here? I mean *really* going on? First yer little 'extraction team' gets double-crossed and almost half of them get killed before they get trapped in that nightclub of yers, and ye ask me to do ye a favor by getting them out. I agree to go in, knowing the Arasakas are waiting for me. Now, a squad of Arasaka goons is just a day at the office, two squads of them is a brisk workout – but there was a whole goddamned platoon of them at Bits! We survived that only because Raven called in the US Marshals. Then Spazz, Red, and I head up to The Gardens, only to find it obliterated by a flight of unmarked AV-9s – who just happen to come back and bloody well try to blow *us* to kingdom come! This isn't the 'trifle,' the 'least of things' you said it was. So tell me, what the hell is it that we have that they want so badly?"

The fury in Blade's voice was so molten in its intensity that Calvin would have hardly been surprised has he been bellowing in rage. Instead, his voice was coldly conversational: only in his eyes – it was amazing, Calvin thought absently, how Blade's cybernetic eye could be just as expressive as his natural one – was the true depth of his anger revealed. He raised his hands in a sort of placating gesture, anxious to reassure the angry Scot and demonstrate to all three of his guests that he was unarmed. The latter was no minor consideration, given that at the moment he was staring down the barrels of three disturbingly steady semi-automatics.

"The VR crystals, Blade, that's what they've been after all along."

"Aw, bollocks! Nobody expends that kind of manpower and resources just to hijack some technology that's going to be obsolescent in three or four years! Somebody's declared war on ye over this, Hobbes – and ye got me caught up in it. Now, think very carefully: apart from me, who else have ye really, really pissed off recently?"

"Dammit, David, if you'll just shut the hell up for three minutes I'll give you all the answers you want! Right now I can't get a word in edgewise because *you're* busy being so self-righteously pissed off at *me!*"

Blade visibly collected himself, but the smoldering anger was still there, ready to flame up again at the slightest provocation. "All right, you have your three minutes."

As Blade predicted, Hobbes had been watching the trio via his security system since their arrival at the Barnett Tower. He'd been a bit disconcerted when Blade's electronic lockpick bypassed not only the building's security system on the private lift, but his own as well. That wasn't supposed to happen, ever, no matter who came calling. *Raven's handiwork again, damn her!*

An array of monitors was laid out before him on the curve of his large, U-shaped work station, situated in the balcony overlooking the enormous great room that occupied most of the lowest floor of his penthouse. It was from here that he oversaw the operations of Cogito Orbis, although in truth, most of the details of the day-to-day workings were now handled by Mycroft, leaving Calvin free to, as he fondly imagined it, "see the 'big picture'" and conceive of new software design paradigms. These days however, as he had been doing for the past three years, Calvin spent most of that time fretting over Project Bowman.

He rarely left his desk save to answer the inevitable calls of nature or toddle off to his bedroom – where he often continued his labors from a small remote workstation. He almost never stepped outside his penthouse; venturing forth to meet Blade at the airport the previous day had been a rare exception to that habit – he had yet to travel the quarter mile that separated the Barnett Tower from

Emory University Hospital where his wife Kim lay in intensive care. His meals were prepared in the Tower's ground-floor restaurant and brought up to him by robotic servitors; housekeeping chores were similarly automated; whatever shopping Calvin needed to do was accomplished digitally. His penthouse was his fortress, his desk his bastion: he had been convinced that from there, as long as he took reasonable precautions, he was protected, invulnerable. The previous week, however, had badly disabused him of that notion. Now, though, at least part of his current nightmare was about to come to an end.

Deciding that it would be uncivilized – and Blade always placed a premium on civilized behavior – to make the Scot and his two female companions walk the entire way across the great room and up the stairway to the balcony, Hobbes rose from his desk and made his way down to the great room, stopping perhaps a dozen feet from the elevator door. Knowing that he was about to have those seven priceless crystals back in his hands, he did his best to control his anxiety, but he couldn't quite stop himself from bouncing slightly on the balls of his feet in his eagerness. This was the moment he'd been anticipating since he'd placed the comm call to Blade little more than twelve hours earlier.

What he hadn't anticipated was, when the elevator doors slid open, finding himself facing an angry Scot, a grim-faced redhead, and a determined-looking blonde. Nor was he prepared to find each of them holding a large semi-automatic pistol, all three pointed with remarkable steadiness at the bridge of his nose....

" – you have your three minutes."

Calvin eyes flickered from Blade's SIG-Sauer to its mate held by Red, to the Korth in Spazz's right hand, and for the briefest of instants, his control cracked, and Blade saw a fear, an outright terror, lurking behind his friend's eyes. Not of the weapons, nor of the man and women holding them, but fear that somehow, some way, they were proof that Blade learned at least a part of something that he was never supposed to know.

Be careful, a still, small voice whispered inside Hobbes' head, *be very, very careful. How you say this is every bit as important as what you say.*

"When I said those what's stored in crystals is a VR program, I wasn't lying, but it's VR unlike any iteration of virtual reality you've ever experienced or imagined. This is not some technology 'that's going to be obsolescent in three or four years.' This is a new expression of VR that is going to be a paradigm shift in how virtual reality simulations are utilized." Despite his best efforts, Calvin's enthusiasm began to show as he warmed to his subject. "What Kim and I were so close to solving was virtual reality's 'uncanny valley.'"

"That sensation that you have when you're looking at a computer simulation that's either too perfect, or not quite perfect enough. That 'something's not quite right here' feeling."

"Precisely, Miss Collins. The problem with simulations like that is that they're never completely immersive – the user always consciously knows that it's a simulation, which means his or her responses are never one hundred percent authentic. We found a way that uses neurological feedback from the viewer to adjust the appearance of the simulation so that it meets the user's expectations of what it *should* look like – to the point where the simulation really *is* indistinguishable from reality."

"The value of just the military and aerospace applications alone would be staggering." Red's voice was pensive, as if she was running through all the possibilities even as she was speaking. "Combat simulators, flight training simulators, orbital spacecraft operations.... Yeah, that would be a game-changer."

"And once the entertainment industry got their hands on it..." Spazz chimed in. "It's starting to make more sense now – why

Arasaka and DisCom would be so desperate to get their hands on it. DisCom would all but own the industry, and Arasaka would be able to more-or-less name their price to defence departments around the world."

Blade looked from Red to Spazz, who were nodding in agreement with each other, and felt his fury, while not entirely abating, becoming more manageable. He turned back to Hobbes, who said simply, "*Now* do you believe me?"

"To a point. It still doesn't explain what happened to Kim."

"Kim got careless, Blade. She was running the system without having all of the safety protocols in place. She knew I hated it when she did that, but she thought they were restrictive and was convinced I was being paranoid. Her take on it was 'Hey, I've never made a mistake yet!' – which in my book is about on par with 'Hey, Bubba, hold my beer and watch this!' She might have even gotten away with it if Judith Rockley hadn't come into the lab and removed the crystals without shutting down the system first. Instead, Rockley just 'pulled the plug,' so to speak, and the shock to Kim's brain drove her into that mental safe room I told you about. I think the only chance I have of coaxing her back out of it is to reintroduce her to whatever VR she was in just before it crashed. So maybe now you can understand that I really was telling you the truth when I said I had a very personal motive for recovering those crystals."

Red nodded again, while Spazz said feelingly, "I guess you really do. And now I finally know what I've gotten myself into." She looked at Blade. "It would seem that my little bout of hero worship has landed me in some deep shit." Blade said nothing, but continued to scowl at Hobbes, even as he slid his SIG back into his shoulder holster; Spazz then put her Korth into her shoulder bag, and Red slipped her SIG into her belt.

Relaxing slightly gestured at the titanium case in Red's left hand. "Is that what I think it is? If so, I'll take it now."

Red looked at Blade, who, after an instant's hesitation – not unnoted by Hobbes – nodded; she held out the case to Hobbes, who took it, turned and walked back to the balcony stairway, followed closely by his trio of...guests. He placed the titanium case on an empty spot – of which there were few – on his desk and examined the locks, then looked at Blade expectantly. MacLaren produced a cyrpto-key from his right breast pocket and held it out to Calvin, who touched it briefly to each lock. A pair of quiet "clicks" were heard, Hobbes opened the lid partway, and looked inside.

The case was empty.

A brief, near-hysterical giggle escaped Hobbes lips, and in a tiny, high-pitched voice he announced, "They're not here," before slamming the lid shut again. Then, abruptly, a grim, almost icy composure asserted itself as he visibly collected himself, glared at Blade, and asked, "Is this your idea of a joke?"

"No, Calvin, it's not."

He did a double-take at Blade's use of his given name. MacLaren had hung the nickname "Hobbes" on him as a shared joke when they'd first met, almost six years ago, and the Scot had rarely called him "Calvin" ever since. The only exceptions were those few occasions when Blade wanted to make certain he had Calvin's full and undivided attention – as he most assuredly did now.

"So what is it, then?"

"It's my way of admitting failure."

Hobbes sighed softly, then fell silent for a moment, but when he spoke again, acid fairly dripped from his voice. "There are 'failures,' Blade, and then there are *failures*. Which do we have here? I can think of several possibilities." He began ticking off items on his fingers. "One, for some utterly incomprehensible reason, you gave the crystals to someone else, say, Compton and Radome – whom, I notice, are conspicuous by their absence as well as their silence – and they reached The Gardens before it was obliterated, so that the crystals now lie buried under an enormous underground pile of rubble.

"Two, they had some sort of traffic accident and are lying dead or dying in a ditch somewhere, with the case holding the crystals flung God knows where along with them and that ridiculous motorcycle of Compton's.

"Three, you gave them to Compton and Radome, who ran afoul of Arasaka yet again, and now the crystals are in Nakajima's hands, aboard some aircraft on its way to Japan at this very moment. How am I doing so far?" Without bothering to wait for a response, he continued.

"Four, you lost them somewhere, somehow, which means that the probability of ever recovering them hovers somewhere between zero and non-existent.

"And finally, five, you're deliberately withholding them from me, for reasons that are unknown to me but which, to you, by whatever convoluted logic and reason you've applied, make perfectly good sense.

"So, please, tell me which one it is. What the hell happened out there, Blade?"

MacLaren grimaced, but continued to face Hobbes squarely. "I guess ye could say I got too clever by half, tried to double-think the opposition. I took it as given that whoever Arasaka has in charge of this op – and yer right, it's almost certainly Nakajima – would assume I would never let the crystals out of my possession once I had them, so I tried a double-blind. I gave them to Radome, then told Compton to take her and himself to The Gardens, expecting Arasaka to follow me and not them. They never made it, obviously."

"Why 'obviously'?"

Blade gave Hobbes the sort of look an exasperated schoolteacher might give a deliberately obtuse student. "Because Mycroft would have told ye the instant they arrived at The Gardens. Or are ye going to pretend that he didn't have the entrance drive under constant surveillance?"

"You're right. He did, and they never arrived."

"Then there's the little detail of Compton's transponder going offline *after* the attack on The Gardens. Maybe ye want to pretend ye didn't know about that, too?"

Hobbes shook his head. "No, I knew that, too." The brave front of righteous indignation he'd thrown up only moments earlier was beginning to erode.

"Then ye also know, despite the fact that Highway 19 – which is the route I told them to take – is at this moment fairly hotching with local and state police in the aftermath of that little chase Red, Spazz, and I just experienced, there hasn't been so much as a single report of anyone finding a wrecked motorcycle or its riders." Hobbes merely nodded, unable to meet Blade's gaze any longer.

"And while we're on the subject of what ye do and don't know, we both know Nakajima can't use commercial airlines anymore, and that if he tried he'd never make it through the real security checkpoints. So if he had the crystals and wanted to leave the U.S., his only option is to hire a charter. Do ye think for a second that I'd believe Mycroft isn't watching every private and chartered flight that's leaving American airspace or filed an international flight plan? He hasn't left yet, because he doesn't have the crystals – and he won't leave until he does.

"As for losing them, that case Red just handed to ye hasn't been out of my sight since we left Bits. And if ye think I'm simply refusing to turn them over to ye, then ye're just bloody daft. I took this job as a favor to ye, true, but we agreed that ye're paying me for it. If I don't get the crystals back, I don't get paid, it's as simple as that. And I really don't like not getting paid."

"You could always sell them to the highest bidder," Hobbes replied, bitter accusation creeping into his voice as he tried to reassert control over the conversation. "I think we could take it as given that you'd make a lot more than whatever amount you're going to bill me for."

"Really? And just what would I be selling? And how? Some of that techno-babble mumbo-jumbo ye just rattled off to me that I'll only half-remember by this time tomorrow? 'Hello, I'm offering for sale seven memory crystals that belonged to Cogito Orbis and Calvin Coleridge. I don't really know just what is stored in them – it may be some new VR software, or it could be Coleridge's private porn stash, I'm not really sure which. Now, who wants to start the bidding?' Not bloody likely, Hobbes."

"All right, then, using your god-like omniscience, tell me what the real situation is."

"You know, Hobbes, when you dial up the snark level that high, all you really accomplish is to sound like a very petty little man. The crystals are out there, somewhere. Nakajima is looking for them, certainly, but *I'm* going to find them before he does – because for Kim, the clock is still ticking. Or had you forgotten that bit?"

"Low blow, Blade."

"I never fight fair if I can avoid it. Blade's Rule Number 43: 'Only an idiot with a death wish fights fair.'"

"So what's your plan?"

Blade passed a weary hand across his eyes: fatigue was beginning to hit him – hard. "I don't have even the glimmering of a plan, Hobbes. I've had an awful lot of adrenaline pumped into my system in the last twenty-four hours, and it's starting to take its toll. Right now, if I tried to plan the takeover of a pub by a bunch of Scots, I'd make so many amateur mistakes I'd bollox up the job – I'm that tired. I need some rest if I'm to have any chance of finding those crystals of yours and getting Compton and Radome back – alive."

"Just find the crystals, Blade. That's what I'm paying for, remember?" The Scot's eyebrows rose at that, as Hobbes' coldly calculating persona began to reassert itself. "Compton and Radome work for me, Blade. They're my people, my responsibility."

"They're my people now, Hobbes. You sent them into harm's way, I'm the one who got them out. Then I went and sent them back into harm's way again. That makes them *my* people."

"All right, I'm not going to argue the point – for now. If you like you can rest here – so can Spazz and Red. I own this entire floor, plus the two above it, so there's enough room for everyone to have as much privacy as they want or need."

"Not a chance, Hobbes. I prefer someplace a lot safer than your penthouse."

"And you think you're going to find someplace safer in Atlanta?"

"I can and I will. It just won't be here. Whether you want to admit it or not, Hobbes, you've got a big, fat target painted on the middle of your back, and I want to be out of the line of fire when somebody draws a bead on it."

He woke up when someone began taking a jackhammer to his head. A second or so later, he could feel a second person hacking into his shoulder with a pickaxe. Or was the pickaxe working on his skull and the jackhammer on his upper arm? They seemed to be switching places periodically. Admittedly the jackhammer and the pickaxe were rather small, just as were the tiny men wielding them, but the pain they were inflicting was unquestionably full-sized.

Compton forced his eyes open and looked about. Or rather, he tried to look about – no sooner had he turned his head a half-inch to the right than the little man with the jackhammer let Compton know he was having none of it. Pain shot halfway down his spine and Compton decided that he would settle for whatever his roving eyeballs could tell him.

How the hell did I get here? Compton wondered. It was a very good question, but an instant later an even better one popped into his head: *Just where the hell is "here"?* He had no idea, of course, although, given that his hands and feet were manacled – chained to the rails of a hospital bed, in fact – he was pretty certain that, wherever "here" was, it wasn't any place on his personal list of potential vacation spots.

He'd been in enough hospitals and clinics over the years to recognize institutional architecture and design when he saw it, and now he saw it. The cheap acoustical tile ceiling ("Tile, Ceiling, Acoustical Mark I" was how he thought of it – some small corner of his mind wondered if there was a single, sole supplier in the entire world who provided every medical facility with their ceiling fixtures), the halogen tube lighting, the pale seafoam paint on the walls, even the bed in which he was currently confined, all could have been found in any second-tier hospital on any continent. In point of fact, the entire room was so stereotypical that it could have come from a movie set, and Compton began to seriously regard the possibility that wherever he was, it really wasn't a medical facility, and what he was seeing was a carefully constructed facsimile concocted purely for his benefit. As to exactly why anyone would go to the trouble of constructing a Potemkin village version of a hospital room just for him was a scenario he had only begun to consider when to his right he heard the sound of a chair being scuffed across the floor.

A hand briefly passed through his field of vision and as he tried to follow it he noticed for the first time that there was an IV hanger stand beside his bed, a half-full bag of clear fluid suspended from it, and a tube leading from the base of the bag was attached to an intravenous shunt in his right arm. After a moment, the pain began to recede toward something like a manageable level, and he was able to turn his head to his right, without the little men with the jackhammer and pickaxe making any effort to increase their exertions.

"Ah, good, you're awake."

Compton focused his eyes on a face not more than five feet to his right. A Japanese face. A Japanese face that he realized he had seen before, although he wasn't yet able to concentrate sufficiently to recollect where he'd seen it. *Whoever he is, this guy is big, especially for a Japanese*, he thought. *I think I'm taller than he is, but from the way his shirt fits, I'd say he's got at least thirty pounds on me. And it definitely ain't flab. And something tells me he's as geared-up as I am. Gotta remember that if I ever get the chance to mano-a-mano with him – I'll definitely be able to hurt him, but he'll be able to hurt me right back.*

The man continued speaking. "We were worried – we thought you might have a concussion, and if you didn't wake up, well, that would not have been a Good Thing. We also couldn't introduce any painkillers to your IV drip until we were sure you'd regain consciousness – they might have just kept you under longer. As you may have noticed, though, I've corrected that situation. I doubt you're actually comfortable, but I'm hoping that the pain has been reduced, at least."

"It has, thank you. I think." There were a few seconds of silence, then Compton asked, "Where the hell am I, how the hell did I get here, why the hell am I shackled to the bed, and who the hell are you?"

The man smiled – it wasn't a particular warm smile, but neither was it predatory. If Compton were ever asked about it, he would have said it was "perfunctory" – provided he would have been willing to admit that such a "25-cent word" existed in his vocabulary. "One question at a time, Mr. Compton. First of all, you are in a private...ah, medical facility that is located...somewhere in downtown Atlanta, shall we say."

"Mind telling me exactly where? Y'know, in case I want to order out for pizza."

"Please, Mr. Hone – oh, you need not look surprised at that. We know all about who and what you truly are. But, as I was saying, you can dispense with the attempts at levity. I have absolutely no sense of humor. I've had it surgically removed, you see."

For a second, the Japanese sat in utter silence, then suddenly burst out in raucous laughter, slapping his thigh and stamping one foot. "Ah, your face just now! Priceless, utterly priceless!" Bringing his mirth under control, he went on. "I do have a sense of humor, as you can see. But, really, save yourself the trouble of the witty repartee. It wastes valuable time, and, well, your last name isn't Moore.... Now, where was I? Oh, yes.

"As for how you got here, I should think that would be obvious. You were brought here in the back of one of the SUVs that were used in our roadblock. You're shackled to the bed – and please, save yourself the effort, the rails have been reinforced, so you won't be able to break them, while the manacles and chains are chromium steel; quite escape-proof, you see. Anyway, I had you shackled to the bed for my own protection and peace of mind. You have no reason to perceive me as anything but an enemy, and while I hope that we can conclude our business without either of us resorting to violence, as you have a reputation as being a man who is 'good with his hands,' as they say, common sense dictates that I take some precautions.

"As for who I am" –

"Don't bother, it just came to me. You're Hideki Nakajima."

"That is correct. There are times when it's nice to be recognized...."

If Nakajima said anything further, Compton didn't hear it. Instead, his mind was fully occupied by a single thought.

I am so screwed.

"So where do we go now?" The question came from Spazz as the trio crossed the plaza to the sadly battered F1, the first words any of them had spoken to each other since leaving Hobbes' penthouse.

"As I said to Hobbes, someplace safe."

"I hope you won't mind if I say this, but it better be pretty goddamned close," she said feelingly, "because I'm really not looking forward to another long stretch in this car."

"Don't worry, it's close enough. Only about six blocks to be exact." He thumbed his remote and both of the coupe's doors swung open, the right with a noticeable groan. "Get in."

Blade eased the F1 out of the Barnett Tower plaza and into the traffic on Allen Blvd, took the first right onto Peachtree Street, and motored sedately south to John Wesley Dobbs Avenue, where he took another right. A near-miss from one of the 20mm shells fired by Chipmunk Whatley just before his demise had torn a very large hole in the coupe's muffler, so that the F1's progress, while slow, was exceedingly loud, hence Spazz's desire to minimize any further time inside it.

Two blocks after making his second turn, Blade pulled into the parking entrance of the LA & P Bank building. Spazz looked up at the logo as they passed beneath it.

"LA & P – huh, I dated a guy with those initials once."

"Ever work with the bank itself?"

"Nah. Why?"

"Curiosity, that's all."

"So this is where we're going to find a safe place to lay low? In a bank?"

"No, this is where we're going to find some friends – or at least a few allies." He offered no further explanation as he swung the F1 onto the entrance drive of the building's parking structure.

Once inside, the noise from the damaged exhaust was overwhelming, so Blade did his best to reach the sixth level before they all suffered hearing damage. It was here that he came to a concrete-and-steel barricade which blocked any further progress; in the centre of the barricade stood a heavy steel gate. To its left stood a Royal Marine in service dress, holding an SA-25 at the ready; there were, Blade knew, at least two more Jollies in concealed positions, ready to support their mate. He stopped the F1 twenty feet short of the gate, shut off the engine, and motioned for Red to get out. "Be sure to keep your hands where they can be seen," he told her, then turned back to Spazz. "Put your hands on top of the dash and don't move until we've been cleared. Understood?"

"Understood. If he's what I think he is, holy shit, do I understand."

"Good."

By now Red had moved well clear of the car, and Blade very methodically made his exit, stood upright, and raised his hands to shoulder level, palms outward. He made no move to advance toward the gate, instead regarding the young Royal Marine with a steady gaze as he called out, "Corporal, keyword. *Per Mare, Per Terram.*"

The young non-com stiffened slightly.

"Sir! Can you validate?"

"I can. Kestrel."

The corporal instantly snapped to the position of port arms, his right boot crashing on the concrete. "Sir! Welcome to His Majesty's Consulate. I'll inform the Consul-General that you're here."

"Calvin, I have Miss Ivanova on comm for you."

"Put her through, Mike. But on voice only."

"Right away." An instant later an indicator glowed green above the audio pickup on Hobbes' desk.

"Ekaterina, thanks for taking my call so quickly," he said.

"Calvin" – her deep, sensuous contralto voice made the way she said his name sound more like "Kahl-vin" – "darling, it's so good to hear from you! It's been just ages since we last talked! Although, surprised I am not that you called. You seem to have slight problem on your hands, no?"

"Katrina, can we dispense with the theatrics and cut to the chase, please? What I'm having isn't a 'slight problem' – what I'm having is a 'Really Fucking Bad Day.'"

"*Da*, I know. But you always enjoy verbal fencing in past, how am I to know this time is exception?"

Ekaterina Nikolayevna Ivanova's English, he knew, was as fluent and unaccented as his own, possibly even better, but she affected the almost cartoonish Russian accent and inflection for theatrical effect. As wily as any coyote, Ivanova was prepared to sound like a *femme fatale* bent on "killing moose and squirrel " if she felt that it gave her an advantage in her business dealings.

"You should know it's an 'exception' because right now I've got a frickin' disaster on my hands!"

"*Da*, that I know also." A subtle shift in tone transformed Ivanova's voice from a coquettish lilt to a soothing purr. "So, please, tell Ivanova all about it."

"At least for the time being, Mycroft's doing a perfectly adequate job of holding the newsies at bay. There's no way, though, I can avoid face-time with local authorities, and I have no idea how high the problem is going to go – the state level at the very least. I may have to personally deal with top level 'talent' in the mainstream media face to face just for the sake of perceived credibility, but for now, it's more important that I make sure my own people know that I'm still in control of the situation. And before I can do that, what I need from you, what I'm hoping you can tell me, is who did this to me – and why."

"Did what, exactly? Destroyed research facility at Gardens? Compromised operation to recover memory crystals from DisCom? Or ordered theft of memory crystals which has brought Project Bowman to brink of failure?"

Calvin choked and fairly goggled at that. *How the hell does she know all that?* he wondered. *Especially about Bowman?* He was especially grateful for having the foresight to make this a voice-only conversation. To someone like Ivanova, the image of Calvin Coleridge staring slack-jawed and buggy-eyed into his comm pickup would have nearly priceless – and not merely for its entertainment value.

As if she was reading his thoughts anyway, Ivanova went on: "Do not act surprised, Calvin. Backchannel has been full of whispers ever since crystals were stolen. Man you hired to assemble mission team to take back crystals, Bordley... Bradley...."

"Bridelow."

"*Da*, Bridelow! Bridelow did good job of keeping details secret when he was recruiting his people, but there are many very intelligent minds using Backchannel who are very good at putting odd bits and pieces together to get answers." "The Backchannel" was the unofficial name for the unofficial communications network – part rumor mill, part jungle telegraph, part Craig's List – which those who were part of or at least dealt with what some snobbishly self-righteous segments of society would call "the criminal underworld" used as their primary communications conduit. Ivanova was one of the acknowledged mistresses of the Backchannel; her stock in trade was that she was among the best of those intelligent minds to which she'd just referred. Her ability to take widely disparate fragments of information and assemble them into a coherent – and accurate – picture was near-legendary, a fact on which her business empire was built and she continued to trade shamelessly. To Ekaterina Ivanova, money was secondary, although she had amassed a considerable personal fortune over the previous two decades; what mattered to her was trading information for yet even more information. She had long ago understood that knowledge in and of itself was *not* power – it was the *use* of knowledge which bestowed power: left unemployed, mere knowledge, regardless of how much or how little of it there might be, was impotent.

Ivanova, then, was what was called "a fixer," a maker of deals, a trader of information, a broker of business connections. The term "fixer" itself dated as far back as the early 1990s and eventually became embedded in humanity's general lexicon. Although only a comparatively small percentage of humanity ever came into contact with a real fixer, everybody knew what a fixer was. And among those who actually did deals with fixers, it was universally acknowledged that Ekaterina Ivanova was among the very best.

"So. People – some people, not everyone – knew that you were going to take action against DisCom almost as soon as you made up your mind to do so. Not difficult call to make, really: you had no choice but to retaliate. I wish I could say that no one gave Big Black Rat warning, but there are always weasels like Bridelow, *da*?" When Calvin made no reply, she went on. "I think everyone was taken by surprise when Arasaka showed up at Atlanta Underground – everyone keeps close eye on Arasaka, for obvious reasons, and while perhaps there may be something that in hindsight points to Arasaka, no one saw it then, not even me. Calling in Blade was very shrewd move: anyone else who might have tried to take advantage of situation backed away immediately.

"Which brings us to airstrike on Gardens, does it not? This puzzles me, as it does everyone else. Sort of what you Americans call a... 'what the fuck?' moment. It is not difficult to see that this is methodical attack on Cogito Orbis, and especially on Project Bowman. There are rumors to be heard that if Bowman fails, Cogito Orbis is done as well. What is unclear is if this attack is personal or just business. Either way, your security is not perfect, and you have leak somewhere. How big is leak, I have no idea. That is your problem, not mine."

"Katrina, I have to know who is behind this. That's the only chance I have of staving off another attack and containing the damage that's already been done. I still don't know for certain if I can recover enough of Project Bowman from this to salvage it and save my company. And, yes, it does exist, there's no point in pretending to you, at least, that it doesn't. Name your price, set a marker, whatever you like, just find out for me who's behind all this."

"When – if – I find this out for you, then I will calculate cost to you. In meantime, relax, Calvin. Keep calm and let Ivanova handle it."

The British Consul-General for the Southeastern United States was Catherine Downing-Carlisle, a petite, bird-like woman in her late fifties, with a bright broad smile, large blue eyes, and mass of coal-black hair parted by a three-inch wide band of pure white. As Red, Spazz, and Blade, all three looking distinctly worse for the wear, were ushered into her well-lit but not overly-large and surprisingly unostentatious office, the bright broad smile was distinctly in abeyance. Though she rose from behind her desk to greet her guests, she did not offer to shake hands with any of them.

"Well, Sir David, I saw on the scream-sheets this morning that you've chosen to bring your distinctive brand of mayhem into my 'turf,' as the Americans call it." Her tone, like her expression, was tart. "Now I'm given to understand that you've invoked a keyword protocol that requires me to render you 'any and all assistance within the limits of my resources' that you may require."

"Yes, Ma'am, I have."

"I won't say that I'm particularly overjoyed to have you here: the newsies have been clamoring for 'comment' and a 'clarification of Great Britain's official position on international vigilantism' ever since the story about Atlanta Underground broke. My press attaché is being harried to a frazzle by those idiots even as we speak – and I've no doubt that somebody noticed your arrival. We certainly all heard it!" She suddenly threw her hands out in a sort of waving gesture. "I'm sorry, I'm forgetting my manners. Please, find seats and take them, all of you." When the trio of visitors had made themselves reasonably comfortable, she continued.

"Ordinarily, Sir David, given that your actions and their consequences are going to cause a great deal of disruption and inconvenience for this Consulate, I would be inclined to offer only whatever minimum amount of cooperation necessary to get you on your way and out of my affairs." Downing-Carlisle snatched up a pen from atop her desk and began toying with it as she spoke; there was an almost palpable air of nervous energy surrounding her. "I am not, however, going to start playing the sort of bureaucratic games that too many of my colleagues seem to believe are required to reinforce their own sense of importance."

"That will be a welcome change, Ma'am," Blade said, allowing himself the hint of a wry smile, "not to mention something of a new experience."

"I imagine so." The fiddling with the pen continued, and now Downing-Carlisle was swinging her desk chair back and forth in small arcs as she spoke. "I'm dispensing with the bushwah because whatever it is exactly that you're doing here in the U. S., Arasaka is involved in it. That adds a personal element into my decision, which leads me to view your current predicament, whatever it is, rather more favorably than I would do otherwise."

"Ma'am?"

"My first husband, Sir David, was Major Charles Henry Downing, of the Paras. He was killed by some of those very weapons Arasaka provided to the Provos eight years ago. That's what makes it personal."

"Yes, Ma'am. I remember Major Downing very well, and with great respect."

"Thank you. Given what you were able to accomplish against Arasaka a few months later, and the consequences, political and economic, for those Jap bastards when the Crown threw them out of the country as a result, inclines me toward charity in your circumstances. I don't like what you've become in the past eight years, but I understand what you've done, what you do, and why.

So, how can I help you and your two associates, who have, I've noted, thus far maintained a discreet but watchful silence?"

"Ma'am, they are, both of them, highly intelligent, most dangerous, and possess very good instincts – including knowing when *not* to say anything. Allow me to make introductions: to my immediate left is Ms. Maureen Collins, to her left is a woman who for security purposes goes only by the name of...Scarlett. Ladies, The Honourable Catherine Downing-Carlisle, His Majesty's Consul-General here in Atlanta." None of the three women rose, or proffered a handshake, clearly the result of a mutual, unspoken agreement that there was no need at this point for such an empty ritual.

"As to what we need, Ma'am, that is simple. First and foremost, we are all three of us *very* tired, and we need someplace where we can rest our heads in safety for a few hours. I need access to a secure communications channel, and if possible, we need ground transportation. My F1 has become a little too conspicuous in the last several hours."

"As if that thing was ever *in*conspicuous," the Consul murmured; Spazz and Scarlett laughed out loud, Blade just grinned unapologetically. "Well...that's certainly a much shorter list than I expected it might be, and certainly easily accomplished." She snatched up the handset on her desk comm, tapped in a three-digit extension, and after a few seconds began speaking. "Eileen, would you come over to my office, please? Yes, now." She replaced the handset in its cradle and wordlessly looked at her three guests.

Not more than twenty seconds passed before there was a knock on Downing-Carlisle's door, who promptly called out "Enter!" In strode a woman, medium in height, thin in build, who moved purposefully but without much grace. Stopping behind the row of chairs occupied by Blade, Spazz, and Red – now "Scarlett," at least for the time being – she looked directly the Consul-General. "You asked to see me, Ma'am?"

"I did." Addressing her three visitors, she said, "This is Eileen Hamilton, my intelligence attaché. Eileen, allow me to introduce you to Sir David MacLaren, Miss Maureen Collins, and Miss...er, Scarlett."

"Yes, Ma'am. I don't recognize either of the two ladies with him, but I do know who Sir David is."

"I would be surprised if there was anyone in our intel community who doesn't. In any event, these three guests have some specific requirements which I believe are best handled by your department, so I'm putting them into your capable hands."

"Yes, Ma'am." Turning her attention to Blade, she said, "If you would specify what you need, I'll get the ball rolling." Looking up at Eileen, Blade got his first good look at her. An ordinary, almost severe face, all planes and angles, it served as the frame for the most intensely blue eyes Blade had ever seen. Contact lenses, no doubt, almost certainly with a few enhancements; there were very few intelligence officers who *didn't* wear them. Her voice, in contrast, was remarkable: Blade thought it was the most pleasant mid-soprano he'd ever heard in his life. Her posture gave her the air of someone who was almost overly athletic, being all knees and elbows, while her figure under the straight lines of her frock was apparently as spare as her countenance. She was no beauty, that much was given, but she positively oozed competence, along with a hint of danger, that Blade found curiously reassuring. Eileen Hamilton was most definitely a professional.

Responding to her question, Blade repeated what he had told the Consul-General, and upon hearing the short list of requirements, Eileen nodded once, and said, "If you'll come with me, we can start immediately." To Downing-Carlisle she said, "By your leave, Ma'am?"

"Of course. Go be about it, Eileen." She rose from her desk, Blade, Spazz, and Scarlett rising with her, and held out her hand to each of them, Scarlett first, Blade last. "Ladies, I'm pleased to have made your acquaintance. Sir David, you have my assurance that as the representative of His Majesty's Government here in Atlanta, I will support you in any way our resources allow. I won't say that it's been a pleasure, but whatever it is exactly that you've become involved with, I wish you good luck at it. We won't personally be meeting again. Eileen will be your consulate liaison, if one is needed, from this moment onward. Good day." With that, she resumed her seat and opened a file on her desk, effectively dismissing Blade from her thoughts and presence.

---------------xxxxx---------------

"As I was saying, there are times when it's good to be recognized, as it simplifies things considerably: I don't have to waste time convincing you that my intentions are in deadly earnest where you are involved." Nakajima smiled at Compton again, and this time, the predator was clearly on display. "In this case, this means I am going to ask you some questions and you are going to answer them."

"OK, OK, I don't get it. I mean, last thing I knew, you – or your people, at least – were trying to kill me, y'know? So, OK, then, why am I still alive?"

"Because for the time being, you're useful that way."

"Uh, yeah, right. And what about Trish – y'know, Radome?"

"The young woman who was your passenger on the motorcycle?"

"Yeah, her."

The big Japanese hesitated for a moment – Compton got the impression he was making a decision of some sort – the spoke in a subdued, almost regretful tone. "I've always found the idea of lying to a man who is going to die soon to be somehow repugnant, dishonourable, even, so I will be blunt. I'm afraid Ms. Crabtree was not as fortunate as you – or rather, didn't have the sort of enhancements which saved your life. She is dead."

OK, that hurt. I liked Radome. She was one of those rare people who never looked at me like I was some kind of Frankenstein's monster. Not that many of them around, y'know? OK, you Jap bastard, I just decided that I'm gonna make this as difficult for you as I can. You've already let me know that you're gonna kill me eventually anyway, and then you went and got my friend killed into the bargain. So I got no incentive to play nice, now, do I?

"OK, Nakajima, let's get on with it. What do want from me?"

"I need your help with a problem I have. "

"Yeah? And just what would that be?"

"Where are the memory crystals, Mr. Compton? The security case that your friend Ms. Crabtree was carrying was empty – it was child's play for my people to crack the locks, by the way. There has been a lot of whispering on the Backchannel about the theft of those memory crystals from Calvin Coleridge's research facility almost since the moment it happened – speculation, rumor, and the like: who was involved, why, and just what was the nature of those crystals that made them so valuable. Today – this afternoon, in fact, those whispers have taken a new turn, and given who has been doing the whispering, I'm inclined to take what they are saying very seriously. The story now is that Coleridge doesn't have the crystals, because Blade did *not* return them to him – he merely handed Coleridge a case identical to the one Ms. Crabtree was carrying, which proved to be equally empty."

"OK, uh, and you're telling me this... why?"

"Because one of my people who wasn't detained by the US Marshals in the aftermath of your little skirmish in Underground Atlanta was able to report to me that she saw your friend Radome carrying a security case during the firefight, but that no one else was carrying one. As I see it, the six of you – I'm going to want to know more about that blonde woman who joined you, by the way – were trying to escape and were taking the crystals with you."

"Yeah, well, you don't need to be a rocket scientist to figure that out."

"True." Nakajima took a pack of cigarettes from his shirt pocket, shook one free, lit it, and drew deeply. "It does help me establish a time frame for when Blade set his little double-blind scheme in motion and introduced the second security case into the scenario. You see, I know – I know, Mr. Compton – that you never stopped – anywhere – once you and Radome left Underground Atlanta. I had a tracer put on your motorcycle, you see."

"So that's how you able to set up that ambush, huh? You knew right where we were and where we were going." A pause, then, "Holy shit! That body beside my bike in the parking ramp!"

"Exactly. One of my *reisen* paid the man $100 to put the tracer in place. He got careless and managed to get himself electrocuted as he did so, but as he was a common street thug it was no great loss. My *reisen* even managed to recover the $100 from the body after you left." He took another drag on the cigarette, then looked quizzically at Compton. "You don't mind if I smoke do you? It doesn't really matter if you do, I'll smoke if I want to, but I thought I should ask, just to make sure all the formalities are observed....

"Getting back to the matter at hand, I'm trying to establish whether or not that security case of Miss Radome's was ever out of her possession. Can you tell me that much?"

Subterfuge had never been one of Compton's strongpoints, which rather complicated the process of trying to sort out all of the possibilities and implications of either lying or telling the truth to Nakajima. The throbbing in his head and shoulder, however much they had been subdued by the pain medication the Japanese had administered, didn't make the task any easier. In the end he decided that telling Nakajima the truth was his only real choice – if he lied and Nakajima knew he was lying, it would only make it more difficult to offer up a falsehood later when it might actually accomplish something useful.

"OK, yeah, I can. That case never left Radome's hands from the minute Blade handed it to her inside Bits."

"Thank you, that's most helpful." Nakajima drew heavily on his cigarette once more. "Now, it's obvious that at some point Blade removed the crystals from the security case and concealed them somewhere. I suspect they're tucked away in that old blue rattletrap he calls a motorcar, but to be certain of it, I have to determine exactly where and when Blade took them. So...I want you to tell me everything you remember from the moment Blade arrived at Bits up to the time you and Radome left Underground Atlanta. And when I say 'everything,' I mean *everything* – don't leave out the smallest detail just because you don't believe it to be important." He looked at Compton expectantly; Compton returned it with a look of his own that mingled disbelief and disdain.

"Nope, sorry, you just used up your quota of cooperation for the day. I'm tired, my head hurts, and just a minute ago you told me that you caused the death of one of my friends. I ain't got all that many left, y'know, so that really, really pissed me off. So...right now I am completely out of fucks to give where you and what you want are concerned."

"You might want to rethink your attitude, Mr. Compton." Nakajima's tone of voice remained as conversational as it had been when he'd first spoken to Compton, but there was a sudden hardening of his gaze, a tightening of the skin around his eyes It achieves nothing for you, in either the long or short term, but you can be assured that you aren't going to like its short-term consequences."

"Oh, look, I just found a fuck to give after all – it's the one that says 'Off,' as in that's the direction I'd like you to fuck, Nakajima. Why should I help you if, y'know, I'm going to die anyway, OK? Doesn't seem like there's a whole lot in it for me, y'know? No incentive in it at this point. So what's the deal?"

"'The deal' is this. You can assist me, and when you're no longer useful, I will guarantee you a quick, painless death.   Being uncooperative, however, will be the most certain way of assuring yourself that you will suffer a lingering, excruciatingly painful demise – one that may take weeks, if I'm fortunate and you're not."

Compton gave a snort of genuine derision. "Dude, I hate to spoil your party and all, but my nervous system got all fucked up when Colonel Crapman damn near got me killed a few years back, OK? The docs rebuilt a lot of shit, but there wasn't much they could do about the nerve damage, y'know? Both legs and both arms are cyber-prosthetics, so is my spine, so apart from my head and shoulders, I don't really feel much pain, even if you start hacking off body parts, OK?. And if you do that, it ain't gonna work too well for your plan to keep me alive for the next round of torture, y'know?"

Nakajima's smile was as thin as it was frosty, and Compton suddenly heard the sound of fingers drumming idly on some hard surface nearby. It was then that he first noticed the cyberdeck sitting on a small table beside Nakajima, who was rhythmically tapping the edge of the keyboard. "I know that, Mr. Compton. But it's interesting that you should mention your cybernetic systems. You are talking pain inflicted from *outside* your body, not *inside* your head. You see, while you were unconscious, I had a surgeon drill a very small hole in your skull, barely the diameter of a human hair, that leads directly to the neural processor unit in your brain which controls those cybernetics. He then attached a very fine antenna to the unit, to which I can transmit at will very specific signals to stimulate very specific portions of the pain centre in your brain. Let me show you what I mean." He pressed a key on the 'deck.

Compton's head exploded. At least, that was what it felt like, there was no other way to describe it. For a few seconds his entire universe was reduced to a locus of pain – there were no other sensations, no thoughts, no emotions, only agony. He screamed, he shrieked, he thrashed against his restraints as he tried to escape it, but to no avail. Then, as Nakajima entered more commands on his 'deck, the pain diminished, not in intensity, but in extent, so that it began to move around his body, from limb to limb, sometimes digit to digit, so that Compton was aware that the rest of his body existed and there was a world outside of the pain, but the focus of his universe remained that excruciating torment.

Finally, gradually – almost reluctantly, it seemed – Nakajima began to reduce the level pain until it merely remained in the background as a reminder. Compton, now soaked in sweat and panting like a trapped animal, looked at his Japanese tormenter with wide, wild, desperate yet comprehending eyes.

"Now, Mr. Compton, please understand that I can do that to you anytime I wish, for as long as I like. You will never know when it's coming, or how long it will last." As chilling as were Nakajima's words, his matter-of-fact, almost conversational delivery was equally frightening. "There is no defence against it, you cannot prepare yourself for it. You will find yourself in a state of constant terror, fearing what agony the next second might bring. Eventually, of course, your higher brain functions will begin to break down under the sheer weight of the sensory assault, and as they do, your mind will begin a process of de-resolution, essentially dissolving. At some point you will reach a state of permanent incoherence, at which time you will become useless to me, and then I will kill you. But – and please try to believe me on this – that point will be a long time coming. And until then, you will become far more intimately familiar with this process than you would ever want to be. Unless, that is, you choose to be cooperative." Nakajima pulled a chair over to the side of the steel bedstead to which Compton was shackled and sat down. "Now, then," he purred, "what shall we talk about?"

----------------xxxxx----------------

Eileen took her charges down a corridor that led directly to the sixth level of the parking structure and pointed toward a pale blue Chrysler Atlantica. "We'll be traveling in that to a secure location."

"A minvan? A *minivan?*" Blade seemed to be completely taken aback.

Eileen regarded him evenly. "A minivan, Sir David. Not just *any* minivan, mind you. It's fully armoured, with bulletproof glass all round, and it has an upgraded suspension and a high-performance engine. But it is, unlike certain other vehicles I know of, very inconspicuous. Who looks twice at a minivan – or who is inside it?" Blade nodded in wry agreement: for more than five decades, their very ubiquity had reduced minivans to a state of near-invisibility aside from being just one more obstacle to be avoided while driving.

"Now, then, if you have any personal property in your car, Sir David, or if the ladies do, please retrieve it now."

Red made a moue and said, "What you see is what I've got."

"My luggage is at my hotel, and I" – Spazz began.

"That will attended to in due time, ma'am. Sir David?"

"My bags and the rest of my equipment are in there. Do ye suppose the corporal could give me a hand?"

"I don't see why not." Raising her voice slightly, she called out, "Lance Corporal Delaney, could you assist Major MacLaren with his kit?" When Blade looked at her, slightly bemused by the ease with which she used rank and military slang, she gave him a smile and said, "My father is a retired Colour Sergeant, he served with The Rifles." Blade nodded in understanding and strode over to where the young Marine stood.

"Let's be about it, Lance."

"Sir!"

It took all of three minutes to extract Blade's baggage and carry it to the waiting minivan, then Blade went back to the F1 for his rifle. When he drew it out of the left footwell, Lance Corporal Delaney gasped.

"Sir, is that a Smelly?

"Indeed it is, Lance. Let's get this stuff over to the other vehicle, then if you like ye can take a gander at it."

"By your leave, Sir?"

Once MacLaren's bags were stowed in the back of the minivan, Blade dropped the magazine out of his rifle's receiver and worked the bolt, then handed the Lee-Enfield to Delaney. The young Marine, in turn, took the proffered magazine, slapped it home, slid the cutoff into place and snicked the bolt closed, then raised the muzzle upward and sighted along the barrel. After a second or so, there was a dry "click" as he squeezed the trigger. He then brought it down to chest level and admired the finish of the stock before removing the magazine, opening the bolt and handing the rifle and magazine back to Blade.

"She's a beauty, sir! They just don't make 'em like that anymore. I like my SA-25, mind you, but somehow it's not a patch on an old Smelly."

"Ye have good taste in rifles, Lance. Thanks for the assist."

"Sir!" Delaney braced to attention.

"Gentlemen, time's a'wasting! We need to get moving!" Eileen called out, though she was smiling as she did so. Blade replaced the magazine, closed the bolt, slung the SMLE over his shoulder and walked to the minivan's offside door.

As he approached, Eileen gestured toward the rifle and said, "Daddy has one of those. Kicks like a mule but it does the job doesn't it?"

"Yer father taught you to shoot an SMLE?"

"He most certainly did! He'll be fair chuffed to learn that I met the 2026 winner of the King's Medal in person. Might even be a bit jealous."

"Give him my best regards, if ye will. Now, as ye say, time's a'wasting, so I guess we'd best be on our way." With that, he climbed into the minivan, pulled the sliding door to after he was seated, and once Eileen was aboard, the minivan began moving.

----------------XXXXX----------------

"I always thought 'safehouses' were cramped, seedy affairs sitting in run-down neighborhoods."

Spazz spoke in uncharacteristically subdued tones as she caught her first sight of Blackbriar Hall, the Altanta consulate's "safehouse". It had been built on West Peachtree Road in 1886, in what was then a semi-rural area north of Atlanta known as Buckhead; over the decades the surrounding area had evolved until it now was the heart of the most affluent – and exclusive, in all definitions – suburb of Atlanta. It had become the property of the what was then Her Majesty's Government in 1992, purchased expressly for the purpose as serving as a secure bolthole for the Crown's intelligence operations and operatives in the southeastern United States. Its existence was an expression of Britain's centuries-old tradition that confidence in one's friends and allies was admirable: blind trust was sheer bloody foolishness....

The whole of Blackbriar's six-acre grounds was surrounded by an eight-foot high brick wall, a measure meant to dissuade prying eyes: no one at street level could actually see the house or grounds – or any of its residents. Spazz's first glimpse of Blackbriar, then, came when the immense wrought-iron gate that closed off the long, sweeping driveway swung open as the minivan approached. It looked to be several centuries older than it was – and on the wrong continent to boot; styled in the manner of Tudor great houses in England, built to an E-shaped ground plan, the house was half-timbered with the spaces between the massive wood framing bricked in. It was covered by a steeply-pitched slate roof which sported numerous gables as well as a plethora of brick chimneys, each erected in its own unique decorative pattern; there were dozens of tall, narrow windows glazed in diamond-pane leaded glass.

"Well, there are safehouses and then there are safehouses, Miss Collins," Blade murmured with just a hint of lordly condescension toward a poor, benighted colonial.

"Bastard, you'll pay for that."

"Best start running a tab, then."

The minivan rolled to a stop before the massive oak portal that passed for Blackbriar's front door. Eileen led her trio of charges inside to the foyer while the driver saw to Blade's bags and rifle. Precisely where the foyer gave way to the house's great hall stood a short, sturdily built woman of an indeterminate age. Full-faced, she sported almost mannishly-short pale blonde hair that framed a round face which was dominated by a pair of sea-green eyes and a thin-lipped mouth.

Eileen made introductions. "Ma'am, this is Ms. Collins, Ms....er, Scarlett, and Sir David MacLaren."

"Thank you, Eileen. Please remind Mrs. Downing-Carlisle to remember to bring her chequebook to our whist foursome on Tuesday. She's going to need it."

"Yes, ma'am," Eileen replied with a grin. Then, with a nod to her three charges, she made a quick exit out the front door. A moment later, the minivan could be heard driving off.

"I'm Veronica Mansfield, the MI6 station chief here at Blackbriar Hall. Mrs. Downing commed and informed me you were coming." Mansfield's voice was husky, though not unpleasantly so. She did not, Blade noted, offer her hand in greeting to any of them. The name rang a bell in his memory.

"'Veronica Mansfield.' Ye're not the daughter of" --

"Granddaughter, actually, Mr. MacLaren, and I make it a point not to broadcast that fact."

"Right, then. Got it."

"Now, as I understand the situation, Blackbriar will be your base of operations for however long it takes to get this – what's the American's term for it? Ah yes – this Charlie Foxtrot resolved. The Consul-General's briefing was concise and thorough, and she made it known that while she would have preferred not to get involved in this affair, it is clear that certain interests of His Majesty's government are involved, which means that I am prepared to put my resources at your disposal. Firstly, you are safe here, and I do mean *safe*. To begin with, this is the single most affluent neighborhood in Atlanta, so people who live here guard their privacy very jealously, and don't think it at all unusual when their neighbors do the same. The physical security at Blackbriar, while you will probably never see it, which is as it should be, is formidable. You'll pardon me, ladies, if I don't go into detail, I'm certain you'll understand why. I believe that if pressed the major here can confirm what I'm saying, however. So you'll not have to worry about ninjas climbing over the walls to garrotte you in your sleep. Not even Arasaka wants to go to war with His Majesty's Government, not after what happened eight years ago. Bloody hell, they'd likely have the Provos and the Irish Army going after them, too, just out of spite. So do your best to relax as far as possible." She paused, looked all three of them up and down, and said, "You know, you look like hell, all three of you."

MacLaren laughed out loud, Maureen seemed annoyed at being characterized so, and Red giggled. She also responded first.

"I'll admit, Ms. Mansfield, that right now I would kill for a hot bath!"

"I believe you – though homicide with malice aforethought won't be necessary. You'll have one very shortly. As far as personal effects, you pretty much need everything, don't you? From shoes to underwear to all that goes on top of it?"

Red spread her hands apart at shoulder height, and said simply, "As I told Eileen here, what you see is all I have."

"We've prepared rooms for each of you on the upper floor of the east wing. My assistant, Carothers, will be along shortly, and you can give her your sizes along with whatever preferences you have; she'll go shopping for you. Miss Collins, if you'll provide us with the name of your hotel and the room number, we'll fetch your luggage and settle the bill for you. Major MacLaren, unless I'm mistaken, you seem to have come well prepared, including your personal arsenal."

"I like to think of it as being thorough, ma'am."

"Of course you do." Mansfield made no effort to keep the tartness out of her voice. Now is there anything else that is immediately pressing, or should I let you go about restoring yourselves to a civilized state?

"I don't know about Red or Blade, but I'm famished!" Spazz said feelingly.

"So am I," Red affirmed. Mansfield looked inquiringly at Blade.

"That makes three of us."

"Understood. I see no reason why the cook can't lay on a quick luncheon for you right now. Dinner will be at nine o'clock. We usually dress for dinner, but we can be flexible about these things when need be, so no one will remark on it if you choose not to do so. And I suppose if you want to send out for Chinese or Indian take-away or some such" – there was a hint of disdain that anyone would consider stooping to such vulgarisms as take-away – "it can be arranged. I doubt you'll find a proper chicken vindaloo anywhere in Atlanta, though."

"Thank you," Blade, Spazz, and Red chorused together.

"Now, if you'll follow me, I direct you to your rooms. Oh, and I must tell you: the west wing is off limits to you ladies – you don't have the necessary clearances to be admitted to that part of Blackbriar. I'm sure you understand."

With that, Mansfield turned and began walking purposefully down the great hall toward the east wing, Red closely in tow. Spazz however, held back, with a gesture indicating to Blade that he should stay behind as well. At the foot of the stairway leading to the second floor, Mansfield stopped, having realized Spazz and Blade had fallen behind. Turning back to them, she called out, in a somewhat vexed tone, "Are you two coming or should I wait for you to finish your little liaison first?"

Spazz offered up her most charming smile. "We'll be along directly, Mrs. Mansfield, no need to wait," she replied in a voice that oozed unctuousness. Mansfield turned away with a "Harrumphf!" that was more imagined that heard and began ascending the stairs. Once she was certain Mansfield and Red were out of earshot, Spazz turned to face Blade full on and said bluntly, "You don't trust him, do you?"

"Who?" Blade was taken aback by the unexpected non-sequitur.

"Your friend Hobbes – Calvin – whatever."

"Now, why would ye say that?" Blade's eyes narrowed dangerously.

"Because you gave in too easily. You knew he was lying."

"That's my friend ye're talking about, lass. Ye'd best explain yourself before I get upset with ye."

"And I wouldn't like it if you got upset with me? C'mon, Blade, it was as plain as if he'd been waving a flag above his head. When Hobbes gave you that song and dance about some new VR system his company was developing, you knew it was bullshit. You don't have a lot of tells, at least not that I've seen so far, but one you do have is that when you get suspicious you get very...still. Not necessarily quiet, just very still, as if you're setting up your next move, mental, verbal, or physical. That's what you did in Hobbes' penthouse when he spun you that yarn. So what tipped you, and why?"

Blade considered his reply for a moment, then decided that this was the time for genuine candor. "There was a moment there, just an instant, really, when his façade cracked. He was afraid of me, and he's never been afraid of me before. Then again, there's never been a reason for him to be afraid of me. But there is now. There's something going on here that he absolutely doesn't want me to know about, and he's terrified that either I already know what it is, or that I'm about to find out. And whatever it is, it's directly involved with those crystals."

"Yeah, about them. Do you know where they are?"

"Of course I do."

"And where is that?"

Smiling unexpectedly, Blade put a finger alongside his nose. "What the eye don't see nor the ear don't hear, the mind never misses."

"So you're not going to tell me?"

"No."

Spazz sighed. "All right, be that way. As far as your friend Hobbes goes, the question is, does he know you know he's lying?"

"Not a chance. He was so busy concentrating on his own acting job that he never had a chance to notice mine."

"So do you think he bought it?"

"Of course he did. Like I said, there's something about all of this that he's afraid we're close to finding out, because if and when we do, there'll be hell to pay. And he's so desperate for us to *not* find out what it is, he's jumping at any chance there is that he's diverted us away from it."

"And do you have any idea what it is he doesn't want us to know?"

"No, but after I get a shower, put on a set of clean clothes, and had some lunch, I'm going to have a long talk with Raven about it. Well, about that and a few other things...."

Chapter 8

"I hope you don't mind my saying this, but good God, David, you look like hell!"

"We can't all be world-class beauties like ye, Ligeia."

"Flatterer!" She had the good grace to blush slightly, then went on. "Still, my point stands: you look like you're headed for the knacker's yard."

No sooner had Blade been shown to his room than he'd set up his 'deck on the small but adequate workstation and sagged into the wingback office chair sitting before it. *I don't care what the damned animal huggers say,* he mused as he ran his hands over the deep-red Cordovan-tanned hide, *these things only feel right when they're done in leather....* After a few moments of indulging in the chair's sinful luxury, he bestirred himself and commed Raven. The sooner he got this out of the way, the sooner he could become intimately acquainted with the unmistakably Sybaritic queen-size, four-poster bed. Blackbriar was evidently almost as comfortable as Mont Creag House.

"I haven't slept in thirty-six hours, just finished my first meal in eighteen, I've been shot five times – I think. The Weclar stopped four of the bullets obviously but they still left some spectacular bruising. I had my leg clipped by what was probably a 9mm, a trio of idjits in AV9's tried to blow me and my car to Kingdom Come, the F1 is a wreck – it's going to cost a small fortune to have it repaired. Do ye have any idea what a replacement silencer for that thing costs? To top it all off, one of my best friends, the man who hired me for this job, just tried to fob me off with a dog-and-pony show as if I were some rube just arrived at the hustings. So if I'm looking a bit less than my usual glamorous self, I think I have sufficient excuse to do so."

"Really? That sound like just a typical day at the office for you."

"Yer fortunate that yer three thousand miles away, wench," Blade growled. "I'll make ye pay for that remark when I get back."

"Oh, I'm all a-quiver with fear and trembling, to be sure" she replied drily. Ligeia's image on the monitor regarded MacLaren levelly, but with a certain primness which he knew meant that she was now being utterly serious. "So, why did you comm me? Keep in mind I've not had much sleep myself in the last twenty-four hours, what with trying to stay abreast of your antics."

"Right then, to the business at hand. First of all, have ye caught on to anything that could give me an idea of where I can find Nakajima?"

"You're convinced he's running this show for Arasaka there in Atlanta?"

"That I am." The conviction in the Scot's voice was rock-ribbed. "The way things have gone down has his hallmarks all over it: heavy-handed and multi-layered. He brought way more muscle to bear at Underground Atlanta than was really necessary – he was trying to send a message to the rest of corporate America at the same time he was trying to get the crystals: 'Don't fuck with Arasaka, we've got you outgunned.' Then the airstrike on The Gardens: he was making certain that even if he didn't secure those memory crystals for Arasaka, whoever had them was never going to be able to use them, because the only facility that could do so had been obliterated. Then he sent those AV9s after me – that was personal. He was able to ID me at the site from the take from that drone I shot down, I'm certain of it, and thinking it would be sauce for the goose, tried to take me out. Aye, that's Nakajima."

Ligeia cupped her chin in one hand, looking thoughtfully at Blade. "I concur. Arasaka wants those crystals, so it follows that they aren't going to leave the task to a second-stringer. And we both know he's not going to give up – his superiors wouldn't let him even if he were. No one is going to commit those resources – materiel and manpower both – to an op like this only to throw up the sponge and walk away empty-handed.

"What really stands out most sharply for me, though, is the exposure Arasaka is willing to risk to get them. It's really quite startling: they haven't been willing to openly use brute, naked force like this for years – especially in America. It almost makes it imperative that they come away with something. And in this case, anything short of complete success amounts to abject failure. Sort of like Monty and Market-Garden. So, yes, Nakajima is going to absolutely tenacious about this."

"Which means I have to pre-empt Nakajima, divert his attention, make him focus on me rather than on Radome and Compton, wherever they are, give him as little time to think as possible. And that means I have to find him."

"Easier said than done." Ligeia sighed in frustration. "Right now he's completely off the grid, which means I have no idea where to begin looking for him. Trying to find him in a city the size of metropolitan Atlanta will be like looking for a needle in a stack of needles." She smiled ruefully at Blade. "I'll keep my eyes and ears open, and of course I'll cast my wicked web as widely as I can in the hope that I feel something quiver, but I'm not terribly sanguine about getting any quick results."

"I know. Ye're a techno-witch, but I suppose it's too much to expect ye to be a real magician as well." MacLaren's eyes took on a distant cast and he went on. "I have an idea, something I'll see if an old friend can help me with...."

"What? Who?"

"I'd rather not say until I'm convinced I'm really that desperate."

"Have it your way." She paused, then frowned, and went she spoke again, there was a decidedly dark note in her voice. "David, there's something I believe you need to know about those crystals that Calvin hasn't told you. And it disturbs me."

"And that would be...?"

"I don't know if Radome had a chance to tell you, but we had the time to look at the directories in each of those crystals. I couldn't open any of them, there wasn't time to download them, but I did get a snapshot of each directory tree. David, every single folder, subfolder, and file is named for some section or function of the human brain."

"*What?*"

"It was Alistair who spotted it first, and we've since gone over the entire contents of all seven directories. If there's a known higher brain function that doesn't have a corresponding file in those directories, we don't know what it is. As for the program that runs these files, well, to you it would be what you so fondly term 'techno-babble,' but the short, simple version for someone as technologically impaired as yourself is this: it most certainly isn't some sort of new virtual reality."

"God's holy trousers," Blade said with obvious – and genuine – apprehension. "Ligeia, I don't like where I think this is heading. "

"And you shouldn't. I can't tell you what it is yet, but I can tell you that there are years of R & D behind this stuff and I've no chance of duplicating it based on what little I have – I'd be working half-blind in a dark room with both hands tied behind my back. But if it's what I think it is, then it's no surprise that your friend Calvin is so desperate to get those crystals back, because he violating whole chapters of American law, PanEuroEcon codes, and about a dozen international treaties – all of which carry penalties that stop just short of the death sentence. In fact, it *would* be a death sentence for Cogito Orbis. Whatever you do, don't let Nakajima *or* Calvin get their hands on those crystals, because I don't know which would be worse in the long run."

"Well, ye certainly know how to brighten up a man's afternoon."

"Oh, I can do that too, thank you, as you well know," Ligeia smiled impishly, then grew sober. "But I'm serious about this, David."

"Point taken."   After a few moments, MacLaren's scowl

deepened, but he said nothing more. Ligeia chose to take the bull by the horns.

"OK, spill it. What else is on your mind?"

"Why do you ask?"

"David, I know you, none better. Even if no one else can see it, I know when you want to broach a subject and can't find a convenient way to do it. So just go ahead and tell me what else is bothering you."

"It's...well.... It's Spazz," Blade said, giving Ligeia a sheepish look. "Ever since she invited herself to this little party, I've been wondering if she's going to turn up to be the joker in the deck. Can you tell me anything about her?"

Ligeia laughed merrily. "Either I'm getting to be as paranoid as you or else I know too well how you think, because I've already started digging into her records. Let me tell you what I've found so far." And with that, she began a recital of Maureen Collins' life story that in every significant particular matched the one Maureen herself had given Blade not twelve hours earlier. There were quite a few additional details, naturally, although the only ones which surprised MacLaren were learning that she'd been married, was now divorced, and had a five-year old son who lived with his father.

"Interesting that she never mentioned anything about that last bit," Blade said pensively, "although, at the time, there was no reason why she should, I suppose." He pinched the bridge of his nose as he sat silent for a moment. "Right then, she seems to be legitimate as far as who and what she says she is. What can ye tell me about her work? What kind of track record does she have?"

"I can tell you quite a lot, actually." Blade saw Ligeia shift her attention away from the video pickup as she consulted another display. "She's been doing solo operative work for the last five years, and her rep is growing. I've found ten ops she's completed in just the last fifteen months, and she never failed at any of them, although there are a couple of others where she's left some question marks behind her."

"Tell me about them – all of them."

"Six of her contracts were active shooters that she appears to have pulled off brilliantly, including two that involved recovering kidnapping victims – alive. Four others that were essentially protective details that went without a hitch or a glitch. Now comes the interesting bits. One contract was pulled by the employer, and there are four additional cases where she took a job and then walked away from it in mid-mission."

"So...she's good at her work when she sees an op through to the end, but if she gets bored, she walks away from it, is that it?"

"That's part of how I'm reading it," Ligeia confirmed, "but there also seems to be an ethical element to it. With Thyssen-Schneider, her attorney filed a claim of 'failure to make full disclosure of mission requirements,' which could mean a lot of things, but since Maureen and Thyssen-Schneider *immediately* settled out of court and the records were sealed, I'm wondering if there wasn't some form of sexual coercion involved."

"Wouldn't be the first time some corporate type thought a female solo should be willing to go 'above and beyond' in accomplishing her mission. What else?"

"The other three incidents, though...yes, you could say she got bored and packed it in. One was a contract with Whitewater Security, a protection detail for a group of PanEuroEcon businessmen in Washington DC. She took one look at who got off the plane at Reagan and resigned on the spot. I've no idea why. That was eighteen months ago. Whatever her reasons, it didn't stop Whitewater from hiring her eight months later for another protective detail, this time for the governor of Mexifornia at a mini-summit in Dallas. It was supposed to be a five-day gig, she walked out on it the second day. Whitewater blacklisted her at that point."

"Understandable from their point of view, although it might be interesting hearing her version of the story."

Ligeia nodded. "Interesting and possibly revealing. Any road, the last one, believe it or not, was right there in Atlanta – three days ago."

"*What?*"

"Yessiree, Bob!" Ligeia affirmed with a cheeky smile. "Somebody named Johann von Poslien. He's some civilian spec ops weenie, consults for the American DoD, who was in town for a convention of some sort. Apparently Spazz told him to shut up and let her do her job, she was tired of being told how he could do it better and having to listen to gun porn."

Blade burst out laughing. "She didn't!"

"She did! Even posted it on her Spacebook page."

After a few more chuckles, Blade got back to business. "And what about the contract that was pulled? Who did that and why?"

"It was a U.S.-based philanthropic think-tank called the January Foundation. I know of them – they keep a pretty low profile, or at least they don't go about shouting 'Be awed, ye masses, by our benevolence and largesse' the way a lot of philanthropies do. They put their money into emerging-technology companies that are in the late start-up phase – basically proven but still developing. Not a bad investment strategy, if you ask me."

"Agreed. Why did they cancel her contract, though?"

"The data that's out there is sparse, and this one *didn't* rate a Spacebook post, so you have to read between the lines a bit, but from what I can see, the situation they hired her to resolve sorted itself out just a few hours after they let the contract, *before* she went into action for them. The Foundation did honour the contract's terms, though, and paid her retainer."

"That's an outlier, obviously, and not part of a pattern, then." Blade drummed his fingers on the desktop for a few seconds, pondering what Ligeia had learned about Spazz. "She certainly knows how to shoot, and she seems to keep a pretty cool head about her when the shite hits the fan, but it would really upset me if I found out that she's been playing me false."

"You like her!" Ligeia exclaimed, both pleased and surprised at once.

"Perhaps. Even possibly. But it's that...erratic...way she has about her that worries me. I can't put my finger on why, and yet I can't help but feel that sooner or later it will lead to trouble. Look at the way she just 'attached' herself to us in Underground Atlanta – she didn't even bother to ask if we could use the help, had no idea who we were or what the situation was, she just jumped in and started popping Arasakas. And before you ask, I'm not entirely buying the tale that she was motivated by a latent case of hero-worship. It makes me wonder if she's truly someone I can depend on, or if she's some sort of flake, and if I find myself working with her again, she'll suddenly decide in the middle of an op that she's had enough for whatever reason and just walk away."

"David, you're going to have to start trusting someone, sometime."

"Perhaps so, but I'm a damned long way from being convinced it's her."

"At least give her a chance to prove that you *can* trust her before you decide you can't."

"That will be up to her. For now, I've got to get at least a few hours' sleep. After that, I need to talk to someone, and I'm not sure where he is at the moment. Would ye see if ye can locate him for me, please?"

"Who?"

"Bruce."

Ligeia grimaced. "He may not want to talk to you, you know."

"I know, but maybe if ye lay the groundwork for me, he'll at least hear me out. Contact him if ye can, tell him I need to talk to him, please?"

---------------XXXXX---------------

He knows. Dear God, Blade knows or else he's about to find out. He's not tech-savvy enough to figure it out for himself, but that bitch Raven certainly can – and she will if she's given enough time. What do I do then?

Sitting at the centre of his workstation, his back for once turned to the monitors, Calvin stared out the floor to ceiling windows that opened out onto the northern Atlanta skyline, looking at but not really seeing the panorama before him. *It's not fair! Six months. That was all I needed, another six months – seven at the most. Just a few more tweaks and I could have gone to beta, finished that and been ready to upload. It would have been over, a done deal. As it stands now, the goal I've been working toward for a quarter of a century is within a whisker of being lost forever. Worse, if that Luddite Blade figures it out, he'll run to the authorities; they'll take Cogito Orbis away from me and I'll probably never breath the air as free man again.*

It was the prospect of losing Cogito Orbis, rather than his freedom, that frightened him the most. He had become so immersed in the company and its work that their identities had blurred and merged to a point where they were indistinguishable the one from the other. It was Cogito Orbis that translated his concepts and ideas into the reality of functional programs; those programs were the building blocks from which he drew new inspirations, expanded the breadth and depth of his concepts. Until the moment he opened the security case and found it empty, and realized that he was fundamentally at Blade's mercy, Calvin had never truly comprehended how small his world had become. The apparently infinite vastness of cyberspace, of which he'd thought himself the lord and master, was reduced to a nutshell: mundane little men and women in the world of flesh and blood could – and, under the right circumstances, would – take it all from him.

For as long as he could remember, the cyber world had always been far more real to Calvin than its physical counterpart – the steady, regular procession of electrons along preordained pathways in processors and circuit boards, and the virtual realities they created, were more appealing than the ceaseless chaos of the material world. There was a beauty in the symmetry, the orderliness, the cleanliness and predictability, the way that those flowing electrons would act and react according to the commands they were issued that had no counterpart in the messy, chaotic world that most people called "real."

From the moment he was given his first computer at the age of eight, Calvin never met a compiler he didn't like, so to speak, nor was he ever unwilling to do bodily harm if need be to anyone who got between him and his machines. He'd graduated from Georgia Tech with degrees in computer science and mathematics, and still was able to minor in linguistics. He'd followed that up with an MBA from the same school, and had actually started Cogito Orbis in his dorm room, designing limited purpose, small-suite smart agents: he made his mark (and his first half-billion dollars, which he'd plowed right back into the company) designing and marketing code refactoring software.

This led him into writing self-modifying code that evolved into his most significant breakthrough to date – the VI, or Virtual Intelligence. In his early teens Calvin became fascinated, even obsessed, by how humans and computers communicated, whether by commands entered via a keyboard and a monitor screen or through a verbal interface. He was continually frustrated by how literal were computers in following instructions they were given, especially their refusal to carry out commands that were not perfectly parsed: they could only do *exactly* what they were told to do, but they could not intuit a user's intentions. His solution to the problem fundamentally altered the computers and users worked together.

Using his refactoring code as a starting point, Calvin developed a program with a vastly accelerated learning curve, one which required only a verbal interface: for all but the most specialized users (and specialized applications), keyboards were now obsolete. Users could actually hold conversations with the operating system that ran their computer; this was *Dennis*, the Digital Neural Intelligence System, a remarkable AI system, robust and adaptive, and it proved extremely popular. In fact, it was *Dennis'* basic program that Calvin used to develop Mycroft. (Raven had actually hacked, sliced, diced, chopped, channeled, and sectioned a copy of *Dennis* into Alistair, although by the time she was finished, Calvin, had he been able to examine her code, would found his original work unrecognizable.) *Dennis* marked the beginning of the age when computers and users could communicate with each other as simply and directly as human beings did with each other. It was a feat that ranked him in the pantheon of computer science gods second only to Alan Turing.

But that accomplishment brought with it an unexpected consequence: what would Calvin do for an encore? Where could *Dennis* lead? It wasn't a question of following the Redmond model of adding whistles and bells in the form of updates, modules, and apps. *Dennis* introduced the closest, most personalized, least restrictive interface between humans and computers that had ever existed; could Calvin take that one step further? More to the point, was there yet another step that could be taken, or had computer/user interaction reached its practical limit, whatever theory might say?

Rather than just continue with a sort of product-improvement development, Calvin changed tack entirely. Few things ever impressed him as deeply as did the fleeting nature of existence, how transitory was intelligence and intellect, the irreplaceable loss to humanity as a whole every time someone died and took all of their accumulated knowledge, wisdom, and experience with them. Was there a way, he asked himself, to preserve all of it instead? *Dennis* certainly was not the answer, but perhaps it could be a starting point. What Calvin wanted to do, though, was go beyond the simple exchange of commands, requests, and information: he wanted to create a way where ideas, concepts, even intuition, could be communicated between a human brain and a computer core without the interference, confusion, and obfuscation of speech. He would create the bridge that directly linked computer intelligence with human intellect.

This little trip down memory lane was interrupted when he heard someone behind him say his name. Spinning about, he realized the speaker was some bubble-headed bleach blonde on INN's five o'clock newsfeed; a scroll at the bottom of the screen identified her as Tegan Porter. The devastation of The Gardens was a major story, at least regionally, so of course the newsies weren't about to leave it alone.

"...has so far not made a public appearance to address this morning's terrorist attack near Blairsville, although his media representative, Mycroft Doyle, did speak with reporters by comm-link earlier this afternoon. I'm told that Amanda Russell, who is presently at the site of disaster, has new information that has come to light since the attack. Amanda?"

The image changed to that of striking, statuesque woman with waves of auburn hair, standing in front of what was clearly a major recovery operation, with several pieces of earthmoving machinery visible in the background, along with several ambulances and paramedics. "That's correct, Tegan, there have apparently been some new developments in the investigation of who attacked the research facility owned by Cogito Orbis known as 'The Gardens,' and why it took place." She half-turned and gestured at the frantic rescue efforts going on behind her. "So far the casualty count has reached sixty-seven dead, twenty-nine critically injured, and first responders can only estimate that there may be as many as two- or three-hundred victims still to be located or accounted for. What has come to light in just the last hour or so is that the wrecks of four AV-type VSTOL aircraft haves been located, one here at the site of the attack itself, the other three at various points to the southwest. Witnesses have come forward stating that they saw similar aircraft flying very low and making repeated passes over the area where The Gardens was located at the time of the attack. One of the federal investigators, speaking on the condition of anonymity, as he wasn't officially authorized to discuss the subject with the media, informed me that certain details recovered from all four crash sites have confirmed that the AVs were owned by the Arasaka Corporation. Other witnesses have said that at the time of the attack or immediately afterward, a dark blue automobile was seen in the car park of The Gardens."

"This is interesting, Amanda," Porter remarked, looking, surprisingly enough, genuinely interested. "The shootout in Underground Atlanta early this morning that seems to have centreed around a nightclub called 'Bits,' which is owned by the same man who owns Cogito Orbis and The Gardens, Calvin Coleridge, also involved the Arasaka Corporation. So I don't think I'm reaching here by suggesting that there's a connection between the two incidents. Can you tell us anything more about that blue automobile?" The screen split, showing both Porter and Russell.

"Yes, I can, Tegan. We're told that witnesses described it as a two-door vehicle, very loud and apparently very powerful, one of the supercar varieties produced in the 1990s and 2000s." Porter paused, consulted her datapad, then went on. "When shown images of cars of this type, they quickly identified it as a McLaren F1, which is known to be the type of vehicle driven by the solo operative and vigilante known as 'Blade,' David MacLaren."

"And this MacLaren person was, you'll remember, identified as one of the instigators of the shooting incident in Underground Atlanta," Porter responded and Russell nodded vigorously. "Obviously there is a lot more to this story that has yet to be uncovered. Thank you, Amanda." Russell's image vanished and Porter faced the camera squarely. "And we here at INN will keep you fully informed of any new developments in this story. Once again, to recap, currently the casualties caused by the terrorist attack on the Cogito Orbis research facility known as The Gardens has reached almost seventy dead and thirty critically injured. Also, the Arasaka Corporation and the international vigilante known as Blade have both been connected to the terrorist attack. We will bring more details as they become known. Now, turning to other regional news...."

Calvin closed the newsfeed window with a snort that mixed derision and annoyance. *Maybe you were right, Blade, maybe I do have a big, fat target painted on my back, especially after that kind of news coverage, but you've got one just as large on your own. You've been branded, if only by association, as a terrorist, while I'm just the hapless victim. I think I'll let Mycroft spin that one around a bit and see how it bounces.* He once again turned his back on the monitors, resumed his vigil of the Atlanta skyline, and returned to his reverie....

As far back as the middle of the 20th Century, "artificial intelligence" had been the holy grail of the computing world, but even then the best minds in computer science understood that true "intelligence," whatever it was and however it was defined, as beyond the capability of any computer. An "artificial intelligence," or AI, no matter what the wild-eyed ravings of semi-literate users, science fiction buffs, or the great unwashed struggling to grapple with electronic technology might maintain, was a flat out impossibility. The reason why this was so lay in its fundamental nature: at core, no matter how elaborate and well-developed, an AI was nothing more than a glorified decision tree. A computer could not employ creativity, or intuition, or make leaps of logic: it could only follow those paths of deduction that were defined by its designer and user. Calvin alone among his colleagues and peers saw the folly in trying to write programs which "imitated" those characteristics – creativity, intuition, and leaps of logic, as they would simply be more of the same, decision trees. Instead, he wanted to deepen the interface between the user and the operating system, an integration of the two, as it were, a process that he called "synthetic intellect." With the success of *Dennis*, in his senior year at Georgia Tech, Calvin plunged head-first into what he knew would be his life's work.

It was then that Kim entered his life. A fellow computer science major, two years Calvin's junior in academic standing but every bit his equal in intellect and skill, she was the physical embodiment of what Calvin had unshakeably believed could not exist: the perfect woman for him. Of medium height, with an athletic build that was just a little too "bouncy" in all the right places to keep her from ever excelling at any single sport, blessed with an oval face, sharply defined cheekbones, a wide mouth that laughed easily, intensely blue eyes, and sandy blonde hair, in appearance she was as far from the stereotypical "computer geek" as could be possible. Appearances could be deceiving, however, and she was every bit Calvin's mental equal, although his ego wouldn't let him admit as much to anyone but himself.

Predictably, perhaps, Calvin and Kim met at a conference on computer imitation of neurological processes. Intrigued by a few comments she'd made in seminar they had attended, he asked her to join him for a drink afterwards. The result was an hours-long discussion of computer science that saw the two of them shutting down the bar. Calvin was dumbstruck: unlike most computer geeks, he was well aware the existence of those creatures known as "females" along with how...interesting...they could be, but he'd never considered the possibility of having his emotions engaged by one. Kim, for her part, found the contrast between Calvin's calm, even arrogant self-assurance within his profession and his bumbling shyness around her irresistibly charming. It was a classic case of total opposites finding total attraction in each other; they married the week after Kim graduated – *summa cum laude*, of course – from Tech.

As it turned out, even more valuable to Calvin, though he didn't realize as much at the time, was that Kim was as socially accomplished as Calvin was inept. As Cogito Orbis grew in size and market presence, Calvin was increasingly ill-equipped to be the public and business face of the company: arrogant, ascerbic, sometimes surly, as Cogito Orbis began to have a presence in the world IT market, Calvin was poised to become his own – and his company's – worst enemy....

As he sat in his "Evil Overlord chair," as his handful of friends and somewhat more numerous colleagues called it, and looked out the windows with unseeing eyes, Calvin smiled ruefully as he thought back to the time, just before her graduation, that Kim called him out on his business manners and consequently became the public business persona of Cogito Orbis. They had been sitting in Junior's Grill, a diner close to the Georgia Tech campus that had been reopened after an eleven-year hiatus and was the unofficial social centre for IT students.

"I don't care if you own the company and that you're the HMFIC of development!" Those intense blue eyes, Calvin discovered, could flash with anger as well as passion or intellectual intensity. "The next time I see you coming that close to blowing up an eight-figure deal, I'm going to whack you smartly on the head – preferably with a two-by-four – and take over from there!"

"C'mon, Kim, he was trying to low-ball me, and I wasn't putting up with his bullshit!"

"Idiot! If he doesn't buy the system from you, he'll just go to Strawberry Software and offer the same deal to old man Fields, who'll be happy to take his money."

"But he was only offering a tenth of a percent," Calvin whined.

"So what? Did you even bother to do the math?" Kim was incredulous. "One tenth of a percent of Silverman-Baggins' gross works out to something close to a half-billion dollars over the next two years. And it was your damned ego that almost lost it for you!" Her eyes bored into his and her voice took on a rock-ribbed tone he'd never before heard from her. "Let me start handling the business of Cogito Orbis and I'll close deals like you won't believe while you keep your Dwalin-like self in the R & D lab where it belongs. Either that or else you can find yourself a new girlfriend!"

Two weeks later, in a quiet civil ceremony at the courthouse, they were married.

Kim was as good as her word, and within two years took Cogito Orbis from the status of "Oh, yeah, those guys..." to that of being one of the world's elite, cutting-edge software companies. Not that Kim was any slow-coach in the research lab; there she matched Calvin mental-stride for mental-stride; it was also where their profoundly different methodologies collided. Calvin had always prided himself on his strict, orderly – some said compulsive – procedures: frequent testing, obsessive documentation, established protocols, and safety precautions – backups – for all of his work. Kim liked to think of herself as more of a "free spirit" who worked and moved however she felt "inspired" to do so. She was far more daring in this than Calvin could ever feel comfortable being, and she habitually ignored whatever limits he set with which she disagreed, regarding them as obstacles – "needless paperwork," she called it. Whenever Calvin tried to reel her in, she insisted that she knew the limits, the problems and the risks, reassuring him that, "Hey, I've never gotten it wrong yet!"

Paradoxically, it was when the moment came to take a new project out of the development lab and introduce it to the world that their roles completely switched. Neither had any fear of shoving the boundaries of computer science out as far as they could go, and then pushing further still. But Calvin ardently insisted that if a new program or system *could* be created, then it *should* be created; if a paradigm could be shifted, then by all means shift it whenever the capability and opportunity to do so presented itself. Kim, on the other hand, constantly argued that just because doing something was possible, it didn't automatically follow that it must - or even *should* – be done. Their arguments over who was right were long, loud, and for those who overheard them, memorable. Naturally, they both enjoyed immensely the making-up process that followed, but the issue remained unsettled between them

As Kim and Calvin worked on Project Bowman, their debate grew sharper until it finally came to a head a little more than a week ago. Calvin had finally written a set of functional algorithms that removed the last obstacle to the working synthesis of a human intellect and a computer's core processor, and he came into Kim's office practically bouncing with excitement, waving a sheaf of printouts over his head.

"Look at this! Look at this!" he exclaimed gleefully. "I've done it!"

"Done what? Finally figured out how to use the printer?" Kim regarded him with wide-eyed innocence. Calvin gave her a very old-fashioned look in return, held it for a few seconds, then went on.

"I finally got the synthesis algorithms to work. Now I know what the eighth day of Creation must have felt like."

"Say what?"

"I mean it! This is what it must feel like creating new life!"

"I thought that was called pregnancy, which you certainly can't feel! You're plumbing's all wrong for it."

"Very funny." From his tone, Calvin plainly didn't find Kim's observation all that amusing. "If I'm not actually creating life, I'm doing the next best thing, I'm creating a genuine synthetic intellect! A human-computer fusion, if you will. It's like a new form of life, and I've created it! It's alive and it's mine!"

"Stop it, Calvin. Have you really thought this through, what you claim you just did, that is? Whether it works or not, right now you're sounding delusional – you're talking as if you've just begun playing God with this!"

"Who's playing? As far as this...this...system goes, I *am* God! And this is Adam in the Garden!"

"No, you're wrong. This isn't Adam in the Garden, this is Nemesis and you're turning into Narcissus."

"You know, you're name should have been Cassandra."

Kim shook her head in dismay. "All right, you want this" – she waved at printouts Calvin had spread across her desk – "to be Adam in the Garden? Fine, it's Adam. And it's yours. But if your going to start putting on the airs and graces of divinity, then let me be Eve. Let me be the conscience that puts her heel on the head of the snake that I know sooner or later is going to appear. If it's really your Adam, put me into that machine."

"No. Not just 'No,' but 'Hell no!' I flat out refuse. You're not going in there, and neither am I. Whoever gets to be the first test subject will be somebody who's...expendable."

Kim looked at him with a mixture of pity and horror. "You know, the fact that you just said that and actually meant it horrifies me. Now get out of here before I say something that both of us will regret was ever said."

Two days later, Kim went into Gamma Lab by herself, without telling Calvin where she was or what she was doing. What came out of Gamma Lab was a living, breathing, mindless husk....

I should have been paying closer attention to what she was saying. So many times while we were writing the code, through all the dead ends and near-misses, she kept warning me that we were on dangerous ground – that even though the map might not say "Here be dragons," that didn't mean there the unexplored territories were safe. And what was my reply? All I could do was remind her that "A man's reach should exceed his grasp, or what's a heaven for?" It never occurred to me that Browning was wrong, that I should have been paying attention to Milton instead. I could never be content with serving, I had to reign. And so I do – in Hell.

And that's the real problem, isn't it, Calvin? This is the first time in how long that you've questioned your own infallibility, the unassailable, unquestionable rightness of your actions, isn't it? This is the first time you can remember when the consequences of your choices and your actions have been measured in human lives, instead of merely lines of code or dollars and cents, isn't it? Have you become so delusional, so enamored of your own sense of near-godhood, that you can convince yourself that, as long as you achieve your goal, human lives don't matter? Is that what you've become?

The longer Calvin brooded, the more convinced he was that the time had come to repent of the whole of Project Bowman concept and the idea of creating a synthetic intellect. It would be so easy to do, especially now that Gamma Lab was gone. Rebuilding it would be hideously expensive, and probably beyond the resources of Cogito Orbis now. The unkind truth was that for the past three years Calvin's time and energy had been so utterly consumed by Project Bowman that the company was stagnating, having introduced no new products in all of that time. Financially, Cogito Orbis was staying afloat solely through sales of Dennis, along with upgrades and new applications. But the release of Strawberry Software's *Gina* ("General Intelligent Neural Automation") system in 2034 introduced unwelcome competition for Cogito Orbis and cut significantly into *Dennis'* new-market share, with a corresponding drop in revenue. Worse, there was nothing new in the pipeline and not even a hint of anything could that be developed in time to turn the situation around and allow him to rebuild Gamma Lab and salvage Project Bowman. No, better to let Blade destroy the crystals if and when he find them; he, Calvin, had already paid too high a price for the lesson that Kim was almost certainly right.

He turned around again to face his workstation and reached for numeric pad on his comm-link. He was halfway through entering Blade's combination when he stopped and pulled his hand away.

No, that's no solution either. Kim paid a terrible price for bringing Bowman so close to its ultimate success – a price she never expected or wanted to pay. If I shut it down, she paid it for nothing: her life, and almost ten years of mine, would go to waste if I did that. The only way I can redeem anything from this disaster is to see it through to the end. Finish Bowman, make it my triumph and Kim's memorial. That's what I have to do.

She deserves no less, and so do I.

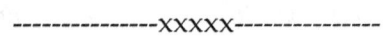

Hideki Nakajima sat sprawled in a large easy chair, a glass of scotch in his hand, a look of mingled frustration and amazement on his face. "This one is stronger than I expected him to be, Umori. Any other man would have told me what I wanted to know after the first demonstration of how much pain I could inflict upon him. Three times this one has compelled me to raise the pain level to its maximum, Umori – three times! Each time he has passed out, of course, but still he refuses to tell me where the crystals are or where I can find Blade, even when he knows what is to come when he regains consciousness."

"Dare I suggest that he doesn't tell you because he truly doesn't know, Nakajima-sama?" Umori replied.

"Oh, he knows, Umori. Of course he knows. If he didn't, I wouldn't be interrogating him, would I?"

Umori knew better than to point out to Nakajima that he was putting forward a circular argument. Instead, he said, "He has to know that he risks permanent brain damage if he persists in withholding the information from you. Why, then, would he continue to do so unless he is unable to tell you what you want to know?"

"Because I made a mistake. I let him know that ultimately I'm going to kill him whether he tells me or not, so to him it's a matter of pride. He knows he can't win – he's determined to make certain that I don't either."

"An interesting conundrum, indeed. With your permission, Nakajima-sama, I will give this some thought while I work and see if I can come suggest a solution." Umori was fussing and bustling about the final details of setting up Nakajima's command centre inside the nondescript office building in Bragg Park that was one of Arasaka "clean sites" – what Westerners called "safehouses" – in Atlanta, the same building in which Compton was incarcerated. No sooner had the situation fallen apart in Undeground Atlanta,

Nakajima and Umori abandoned their suite in the Centennial Plaza Hotel and moved here, lest some unanticipated detail betray them: Nakajima was wanted by not only the FBI and the US Marshals, but by law enforcement agencies in most of the fifty states as well. He couldn't openly show his face in public without risking being identified by some overly-observant policeman; at the same time he had to make sure, even while lying low, that he did nothing to attract attention to himself. A pair of Japanese businessmen working out of a hotel suite for a few days would be unremarkable; those same two businessmen never emerging from that room for a solid week or more would start raising eyebrows. So he and Umori had decamped from the hotel and set up their op centre in the clean site. He still had a mission to complete, and he could do so from here just as easily as from the Centennial Plaza; not as comfortably, perhaps, but one precept that the Japanese and the western *gaijun* shared was that a little suffering was good for the soul.

He looked at his watch and sighed. "I believe in another half hour it will be time for me to once again have a talk with Mr. Compton."

Five hours after he'd spoken with Raven, Blade was once again in front of the monitor sitting on the work station in his room, this time comfortably clad in black trousers and a maroon golf shirt. He was rested now and reasonably relaxed. The luncheon had been only a cold buffet, but it had more than sated his hunger, he'd taken a long, hot shower, and managed four hours of uninterrupted sleep. He didn't imagine for moment that he was going to enjoy the pending conversation, though, but at least he felt ready for it. He entered the comm code Raven had provided and waited for the request to be accepted. Within seconds, it was.

The years had not been kind to the face that looked out from the monitor screen at MacLaren. Impending jowls muted the once-square jaw line, age spots had taken up residence, and what had been a full head of black hair was now resembled nothing so much as a white battle-line in full retreat. But the dark eyes were still clear, still the eyes of the predator the man had once been.

"Yes?"

"Bruce, it's Blade."

"Hello, David. Raven told me to expect a comm from you." His voice had gotten raspier as the years passed, now it sounded as if someone had sandpapered his vocal cords. "She even convinced me to take the comm when it came through."

"I'll have to thank her for that."

"So to what do I owe this...dubious pleasure?"

"I need yer help."

"Me? And just how can a broken-down, old, idle layabout help you? These days, you're the one with all the wonderful toys and the techno-wizards helping you." Blade thought he could hear a faint echo of envy and bitterness in that voice.

"Does the name Hideki Nakajima ring a bell?"

"Nakajima? That piece of work? It certainly does."

"I need to find him – quickly. Once upon a time ye were able to tap into the cyber-surveillance system of an entire city using the wireless net to find one man. I need to know how ye did it – I need the software ye wrote to do it – so I can duplicate that system."

"Why? So you can use it to go out and kill more people?"

"I'm hoping it won't come to that. But this much is certain: if I *don't* get it, other people – good people – *are* going to die. By Nakajima's hand."

"David, you know damned well that I don't condone your methods, and I won't be party to them. Vengeance achieved is always a hollow victory – nobody knows that better than I do."

"This isn't about vengeance, Bruce" –

"David, when Nakajima is involved, with you it's *always* about vengeance!"

"Dammit, Bruce, if this *was* vengeance, I wouldn't bother worrying about the two people he's holding, I'd just wait until he popped his head up again after he was through with them and go after the bastard once he did!"

"And if you do find him, you intend to kill him."

"I intend to *execute* him! There's a difference! The man is a walking crime against humanity – no one with a moral compass can say he isn't – so it's not as though he hasn't earned his punishment."

"Then let him be accountable to humanity, Blade, not just to one man. I will *not* help you play judge, jury, and executioner and kill yet another human being. The answer is 'no'." There was a finality in the way he said that last word.

"So ye're willing to let him kill more people until every legal 'i' is dotted and 't' crossed?"

"No, I'm not and you know that. But I'm not willing to let you throw the law right out the window because it's an inconvenience for you. I'm not as good as you are, Blade, when it comes to deciding who deserves to live and who needs to die!" There was a bitter fury in Bruce's voice now.

"And I'm not as good as ye at shrugging off 'collateral damage' so I can pretend my lily-white morals are still pure." Blade shot back, his anger matching the other man's; both were raising their voices now.

"God knows my morals were never lily white, David." He gave a sudden snort of derision. "That surveillance system you want – do you know how illegal that was? Dear God, I was so far on the other side of the law when I created it I almost lost sight of where the line was! Hell, *most* of what I did before I 'disappeared' wasn't even *remotely* legal. Searches without warrants, flaunting jurisdictions – local *and* international, I might add – I shredded the whole idea of due process! And there were so many cases of assault and battery that if I'd ever been arrested I'd have been put away for a dozen lifetimes. I was only allowed to get away with it because of the results I got and even then I realized that there was a point where the results couldn't justify the means I used to get them. No, I never claimed that my hands were clean, David – I just wasn't prepared to keep on soiling them as willingly and as often as you do yours."

"Bruce, we're not going to have this argument again. Yes, ye drew yer moral line in the sand, and no, ye never crossed it, well, hoo-bloody-ray for you! Hundreds of innocent lives were lost because ye refused to put an end to the life of one man! *One man!* Somebody else had to finally stop him for good, all because of yer misplaced sense of self-righteousness!"

"And how many people have died because it was simpler for you to put a bullet in their brain instead of their kneecap? How many died because of who they worked for, or what they knew, or just because they were some minion who got in your way?" Bruce shouted back at him.

"Right, I said we're not having this argument again, and we won't. But I still need yer surveillance system – if I don't find Nakajima soon, two of my people are going to die."

"You're serious, aren't you? You really do want that system!"

"Did ye hear what I said? The lives of a good man and a good woman are at stake here! People who *trusted* me!" Blade was now matching Bruce decibel for decibel. "If I can find Nakajima, I can find them; if I find them, then there's still a chance I can save them. And if I can't do that, then I can make damned sure Nakajima pays for it – him and everyone involved with him."

"And that's precisely my point, David: if you can't have justice, you'll always accept revenge in its place!" Bruce abruptly stopped shouting, visibly gathered himself, and went on in an almost conversational tone. "I drew that 'line in the sand' to keep myself from making that same mistake. I always worried that one morning I would wake up to find that I'd given up what made me good for what made me right. Thank God it never happened to me – I don't want to see it happen to you."

There was a long pause before Blade spoke again, and when he did, he was equally subdued. "All right, I'll grant ye that – that's someplace I never want to go either. But answer me this: if ye're not prepared to trust me with yer surveillance system, are ye willing to trust Raven with it?"

"What part of 'no' don't you understand, David?" Bruce was well and truly incredulous. "I won't let you or anyone else – including Raven! – have it. I created that system with a self-destruct because I knew even while I was building it that if I didn't, the temptation to keep on using it would be too great to resist. I deliberately took it away from myself – I'm not about to turn around now and give it to someone else."

"And that's yer final answer?"

"It is."

"Then God have mercy on yer soul, Bruce, if I don't find Radome and Compton in time. Because *I* won't." And with that, he broke the connection, sat back in his chair, and passed his hand across his eyes. *God, I need a drink.*

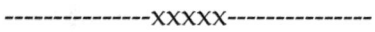

Blade pulled the door closed behind him, turned, and saw Spazz standing perhaps ten feet down the corridor, leaning against the wall, arms and ankles crossed. Her face showed a mixture of amusement and concern as she raised an eyebrow at him.

"He said no, didn't he?" she asked.

"Who?"

"Your friend Bruce."

"You heard it?"

"Most of it."

"Eavesdropping, were ye?"

"More like I didn't have any choice. I think the whole damn east wing heard you – if not the whole house."

"I didn't realize we'd gotten that loud."

"You did. Trust me."

Blade thrust his hands into his trouser pockets and sighed. "I need a drink. Want to help me find the bar? And to answer your question, ye're right: he said no."

She moved closer to him and laid a long-fingered, carefully manicured hand on his arm, as if to reassure him in some way. "I could have told you he would."

He looked at her, startled. "How do ye even know about him? He 'vanished' twenty years ago."

"I used to work in international finance, remember? He never really went broke, you know – he had money stashed all over the world. Over the years a few of us figured out who he was – or who he'd *been*, at least. We've just sort of decided to keep our mouths shut about it and let the guy enjoy his 'retirement.'"

"Ye're just full of surprises, aren't ye?"

"You have no idea," she purred.

"Miss Collins, ye're a lot of trouble."

"Oh, I hope so!" She slipped her arm through his and they began walking. "He's wrong, you know."

"What do ye mean?"

"Bruce. He's wrong: you're not someone who randomly kills people just because they're in your way. That's what a psychopath does. That's what your pal Nakajima does. That's not you, though – I've followed your whole career, remember? But Bruce...Bruce doesn't understand – or maybe he doesn't *want* to understand – that you and he are very much alike. You both made choices as to who you would be, drew your own boundaries, and each of you have, in your own ways, never crossed them."

"And just what do ye see as being *my* choice?"

She stopped, turned him to face her directly, then looked into his eyes for second or two with a very level gaze. "You decide that sometimes, someone has to die in order to let better people live."

"And Nakajima, did he make a choice?"

"I honestly don't know, Blade. I sometimes wonder if some people are just born wicked – like Democrats, for instance – and never choose to be anything but. Other people, though, do make that choice."

"Ye're starting to sound like a Scottish Presbyterian."

"Nope!" She gave him a breezy smile. "Lapsed Roman Catholic."

"Ye gods, I'm consorting with a papist!"

"Yep! There goes your reputation right out the window." She stopped, reached out, and turned Blade to face her directly, serious once again.

"Look, lemme 'splain sumthin' to you. There really *is* a difference between someone like Bruce and people in our line of work. I don't think you've ever articulated this idea to yourself because it's probably fucking hardwired into your psyche, but here it is. There's a legal concept that both British and American law share: the idea of the outlaw. Some asshole who, simply by their utter indifference to the law and how grossly they've violated not just the legal but the moral precepts of civilized society, placed themselves outside of not only the justice but also the *protection* of the law. They don't just mock the system, they mock the society that built the system, they mock that society's very existence. These aren't people with broken minds, these are people who know *exactly* what the fuck they're doing – and do it anyway. There's an old saying down in Texas, that 'Some people just need killin'. Those are the people you and I hunt down and destroy." She looked deep into his eyes, holding him in place with an intensity he'd not imagined she possessed.

"Bruce...well, Bruce spent most of his time squashing ordinary, decent criminals. Gangs, the local Mob, the occasional twisted genius who thought because he was smarter than anyone else he could ignore the laws meant for the 'little people.' But they weren't outlaws, not really, even at their worst. Bruce only ever had to face one real outlaw, Blade, *and he lost*. He lost because he could never quite take that last step and recognize that there *are* exceptions to the rules, and the outlaws are the exceptions. Bruce won't help you, Blade, because somewhere deep inside he realizes that you're willing to go where he never could, and that even when you do, you still never lose yourself. What he sees, Blade, is that you're doing the sort of job he should have been doing twenty years ago." She finally fell silent but never took her eyes off his.

"Are you finished?"

"Yes...yes, I am.

He gave her arm a squeeze of genuine affection and said, "Thanks, Maureen, I needed that. I still need that drink, too, though. Want to join me?"

"Lead on, MacLaren."

Chapter 9

"Oh, it's you again."

When he walked into the room where Compton was being held, the last thing Nakajima expected was Compton's curled lip and sneering tone. By every measure he'd ever understood of human suffering, and few people currently alive knew more about inflicting it, Compton should, by now, be well along the road to sheer, paralyzing terror, the very sight of Nakajima and the agony he could – and almost certainly would – bring with him being enough to reduce Compton to whimpering helplessness. Instead, there were still notes of defiance and disdain in his voice. Nakajima found this distinctly unsettling, although he was careful not to let his discomfiture show.

"Yes, I've returned, and I hope that you've decided to give up this pointless intransigence and tell me where I can find Blade and those storage crystals. You don't you really imagine that I'm not exploring every possible source of information available, do you? You just happen to be the most direct, I think. All the same, believe me, I don't enjoy inflicting the sort of suffering I've subjected you to. It's unprofessional." The lie came out so effortlessly and with such sincerity that most people would have taken it at face value; Compton knew better. "And you have to realize that the longer this goes on, the closer the possibility of permanent, crippling brain damage approaches to certainty. This will kill you if you persist long enough in being obstinate."

"OK, y'know, so fucking what? You've already said you're gonna kill me anyway, so what's the point? Why should I care about brain damage when you already told me you expect me to die."

"No, Mr. Compton, I expect you to talk." Nakajima sighed in apparent weariness and settled into the chair beside Compton's bed. "I made a mistake, a miscalculation. I expected that the fear of death would provide motivation for you, that knowing you're demise was inevitable would compel you to...'spill your guts,' as you Americans say, in the hope that I would find some scrap of gratitude that persuade me to let you live instead.

"The mistake I made, which I didn't recognize until I reviewed your data files this afternoon, was that I did not understanding that, for you, the prospect of dying holds no fear. *Living* is what you're truly afraid of. You view yourself as damaged goods, a potentially lethal danger to everyone about whom you care. Death would be a release, almost a redemption, for you, something devoutly to be wished. What would truly punish you for withholding that which I wish to know would be to reduce you to mental wreckage, with just enough wit remaining for you to recall why you are the way you are. A curious juxtaposition, is it not? That death is the reward, life the penalty?" He turned to the computer deck sitting on the small bedside table, and entered a few commands; suddenly every inch of Compton's body began to ache. "So. Let's begin again, 'from the top,' in the American idiom. Where are the storage crystals, and where can I find Blade?"

----------------xxxxx----------------

The interrogation continued for another thirty-five minutes, with Nakajima endlessly repeating, with subtle variations, those same two questions: where were the crystals and where was Blade? Gradually, delicately almost, he elevated the level of pain inflicted on Compton, keeping a close eye on the EKG, pulse rate, blood pressure, and temperature monitors to which the younger man was attached. It would do no good for his heart to suddenly go into arrhythmic tachycardia, or there be a stroke-inducing spike in his blood pressure, or an abrupt rise in body temperature begin inducing brain damage that might reduce Compton's ability to sense the pain. Nakajima was nothing if not a methodical sadist.

Eventually, Compton passed out yet again; this time Nakajima noted a slackening, a feebleness almost, in the way Compton thrashed his limbs about before succumbing to unconsciousness. He took that as a sign that he was slowly eroding Compton's ability to endure the pain, an indication that the young black man was giving up the struggle, was close to the breaking point.

What Nakajima never imagined was that far from giving in to the pain, Compton was reaching out to embrace it. Unknown to Nakajima, when his surgeon inserted the antenna into Compton's neural processor, the procedure accidentally disrupted a circuit in the unit, one connected to a small, replaceable module at the base of Compton's spine. That module had been implanted to release metered doses of the psychotropic cocktail which Compton required to avert the onset of cyber-psychosis directly into his bloodstream. In most cases, such medications would be introduced at four or six hour intervals: for Compton, however, his reconstruction had been so extensive, his potential for cyber-psychosis so pronounced, that when his surgeons worked on him, they had, on the advice of his psychologist, implanted a unit that triggered smaller doses at ten minute intervals.

The psychologist had feared, rightly so, that repeated spikes of medication followed by long periods of declining levels might actually aggravate the onset of a cyber-psychotic incident. It had happened before, it would happen again, and the psychologist was determined to see that it didn't happen to Compton. Instead, he posited that smaller doses at much shorter intervals, eliminating both the spikes and the hours-long tapering-off periods, would allow Compton to be far more stable emotionally. That worthy could have never imagined a scenario such as the one in which Compton now found himself, however: nearly eight hours had passed since the last traces of the medications had been purged from Compton's system, who was now teetering on the edge of a full-blown outburst of paranoia.

As consciousness returned sometime later, Compton began to gradually realize, or at least so he thought, that Nakajima's persecution of him was not an attempt to extract information, but rather was an effort at breaking him, personally. Nakajima didn't truly care as to the whereabouts of Blade or the crystals, this was all part of some sick, elaborate game of domination. Nakajima was *afraid* of him, so frightened that he felt compelled to establish his dominance over Compton, to subjugate him, before he destroyed him. The pain was simply the tool through which Nakajima would work his dominance.

All right, you Nip sonofabitch, you wanna see how pain works? You wanna find out who's top dog? Let's see you dominate this! As he finished his thought, he savagely pulled his forearms up toward his chest.

Compton was pretty certain that even Nakajima didn't know what was truly par for the course when it came to his sadistic little game, so for the last two "interrogations" he'd been taking a chance. Even when the pain was still at a level that he found tolerable – really, really uncomfortable, but tolerable, he could still think rationally if he concentrated hard enough – Compton began to subtly exaggerate his reactions, writhing a bit more than he might have, pulling hard against his chromium-steel restraints.

Contrary to what videos, comic books, computer games and role-playing systems misled generations of nerds and geeks, along with countless thousands of otherwise rational people to believe, cybernetic implants and enhancements do not confer "superpowers" on their users. Cybernetic eyes don't bestow x-ray vision, cybernetic audio implants don't allow the wearer to hear conversations taking place miles away, and cyberlimbs do not impart "superhuman" strength. No one with cyberlegs can run a two-second hundred-yard dash, or leap tall buildings in a single bound. Nor will someone with a cyberarm toss a half-mile shotput, uproot lightpoles with their bare hands, or toss around automobiles.

Molycirc – molecular circuit – muscles can give their users something approaching four times the strength of organic muscles, but just as in everything else in life, the laws of physics can't be defied or broken – nor even bent more than slightly. Mass and momentum – or mass and inertia, whichever is greater – always wins, and all the cybernetics in the world can't make an organic joint or contact point superhuman. A cyberlimb's owner's abilities are limited by the weakest link in the system, which is invariably his or her own body – bones, tendons, and ligaments – which must be able to able to cope with the torque, sheer, flex, and compression stresses imparted by the cyberlimb. Then there are the limits of the materials used to produce the limb. Even titanium alloys, long the mcguffin of choice for purveyors of cybernetic fiction, and in particular cyberpunk fiction, has its physical limits. So do nickel-martesitic steel, inconel, nanocomposite metals, and carbon-composite-based materials. All can bend, or break, or fail through abuse, misuse, or neglect. And just like their flesh and blood counterparts, they aren't invulnerable: repairing damage to cyberlimbs, almost all of which are custom-made for their user, can be just as time-consuming, expensive, and complicated as the human body's natural healing process.

But while there are damned few exceptions to the laws of physics and chemistry, there are now and again exceptional *circumstances*. And it was just such a circumstance that now presented itself to Compton. Using his elbows as the fulcrum points, he levered hard, pulling against the chains that attached his manacles to the bedrails, carefully overstressing the rails of the bed to which he was shackled. More precisely, he was straining the weld points where the various pieces of the railings were assembled. Since his reconstruction, Compton had become something of a self-taught expert on structural metals and alloys and so he'd almost immediately noticed when he'd first regained consciousness that while the chains and manacles holding him to the bed were made from a nanocomposite high-carbon steel, the rails themselves were fabricated from ordinary stainless steel. Stainless was always something of a problem child in welded steel, and usually there were flaws in the welds that if subjected to sufficient stress in the right places could be counted on to fail. In Compton's case, the very manacles which bound him worked to his advantage, allowing him to even more precisely apply the force he was bringing to bear on his restraints.

After several minutes – Compton would never know how long – he felt first one, then the other, railing begin to give. Heave, relax, heave, relax, he repeated the process over and over until fatigue set in – not on himself but on the metal rails. Almost simultaneously both welded joints failed and Compton was free. He tore the blood pressure cuff off his arm and ripped the EKG and temperature sensors away from his chest. Looking to his right, he saw Nakajima's 'deck sitting on the bedside table; in a matter of seconds he pounded it into scrap, strewing the shattered components across the room. Then he crossed to the doorway, found it locked, and crouched down beside it on the hinged side, his mind racing erratically.

We tried it your way up to now, motherfucker. Let's see how you like it my *way. No more Mister Nice Guy. You want a pissing contest? I got a pissing contest for you. I'm gonna get* you *before you have a chance to get* me. He looked around the room, hoping to spot the surveillance cameras that he knew had to be there – people like Nakajima *always* had surveillance cameras. OK, so maybe he couldn't see them, but he knew they were there – they made those bastards really, really small these days, and those goddamned Japs were good at miniaturizing electronics. Probably had microphones, too. Yeah, there'd be microphones. Eyes wide, pupils dilated, nostrils flaring, chest heaving, pulse pounding, he knew Nakajima would be coming for him. Whatever Nakajima's real grudge against him might be – and he was absolutely certain it had nothing to do with Blade or those fucking crystals, it was personal, dammit! – he'd want to settle this thing once and for all, so, yeah, Nakajima would be coming. Compton was pretty sure that he wouldn't have to wait very long.

She woke up with a splitting headache.

At first, just opening her eyes was painful enough. The overhead light shone directly down on her, and for some reason her right eye was way too sensitive to it. Gradually, mostly by either squinting or simply keeping her right eye shut, she was able to take in her bland, sterile, institutional surroundings.

What the heck am I doing in a hospital room? How did I get here? What hospital am I in? She tried to reach for the nurse's call switch that by rights should have been clipped to the sheet next to her head, and it was then that she realized she was handcuffed to the rails of the hospital bed in which she lay. That brought her up short, and she began to reassess her surroundings.

OK, this is no hospital room. For one thing, it's too big. The lights are all wrong, and so's the colour of the walls. And that ceiling! Ceilings like that went out of style twenty years ago! And why am I wearing handcuffs? Well, that much at least I can take care of right now. She calmly, carefully dislocated her left thumb and slid her hand out of the encircling steel bracelet, reset her thumb, then repeated the process for her right hand. *Amateurs!*

She then tried to sit up, and instantly regretted doing so. The room began spinning on at least three axes, and she was immediately and unexpectedly grateful for the siderails, as they kept her from rolling off the bed and onto the floor.

Whoa, there, Trish! Don't do that again! Rather more methodically this time, she gradually reached an upright position and found the world a bit more stable than it had been a few moments earlier. Not much, but a bit. She eased her legs over the side of the bed, groaning as she did so. *Holy crap, I hurt in places I never knew I had places! What the heck –?*

It was then that she remembered, sort of, the chase up through the backroads of north Georgia, the ambush on Highway 19, and the crash of Compton's bike. She recalled the sensation of flying through the air, but after that, nothing, not until she woke up here, at least.

Crap, what about Gerry? I remember flying straight toward a ditch, there must have been enough soft debris and ground cover to cushion my landing, but what happened to Gerry? Looking down at herself she realized that she was still wearing the same blue jumpsuit she'd had on at the time of the ambush, and that her cuts and scratches, of which there were many, hadn't been treated in any way. *So I was right: this* isn't *a hospital. This is what somebody thought a hospital room should look like after watching too many straight-to-streaming movies, and they're doing this for some sort of effect. So, where am I and why am I here?*

At least it didn't require rocket science to figure out *who* brought her to this place, wherever it was. Arasaka. Of that much she could be certain. Then it struck her. The crystals! Oh my God, that's why I'm here! They want to find out about the crystals. They must have been waiting for me to regain consciousness. Which means some Arasaka goon could come walking through that door any minute. In an instant, her situation took on a whole new level of urgency.

Her vision was improving, slightly, although the right eye still wasn't focusing properly and remained far too sensitive to the light. She also felt, well, a bit woozy, as she called it, almost as if she were drunk. That was something she never enjoyed, as she had no head for alcohol. Her friends never let her forget that party at Gitmo, where, after just two glasses of champagne she was up dancing on the table. Fighting off the nausea and dizziness, she began to take a larger inventory of her surroundings, noting a pair of classically institutional chairs by the side of the bed, along with what the decorator must have deemed to be the stereotypical bedside table. On it lay her deck, the top obviously bashed in, no doubt by a rifle butt. *Dammit! Dammit! Dammit! Why is it every time I finally get a deck tricked out exactly the way I want, some bullet-headed, jackbooted thug has to try and bust it up? Or if it isn't a cop, it's some two-bit punk looking to score a quick snatch-and-grab.* At that, her fingers twitched involuntarily as they sought to fit the grips of the BERSA semi-automatic she usually carried, but that, of course, was gone.

With a sigh, she half-slid, half-slithered over to the chair closest to the small table, and as she did so the pain in her head spiked sharply. Reflexively she raised her hand to her temple, then cried out in pain as her fingertips touched her skin. Gingerly exploring the right side of her face, she realized that much of it was one massive bruise. *That explains the wooziness and the vision problems. Radome, my girl, you've most likely got yourself a concussion. I guess the landing wasn't as soft as I thought. Thank God I was wearing a helmet!*

Once the pain subsided, she began examining her deck. It was of a type called a "combat deck," built to milspecs and extremely rugged. At some point someone had tried to boot it but failed: her basic encryption key was sitting in one in the pair of key slots on the side of the deck. Somebody had gone through her pockets and found it. But her system required two separate keys, and whoever tried booting it had been thwarted when the deck failed to cooperate. *That probably explains why the top's been smashed in,* she thought. *Somebody got frustrated and threw a hissy fit.* A half-smile crossed her face as she very gingerly reached down inside her left boot and drew out the second key from a tiny, velcro-sealed patch on the *inside* of the boot's upper. Barely a half-inch square and less than a quarter of that thick, the key was undetectable unless her boots were removed and examined very carefully. From the bits of dried leaves and mud still caked on the laces, she was certain that wasn't the case.

Within seconds the deck was powered up, though it was most definitely in poor health. At least two-fifths of the screen was completely dead, despite having been made of top-of-the-line armoured flexiglass, and that part of the display which still worked flickered ominously. She thought she caught a whiff of ozone and fervently hoped she was wrong. *Just let me get to the POST screen*, she prayed fervently, hoping that St. Cappello Rosso, the patron of computer geeks, was listening. *OK, c'mon, baby, c'mon! Aaaannnnd – gotcha! Now, run the fastest damn diagnostic cycle you've ever run, baby!*

That faint hint of ozone wasn't quite as faint as it was a few minutes earlier, and Radome reached into her right boot and pulled out a small multi-tool. Fingers flying even as she was shaking her head to clear her vision, she had the back panel of the deck open in seconds, and quickly scanned the components.

"Definitely ozone," she muttered, "but where?" Leaning closer, she realized the smell was coming from the display screen. "OK, that's not good. Come on, baby, tell mommy what she needs to know!" Her fingertips drummed impatiently on the tabletop as she waited for the diagnostics to finish their test cycle. Finally, the report began scrolling across the screen, although she had to keep using the touch-pad to move the image back and forth out of the dead space on the display.

Power cell is at 18 percent...what the hell *drained it so fast? Uh-oh, two compartments in the cell have been compromised, that explains it. I've got one cell left. Half my memory isn't working, or at least it isn't talking to the rest of the machine, and – shit! I thought these solid state drives were supposed to be unbreakable! Milspec, my ass! Somebody's gonna get a very strongly-worded letter about this when I get out of here. Wireless...wireless.... Oh, damn!*

The transmitter in her wireless strip was showing as fully functional, but the receiver tell-tale kept flickering between "on" and "off." As soon as she'd realized she could power-up the deck, she'd been counting on using the wireless to call somebody for help: concussed, lost, and unarmed, there wasn't a whole lot she could do on her own other than sit tight and hope the cavalry came charging over the hill. She could still try to reach out and touch someone, but if the receiver failed, she'd never know if the message got through.

Even so, she had little choice – well, really, she had no choice. The flickering on the display was growing more pronounced, and she was down to 16 percent power. *Get on with it, girl. You have no idea when somebody's gonna stick their nose in here, and if you futz around much longer, you won't have enough power to be able to put out a signal strong enough to be picked up across the street. OK, let's be about it, then.*

Radome didn't know it, but at that moment Fortune was smiling on her. Her wireless signal was just strong enough to reach through the walls of the building where she was trapped to a hot spot in a Stubb's coffee shop two blocks away. No sooner had she established the connection than she began entering a comm combination – her deck's VOIP was shot, collateral damage, she assumed, to the battering the display had taken.

Of all the comm combinations she knew – and she knew hundreds if not thousands of them – there was only one that she could recall just then. A product of the concussion no doubt, and she fervently hoped her memory wouldn't suffer any long-term effects, but she also knew that the one code she did remember was enough. The instant the connection opened, she started typing, hoping that, despite the dead key clusters on her keyboard the recipient could make some sense of what she sent...

RVN, IT' RDOME. I DON'T KNOW HR I M, SO IF YOU CN, PLESE LOCT THE IGNL OURCE, I'LL B CLOE BY. DCK I DMGED CNNOT RECEIVE. RSK H ME, I DON'T KNO HR COMPTON I, BUT I'M PRTTY URE TIME I RUNNING OUT. ND TH CVLRY. HURRY.

Time to get the hell out of Dodge while the gettin's good, she thought, breaking the connection and tucking her deck under one arm. *Somebody screwed up big time by not permanently disabling my deck. Now let's see what else these gumballs got wrong.*

She crossed over to the door, which was more of a challenge than she expected it to be; the concussion was definitely affecting her equilibrium. Leaning against the wall for support, she gave the lock a quick once-over, and snorted in disgust. *A standard Japanese-made MIKAWA electronic lock. Really, guys? Really? Yeah, it would be a major obstacle to most people, but for yours loveable truly? Puh-leeze!*

Carefully setting her deck on the floor, she whipped off her belt and popped the snaps by the buckle. Two short, gleaming copper stubs greeted her eyes. She pulled on both of them, extracting two bare 16 gauge copper wires, each twenty-four inches long, then turned her attention to the lock plate on the inside of the door. Apart from the manufacturer's name laser-etched on the face, the plate was featureless, but it wasn't really the plate Radome was interested in. She was focused on the seams where the edges of the plate met the face of the door. With an assurance born of long practice, she eased one end of the first wire under the bottom edge of faceplate, then repeated the process with the second wire, this time on the left hand edge of the lock plate.

She picked up her deck, turned it upside down, and, muttering "Tampering by unauthorized personnel invalidates the manufacturer's warranty" as she did so, slid the loose ends of the wires into a pair of tiny, unassuming holes in the bottom of the deck. A muted "fffzzzzt" and a hint of smoke issued from the edges of the lockplate, followed by a very satisfying "thunk" as the bolt slid open. She rose to her feet, dug her nails into the gap between the lock plate and door face, and pulled. The door swung open easily, causing her to almost lose her balance. She shook her head and murmured, "You guys really should have bought American," reached down for her deck, then as quickly as she could on unsteady feet, edged out into the awaiting hallway.

Here goes nothing! Best get that cavalry moving ASAP, Raven, because I really don't wanna die here!

---------------XXXXX---------------

Blade was sleeping the sleep of the just, or at least the thoroughly sated. Dinner had been memorable – and the food had been pretty darn good, too, although for the rest of his life, Blade would never be able to recall a single dish that was served.

What *had* left an indelible impression – and memory – was that moment when he saw Maureen descending the staircase from the second floor of the east wing. She was more than just beautiful, she was breathtaking. She had unquestionably chosen to disregard Mansfield's indulgence in regard to dressing for dinner, and appeared wearing a floor-length, backless dress of emerald green, cut to emphasize her slender figure so that it looked as if it had been molded to her body. Her neck was circled by a single strand of pearls, her earrings were single-pearl studs, her make up muted but flawless. MacLaren smiled to himself as he realized that in the green pumps that matched her dress, she was easily six inches taller than he. *You know*, he mused, *there's something intriguing about a woman you have to look up to.*

"I suppose I don't have to tell ye how beautiful ye look," he said, offering up his most charming smile and his left arm as she reached the bottom of the stairs. The whiff of Chanel's "Allure" that he caught as she approached made the image perfect, in his opinion.

"No, you don't have to, not really, but it's nice to hear anyway. And I have to admit, Blade, that you clean up pretty well yourself."

She had a point. MacLaren had brought his regimental mess dress with him, and now stood in scarlet mess jacket, complete with shoulder boards and miniatures, Black Watch tartan kilt (with rosettes!), sporran, skein dubh, diced red hose and black buckled brogues. *Some men can wear the kilt, others can't*, Maureen reflected, *and he definitely can. Somehow, I think he knows that....*

Blade cocked a wry eyebrow at her. "Let me guess. Ye just *happened* to find that in your luggage?"

She let out a throaty laugh. "No, I didn't. And I don't play the 'What? This old thing?' game either. I brought it with me because before I told Johann von Poslien where he could put his protection contract, I knew there was at least one dinner party on the schedule where I would have to show up wearing a full-length dress."

"Right then, you came well-briefed and well-prepared."

"No, no briefs, not in this."   She burst out laughing at MacLaren's double-take at her remark. "Gawd! You're blushing!"

Composing himself as best and as quickly as he could, he replied, "I have to admit I have absolutely no idea where you could hide your sidearm. I mean, you said it was a protection contract."

"Oh, you might be surprised what happens when a girl decides she needs to resourceful, MacLaren. Besides, I'm very good at *aikido*."

"I see the two of you are already enjoying yourselves."

The voice came from above and behind them, and Maureen and MacLaren wheeled together to face the speaker. Both stared for a long second, then their jaws dropped in unison. If Maureen looked gorgeous, and she did, Scarlett looked spectacular. She wore a deep amethyst off-the-shoulder dress, trimmed in black velvet, that sported a rather intriguing cut up each side; her shoes matched the accent on the dress. Her auburn hair had been brushed until it all but glowed and fell across her left shoulder; scarlet lip gloss added a touch of 1940's Hollywood glamor. She took in their expressions and allowed an amused expression to play across her features as she descended the stairs with a sinuous (and sensuous, Blade allowed to himself) grace.

"But where...?" Maureen asked.

"But how...?" MacLaren asked.

Scarlett smiled mischievously at their discomfiture.   "Mrs. Mansfield, if you must know. She came to my room a couple of hours ago and handed me the dress, shoes, and a cosmetics case. She said 'It's my daughter's, she left it here when she went back to England for the summer, and since she and you favour each other in height and figure, I thought we could put it to good use.'"

Maureen looked at MacLaren. "Makes sense. She is British

Intelligence, and you people do have a reputation for being resourceful."

"I know – I just never guessed *how* resourceful." Addressing Scarlett directly, he said, "I've never really regarded ye as an eyesore exactly, ye understand, but until now I didn't fully comprehend what a remarkable-looking woman ye are." He offered her his free arm. "Now that we've all had our wash-and-brush-up, why don't the two of you dazzle them in the dining room and I'll just bask in yer reflected glory."

Scarlett giggled. "Fine by me. Spazz?"

"Lead on, MacLaren."

MacLaren was no stranger to the company of lovely women – anyone who ever met Ligeia could attest to that – and had Maureen been his sole dinner companion he would have been hard put to recall any time he had been in such beautiful company. Seated at table across from Maureen with Scarlett to his right, though, he could have been forgiven if he'd imagined that he'd died and gone to heaven. As formal dinners went, this one was a rather simple affair of only seven courses, though everyone at the table seemed inclined to linger over each one. For a few comparatively brief hours, and the first time since he'd met either woman, Blade felt truly relaxed in their company, as they laughed and chatted their way from the consommé to the port. Even the redoubtable Ms. Mansfield dropped her façade of formal reserve and fully joined in the conversation, as did her four section chiefs; by an unspoken mutual consent, no one talked shop.

It was almost midnight when, the loyal toast having been drunk and the last glass of the Semillon consumed, the three of them made their way upstairs again. At Scarlett's door, she and Maureen exchanged the obligatory air kisses, while Blade simply took her hand – and perhaps held a bit longer than was absolutely necessary before she said her last goodnight and closed the door. Sauntering to the door of Maureen's bedroom, they stood in a moment of wordless silence, then Maureen startled him when she leaned forward and planted a quick kiss on his cheek. Her eyes were laughing at him when she said, "Good night, MacLaren. It was lovely. Maybe you're not such a complete barbarian after all."

He mock-glowered at her. "Ye, Miss Collins, are a lot of trouble."

"You have no idea...."

"Goodnight, Maureen."

"Good night." Her door closed quickly and quietly.

A dozen strides later, Blade was closing the door to his room behind him. He leaned against it for a moment, shook his head, and muttered. "A lot of trouble, indeed."

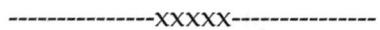

Blade woke up instantly, the shrill, atonic sound of the Royal Navy's Emergency Action Stations alarm shrieking from the comm-link beside his bed. No one could ever sleep through that piercing, nerve-scraping sound, and so after the first time he'd heard it while on detached duty with the Royal Marines, he'd adopted it as his own personal wake up call in emergencies. Few people knew how to activate it; those who did knew precisely when to use it.

Slapping at the alarm, he slipped the earbud into place, then said, "Call accepted. Who is it"

"David, it's Raven. There's no time to waste on preliminaries. Radome's alive. Compton may be. And I know where they are."

Blade slid out of the bed, already reaching for the battledress that the Blackbriar staff had laundered for him. "Keep talking, Raven. I'll listen while I get kitted out."

"I got a text from her not three minutes ago. It says, 'Raven, it's Radome. I don't know where I am, so if you can, please locate the signal source, I'll be close by. Deck is damaged, cannot receive. Arasaka has me, I don't know where Compton is, but I'm pretty sure time is running out. Send the cavalry. Hurry.'"

"Right then, where is she?"

"She's in southeast Atlanta, a section called Bragg Park. I've got the exact location pretty well pinned down. The comm came through a hot spot in a coffee shop, but if she was there, she wouldn't be calling for help like this. I'm convinced she's in an old unused office building two blocks away."

"Why do ye think so?"

"Because according to Atlanta city tax records, that building has been unoccupied and unused for the past three years. It's the only 'unoccupied' building in a four block radius of that hot spot, and Radome's deck doesn't have the power to reach outside that radius."

"So it might be one of Arasaka's 'clean sites'?"

"I can't guarantee it, but I'd say that's the way to bet."

"Is it a trap, d'ye think?"

"I honestly don't know – but can you afford to assume that it is and ignore it?"

"Not a chance in hell. I got the two of them into trouble, and like I told Hobbes, it's my responsibility to get them out. I'm going to commandeer a motorcar, have Alistair feed me the GPS once I'm on the road, will ye? While you're at it, wake Spazz and tell her to saddle up."

"And Red – er, Scarlett?"

"No, I'd rather keep her out of the line of fire if I can."

"David...." There was a distinct cautionary note in Ligeia's voice.

"Look, Ligeia, I have my reasons, and they're not what ye might think they are, all right?"

"If you say so."

"I do. Tell Spazz she's got five minutes."

Four minutes and forty-nine seconds later, there was a knock on Blade's door. When he opened it, he found Maureen standing there in high-laced black boots, denim jeans, a dark gray wooly-pully, and a matching hunting vest. Her holstered Korth was strapped to her waist, and she was holding what looked to be a cut-down 12-gauge shotgun in her right hand.

"How the hell did ye" – he began. She cut him off in mid-question.

"Your fucking alarm woke me up, dammit," she said reproachfully. "I started getting dressed as soon as I heard it, because a goddamned noise like that can only mean trouble. Then Raven called me and told me I had five minutes to get ready, we're going into action. So here I am."

"Damn."

"She also told me that we're going to try to rescue Radome and maybe Compton, if he's still alive. Those are good people, Blade, and like you, I don't want to leave 'em behind."

"Right ye are." He buckled his utility belt, slipped into his shoulder harness, adjusted his ruck, made sure the SIG was securely seated in its holster, picked on his SMLE, and finished by plopping a dark blue beret-style hat on his head.

"A Balmoral? Red dingle-ball and all?"

"The 'dingle-ball' is called a 'toorie,' and this is the best way I know to make sure ye know it's me in poor light." He nodded at the shotgun she was cradling, an Ithaca Model 37. "Helps keep ye from blowing my head off by accident with street howitzer of yers."

"OK, I'll concede the point. Are you ready?"

"I am. Let's go find some transportation."

They were halfway down the corridor when Scarlett came out of her room, dressed in khaki drill trousers and shirt.

"Let me guess: ye heard the alarm, too." Blade made no effort to hide his exasperation.

"I did, and I'm going with you!"

"No, Scarlett, ye're not."

She started to protest, but Blade cut her off with a decisive shake of his head, his tone of voice adamant. "No, ye're not. It's for yer own good, lass. From what little bits and pieces ye were able to tell me about yerself, I suspect that somebody – probably DisCom – had something very bad in mind for you, something I don't even want to think about at the moment. Ye were likely going to be a guinea pig, probably in one of their bionetics programs. I know it sounds absurd, but if ye spend thirty seconds thinking about the sort of rabbit hole we've fallen down in the last two days, 'absurd' and 'impossible' aren't exactly synonymous, now, are they?"

"You know he's right, Scarlett." Spazz was most emphatic in support of Blade. "And not just about DisCom. You're the last person a corp like Arasaka, or somebody like that sick bastard Nakajima, should ever get their hands on. And I suspect that Blade here has an ulterior motive: I'll bet he thinks it would be nice if you had a chance to find out who you really are before you go getting your cute little ass – which, by the way, I think I'm jealous of – blown off. I happen to agree with him."

"But" –

"'But' me no 'buts' on this, Scarlett," Blade's voice was unexpectedly gentle. "I've put enough people in harm's way on this job, and I'm not putting anyone else there."

"Then explain why Spazz is going with you."

"Defective mental equipment – she volunteered." He held up an admonishing hand. "And before ye tell me ye're volunteering, this is me telling ye that I'm 'unvolunteering' ye on this."

"And if he wouldn't, I would," Spazz affirmed.

Scarlett looked from Spazz to Blade and back, and said, "The two of you intend to be stubborn about this, don't you?"

"We do," they replied in chorus.

"All right, I'll stay behind. But I'm warning you: as soon as I can figure out who to file it with, I'm filing a complaint!"

"Wouldn't expect any less of you," Spazz replied, grinning.

"I'll have Alistair keep ye updated." Blade assured her, then looked at Spazz. "Now that that's settled, let's get started."

The Charge of Quarters, a tall, middle-aged, impressively-mustachioed chap who had "retired Brigade of Guards sergeant" written all over him, was sitting at a small desk in an alcove off the side of the entrance foyer. He stood as Blade and Spazz approached, coming close but not quite snapping to attention; Blade had to work hard to suppress a smile.

"How can I help you, sir!" Somehow the way the man said it, the words clipped and correct, made it more of a statement than a query.

"Charge, we need a car and we need it now. It's literally life or death."

"I can see that just by looking at you, sir," he replied, with a nod toward Blade's SMLE and Spazz's Ithaca. He pulled open a side drawer in his desk and produced a key fob. "Here you are, sir. Just around the corner to the left maybe twenty yards, there's a lovely Jaguar Mk 12. Two-tone grey. I believe she'll be just the ticket for you."

"Fast?"

"The usual Company mods, sir. Fast and quiet."

"That'll do. My thanks, Charge." Turning to Spazz, he said, "Let's roll."

They found the Jaguar exactly where the Charge of Quarters said it would be. They settled in and Blade started the motor, then he looked carefully at Spazz.

"Ye're sure ye want to do this? I realize I sort of 'volunteered' ye for this, and I really shouldn't have done that. So I'm offering ye an out if ye want it."

"Blade, I could have said 'no' when Raven called me. *I* came to *your* door, if I remember correctly. I'm in."

"Just so ye understand that we're all by our lonesome this time. There won't be any cavalry coming to the rescue if things get well and truly buggered up."

"Look, we're wasting time. According to the GPS, it's twenty-two miles to Bragg Park...."

"We've a full tank of petrol...."
"I've got a half-pack of cigarettes...."
"I've got three cigars...."
"It's dark and you've got night vision."
"Let's hit it."

---------------XXXXX---------------

Aiko Kurita glared out from the computer monitor, her expression grim, her eyes hard set in anger, her lips a taut, almost invisible line slashed across her face. It was, Hideki Nakajima admitted to himself, the most frightening visage he hd ever seen, all the more so because he was the focus of her fury.

"Nakajima-san, I have neither the time nor the patience to waste on the usual circumlocutions and formalities." Sitting in her office in Kagoshima, she idly swung back and forth in her chair. "The American *gaijun* have a wonderfully vulgar turn of phrase that describes your situation perfectly: you have 'screwed the pooch,' as they say, 'by the numbers.'"

Nakajima, who was standing facing the monitor, bowed low. "Kurita-sama, I assure you that is not so. I have been scrupulously faithful in carrying out your instructions, and success is almost within our grasp! The *gaijun* Compton is very near the breaking point, and he *will* tell me where I can find the storage crystals. Even if he does not, we have the other gaijun, the one they call Radome, who we can begin interrogating as soon as she regains consciousness." He bowed again, this time a little lower than before. "I simply need a little more time."

"Oh, please, Hideki, if you're going to act like some overly-obsequious minion, first buy some yellow face paint and a pair of goggles. Those crystals are no longer the issue – in fact, our employers have decided they have no use for them. I don't pretend to understand all of the technical details – computer people do so love their jargon and cant – but the gist of it is that there is a fundamental danger in what the program they carry is designed to do, a danger so grave that no one wants to touch it. The *Yanki Jigyo* is terminated."

"But...but...how? Why?"

"'How' and 'why' are questions you need no longer ask. I'm formally notifying you, both in my capacity as a member of the Board of Directors of Arasaka Corporation, and in my...other persona...that your operations in North America are to be closed down, immediately, and you personally are to return to Kagoshima as soon as transportation out of the United States can be arranged. Once here in Kagoshima, you will report to me, and explain why you have dishonoured me as well as yourself by deliberately disobeying my orders."

Nakajima's mouth gaped like that of a landed fish as he struggled to frame a reply. Finally he blurted out, "What do you mean, 'disobeyed your orders'?"

"Please, Hideki, are you really so stupid as to think you are my only source of information about our operations in the United States?" Scorn practically dripped from Aiko's voice. "I seem to recall strictly charging you to take care of my nephew, Tomiyashi Yashida. And yet I was given written confirmation not twenty minutes ago that one of the four AV pilots we lost yesterday was my own Tomiyashi. That was a mistake, Nakajima-san, a very bad one. But what makes it even worse, makes it a mistake for which your life will be forfeit, is that he died *while trying to kill David MacLaren*!" She shot up out of her chair like a striking snake, and Nakajima recoiled from her image in spite of himself.

"He died trying to kill Blade – on your orders! You defied me, Nakajima! You openly defied my explicit instructions!" Aiko was shrieking like a harpy now. "I explained to you that our organization has plans for him – he's the sacrificial piece in a gambit that's only begun to play. And you, with your overblown ego and obsessive hatred of the man, almost undermined the whole strategy, because you so desperately want to kill him yourself!" Nakajima had no idea how much of Kurita's tirade was honour and how much was genuine anger, but he was disinclined to count on it being much of the former. "The *gaijun* have another phrase, one which describes you perfectly, Nakajima. 'A loose cannon.' That is what you have well and truly become: you're dangerous not only to yourself and your underlings but to your superiors as well. I do not – *do not!* – care about what happens to your *reisen*, they were born to be expended. I do not – *do not!* – care all that much about you if your own stupidity gets you killed. But I will *not* make any more excuses for you with our superiors or protect you any longer."

"Kurita-sama, I can" –

"*Shut up!* Don't you dare interrupt me! You may speak to me only when I say so!" Aiko drew a deep breath and visibly struggled to regain her usual composure. When she finally spoke again, her voice could have created icebergs in the open ocean. "You have no idea, Nakajima, of how disruptive the sort of self-indulgence in which you seem to revel has become for us. I have neither the time nor the crayons to explain it all to you, but I will tell you this: had you succeeded in having MacLaren killed you would have undone years of patient work in both Europe and America. You have exhausted my patience and my good will, Hideki. I will expect you in my office within twenty-four hours. Bring your *tanto*." Nakajima sucked in a breath, hissed sharply as he did so, at the last three words, but Aiko cut the connection before he could respond. For several seconds he stood motionless, staring with unseeing eyes at the blank monitor, then he collected himself and turned to Umori, who had overheard the entire conversation.

"Well, *Fukuro*, it seems that I am disgraced. Not just personally and privately, but openly and officially. Dishonoured by my own lack of self-control and that *gaijun* bastard, Blade. I am to close down all of my operations here in America and return to Dai

Nippon immediately."

"I heard it all, Nakajima-sama." Umori stood and offered a bow of genuine respect, then faced Nakajima squarely with an expression of defiance. Not of Nakajima, but of whatever fate awaited him. Though he could never say as much, Nakajima was profoundly touched by the younger man's display of loyalty. *He, at least, has learned what it means to be* samurai. The thought gave Nakajima a surprising measure of satisfaction.

"What are your instructions, Nakajima-sama?"

"Find the others, tell them that Compton – and that woman, Radome – are of no further use to us and are to be executed immediately. If our people have any personal equipment they want to take with them, they must collect it immediately and then leave the building. Once you've confirmed that the two *gaijun* are dead, start the timers and evacuate yourself. You know where to go. I want to be well away from here when the fire rises."

"I will make it so, Nakajima-sama!"

Compton heard doors opening and closing somewhere in the building, then the approaching sound of at least two sets of footsteps. Mingled anxiety and anticipation as they drew closer made him suddenly aware of how utterly exhausted he was; he'd been running on adrenaline for far too long already, and Nakajima's little torture fests had drained him even further. The tank was almost empty, as it were, but before it ran dry, he was going to get out of this...this...*place*, wherever and whatever it was, and fuck up a few Arasakas in the process. The footsteps stopped at the door to what he had come to think of as his cell.

OK, right, you bastards, time to party hearty!

With a loud "clunk" the door unlocked and swung open. The first Arasaka sashayed in, holding a large-caliber semi-automatic at his side, looking toward the now-vacant bed. In the half-second it took for the *reisen* to realize that it was empty, Compton burst from his crouch, driving his shoulder into the door, catching the second reisen as he was halfway through it. There was a satisfying *crunch* as the *reisen*'s head, turned at an awkward angle, was caught between the edge of the door and the doorjamb, simultaneously crushing his occiput and caving in the right side of his face. The first *reisen* began to turn toward Compton, who was already reaching for him. Clamping the Arasaksa's right hand in his own, Compton launched a straight left that simultaneously dislocated and broke the man's jaw. Out on his feet, the *reisen* took one involuntary step forward then collapsed face-down on the floor. Compton didn't hesitate, leaping into the air and bringing both feet down on the unconscious reisen's skull, the heels of his boots reducing the head to a misshapen lump.

"How'd you like that, meatjob?"

Stooping, Compton snatched up the *reisen*'s pistol, a Glock 54 – "You won't mind if I borrow this, will you? I mean, you won't be needing it for a while, y'know?" – quickly checked the body for spare magazines, found none. Turning to the other Arasaka, he performed a similar search, found an identical Glock, a which he stuck in his waistband, and discovered that this *reisen* at least had the sense to carry a second magazine as well. Compton noted that the man was still breathing, barely, and for a split second thought about finishing what the door had started.

"Nah, you're as good as dead anyway," he muttered. "Better save the ammo."

Easing his head out into the corridor, he looked left, then right, saw no one else, and mentally tossed a coin as to which way to go. Left, he decided. The lighting was dim, with only perhaps one in five of the overhead lamps illuminated. It took only a few moments to realize that the building's floor plan was square, with two parallel corridors, perhaps eighty yards long, running the full length of the building, flanked on both sides by offices and cubicle galleries. Two shorter right-angled corridors connected them, flanking the central core of the building, which enclosed four elevator shafts and, presumably, the HVAC ducting.

Once he knew the tactical situation and confirmed that he was alone on the floor, Compton walked rather than ran toward the end of one of the long corridors, where a window awaited him. Running when no one was shooting at you was, he knew, a really bad idea – all it took was one foot-fart and you were flat on your face with your ass in the air. Reaching the window, he looked out as he pressed himself against the wall – no FNG-like silhouetting himself in the window for Mama Compton's baby boy, thank you very much – and took in as much of the view as he could.

What he saw wasn't encouraging: he estimated that he was six or seven stories above ground level, and he didn't immediately recognize the skyline, which left him with no idea where he was. He couldn't even be certain he was still in Atlanta; for that matter, he realized, he also didn't know what day of the week it was. At least he knew now that it was nighttime, but that was all.

OK, so I'm, like, seventy-five or eighty feet above ground. So much for slipping away into the night, y'know? Then again, since that also means I'm probably gonna have to fight my way out of here, that just gives me more opportunities to dance with some Arasakas, maybe even Nakajima himself. Works for me! Start the music! Now, where's the goddamn stairs?

----------------xxxxx----------------

Holy crap! I must be at least eight floors up!

The thought caused Radome some trepidation, even while it gave her some measure of relief, as it resolved some tactical dilemmas for her. She had to get out of the building, that much was clear: hanging about waiting for the cavalry to arrive in a building that belonged to the bad guys qualified as Very Bad Idea. So, she had to get down to ground level, outside, and hope whoever Raven was able to send her way could find her there. That, of course, meant either taking an elevator, or negotiating the emergency stairs.

OK, so I know taking the elevator is never a good idea when there're gomers around, but there's no way I can face eight flights of stairs when I can barely see straight and my equilibrium is out of whack. I'm just gonna have to hope I get damn lucky, I guess.

With that, she returned to the pair of elevators she'd passed only a moment or so earlier. She felt a wash of relief come over her when she pushed the call button, saw it light up, and heard a motor spin up somewhere above her. A fifth – maybe a quarter, if she was feeling generous – of the ceiling lights were working, in no discernable pattern, which she took to be the consequence of neglect rather than a deliberate decision on somebody's part. The building smelled old and unused, and most of the rooms which she'd found unlocked were completely devoid of contents or furnishings.

The elevator's arrival was announced by a rather anemic *ding*, and the direction indicator on the doorframe seemed dim. She was relieved to find the lights on in the elevator car when the doors groaned opened. The floor selection button started at "1," immediately jumped to "6," then ran consecutively to "12." *Split level access. This must have been one busy place once upon a time.* Noting that she was indeed on the eighth floor, Radome pushed the first floor button. The doors wheezed closed and the car began its descent.

The trip was short, however. Upon reaching the sixth floor, the car stopped, and despite Radome's repeated stabs at the ground-level button, refused to budge further. Buildings that sit long unused slowly decay, their internal workings succumbing to neglect; such was the case with the building she found herself in. Whatever mechanisms or contacts were supposed to keep the car descending further were no longer working. The doors finally opened and, realizing she had no real choice about it, Radome stepped out of the elevator. Realizing that there had to be another set of elevators that accessed the lower levels, and thinking there would likely be some overlap in the floors served by both sets, she began walking around to the other side of the building's central shaft, which held not only supported the elevator shafts, but was also the building's structural spine. Coming around the last corner, she literally walked right into Compton.

She didn't realize it actually was Compton at first, but as she recoiled from her impact with his solidly built chest and was on her way to planting her backside on the floor, she recognized him, and had just enough time – and presence of mind – to call out as he brought the muzzle of the semi-automatic he was holding to bear on her.

"Compton! Gerry! It's me – Trish! You know, Radome!"

The handgun snapped up to the vertical. "Radome, Jesus! You were, like, y'know, about seven pounds of pressure away from a better world. Or at least a different one." He held out a hand and helped her to her feet. "They told me you were dead!"

"Yeah, well, the rumors of my recent demise et cetera, et cetera. A bit worse for the wear, mind you. I'm pretty sure I've got a concussion, I'm not seeing so good out of my right eye, and my balance is off." Taking him in with a quick up-and-down glance, Radome noted the wide, wild eyes that were constantly flicking here, there, and everywhere, the even twitchier demeanor, and the manifest exhaustion. She'd seen the symptoms before and knew he was well down the road into cyber-psychosis, with the throttle wide open. "On the other hand, compared to you, I'm in great shape. I hate to break this to you, Gerry, but you look like hell."

"Yeah, OK, well, I feel like hell, too. Nakajima's come up with a new method of torture that makes you feel like you've been waterboarded, racked, hung, drawn, quartered, electrocuted, flayed alive, and burned at the stake all at the same time."

"You mean he made you watch old Hillary Clinton speeches?"

"Worse."

"I didn't think that was possible. Wait a minute. Nakajima's here – in the building?"

"Yeah, he is. Him and some of his flunkies, y'know? Although there isn't quite as many as there was a while ago, as the song says. I took down two of them busting out of my cell, OK? A very satisfying experience it was, too."

Radome didn't like the sound of that – it wasn't the Compton she was used to – so she changed the subject. "You can tell me about it later. Right now, though, we gotta get out of here."

"Yeah, OK, right, it would kinda help if we where 'here' is, y'know? I got no idea where we are."

Radome pointed down the corridor. "If you look out that window you can see the Atlanta skyline. From the look of it, we're somewhere south of the city, between the Perimeter and Hartsfield."

"Oh." Compton pointed in the opposite direction. "OK. I looked out *that* window, and didn't recognize anything."

"No biggie. What's important is that I was able to send out an SOS." For the first time since the ambush, Radome actually smiled.

"Really? I mean, like, I know you're supposed to be a miracle worker and all that, but how?"

She tapped the deck she was still clutching to her chest. "Somebody tried to bash it in after they tried to hack it and failed, but I was able to get it up and running for a few minutes. I got a message out to Raven."

"Raven? You mean, like, Blade's Raven?"

"Yep! If Blade himself isn't coming, you can damn betcha somebody is. That woman draws a lot of water."

"I think it helps to know where all the bodies are buried, y'know, especially when you helped Blade put 'em there. How long, d'ya think?"

"Oh, a half-hour, maybe forty-five minutes."

"Good. Just enough time to take care of a few more Arasakas, y'know?"

As if in response, the elevator by which they were standing dinged and the doors slid open, revealing a pair of *reisen*. Compton leveled his pistol even as he was shoving Radome back around the corner, and squeezed off a quartet of shots, putting two rounds into the head of each Arasaka. Yet before the bodies had slumped to the floor, the doors to the second elevator opened, and four more reisen appeared. They began firing even as they crossed the elevator threshold, forcing Compton to duck around the corner himself. Fumbling in his waistband, he produced the other Glock and handed it to Radome, saying, "Hey, watch my six, OK?" then popped two shots around the corner, just to keep the Arasakas honest. A minor fusillade of bullets answered him.

"I told you I can't see all that well right now!" Radome shouted.

"Don't worry about it. We stay back-to-back, so if it's in front of you, it ain't me, y'know, so just aim centre mass, OK? That'll be good enough for government work!" He took a quick glance around the corner, just in time to see one of the *reisen* make a move toward one of the empty offices across the corridor. He snapped off two more shots and the man went down hard and stayed down. He heard Radome rip off five or six shots of her own and knew he'd been right – the Arasakas had split up and tried to flank them from behind.

"How many did you get?"

"Two."

"So that means there's just one left. OK, I got this." He stood up, leveling his pistol, holding it at full extension, and stepped around the corner. The remaining *reisen* squeezed off a single shot, which barely missed Compton's head, but came close enough to nick his right ear. His hand flew up to the side of his head and came away red.

"OW! That hurt, motherfucker!"

The *reisen*, seeing the slide on his pistol locked back on a empty magazine, desperately tried to reload. He never had a chance.

Compton grimly put two bullets into the groin of the hapless *reisen*, who collapsed with a shriek of agony.

"*Anata wa chodo watashi no kogan o ofushotto!*" the man screamed.

"OK, yeah, like, I'm not sure, but I think that was Nip-speak for 'You just blew my fuckin' balls off,' right? Well, Happy Chinese New Year, motherfucker!" Compton's Glock barked one more time before he turned to face a horrified Radome. "What? It's not like he didn't deserve it!"

Radome was no stranger to violence, obviously, but the sheer unmitigated malice and sadism of Compton's action appalled her, and she physically recoiled as he approached her.

"Hey, relax! I'm not gonna hurt *you*, OK? I'm just settling a couple of scores, y'know?" Radome looked dubious and Compton shook his head in resignation as he rifled two of the bodies for spare magazines and was rewarded with one from each. "OK, whatever. Look, let's just find the emergency stairs and get the hell out of here. I can, like, help you keep your balance, y'know? I think Arasaka's just demonstrated that the elevators aren't a viable option for us."

The emergency stairs were at the end of the opposite corridor, so they moved as quickly as they could – Radome found herself leaning on Compton a bit more than she really wished – to the other side of the building and down to the end of the corridor. There they found an expanse of glass identical to all of the other corridor ends on the floor, but to the left of it was the doorway to the emergency stairwell. Compton hit the release bar and shoved his shoulder hard against the door, to no avail.

"Shit! What the hell?" Compton threw himself against the door, which moved exactly the same distance it had previously, that is, not at all. Realizing that simply battering himself against the door was a pointless exercise, he took a moment to examine the doorframe. What he found made him throw up his hands in disgust.

"Dammit! Just dammit all to hell, y'know?"

"What is it?" Radome moved over beside him and began

examining the doorframe for herself.

"Is that...?"

"Yeah, it's been welded shut. Not just spot welded, OK? Some Jap motherfucker ran a bead around the entire door frame! Not even *I* can break through that!"

"Looks like Arasaka just demonstrated that the stairs aren't a viable option for us, either."

They heard the elevator chime sound in the other corridor.

"Hey, Radome, did you, like, y'know, order a pizza or anything?"

"Uh, no."

"Yeah, me neither. So that 'ding' ain't good news for us, OK?" He moved over to the nearest office door, pushed it wide, and saw that it was once a cubicle bay, the partitions still standing in place. Looking at Radome, he jerked his head toward the empty office space. "Get in here, just don't get too far in you get trapped. How are you doing on ammo?"

Radome thumbed the release on Glock's frame, caught the ejected magazine, and gave it a once-over. "I've seven left."

"Here, take this one." He thrust a spare magazine at her.

"But what about you?" she asked as she took it from him.

"I got two more spares I pulled off the first guy I shot at the elevator, plus two more that changed ownership just a few minutes ago." He grinned at her. "Just because someone's dead doesn't mean they can't still be helpful!"

"What do we do if we run out?"

"Hope some of these guys will be just as accommodating. Get ready."

The big grey Jaguar Mk 12 came growling up to the entrance of the parking lot. A dilapidated sign out in front of the building read

"Spayth Building" – at least it had at one time; now the "ild" was missing. A pair of halogen street lamps made a feeble effort at illuminating the car park, while only a faint glow showed from a handful of floor to ceiling wall panels of the building's facade.

"Alistair, are you sure this is the right place?"

"Aye, Miss Collins, Ah am. The only public-access hot spot in this area is twa blocks behind ye, and accordin' to APD surveillance systems, the only other building within four blocks frae which any EM emissions have come in the last hour is this one. Yer Miss Radome has to be here."

"But how the hell are we supposed to find Radome in this?" she asked, waving her hands about to indicate the darkness.

While Spazz talked, Blade was studying the building. "I think I found her."

"What? Where?"

"Four, five, six, aye, sixth level, left corner."

Spazz followed Blade's directions and then she saw it too: a succession of intermittent flashes of light, dulled by the tinting on the windows, along with years unwashed grime. She recognized it immediately

"Firefight."

Blade nodded. "Looks like Compton is with her, most likely. At heart Radome is a techie, not a shooter."

"Then what are we waiting for, an engraved invitation?"

"This time, Miss Collins, I believe I like yer brand of trouble."

"Now you're starting to get the idea."

Their doors flew open and Spazz jacked a shell into the chamber of her shotgun; Blade already had a round up the spout of the Enfield and opened the magazine cutoff. Now he drew his bayonet and *snick*-ed it onto the business end of the rifle. Scanning their front as they advanced, Blade to his left, Spazz to her right, the trotted toward the main entrance.

"Locked do you think?" Spazz called out.

"Probably, but I'm not going to waste time finding out." With that he put his first shot through the left hand double door, shattering the glass. Spazz gave him a sidelong look.

"As good a way of announcing 'Here we are!' as I can think of, bar shouting!"

"I'm pretty sure it doesn't matter much at this point!" *Click-clack, clack-click,* BOOM! Blade fired at a *reisen* who had come running toward the entrance, gun drawn, the spiky hair and boxy black suit making the man's identity obvious. Blood, brain tissue, and skull fragments blew outward from the back of his head – rather than the composite-design bullets he usually employed, Blade had brought dum-dums for tonight's work. Moving quickly, they passed through the now-empty doorframe and advanced toward the elevators.

BLAM! BLAM! Spazz's first rounds made short work of yet another reisen who was standing in the elevator, trying to take what cover it offered. They moved forward, wary of anyone trying to lurk in ambush; the sound of gunfire somewhere above them was unmistakable. "Elevator or stairs, Blade?"

"The lift – er, elevator. If we take the stairs, we'll walk right into the line of fire."

"How do you know?"

Blade reached down and grabbed the collar of the reisen lying across the lift threshold, dragging the body out of the lift car. He and Spazz stepped inside together, and Blade pushed the button marked "6." "Because I noticed that the ground level exit for the emergency stairwell is in the same corner where all the shooting seems to be taking place. We're not going to do Radome and Compton much good if we get pinned down as soon as we arrive, and I doubt we have the time to go pussy-footing around to find the other stairwell. So if we're going to come in behind them, let's get *right* behind them. Besides, with all that racket going on, they'll never hear us arrive."

Spazz nodded absently as she reached into the right breast

pocket of her vest and pulled out a pair of fresh shells to top off the magazine on the shotgun; with a single swift, smooth movement she slid them into the feed. Watching her, he asked, "What load are ye using?"

"Buck-and-ball. Malorite UDX-3's."

"I think I'm beginning to like ye."

The dinky little chime sounded and the doors began to open. "Ready on the left," Blade murmured, but Spazz, crouching low, opened fire before the doors were more than six inches apart: an unfortunate Arasaka who happened to be standing in front of the door, took the shot at hip level, his pelvis shattered. The man fell to the floor, thrashing about in screaming agony for a few seconds before succumbing to unconsciousness. She never noticed. Together she and Blade each took a long stride into the corridor and pivoted to their left, Spazz staying low, Blade going high. They took two more strides and then turned left again. A double-handful of Arasakas were huddled in the short corridor, a few anxiously peering around the corner as the snarl of gunfire sounded to their right.

Spazz had once remarked to Blade that she wished she'd been born of Swedish blood, and in the next few seconds he came to wonder if that wish hadn't been granted after all, as he was convinced he was watching a female berserker in action. Dropping to one knee, she slam-fired all five shells in the Ithaca's magazine, holding down the trigger and racking the slide as fast as she could. At least one Arasaka went down with each shot, and Blade was pretty sure that she'd scored daily-doubles on her third and fifth. Meanwhile he was working the bolt and squeezing the trigger on the Enfield as fast as he could, taking out four targets of his own. Then he ran forward, impaling a *reisen* who had been crouching around the corner, but was now looking back, only beginning to understand what was happening. He gave a quick twist of the rifle and recovered, then butt-stroked yet another before ducking back around the wall. He looked at Spazz, who worked the pump on her weapon and nodded at him in return.

"Damn, that was fast! How'd ye do that?"

"Practice, practice, practice!"

In the back of Blade's mind his respect for the woman kicked up another notch. He'd known far too many solos, most of whom were now dead or medically retired, who'd neglected to spend time learning to do combat reloads – clearly Spazz wouldn't find herself numbered in their ranks.

"Ready?" he asked. She nodded. "Right then, time to be among them."

Sprawled on the floor to present the smallest possible target, sheltering as best he could behind the half-closed door to the cubicle gallery, Compton had been exacting a steady toll on the Araskas. The four nearest to him, none of them closer than thirty feet, lay face-down on the mildewed carpet. Radome watched in horror as Compton had methodically knee-capped each of them, then carefully killed – no, that wasn't the right word – *executed* them with carefully placed headshots. Each man had known he was about to die, as Compton's face was split wide in a rictus-like grin, his teeth gleaming in contrast to his coffee-coloured features.

"Why, Gerry? Why do it that way? That was as sadistic as hell!"

"Hey, it wasn't anything more than they deserved, right? I just wish one of 'em had been that bastard Nakajima! Now just stay behind me, Trish, OK? Watch my six, will ya?" Radome nodded, her eyes filled with concern for her friend. Unmistakably he was far gone into psychosis – he was enjoying this too much. What he was doing wasn't just defending himself and her, he was executing any Arasaka he could capture in his sights. *Please, God, don't let Gerry be so far gone that we can't get him back again once we're out of this!*

For his part, Compton was content in the moment. His world, his entire universe, at that moment was reduced to two elements: protecting Radome – keeping her alive until Blade or whoever was coming actually arrived – and killing Arasaksas, especially *these* Arasakas. The remaining Japanese who still faced him had become the personification of everything that was wrong with the world, everything that was wrong with his life, every person who had ever wronged him, whether because of the colour of his skin or the cybernetics that had prevented him from being turned into a quadruple-amputee freak even as they turned him into another kind of freak, or who had wronged him out of sheer stupidity and incompetence, like the late and very unlamented Lt. Colonel Cartman.

It was more than simple revenge, although he was dishing that out with a glacial frigidity that would have been the envy of any Sicilian. It was a validation that had finally been awarded him, a redemption of a sort, the knowledge that he'd "kept the bridge," while "facing fearful odds." Maybe, like the Thane of Cawdor, nothing in his life would so become him as the leaving of it, but if that were so, he could be content with it. He'd finally discovered within himself something which transcended paychecks, street rep, or any kind of personal gratification. *God, if You're there and You're listening, get Trish out of this, please. We can talk about me later.* He took aim, squeezed the trigger, and saw another *reisen* go down. His grin grew even wider.

Yet it could never last, and he knew it. He was down to his last full magazine – Radome had long since given hers to him – and there were more Arasakas out there than there rounds remaining. Probability alone dictated that the sheer volume of fire coming in his direction would eventually take its toll, and it did. Two more *reisen* had gone down when a .40-calibre bullet tore into his left shoulder, the same one that been injured in the ambush south of Blairsville. The bullet traveled down inside his rib cage, tearing open his left lung and bisecting his spleen as it did so, before exiting just below his lowest rib. He grunted at the impact, though there was surprisingly little pain, and suddenly his left hand no longer had the strength to raise his Glock once more, or even keep his grip on it.

It took Nakajima a moment to realize that there was no longer any return fire coming from the far end of the corridor. He had been part of the second wave that responded to the exchange of gunfire on the sixth floor, but had held back, seeing no reason why he shouldn't let the hired help do exactly what they'd been hired to do: shoot and die. Now, sensing Compton's helplessness, he shoved his minions aside and dashed down the corridor, covering the distance to his enemy's position with astonishing speed.

Compton saw Nakajima coming and tried to rise to his feet, but the tank was finally empty – there weren't even fumes left for him to run on: trauma, pain, adrenaline, and exhaustion had all taken their toll at last. Nakajima saw a terrified Radome scuttling backward, deeper into the cubicle gallery, but ignored her for the time being as he loomed over Compton, who had barely made it to his knees. With his left hand Nakajima took hold of the front of Compton's shirt, hauling him to his feet, while with his right hand Nakajima reached behind his back and produced his *tanto*, its blade gleaming fitfully in the low light. Compton raised a hand in ineffectual protest at what was coming. Nakajima was about to strike when a fusillade of shotgun and rifle fire exploded behind him, and turning to look back, he saw *reisen* – and parts of *reisen* – falling in all directions. Another round of gunfire was followed by the appearance of a man of medium height and stocky build, wearing black combat dress and carrying an antique rifle at the ready, accompanied by a tall blonde holding some sort of shotgun in a manner which said unmistakably that she knew how to use it.

"Blade," Nakajima snarled, "you and that soggy bint with you are too late." With that, he spun back around and drove the knife deep into Compton's left side, jerk it hard to the right, then pulled it free. By the time Blade squeezed off a shot, the big Japanese was already moving, not toward these fresh assailants, but away from them; the .303 bullet was stopped by the anti-ballistic fabric of Nakajima's jacket. Spazz, holding her fire until she was certain that Nakajima was clear of Compton, pumped out two quick rounds just as Nakajima went crashing through the window at the end of the corridor. She hoped she'd hit him, she doubted that she had.

The dive out the window had been a calculated risk on Nakajima's part, but one that was well-calculated. He was counting on the smaller branches of the trees that ran around the perimeter of the Spayth Building to cushion his fall somewhat, and slow the speed of his descent to something his cybernetic skeleton could absorb. He got more than lucky, landing in a patch of soft earth after encountering not even a single large branch or bole that could have been potentially damaging, cyber-parts or not. By the time Blade and Spazz reached the shattered window, Nakajima had vaulted over the cinder block perimeter wall that surrounded the property and was out of sight, blending into the darkness as he put as much distance as possible between himself and the tower.

Blade wasted no time on recriminations, but immediately turned back to Compton. Radome had come forward and was cradling Compton's head in her lap, while Spazz was pulling a pair of field dressings from one of the larger pockets on her vest. She slapped them down hard on Compton's wounds, but they were saturated in seconds – there was blood everywhere, and Spazz could see it seeping between her fingers as she tried to keep pressure on the knife wound. Even as she did, she knew that it was a losing fight, however. The blood surged ominously in time with Compton's pulse, and even as she watched his pulse was noticeably slowing.

Blade dropped down beside her, pulling yet another field dressing from his ruck, applying this one to Compton's shoulder. Looking up at Radome, he said, "Yer shirt, take it off, give it to Spazz to use as a bandage!"

"Take it off? I" –

"Look, ye've got a t-shirt on underneath it! There isn't time get all modest on us, we've got to get the bleeding slowed or we're gonna lose him!" Suddenly nodding her understanding, Radome pulled the buttons apart with one swift, hard jerk, the dragged the shirt off her shoulders and handed it to Spazz. Compton opened his eyes and looked up at Radome.

"Giving me the shirt off your back, Trish? Must be true love...." Radome said nothing, just bit her lower lip.

"Shut up, ye gobshite!" Blade snarled, although his heart really wasn't in it. "This is no time for cracking wise. We're going to get ye downstairs and into the Jag, and then find the nearest chop shop where they can go to work on ye." He raised his voice slightly. "Alistair, are you monitoring this?"

"Aye, Sir, Ah am!"

"Find the location of the nearest emergency treatment centre, feed the route into the GPS on the Jaguar."

"'Twill be waitin' for ye when ye get there, Sir!"

Compton coughed, spitting up yet more blood as he did so, and suddenly Blade knew the awful truth: at some point in that firefight Compton had also taken a shot to the chest. No matter what they did here, by the time they got him to an emergency medical centre, Compton would be dead, either through bleeding out or by drowning in his own blood.

Compton himself had seen enough combat to recognize the truth when it stared him in the face, and as he looked at his three...buddies, yeah, that was the right word, they were buddies, in the way only someone who once wore a green suit or a blue one understood – they'd put it all on the line for him...as he looked at the faces of his three buddies, he felt nothing but respect for their refusal to try to put a brave front on what was about to happen. Radome – Trish – was softly crying, while Spazz's expression was bitter with unshed tears; Blade's face was grim-set.

"Hey, Blade, I know I don't have to tell you this," he said, his breath ragged and punctuated by unnatural wheezes and burbles, "but get that Jap motherfucker for me, OK?" Blade nodded in confirmation. Turning his eyes upward to Radome, Compton said, "Hey, Trish, it was fun, y'know? Glad you made it." He paused, and then a perplexed look came over his face. "Oh, wow, this isn't...." was all he got out before his eyes lost their focus and his head lolled to one side.

Trish let out a single sob, then returned to her silent weeping. Spazz got to her feet, leveled the whippet, and walked back to the spot where the dead Arasakas lay sprawled, almost as if she was looking for something else to shoot. Blade stood, looked down at Compton, muttered, "Aw, shite..." and said nothing more.

Everyone froze in place as they heard a succession of small "bangs" come from somewhere below, then Blade and Spazz went to their knees as a heavy explosion shook the building. A wave of heat and smoke came through the shattered window; Blade stood up and went over to it, peering out and down. He watched as, to the accompaniment of yet another series of bangs, a procession of small explosions made their way around the base of the building.

Standing back from the window, he looked first at Radome, then at Spazz, and said, "I think the bastard rigged the building to blow up on us – or else come down on top of us."

Spazz, sniffing suspiciously, shook her head. "I don't think so. Take a whiff, what do you smell?"

Blade inhaled deeply, then his eyes went wide. "That's JP-9!"

"Yep. Jet fuel." Spazz nodded, her mouth set in a bitter line. "Your pal Nakajima doesn't want to blow the building up, he wants to burn it down – with us inside it."

Part Three

The Good, the Bad, and the Crystals

Chapter 10

" ... he wants to burn it down – with us inside it."

"That may be what he wants, but I'm not feeling particularly cooperative where he's concerned. At the very least, I won't let myself be caught here, taken like an old badger in a trap." Blade slung the Enfield across his back, muzzle down, stepped over to the door to the emergency stairs and pushed. When nothing happened, he pushed harder. Still nothing. "What the" –

"Don't bother," Radome said, still kneeling on the floor, cradling Compton's head in her lap. "The exit doors to the stairwells are welded shut."

"Damn!"

"OK, that's not good," Spazz opined. "That means it isn't some jerry-rigged self-destruct down there that Nakajima's minions slapped together Tuesday afternoon. This was planned well in advance."

Blade nodded agreement then looked down at Radome. "How did ye get up here in the first place?"

"I didn't. I came *down* here: when I woke up I was in a room on the eighth floor. I took the elevator down here because I was afraid to try the stairs." MacLaren lifted an inquiring eyebrow. "I've got a concussion, Blade," she said matter-of-factly. "My right eye isn't focusing very well and my balance is twonky. Stairs didn't seem like a good idea at the time."

"No argument there, then. Looks like taking the lift is what we'll have to do, too."

"Blade," Spazz called out, one hand on the facing wall of the lift bank. "If we're taking the elevator, we'd better get our asses in gear, because it's getting a little warm over here!"

"What do ye mean?"

"These walls" – she tossed her head to indicate the banks of lifts

– "are definitely heating up. Not hot exactly, but a helluva lot warmer than they should be." Blade hurried over and laid a palm alongside hers.

"Shite! The central shaft's acting like a chimney, creating a draft that's fanning the flames on the lower floors." He stepped back and looked down the corridor toward Radome. "That really complicates things. I need to think."

Spazz scowled at him. "Blade, in case you hadn't noticed, we probably don't have a whole lot of time here!"

MacLaren whirled on her, raising a hand, index finger upright. "Blade's Law Number Two: there's always time to think!" He scowled at her. "Ye should know that by now. It may not be much, maybe only a second – maybe only a fraction of a second – but there's always time to think!" He fell silent for perhaps a two-count, then his face cleared and he said decisively, "We go up. It'll be dicey as hell, but we don't have any choice."

"Can't we just go out the window like Nakajima did?"

"Lass, it's at least a seventy-foot vertical drop out there. If ye want to trust a bunch o' branches and tree limbs ye can't even see to slow yer fall so ye don't break half the bones in yer body when ye land, be my guest. As for me, well, I forgot to bring my titanium skeleton."

"Then we go down to one of the lower floors, bust out a window there and take our chances."

"Too risky. We don't know how high up the fire's gotten. We could wind up opening the doors onto a solid wall of flames – and that draft would blow it right into our faces."

"And there's nothing helpful in that goddamned bag of tricks of yours?"

"Nothing that will help us right at the moment. We go up, that's final. Call the lift." Spazz moved over to the call-button panel while Blade went back down the corridor to collect Radome.

She was still kneeling, cradling Compton's head in her lap.

She'd stopped weeping, though there were still unshed tears in her eyes as she looked up at him. He held out a hand to her.

"Come, lass, time to go."

"I know. But I don't want to leave him. He – he protected me. Put himself between me and them. He was my friend, MacLaren. I only knew him a couple of days, but he was my friend. It just seems...*mean* to leave him here like this. Nobody will even find his ashes."

Blade never thought of Radome – Trish – as particularly delicate, certainly not given what went down in Bits and afterward. But for the first time he saw that she was a truly gentle soul, and now was not the time to be bellowing commands at the woman. This was a fragile moment for Radome, and no matter how urgent the situation, Blade was not about to inflict more injury on what were already raw and bleeding emotions. So instead, he spoke softly, firmly.

"I can't say ye're wrong, lass. I think, though, that wherever he is, he's still pretty sure ye're worth protecting, and he made it my job before he left. And every second we waste is just going to make that job harder. So what say we finish what he started and be about it, all right?"

Radome didn't reply, but instead raised her fingertips to her lips, then pressed them to Compton's, murmured "Goodbye," and then gently laid his head on the floor. She took Blade's outstretched hand and slid to her feet, then gave Compton one long, last look. Biting her lip, she visibly struggled to keep a grip on her self, but when she finally turned back to face Blade, there was a surprising steadiness in her voice when she spoke.

"I'm good now. Let's go."

Spazz was holding the lift door open, waiting for them. "C'mon, you two. It's getting fucking hot in here!"

As soon as they were inside, Spazz pushed the button for the twelfth floor, and the car started moving upward.

"Christ, yer right, it *is* bloody hot! At least it will be cooler up top. Quieter, too." The rumble of the flames only a few floors below was steadily rising in volume.

"What do we do when we get there?" Spazz asked him.

"What do ye mean?"

"I'm assuming you have some sort of plan. Or are we just postponing the inevitable?"

"When we reach the twelfth floor, we go up through that maintenance hatch there" – he pointed at the ceiling, where a rectangular hatch was clearly visible – "which should give us access to the winch house. From there we go out onto the roof."

"And then what? Once you get us up there, don't you have a plan for getting us down?"

"I'm not planning to die there, if that's what ye mean." He touched his ear bud, activating him comm. "Alistair? We could use a little help here."

"Aye, Sirr, Ah ken," the VI responded immediately, "but there's nae onyone tae be helpin'."

"You'd best explain that."

"Somebody with access to the Atlanta Emergency network blocked the initial reports of the fire at yer location from reachin' the AFD. Then at least twelve reports were made in the next ten minutes aboot fires in yer general area. Some were false alarms, some were real fires – all o' then in occupied properties. AFD doesnae have ony time tae waste on abandoned buildings. So, nobody is respondin' tae yer location, Sir."

"That sonofabitch!"

"Sirr?"

"Nakajima. Ye can bet real money that this was all preplanned – mainly to make sure this building was totally destroyed, along with anything in that could tie this location to him or Arasaka. Now it just has the added bonus of having the three of us trapped inside. Bastart!" Blade drew a deep breath, then went on.

"Right then. Whistle up whatever help ye can, Alistair, ASAP.

We're headed up to the roof, and we're going to be a bit busy for a wee while. Let me know when ye've got anything."

"Will do, Sirr! I'm clear."

With no warning, the overhead lights went out and the car gave a sickening lurch as, from above, the sound of the electric motor-driven winch died; the dim emergency lighting in the car snapped on.

"The fire must have taken out the electrical mains," Radome said.

"Did either of you see which floor we last passed?" Blade asked.

"It was the ninth," Radome answered, "so we're either just level with the tenth or just below it."

"That's not good," Blade said, as Spazz cocked a knowing eyebrow at him, "but, then again, it could be worse." Hardly had the words left his mouth then the car lurched again, falling a few inches downward as a groaning sound came from somewhere above their heads. Grabbing onto a handrail, Spazz pursed her lips, then announced:

"It's worse."

By now, all three of them had noticed the tendrils of smoke that were creeping through the gap at the bottom of the doors. Time was becoming very much of the essence. Blade climbed up and stood on the handrails in left-rear corner of the car, shoved aside the plastic light-diffusing grating above him to reveal a maintenance hatch in the lift car ceiling. Bracing as best he could, he slammed the palm of his left hand against the release lever on the hatch and heaved upward. With a groan of protest the oil-starved hinges gave way and the panel opened. Grabbing onto the hatch coaming with his right hand, Blade held out his left to Radome. "We've got no time to waste. Spazz, give her a boost up, will ye?"

Spazz interlaced her fingers and formed a stirrup, which Radome stepped into, then boosted herself upward, extending her hand to Blade. Spazz pushed, Blade pulled, and as she rose, Radome caught the hatch coaming, levering herself up onto the roof of the lift car. Blade turned back and held out his hand again, this time to Spazz. Even with the urgency of the moment, he couldn't help but admire her catlike grace as she stepped up on railing then pulled herself up through the hatch.

"I take you're planning to join us up here eventually, MacLaren?" Spazz called down impatiently. Blade glared at her for a second, then grabbed the edges of the coaming and pulled himself up to join his two friends. Like Spazz and Radome, he took hold of one of the cables supporting the car, the better to keep his footing. Looking down he could see flames reaching up past the sixth floor, and even as he watched, it seemed that the fire was increasing in intensity. Looking up, he could see that the other lift car was at the very top of its run, the twelfth floor. Behind him was a solid metal wall, ventilation ducting from the look of the airchests that branched out of it at each floor. Even though he was standing a good eight feet from it, the metal was already giving off an uncomfortable amount of heat. Indeed, he, Radome, and Spazz were all beginning to perspire heavily, and the smoke was starting to rasp at their throats.

In the fitful illumination of a quartet of emergency lights, the trio standing on the lift could see, thirty feet above them, the cables, catwalks, and frames that surrounded the lift equipment. It took Blade a few seconds to make sense of what he was seeing, as he searched for...there it was – the door that gave rooftop access from the winch house. Turning to Spazz and Radome, he pointed up at the door.

"That's where we're going! I'm going to get a line up there, it'll take us out onto the roof. Radome, ye're the lightest, ye'll go first, Spazz, ye'll go second." He had to raise his voice, as the noise of the flames below was rapidly rising; so was the heat. The car abruptly jerked downward another few inches, and from below metallic moanings and groanings could be heard above the noise of the flames.

"We've got to hurry! The brakes are going." Radome's voice was thick with urgency, and Spazz's eyebrows rose in an unspoken question. "The heat's starting to do a job on the brakes on the counterweights," Trish explained, "and with the power out, there's no braking on the winch up there. When they lose their grip, the car is going to fall all the way to the bottom."

While Radome spoke, Blade rummaged about in his ruck for a few seconds, then first produced a dull metal cylinder, perhaps six inches long and two in diameter, that sported a skeleton handgrip and what looked to be a folded grapple tucked into its front end. Next came length of small-diameter black line, no more than a few millimeters in diameter – made of carbon nano-fiber, it was every bit as strong as nylon line ten times its diameter. One end was fixed to a carabiner, which he snapped into a ring on the forward end of the grapple.

"What is that thing?" Spazz asked.

"It's a one-shot hand-held line gun. The Royal Navy uses them for evacuation and rescue work at sea."

"Why didn't you try using it when we were down below, so we could escape out one of the windows?"

"It's not exactly a paragon of accuracy, Spazz, and it's a single-shot device, which means I don't get to take a mulligan! If the grapple didn't snag a secure anchor at ground level the first time, it would have been damned well useless! Which means we still would have found ourselves atop this lift car, with no way to get up to the roof, waiting to find out if we would all die from smoke inhalation before we fried! Any other damned stupid questions ye'd like to ask?"

Taken aback by MacLaren's sudden vehemence, Spazz lapsed into an uncharacteristic silence while he looked upward, studying the layout of the shaft; Radome wisely chose the better part of valour and said nothing.

"Admittedly, an entire ceiling is hard to miss," Blade said after a few seconds, "so I don't see a problem here. Now, shield yer eyes, both of ye!"

With that, he opened the grapple and raised the launcher over his head, pointed to the vertical, turned his face aside and squeezed the firing stud. There was a loud *whoosh* and the grapple shot upward, somehow missed the trusses supporting the two big winches that raised and lowered the elevator cars, then caromed off the winch house ceiling, and snagged a small I-beam perhaps a foot from the wall. The grapple's momentum caused it to wrap around the crossmember, within easy reach of a service catwalk, and with a couple of hard tugs, Blade was satisfied he had a secure attachment.

"Nice shot!" Radome said, with a nod of approval.

"Just lucky, I guess. Right then, now to work." He pulled the line taut, stooped and looped a quick-release knot around a grab-handle by the roof hatch. Dipping into one of the pouches on his utility belt, he produced a large carabiner, along with a pair of small ascenders, modeled on similar devices used by mountain climbers, but modified to fit the 4mm line he was using. Motioning Radome over to where he stood, he clipped the ascenders to the line, then just below them snapped the carabiner over the line and around her belt.

"This way, ye won't get separated from the line in case ye have a problem on the way up." He grinned at her. "Now, if ye fall out of yer own *pants*, it's not my fault, ye ken?" She smiled back and nodded. "Have ye used these wee beasties before?" he asked, indicating the ascenders.

"Start with both clamped on, release the upper one, slide, clamp, release the lower one, slide, clamp, rinse, repeat as needed," she replied confidently. Blade was impressed by how quickly she'd regained her composure – no doubt it would take a lot to permanently rattle this woman.

"Ye got it. When ye get up top, slide the carabiner and the

ascenders back down to us. Now on yer way with ye." As if to emphasize the urgency, the elevator car again shuddered underfoot.

Wasting no time, Radome began her ascent. Her movements were sure and deliberate, and she made steady progress, though she had to stop twice. Both times Blade and Spazz could see her shaking her head as though she was fighting off a bout of vertigo: however determined she might be, she couldn't entirely ignore the side effects of the concussion. All the while Spazz and Blade were mentally urging her on – they could hear the groaning steel, see the flames rising beneath the elevator car, feel its tremors and shifts. After what seemed an agonizingly long time but was in truth barely more than a minute, Radome reached the catwalk and swung herself onto it.

"Ready, Spazz?" she called down.

"Send 'em!"

The carabiner and the ascenders came whizzing down the line, and Spazz quickly had the carabiner looped through her own belt. She ran the ascenders up and down the line to get a feel for them, then looked at Blade, who was watching her carefully.

"I've got this – I've been rock climbing since I was ten."

"Off ye go, then." He was startled when, without warning, Spazz reached out, pulled him close, and planted a quick kiss on his lips. "Good luck!" she said.

"Thanks, yer Highnessness."

With the experience born of long practice, she slithered up the rope, like Radome using her feet and ankles to lock herself in place as she moved the ascenders. Her long legs and arms allowed her to climb more rapidly than Radome, and in barely half the time Radome had needed, she too was up on the catwalk.

"OK, gardy-loo or mind your head or whatever the fucking saying is!" she called out, and the ascenders and carabiner once more began their slide down the line. No sooner had they reached Blade's outstretched left hand and he locked the lower one in place than the elevator car started to drop. Instantly, Blade reached out with his right hand to yank free the quick-release knot – even as he did so he could feel the line stretching and growing tauter. Trailing a tangle of heavy cables, the car began to drop away, disappearing into the mass of flames below, and is it did a wave of furnace-like heat washed over McLaren as he found himself dangling above damn-all in the cavernous maw of the lift shaft.

That was too damned close, he thought bleakly.

Unfortunately, the shaft wasn't *quite* empty, and as he swung gently back and forth while he grimly worked the ascenders, an eldritch screech of metal came from somewhere above him. Looking up he saw one of the two I-beams that supported the elevator winch give way: the plummeting car below, still attached by its cables to the winch itself, was subjecting the whole structure to stresses and strains it had never been designed to withstand. The other end of the I-beam broke, and Blade watched in fascinated horror as the remaining beam twisted, then fractured, and the whole multi-ton mass of metal came hurtling down at him.

Had he been suspended in the middle of the shaft, or even close to it, the winch would have struck him directly, effortlessly brushing him off the line to which he was clinging, consigning him to the flames below. Not that it would have mattered, the impact alone would have killed him. As it was, the winch was tumbling as it fell, and as it passed, one of the I-beams struck him a glancing blow in the side, "glancing" being a relative term, of course, and he felt at least two of his ribs break under the impact. He hit the outer wall of the elevator shaft hard, and as he bounced away, a reddish haze formed before his eyes that had nothing to do with the flames rising to meet him. He barely maintained consciousness, but some still-alert corner of his mind kept his left hand clamped on the ascender with a literal death-grip. It was the unnatural strength of that cybernetic hand which saved him – for the moment at least.

"*DAVID!!!*" He heard Spazz scream in horror somewhere above him, and realized with an odd detachment that it was the first time she'd ever used his given name.

"Goddammit, MacLaren," she shouted, "if you fall, I'm gonna die in here, and if you let me die, I will *never* fucking speak to you again!"

Nag, nag, nag, he mused, but there was something about the way she'd said it that brought with it a measure of clarity, and he began to haul himself up the line he was grasping. It was an agonizing undertaking. Every time he reached up with his right arm, lights flashed before his eyes and he imagined he could literally feel the ends of his broken ribs rubbing against each other as a fresh jet of pain shot across his chest. Even the simple act of breathing, already made difficult by the rising heat from below, was its own Tartarus. With literally agonizing slowness Blade worked his way up the line, moving first one ascender, then the other, then locking his ankles about the line to thrust upward with his legs so he could move the ascenders again. Every few feet he had to stop and breathe as deeply as the pain would allow – he found he literally could not climb and breathe at the same time, the agony was simply too great. Spazz and Radome shouted encouragement as he rose, and, after what seemed like a considerable fraction of eternity, reached out helping hands to bring him over the lip of the catwalk.

He sprawled there, momentarily exhausted, gasping for air. Spazz stood, and looked down at him, an expression he'd never seen before playing across her face. "Are you planning on lying there all night?" she asked.

"I'm taking it under advisement, aye."

"Trish and I are going out on the roof to get away from this goddamned heat. Feel free to join us when you like."

With a groan that was in no way theatrical, Blade got to his knees, and opened his mouth, mustering a reply, but Spazz spoke first.

"Oh, and I trust you got a sufficiently good look at my ass while

I was climbing."

"Was it that obvious?"

"It most certainly was. I'm surprised your eyes didn't pop out of your head."

"Damn."

"Just remember, MacLaren, that, yes, I *am* Maureen Collins," she purred, "and I *am* a lot of trouble." With that she turned and sashayed to the winch house door, leaving a thoroughly bemused Blade shaking his head.

"So that's what that feels like," he muttered.

Spazz delivered several hard kicks to the winch house door – evidently someone had taught her sometime, somewhere, that firing high powered bullets at metal locks on metal doors qualified as a Very Bad Idea. At last the lock gave way, and as the door swung open, the flames below Blade surged higher in the now-stronger updraft. Climbing to his feet, he hurried as best he could to catch up to Radome and Spazz, slamming the door shut behind him once he was through, leaning against it, gasping for air.

For some moments, no one would remember how long, they simply stood there, looking back and forth between themselves, at a total loss for words as it slowly dawned on all of them that there was literally nowhere else to go now. Finally Spazz broke the silence.

"Well, we're here. Now what? I mean, what options do we have besides waiting for the goddamned roof to collapse under our feet? If you'll pardon the really bad pun, this looks to be pretty much a dead end."

"I know, and I'm truly sorry for it," Blade replied. "I was trying to buy us some time, as much as possible, hoping Alistair could make something break our way, find a friendly close enough to be able to help us. He didn't, obviously, and I'm sorry. Ye really don't deserve this, Maureen." He turned to look at Radome. "And I'm sorry for ye, too, Trish. We really meant to get ye away from here.

I never imagined it would turn out like this – I never imagined it *could.*"

"You know what they say, Blade: shit happens." She made a half-hearted attempt at smiling. "You tried, you gave it your best shot, etcetera, etcetera, you know, all those platitudes people spout to make other people feel good when the wheels come off the wagon." She shrugged expressively. "I'm not liking this, not one bit, and yet, even though it's very small comfort at the moment, at least I have the satisfaction of knowing that prick Nakajima never got to go to work on me."

Blade nodded. "Ye'd have been just as dead in the end, it would have been even more painful, and it would have taken a lot longer for ye to get there." He looked about, noting the occasional tongue of flame that licked at the ventilator gratings on the walls of the winch house. Before long the fire would weaken the ceiling sufficiently that it would collapse, and when it did, the whole shaft structure would be one vast, open chimney; then the flames would grow even hotter, and begin to attack the structural steel, softening it, distorting it, until it gave way under its own weight. When that happened, the entire building would collapse in on itself, bringing the roof down with it. Already he could feel the occasional tiny tremor underfoot, as the heat at the lower levels began subtly distorting the beams and pillars that held the Spayth Building upright. He slowly walked over to a small air conditioner unit and sat down on it. Spazz joined him.

"Radome's right, MacLaren, this really isn't your fault. Still, to be honest about it, I really hate your ass right now."

Blade gave her a crooked smile, but didn't respond directly. "One of the things I've always disliked about big cities," he said, looking skyward, "is how at night ye can never properly see the stars – too much light pollution. Now, if we were at my home in Scotland, we could be sitting out on the terrace – or, better yet, up on the tower roof – watching the whole Milky Way go by in all its glory.

A good cigar in one hand, a good single malt in the other, a good woman at my side, that's the way a man should – "

"Mad Scot, Mad Scot, if you copy, this is Cardinal One. Please respond. Over." A very familiar female voice affecting an Appalachian drawl spoke in Blade's earbud.

Activating his comm, Blade replied, imitating the accent as best he could, "Uh, roger, Cardinal One. This here's the Mad Scot. What can I do fer y'all? Over." Spazz and Radome, neither of whom were on the comm channel, were looking at him as if he had suddenly lost his mind.

"Mad Scot, be advised I am ninety seconds out from your position, bearing three-five-two true at an altitude of one-five-zero feet. I'm flashing navigating lights now. Please advise when you have eyeballs on me. Over."

Blade jumped up – a move he instantly regretted as his ribs filed a very strong protest at being disturbed yet again – and turned to the north. Triggering the telescoping function his cyber-eye, he began scanning a narrow arc at just about the same level at which he was standing....

There! He could see it. "Uh, roger, Cardinal One, y'all're approaching at three-five-two true, altitude one-five-zero feet. I have you on visual. Over."

"Roger that, Mad Scot. You and your companions should be prepared to get your slow, sorry asses aboard soonest I arrive. Will be light on the skids when I touch down on rooftop. Over."

"Roger, Cardinal One." It was all Blade could do to keep from laughing out loud. "Will have slow sorry asses aboard soonest y'all arrive. Over."

"Roger that, Mad Scott. Over and out."

Forty seconds later, a grey-painted AV7 bearing no markings whatsoever, civilian or otherwise, came swooping in and settled onto the roof, its turbo-fans spinning just fast enough to maintain vertical station-keeping. Sitting in the pilot's bubble, wearing a headset and an utterly archaic leather flying jacket as if she been doing so all her life, grinning from ear to ear, was Scarlett.

It took only a matter of seconds for Radome, Spazz, and Blade to clamber into the small passenger compartment behind the cockpit, and no sooner had Blade slammed shut the rear hatch than Scarlett opened the throttles, lifting up and zooming away. Spazz and Blade stared out a viewport, and as they watched, flames burst through the top of the winch house and shot skyward. Within seconds the entire rooftop began to cave in as the central core of the Spayth Building collapsed. Radome couldn't bring herself to look: she would always remember the blazing tower as Compton's funeral pyre. As the AV7 banked northward, Blade caught one final glimpse of the upper-level walls begin to fall inwards. By sunrise all though would remain would be a pile of smouldering wreckage.

What Blade didn't see, couldn't have seen, was a figure standing atop a small knoll perhaps a quarter-mile from the burning building. As the AV7 zoomed directly overhead, Hideki Nakajima, for perhaps the thousandth time in his life, cursed the name of David MacLaren.

"I swear, when I began responding to yer comm, with all those 'Cardinal One' and 'Mad Scot' and 'Roger' and 'Over' bits, these two" – Blade pointed at Maureen and Trish – "both thought I'd gone completely potty!" All three women – Scarlett, Radome, and Spazz – cackled mercilessly at Blade's expense.

"We did, we truly did!" Spazz confirmed. "I'm sitting there thinking, 'OK, MacLaren's gone off the rails, he knows he's about to die, so he's having a fucking death fantasy right before my eyes!'"

"I was waiting for the soul-stirring rendition of 'I'm a Little Teapot,' or something like that." Radome looked at Blade, her blue eyes twinkling with mischief. "I would have paid good money to see that."

The four were sitting in a small drawing room on the ground floor of Blackbriar, Blade just having undergone the less-than-gentle ministrations of Dr. Smythe-Matthews, a local British ex-pat who had been a medic in the Paras before going to medical school and moving to the United States. At one point, after first confirming that Blade did, in fact, have a pair of fractured ribs, he brought sufficient enthusiasm to the task of placing a flexible brace around the Scot's chest to cause Blade to wonder if he would be able to breathe. Turning to Smythe-Matthews, he asked, "It is really necessary that it be *that* tight?"

"I assure you, Major, it's absolutely necessary. You'll adjust to it soon enough, but in the meantime you don't want those ribs wandering about."

"Well, I suppose if you ever lose your medical license, you'll have a job waiting for you at Helga's House of Pain." The physician politely ignored him.

Smythe-Matthews had been far more solicitous in tending to Radome. After a quick but thorough examination, and listening to a recounting of her ordeal, as well as how she came by the various cuts and bruises she had about her person, he assured her that the concussion she did indeed have showed no indication that it would produce any serious, lasting brain trauma. Since Blade had heard no screams of agony or pleas for mercy coming from the small room where Smythe-Matthews tended to Radome's injuries, he concluded that the good doctor was selective in his application of sadism...

Now, with the pill-roller at last safely out of sight, all four of them were recounting their recollections of the events in the Spayth Building. Blade paid particularly close attention to Radome's telling of her experience, along with what details she could supply about Compton. Blade was beginning to feel a keen regret for the younger man's death: in the brief time he'd known Compton, Blade came to regard him as a good man to have on one's "six." There was no higher compliment Blade could pay someone, in his opinion, and so he figuratively raised a glass of the Highlands' finest to Compton's memory.

That he raised no such glass in real life was due to the pain-killers Dr. de Sade – er, Smythe-Matthews – had given him: alcohol was strictly contraindicated, and as MacLaren had no desire to wake up dead in the morning, he accepted the physician's enforced temperance. So it was that instead of his accustomed single malt, in his hand was a glass of tonic water and soda, with a twist of lime; at least he had the consolation of a good cigar. Spazz and Scarlett were sipping white wine – Blade was vaguely pleased to see that Maureen had given up her "Dead Nazis," at least for now – while Radome was paying court to what was, in her opinion, a very nice Amontillado.

"Any road, what I still don't understand is what ye were doing down there in the first place. I mean, how? How did it all happen? *What* happened? When did ye learn to fly an AV?"

"Well, that's the thing, isn't it?" Scarlett was clearly uneasy with the situation. "I don't know. I just did."

"Tell me what happened."

She shifted in her seat, tucking one leg under her, then folded her hands across her knee. "Alistair was feeding me a running update on what was happening with you, told me about losing Compton." She looked over at Radome. "I'm really sorry about that, I liked him, too. Anyway," she continued, returning to Blade, "he told me about how you were trapped when the building started burning. I expected the police and fire department would respond, but when Alistair explained the situation, I realized that wasn't going to happen – by design."

"Yeah, about that, MacLaren, just what *was* going on there?"

"Do ye mean specifically or in general terms, Radome?" Blade asked in return. "Specifically, I don't know. Generally, ever since Red China fragmented back in 2022, the Japanese have been trying to move into the vacuums the Chinese left behind, and not just the economic ones. The four 'Little Dragons' – Taiwan, South Korea, Hong Kong, and Singapore – all saw an opportunity to cash in and reclaim world-wide market shares they had lost to the Chinese in the first decade of this century. The Japanese went even further, and put in a lot of effort in regaining the political influence they lost back in the 90's – but this time they didn't bother trying to buy American senators and congressmen: after yer Social War, those people just didn't draw the same kind of water as they used to do. Instead the Japanese went after state and local politicians, and Atlanta was one of the cities they went all out in trying to 'buy.' I'm guessing that Arasaka has its hooks even deeper in local government officials than anyone ever suspected. That would explain why APD is so hostile to me, and it accounts for the APD and AFD being selectively blind this morning: somebody told them to look the other way, and they did."

"It would have to be something like that," Spazz nodded in agreement. "There are a lot of good first responders out there, and the only way they would ignore a situation like the one we were in would be if they were *told* to ignore it."

"Any road, we're getting off the subject." Blade turned back to Scarlett. "So what happened next?"

"What happened was I got pissed off, Blade. I mean, I didn't think there was anything I could do, but I thought that *somebody* here might be able to help somehow. So I went down to see the Charge of Quarters, you know, Colour Sergeant Bourne?"

"So that's his name...."

"Yes, it is, and he's a very nice man. I explained what was going on and asked him if there was anything we could do. He said he didn't think so – there was an AV7 kept at the ready in the carriage house – it's really a hanger in disguise – but the pilot was back in England on maternity leave, so there was no one to fly it. I asked him to show it to me – don't ask me why, it was just an impulse thing, but there was this crazy idea starting to take shape in my head – and he did. Once I saw the cockpit, I knew – I just *knew* – that I could fly the thing, and I told him I could. He said it was against the regulations and all and I told him he was welcome to try and stop me if he really wanted to."

"You didn't!

"Yes, Spazz, I did!" For a moment, Scarlett's face lit up with a mischievous grin. "He said something about being middle-aged and all and not hearing and seeing as well as he used to, and then just walked away. So I said 'Screw it!' and strapped the thing on. It was like riding a bicycle: the preflight, the start up, my hands just knew where to go, when to go there, and why. I taxied out of the carriage house, lifted off, and – well, you know the rest."

Blade gave her a considering look and said nothing for some seconds, then asked, "It was just that easy? Truly?"

"It was. It was as if I'd spent hundreds of hours in an AV cockpit – all of a sudden the knowledge was just *there*! And that's the really scary part of it. I'd remembered it all in an instant. It wasn't like someone just poured the knowledge into my head and 'poof!' there it was – I *remembered* it! It came back to me as a *memory*, Blade. That's what my life is like now – I'm tantalized by the thought that there's so much out there that I know, but I can never quite connect with it. It's like I'm inside a room where I know there are doors in it, but I can't see them, and then suddenly a door opens up and lets me into a new room – and this one doesn't have any doors that I can see either, except the one I just came through. I was wrong just now: it's not scary, it's as terrifying as hell. Am I crazy or just an amnesiac?"

Spazz was watching Blade closely as he listened to Scarlett's account. *She still worries him. He's still not convinced her "I don't remember anything from more than two days ago, not even my name" act isn't just that – an act. And every time she "breaks character," it makes him wonder even more. Where do all these skills come from? Where did she learn to shoot like she does? How she acquire her hand-to-hand skills?*

Who taught her to pilot an AV – and where and when? He's worried that he's being played, and that he's missing some tell that should give him a clue that he is. And if he is being played, who's doing it and why?

And why do I care?

"I don't think ye're crazy, Scarlett, but as for just what it is going on inside yer head, I'm not qualified to say. All I know is that I don't envy ye one bit."

"Neither do I," Radome agreed.

"Nor I," Spazz echoed. "On the other hand, whatever it was that threw the switch inside your head, I have to say that I'm pretty damned grateful that it did. I like having a good tan, but given what would have happened if you hadn't shown up when you did, well, let's just say I don't like tanning so dark I wind up charred."

Radome chimed in, saying, "OK, one last question then I'm off to bed: what was with all the call signs and the 'Roger, wilco, over and out' stuff?"

Scarlett laughed. "Oh, that! The one thing I didn't know how to do was set the encryption on the comm equipment. Whatever you Brits use – " she nodded at MacLaren – "is different from whatever it was I was used to, apparently. So I knew I'd have to be transmitting in the clear and I didn't want to give the show away to anyone who might be listening who shouldn't have been."

"That's good enough for me," Trish said, "and with that, I'm off to bed – wherever that'll be."

"I'll help you up the stairs, Radome," Scarlett offered. "Colour Sergeant Bourne already told me what room is going to be yours."

"Thanks, I appreciate it. Good night – no, make that 'Good morning' – everyone." With that Radome and Scarlett departed.

Maureen looked at Blade. "That's our cue, MacLaren. You best get yourself off to bed as well. You definitely need the rest."

"Going to tuck me in, are ye?"

"In your dreams, 'Mad Scot.' I'll make sure you get up those stairs safely, but after that, you're on your own."

Blade let out a deeply theatrical sigh. "Well, it was worth a try,

I guess."

"If at first you don't succeed...."

Blade looked at her hopefully as she let her voice trail off. She grinned wickedly back as she finished the thought. "...give it up and find something else to do."

"You, Miss Collins – "

"Don't even say it. Besides, I told you: you have *no* idea...."

Safely back in his room once more – Maureen had been as good as her word and had given him an arm to lean on while negotiating the stairs, then had bid him good night at her door – MacLaren quicky doffed his battledress and drew on a set of light silk pajamas. He'd just finished his routine ablutions when his comm chimed, the "Incoming Message" prompt appeared on the workstation monitor, and Alistair's voice buzzed in his ear.

"Sir, ye have an incomin' comm. From The Russian."

"Accept it, Alistair."

"Aye, Sir."

Ekaterina Ivanova's face appeared on the screen, and she bestowed her most dazzling smile on MacLaren. "Hello, Blade."

"*Keterina, lyubov' moya, s kazhdoj vtrechej ty vsjo prekrasnej!*"

"*Blajd, dorogoj, ya ocharovana tvoej pesnej, hotya po-russki ty mekaesh' kak' bosnogogij orlovskij kolhoznik s nogami v navoze!*" At that they shared a laugh, then Ivanova switched to English.

"I am told you had very interesting morning, Blade."

"*Da.* 'Interesting' in a Chinese sort of way." MacLaren allowed. "I take it that wasn't a wholly rhetorical question, was it?"

"No, it was not. The Backchannel is full to brim with rumor and hearsay about what happened to you this morning. To point that almost no one is talking about anything else."

"Indeed. And why would one little incident like that attract so much attention and comment?"

"Because word is now out on street that your friend Nakajima has been disavowed by his superiors at Arasaka. It is said that Aiko Kurita herself demanded that he report to her in person within forty-eight hours – and that he is to bring his...'tonto,' is it?... with him."

Blade sat bolt upright, his bare feet hitting the floor with a thump. "Katya, did ye say she told him to bring his *tanto* with him?"

"*Da*, that is word, *tanto*. Yes, he is to bring his *tanto* when he faces her."

"Shite!"

"Nakajima has apparently disgraced himself and his superiors. Rumor is he disobeyed orders – orders which explicitly forbade him to even attempt to kill you." Ivanova leaned forward, her expression intent, and all trace of her theatrical Russian accent vanished as she slipped into the fluency MacLaren already knew she possessed; he had rarely seen her in such dead earnest. "Blade – David – there are an alarming number of things happening right now that all spawned from whatever it is that's going on in Atlanta. I'll send you a packet that outlines exactly what they are, but the most important is this: your friend Calvin is in...what's the phrase...'deep shit'?... Calvin is in deep shit and I doubt that he's truly aware of it."

"What do ye mean?"

"I mean that Arasaka has not only washed their hands of Nakajima, they've also shut down what they called the 'Yankee Project,' their attempt to acquire those memory crystals you have."

"What makes you think I have them?"

"Please, David, can we dispense with the pretenses?" Blade was intrigued by the way a woman as striking as Ivanova could contrive to make a look of withering disdain appear so sensual. "Arasaka is trying to put as much distance as possible between themselves and Nakajima; they're even going so far as to suggest that Nakajima may have been working a third-party agenda, though they haven't gone so far as to suggest who that might be. In any event, they've let it be known that they are no longer interested in the crystals – at all. In fact, almost *no one* is interested in them anymore. Every IT corp in the world is falling all over itself trying to distance itself from those crystals, whether they've ever been interested in them or not. Rumor has it that there's something about them that grossly violates the Bill of Humanity – and we both know what could mean for Calvin. If it's true, the American government will lock him up and throw away the key – well and truly throw it away."

"I wish I could say that surprises me but I can't. He's always had this sense of innate superiority, of entitlement. Laws were meant for other people, 'the mundanes' he likes to call them; for himself, laws are more what ye might call 'guidelines' than actual binding provisions, if ye catch my drift. And he's never more self-righteous than when he's developing some new tech." He fell silent for a moment, then, "Wait a minute, ye said 'almost no one' was interested in those crystals now...." His voice drifted off, its rising inflection at the end making a question out of the incomplete statement.

"There are two, perhaps three players still at the table, and I can't make out the faces of all of them. Thirteen forty-seven is where I believe you should start, David. The answer is 1347. Think about it very carefully. I don't dare name names – I'm more vulnerable than most people realize, and I don't want to risk the possibility that someone might be eavesdropping. Just think about it – then talk to your friend, Houston. Be careful out there, David. I'm clear." And with that, Ivanova's image vanished from his monitor.

MacLaren leaned back in his chair, his fingers steepled at his lips, lost in thought for several minutes. Then he stood up, and began turning out the lights in his room.

"Alistair, contact Raven and ask her to dig as deep as she can into Cogito Orbis' finances over the last ten years. Tell her to use the number 1347 as a starting point." He yawned hugely as the painkillers and fatigue made common cause in overwhelming his ability to remain awake. "I've got to get some sleep."

"Shall I gi'e her an update on yer condition, Sirr? She'll be awfu' worried aboot ye. She's like that, ye ken."

Blade chuckled. "Where would I be without ye, Alistair?"

"Most likely chasin' sheep up in the Highlands, Sirr."

"Ye're an ungrateful bastart."

"As Ah said before, 'tis nae my fault ye and Miss Ligeia aren't wed."

"Goodnight, Alistair."

"G'night, Sirr."

Six hours later, Blade's com chirped. He was instantly awake, and made to quickly sit up, which proved to be a mistake as his ribs rather vehemently protested the sudden movement. Moving a bit more carefully this time, he slipped his earbud in place and said, "Accepted."

Ligeia's face appeared on the monitor, looking unwontedly serious. "David?"

"Yes?"

"It would appear that we've both had rather interesting mornings, although mine wasn't so...physically rigorous as yours, from what I understand from Alistair. Still, I have a couple of things here that I believe you'll find interesting."

"'Interesting' as in 'My word, Ligeia, that's fascinating!' interesting, or interesting as in 'Chinese interesting'?"

"Yes."

"I was afraid ye were going to say that."

"First of all, I had the most intriguing packet appear in my email. It was sent through an anonymous re-mailer, and signed 'Meow,' nothing more."

"And what was in it?"

"An electronic surveillance suite that's quite possibly the most dangerously illegal thing I've ever seen. I mean, handling-raw-plutonium-in-the-nude levels of dangerous."

"Ye have no idea what sort of interesting visuals are running through my head right now because of what you just said."

"David, I'm serious! And something tells me that somehow this is tied to you and what you're doing there."

"Before I respond yea or nay, explain what ye mean by 'handling-raw-plutonium-in-the-nude levels of dangerous'."

"I mean, David, that I committed an undetermined but substantial number of indictable offenses just by reading it, the sort of offenses that don't put me *in* prison, they put me *under* the prison. So, before I delete it and erase any traces of ever having been in possession of it, I need to know just how important this bit of toxic cyber-waste really is."

"It *is* important, Ligeia – life or death important. Nakajima was always something of a loose cannon, but without Arasaka to keep him on a short leash, he's a bigger threat than ever. The man's a sadistic bastart, and now that he answers to no one, he'll kill people in job lots just for the sheer, sick pleasure of it. I have to run him to ground once and for all. This isn't personal anymore, it's become my job. I need to find him – quickly – and I need that surveillance suite to do it."

Ligeia leaned forward at her workstation, tapping a fingernail against her teeth. The silence drew out as Blade allowed her to work through whatever decision she was making. Finally she sat back in her chair with a heavy sigh. "All right, David, here's what I'm willing to do with this...this...travesty. I don't dare run it from here – no matter what clearance I hold or what work I do for His Majesty's Government, I'm technically a private citizen, so I have no legal protection if the authorities find out that I've been running it.

"You, on the other hand, and, more importantly right now,

Radome, are on what is technically British soil within a sovereign foreign country – you've got diplomatic immunity, and if she's pressed on it, the Consul-General will almost certainly grant Radome asylum if she asks for it. That way the Americans can't touch her, and that means Radome can run this thing from Blackbriar. So...I will send this packet to you right now, and once I've confirmed that you have a clean copy, I'll delete mine and start erasing footprints. What you and Radome decide to do with it is up to the two of you."

"Thank ye, Ligeia." Blade's gratitude was almost palpable.

"But understand this, David: I am really pissed off at you right now. I don't like being used like this, or being put into this sort of position; you've just really strained our friendship. Do it again, and that friendship ends."

"This isn't my doing, and you know it. We both know who sent that packet, and we both know she's never felt as strongly about Bruce's methods and boundaries as he does. *She* decided to send that to you – I didn't ask her to do it."

That seemed to mollify Ligeia – a bit. "In that case, maybe I don't hate your arse as much as I did a minute ago."

"Why is this the morning for beautiful women to hate my arse?" Blade threw his hands up in resignation.

"What?"

"Never mind. What else do ye have for me?"

With a classic female mercuriality, Raven unexpectedly smiled. "You asked me to look into Calvin's finances – well, Cogito Orbis' finances, which amounts to the same thing."

"Right."

"You won't believe what I found."

"Tell me."

"For the last eight years, the six largest investors in Cogito Orbis have been AmCom Bank, the January Foundation, the Jamieson-O'Connell Research Foundation, the Waterbridge Company, the

Grant-Neuman Partnership, and Northern Commonwealth Bank."

"And...?" Blade asked after a pause.

"It's the last two that are really...interesting," she replied, with a careful emphasis on "interesting."

"How so?"

"They used to call it a 'paper trail,' she answered in an apparent *non sequitur*, "but now it's more of a paper maze." When she saw Blade's slightly baffled look, she giggled then went on, "What I mean is that there are so many layers, dead ends, cutouts, and diversions in some of these companies that sometimes I feel like a female Theseus negotiating the Labyrinth. In any case, what it comes down to is that the Grant-Neuman Partnership, while it does a lot of legitimate investing for genuine clients, corporate and individual, is an elaborate front for PanEuroEcon."

"Holy shite! Are ye sure of this? Stupid question, of course ye are, otherwise you wouldn't be telling me this. Just a moment, didn't ye tell me that the implant in Bridelow's body was made by PanEuroEcon?"

"That I did."

"Fascinating."

"Told you so."

PanEuroEcon was the colloquial shorthand for the PanEuropean Economic Partnership, a multi-national cartel that had been formed in the wake of the European Union's slow disintegration that began in 2016. It was in many ways Europe's equivalent of Arasaka Corporation, or America's National Motors – essentially corporate thugs in expensive three-piece suits, although PanEuroEcon was as a rule more refined in its ruthlessness. In the countries where it was based, primarily France, Germany, and Italy, PanEuroEcon prospered, generally by first marginalizing, then eliminating, competition. In countries where something that even remotely resembled a free market existed, PanEuro never did well when it operated openly. So instead it relied on proxies and surrogates to establish bridgeheads, as it were, some of which thrived, others withered on the vine. The news that PanEuro had a foothold in Cogito Orbis disturbed Blade on several levels, not the least of which was that Hobbes was almost certainly aware of it and never bothered to inform him.

"Right then. What about Northern Commonwealth Bank?"

"Your friend Spazz would love this – it's right up her alley, as the Americans say. Northern Commonwealth is an offshore bank based in the Turks and Caicos. Well, its corporate charter says that it's a bank. The truth is that it's a money laundering front for just one client: DisCom."

Blade's jaw dropped. For more than century, DisCom had publicly prided itself on its "squeaky clean" corporate image, with nary a hint of any genuine criminal taint to besmirch it. True, the company had always been oppressively litigious in protecting its intellectual property rights, real or imagined, often to the point of destroying smaller companies and ruining thousands of creative careers in the process. And the company's reputation had become somewhat murkier in the 21st Century, but then again, the whole world had become somewhat murkier in the 21st Century. The Black Rats were a reality, an open secret of which no one spoke publicly, yet there was always the justification – or at least rationalization – that they existed to protect the company from the depredations of other corporate strong-arm divisions.

Yet, while DisCom could no longer be said to be the worldwide purveyor of unalloyed happiness that its founder intended it to be, and while some of its corporate undertakings may have ventured far into the gray areas of the law, no one had ever suggested that DisCom was involved in anything so criminal that it would have need of an offshore bank to hide illegal gains. This was explosive information, Blade realized, and of course Raven knew it as well. He was absolutely confident that once she had confirmed her findings – and Raven was nothing if not thorough – certain interested parties in His Majesty's Government as well as in Washington DC were shortly going to receive some utterly fascinating hand-deliveries.

Of more immediate concern to Blade, however, was fitting this new information into everything that had already transpired involving those seven memory crystals. Two questions suddenly nagged at him. The first was why had DisCom tried to steal a technology that it had already funded and, in effect, already owned, at least in part? The second was even more disturbing: why had Red – now Scarlett – been in that R & D laboratory when the ill-fated extraction team arrived?

"Ligeia, this opens up some avenues that I really don't like the idea of going down, even though I'll have to do just that, and very, very soon. Right then, one more question: any luck with '1347'?"

"None at all. I've run every analytic I can think of through all the data I've collected, and nothing correlates to 1347. Nothing."

"Strange. Ivanova doesn't make mistakes like that. Keep worrying at it – she wouldn't have mentioned it if it wasn't truly important. Something is bound to unravel, hopefully sooner rather than later. In the meantime, though, your comment just now about PanEuroEcon made me realize that sometime soon I need to see an old cowboy about a cyber-horse. I'm clear."

"Good luck, David. Be careful, please! Clear." And with that she broke the connection.

Chapter 11

"Loyalty was a virtue, *Fukarō*, that once made *Dai Nippon* great. From the peasant to the *samurai*, the *samurai* to their lords, the lords to the *shogun*, later to the Emperor, loyalty was given without question. It was returned, in the form of protection, leadership, a sense of purpose from the Emperor down through his vassals and the *samurai* to the peasants. Obligations were as binding on masters as on serfs." Hideki Nakajima took a pull from the glass of Suntori whiskey in his hand as he sat in the living room of a Dunwoody condominium, looking out at, appropriately enough, a sunrise. He and Umori were comfortably ensconced in what Nakajima preferred to think of as his "Southern Bolthole," a split level condo in Dunwoody, a fashionable but not overly-ostentatious northern suburb of Atlanta. The property was owned – in name, at least – by a woman who worked as a flight attendant for JAL, and who, so her cover story went, was Nakajima's mistress, a pleasant arrangement to which he was willing to lend as much verisimilitude as necessary. More importantly, she was one of his personal operatives, unknown to Arasaka or anyone else.

"The virtues of the *samurai*," he continued, "their strength, their courage, their wisdom, the spirit of the *bushi-do*, gave form and substance to the spirit of the *Yamato*, guarded them from the incursions of the *gaijun*." Nakajima conveniently forgot that for most of Japan's history, those same *samurai* and their lords had waged near-constant – and very bloody – intramural warfare. "And greatness... there was a time when *Dai Nippon* was not simply the *gaijun*'s toybox, producing their automobiles and electronic trinkets, a nation of shopkeepers and tinkers. Once other nations feared *Dai Nippon*, feared our spirit, our strength of will, the power of our arms and armaments...." His voice trailed of despondently.

"And now, Nakajima-san, 'virtue,' 'loyalty,' and 'greatness' are all hollow words," Umori responded; like Nakajima, he held a glass of whiskey. "The men who lead our businesses and industries have abandoned Japanese tradition for Western expedience, and honour for profit. They posture and strut like modern-day *mikado*, and yet they have no real power: they must negotiate for what their grandfathers and great-grandfathers would have demanded and taken." Neither man mentioned Arasaka by name, neither needed to do so: they were both fully aware of the object of their shared scorn.

Umori set his whiskey glass on the side table to his right. "Enough theatrics, Nakajima-san. I've been in your employ for fourteen years now, long enough to know that wallowing in self-pity and pathos has never been your style. I can always tell when you're planning something, which is what you're doing now. What you were saying just now, that was why you wanted – and still want – those memory crystals so much, isn't it? Because you see them as the key to a revival of Japan's imperium, giving *Dai Nippon* the power to once again demand and take. And you're still determined to get your hands on them. So, tell me: what is it you have in mind?"

Nakajima chuckled. Of all the people he had known in his life, all the employees who had come and gone – or been disposed of – Umori, his old compatriot *Fukaro*, the Owl, had come the closest to being a real friend. For the first time ever, now that he was utterly abandoned by those same Arasaka executives to whom he had given so much loyalty for nearly three decades, he realized just how much he valued Umori.

"You do know me too well, *Fukaro*, and you're right, I am planning something." He set his own glass down and turned his chair so that he could face Umori directly. "Aoki Kurita and the rest of Arasaka's directors don't know it yet, but they have made a terrible mistake by disavowing me –"

"– And you wish to teach them a lesson."

Nakajima shook his head. "No, Umori, I don't; there's neither honour nor purpose in that. Let me finish. Their mistake was not simply disavowing me but also letting MacLaren – Blade – live. That man is dangerous, *Fukaro*, far more dangerous than they realize. He's not just the enemy of their methods, he's the enemy of everything they are trying to achieve. He's the enemy of progress, of the future."

"Please explain yourself, Nakajima-san."

"The man is a walking anachronism. Everything about him, his values, his morals, his loyalties, belong to another century. His weapon of choice is an antique rifle, the car he drives is older than he is. He lives in a stone pile in Scotland that was built in the 19th Century!"

"So he's a glorified eccentric with guns." Umori shrugged. "Aside from his skills as a solo operative, which I must admit are considerable, I don't see how he's dangerous, certainly not to the degree that you seem to believe he is. Where's the threat?"

"The threat is in those very ideas he clings to, outdated ideas like self-determination, the individual right to exercise free will, that laws and governments exist to serve their people, rather than the other way around. There was a truly prescient American politician – she's dead now, sadly – who, about twenty years ago, said 'We must stop thinking about the individual and start thinking about what is best for society.' That was something Japan got right from the very beginning: the weak exist to serve the powerful, and the powerful exist to maintain their power while doing what is necessary to keep the weak docile, servile, and content." There was an earnestness, an intensity, in Nakajima's voice that Umori had never before heard.

"Humanity craves order, *Fukarō*, and humans crave orders. Only fools think otherwise. But Blade is persuasive as well as deadly, and he makes others believe in the foolishness he embraces. And that is where my former superiors at Arasaka failed by refusing to allow me to destroy him once and for all, whatever it took."

Umori frowned. "I'm afraid I'm not following you."

"The crystals, Umori, the crystals! That idiot Coleridge hasn't a clue as to what he's actually created – he imagines it to be nothing more than another one of his cyber-toys, another 'Dennis' or 'Mycroft.' But Blade *does* understand it, as difficult as that may be to believe, and that is why he will never willingly let them out of his possession. What he's realized, somehow, is something that I knew from the very beginning: stored inside those crystals is everything necessary to construct a master Virtual Intelligence, one that can subordinate every other VI on the planet, and direct them to its own purposes. To the purposes of the person who controls that master VI." Nakajima leaned forward, as if to impart some of his own intensity of feeling to the other man.

"As it stands, VI's run the world already: they control the day-to-day operations of every major industry and business, and most of the minor ones. But they do so at the whims of their individual owners – and as often as not they're working at cross purposes, because they lack a central, guiding hand! Provide them with that guiding hand, with someone possessed of sufficient vision and determination, someone who understands that nation-states and national governments are obsolete and that the corporations should, and of a right ought to, have charge over humanity's future. Do that and a whole new order for humanity's future replaces the chaos we have now. That is why I must have those crystals – to put them into the hands of those people best qualified to make that happen! And by that I don't mean *my* hands – I know my limitations. I mean the hands of those who employ us."

"But, how do you know all this?" Umori was baffled: he'd never seen Nakajima so openly determined about anything, and he found himself wondering if his disgrace had...*unbalanced* wasn't the right word...skewed, yes, that was it, something had skewed Nakajima's thinking into wishful thinking, even fantasy. Yet at the same time he wasn't speaking like a man in the throes of either desperation or dementia. Despite the events of the last twelve hours, Nakajima was as coolly confident as Umori had ever seen him to be. "How are you so certain of exactly what is stored in those crystals and what it can do?"

"We've had someone inside Cogito Orbis from the very beginning of Coleridge's 'Project Bowman,' *Fukaro.*"

"'We'? Do you mean Arasaka Corporation?"

Nakajima shook his head and gave Umori a chiding look. "You know better than to ask questions like that," he said simply.

"Consider the question withdrawn. That still leaves the question of how you intend to get those crystals out of Blade's hands and into yours."

"We play on Blade's greatest weakness, Umori, his altruism. We create a situation so terrible that it will be beyond his capacity to contain, or even cope with, and then we let him know that it will end only when he surrenders the crystals – and himself – to me."

"And to do that...?"

"To do that, we'll create our own little reign of terror, one that starts here in Atlanta, and let it spread outward."

"I can see by the expression on your face, Nakajima-san, that you've already created a plan to do just that." Umori picked up his whiskey glass. "And that means you have work for me to do...."

"Correct." Nakajima drew his comm unit from an inner jacket pocket and began touching keypoints. "Here is a list of resources we will require, along with a list of contacts for hiring expendable help. See to it." He turned his attention back to his comm display, scrolling through names, tagging several as he did so. "Fudokome, Yamashita, Homma... Mifune is too far away...Ito...yes, Yamaguchi, too...." He glanced up, then made a shooing motion at Umori. "Get to work! Have as much of the equipment as possible sent to the clean site in Canton as quickly as possible. I intend for us to be on our way there within the hour. My senior operatives will be joining us there by 9:00 PM tonight." His face transformed for a moment into something almost vulpine. "We will find out how many dead *gaijun* it takes for Blade to give up, Umori. Hopefully it will be quite a few."

----------------xxxxx----------------

"Calvin...."

"What is it, Mycroft?"

"You have an incoming comm...from The Russian."

"Wha – ? Why the hell would *she* be comming *me*?" Calvin was sitting at his workstation, his back uncharacteristically turned to his monitors, looking out floor-to-ceiling windows at the late-August morning spreading itself across the city of Atlanta, much as Hideki Nakajima was doing just a few miles north of him. Unlike Nakajima, the vista before him brought no pleasure – in point of fact, he really wasn't seeing it at all. The past thirty-six hours had been a mental and emotional roller coaster, the like of which he had never before experienced – and devoutly wished to never know again. The fear of losing those crystals, the anxiety of that near-run affair in Underground Atlanta, the euphoria at the news that Blade had successfully secured the crystals, the shock of the devastation of The Gardens – which was redoubled when Blade informed him that he did not, in fact, have the crystals – and the numbing sense of betrayal when he realized that Blade was probably double-crossing him, had whipsawed Calvin's mind and spirit almost to the breaking point.

It was Mycroft, faithful as always to his primary mission of doing what was best for Calvin Coleridge and Cogito Orbis, who had saved his sanity, Calvin was sure of that. Mycroft had interposed himself between Calvin and the newsies, and dealt with the numerous local and state officials who were, with due and proper diligence, or so they believed, "investigating" the airstrike on The Gardens. But the Feds, well, Mycroft couldn't handle the Feds; try as he might to divert them, delay them, fob them off with excuses, smoke, and mirrors, they wouldn't be dissuaded from their determination to "interview," as they so politely put it, Calvin directly. Worse, they insisted on doing so in person. Here. In his penthouse in Barnett Tower.

But worst of all was that God alone knew how many of the alphabet soup agencies would show up, what they would want, or what lies, falsehoods, and distortions they would fabricate to achieve their goal, and God apparently wasn't prepared to vouchsafe that knowledge to Calvin. They would be arriving, Calvin knew, just after lunch.

But it seemed that something even more immediate was about to impose itself on him.

"All right, Mike, put her through." He spun about in his chair to face the monitors, and by the time he did so, Ekaterina Ivanova's face had already appeared on the centre screen.

"Hello, Calvin. You look like hell."

Instantly he noticed that Ivanova had dispensed with the exaggerated Russian accent. *Whatever this is, it isn't good,* he thought.

"Hello, Katrina. It's good to see you again, although I was a bit startled when Mycroft announced your comm. And yes, I probably look like hell because right now I feel like hell. I'm working on about four hours' sleep in the last forty-eight, and I've got an incipient migraine trying to make its way through my meds. Plus I have a meeting with an undetermined number of Federal officers in about five hours. So, yeah, if I look like hell, I at least come by it legitimately."

"I'm sorry to hear all of that," she said with genuine concern in her voice, "and I wish I could be the bearer of some good news to alleviate some of the bad, but I'm not, as I'm certain you've already surmised."

"Yeah, the thought did cross my mind: people come to you *for* information, you don't go to them *with* information."

"In this case, I'm making the exception to the rule. You've always dealt with me fairly, and you did so with my father, as well. That's not something someone in my line of work can say about very many people. So consider this a freebie."

"And 'this' is...?"

"You are, to put it bluntly, in deep shit." As he heard the words, Calvin realized he had never seen Ivanova look so serious, even grave. "Or, to put it another way, you have screwed the pooch." She held up her hand as he opened his mouth, cutting off whatever response Calvin was about to offer. "Word started spreading on the street last night, and I've been able to confirm it, that almost everyone, including Arasaka, has lost any interest they may have had those crystals of yours. Every IT corp in the world is practically begging their national law enforcement agencies to listen to their protests of innocence and disinterest."

Calvin shrugged. "I don't see how that's a problem. If anything, that makes my life easier, knowing that half the IT world isn't gunning for me, figuratively or literally."

"Calvin, listen to me. There is a *very* strong rumor that information in those files are in gross violation of the UN Bill of Humanity – and that there's enough information there to give someone with sufficient talent, determination, and resources the capability to build a program that essentially replicates, even if it doesn't exactly duplicate, your 'Project Bowman.' Whatever this program is, Calvin, it is enough to, as a friend of mine likes to say, put you not in a prison but under one."

"Bullshit."

"You are *nekultury*, Calvin."

"Katrina, all those crystals contain is a brain scan of my wife, Kim," he said wearily. "An extremely detailed scan, more detailed than anyone else has ever done, yes, but that's all it is. Somehow this whole mess has gotten blown out of proportion – it's like some goddamned urban legend that keeps growing. The crystals can do this, they crystals can do that, they can steal your passwords and wipe out your operating system if you get too close to them, looking at them will hypnotize you and let them read your brain waves! They'll rewrite your DNA and make you grow two heads! I'm surprised that no has gotten around to saying they hold the cure cancer, can turn water into wine, transform lead into gold, and alter the orbit of the Earth around the Sun!" He snorted derisively. "It gets more layered and more detailed and more complex, not to mention more sinister – to say nothing of more *stupid*! – every time somebody passes it along. But there's nothing illegal about it!"

"I hope you can convince those federal officers who will be visiting you this afternoon of that," she replied, her skepticism unmistakable.

"What? How did you know – ? Never mind, silly question. I *will* be able to convince them, assuming, of course, that between the lot of them they can muster up a three-digit IQ."

Ivanova marveled at the man's arrogance, then suddenly realized that it was all he had left, his only defence. He was, she knew, all too aware that his entire world was probably about to come crashing down around him. He showed a brave front, but behind his arrogance Ivanova saw fear.

"Don't underestimate them, Calvin: they're listening to the same Backchannel chatter that I hear."

"Look, Katrina, I'm telling you, there's nothing illegal about what I've done. The bottom line is that I collected data – data, that's all! – and in a situation like this raw data is meaningless. It's like pure knowledge – what matters is what you do with it, not the data itself! And now that my Gamma Lab at The Gardens has been destroyed, none of the data in those crystals is going to do anyone a single goddamn bit of good anyway! Not even the Feds can prosecute me simply for possessing data that I can't do anything with."

"You know as well as I that despite all that has happened since the Social War, one thing about the *federal'nyy* has not changed: if they want to convict you of something, they will, innocent or not."

"Besides," he went on, as if he never heard her, which was likely, given his state of mind: he seemed to be talking more for his own benefit than for Katrina's, "I don't even have the crystals – the man I hired to get them back for me tells me he's lost them and has no idea where they are."   At that, she gave him a sardonic look. "Really, that's what he told me. Look, all I want to do is get my wife back."

"It's a bit late to start playing that tune, isn't it? Don't you think you should stop spinning yarns and telling tales, at least to me?"

"What do you mean, 'spinning yarns and telling tales'? I'm telling you the truth!"

"In the same way you told Blade 'the truth'? Or should I rephrase that and ask 'Which version of the truth you told him do you mean – the first one or the second?'" That brought Calvin up short: he'd never suspected MacLaren would no idea Ivanova's voice took on a sharp edge as she went on. "   That man is thoroughly pissed off at you because you lied to him not once but twice about those crystals. I know that he's your friend, and I *think* he still regards you as his, but I'm warning you, Calvin, play that man for a fool – or even cause him to think you tried – and he will find ways to hurt you that you never even knew existed."

"Katrina, he's a hired gun with style – those are his own words. He's useful, but he's hardly a danger to someone like me. We don't even live in the same worlds."

"On your own head be it, Calvin. Just make certain that the world you're living in is the real one. I'm clear." Ivanova's face vanished from the monitor.

Calvin sat back in his chair, perplexed. On the surface, there was no reason for the conversation that just occurred to have taken place – but Ekaterina Ivanova never did anything without a reason. So *why* had The Russian commed? Then it struck him: even as she acquired a few more pieces of information for herself, she'd sent him a message. Somehow she'd discovered that he had sold Blade a bill of goods about the crystals – and had done so not once but twice. Even if she hadn't been absolutely certain of that before she commed, his reaction had confirmed it for her. But as for the other side of that coin....

"Mike!"

"Yes, Calvin?"

"We've got another problem."

"Oh?"

"Ivanova just told me in so many words that she knows I've been lying to Blade about the crystals."

"I know, I was monitoring the comm."

"So, how does she know that? Blade wouldn't have told her, he's too security conscious to have done that. Hell, he won't tell his own doctor what he had for breakfast if he thinks it'll violate op sec. It wasn't Raven – she knows about the first cover story I gave Blade, but not the second. And those two women who were here with him yesterday know about the second cover story, but not about the first. Which means...."

"Which means that, as you say, we have another problem."

"Yeah, we do. We've got a fucking leak somewhere. My private security data has been compromised. Somebody's been running their goddamned mouth. Find them, Mycroft, find out who it is. I want you to isolate this bug so we can fix it."

"Holy crap! This is even better than mine was – and that was a custom-built 'deck!" Radome exclaimed when Blackbriar's elint tech appeared unannounced at the office she'd been assigned and handed her a sealed, grey-metal 'deck, along with a small sheaf of documentation. She'd opened the deck, booted it, then checked out the unit's specs – which elicited her exclamation of surprise. "And you're telling me that this is standard issue for you people?"

"Yes, ma'am, that's correct," the tech replied with a slight smile. Being of a kindred spirit to Radome, he understood her kid-on-Christmas-morning-like glee.

"OK, where to I sign to join up?"

"That, ma'am, you'll have to discuss with Ms. Mansfield – or the Consul General herself. Now, if you'll excuse me, I'll leave you to your work and return to my duties." Unspoken but present in his tone was the message that he was not supposed to know what it was that Radome was going to do with that equipment.

Radome smiled broadly at the man, who grinned in return then left the room, closing the door behind him. Even before he was gone, Radome was already elbows-deep in the process of getting acquainted with her new toy. The tech had assured her, when she'd asked earlier, that bandwidth and storage – both of which would be in high demand by the surveillance program Raven sent her – would not be an issue. According to Ms. Mansfield, the Consul-General's instructions had been, "Give the woman whatever she says she needs: genuine national security issues depend on her success." Within less than a minute, Radome finished the basic set-up of the 'deck's POST, had the blink drive given her by Blade linked to the deck and was busily downloading and installing the surveillance program it contained.

Actually, the surveillance "program" wasn't a program so much as it was a suite of tools that could all merrily chatter away to each other while coordinating their particular specialities and report their results to what Radome liked to think of as the "concert master" – she of course, was the orchestra's conductor. The suite had tools designed to unobtrusively burrow into local, state, and federal CCTV and CCAM systems, rifle through their face- and voice-recognition files, even as other tools monitored the live feeds from video and audio pickups in real time. Still other tools accessed the records of national and international telcoms, correlating the date, time, location (by contact node) and comm combination of all incoming and outgoing comms. They would then follow the routing of comms on those domestic combinations that could not be confirmed as unrelated to the search currently underway. At the same time, another system correlated the origins and routes of calls coming in from or going out to Japan via, say, Las Vegas that were then redirected to other comm units, one of which may or may not be Nakajima's phone.

After a few minutes passed, Radome was joined by Blade and Scarlett; Maureen was off in some nook somewhere, poring over the Cogito Orbis financial documentation forwarded to her by Raven. They watched in fascination as the petite, platinum-haired woman's fingers danced about her keyboard display or flitted and flicked across her monitor screen as she set up the suite then tweaked it to her satisfaction.

Scarlett leaned close to Blade and murmured, "How long do you think it will take, once Radome has it up and running, for this surveillance program to find anything – or anyone?"

"It may take a while, there's a lot of information that has to be sorted, sifted, and evaluated. There will hundreds of millions, possibly a couple billion, of false hits and dead ends – even I know that much – every one of which has to be positively eliminated. Nakajima's trying to get lost in the clutter, counting on the sheer volume of traffic to make him invisible."

"Blade's right," Radome affirmed, glancing back over her shoulder at Scarlett. "What you would call the 'signal-to-noise ratio' is incredibly high. There are filters and discriminator routines in here that'll sort out the false hits and then ignore them if they come up again, but they have to make that positive-false ID first. And I can't just assume that every one of Nakajima's comms – outgoing or incoming – went directly to Japan. Some of them may have been redirected once they were outside of the U.S. electronic border. So there's a lot of comms to sift through. Oodles of them, in fact. That's a technical term, you understand – 'oodles.'" Blade and Scarlett shared a smile at that. Radome turned to look at them directly. "What that means, guys, is this is gonna take some time. As soon as I've got this suite tweaked to my satisfaction and I'm sure that everybody is playing nice with everyone else, I'll hit the 'GO' button and let it do its thing. But it could be minutes, it could be hours, it could be days before I get any results – so don't start holding your breath, all right?"

Scarlett grinned. "We can take a hint." She turned to Blade. "Why don't we see if we can find a decent cup of coffee somewhere in this house?"

"Not a bad idea. We'll check in with ye around lunchtime, Trish. See ye then."

Stepping out into the hallway and closing the door behind them, Blade and Scarlett made for the main staircase. "So if that program can access government databases, why don't the Feds use something like this to find Nakajima themselves and bring him in?" Scarlett asked.

"Oh, they do, after a fashion." Blade's smile was sardonic at best. "Which is why it's so damned illegal for a private citizen to have a copy of that program. Ye ken how much governments hate competition." His voice suddenly shifted into an exaggerated English upper-class drawl. "You do understand, don't you, that it's illegal to tell the world about what your own government is doing illegally?"

"I'm not following you."

"What Radome is using is too much like the old TIA program the American NSA created back around 2003 as an anti-terrorism tool. It was designed to collect just about every piece of data that was ever recorded about every living person in the United States – and more than a few of the dead ones."

"You make it sound like it doesn't exist anymore."

"It doesn't, because it was too good at what it did. People went absolutely daft over it, ye ken, because it was the sort of privacy invasion that would have done Orwell proud."

"So...what happened?"

"Enough people started screaming about it – nutters on the left, nutters on the right, religious nutters, atheist nutters, nutters of every social, economic, ethnic and racial persuasion you can imagine – and rightly so. Worse, people who weren't nutters but were perfectly sane and capable of thinking for themselves were as furious as any of the nutters. They didn't stop screaming until yer Congress cut off the R & D funding for the program and broke it up."

"But that's not the end of the story is it?"

"No, it isn't, because all the NSA really did then was very quietly subdivide TIA into separate programs that monitored specific groups of data, and then parceled out those programs to other agencies. The idea was that the NSA would be sort of clearing-house for what was collected. Slightly different method, but in the end it would get the same results."

"All right, I understand all of that. But my original question still stands: why haven't the Feds already done what Radome is in there trying to do?"

"Two reasons. First, pure inertia. There's so bloody much information being collected and collated that it overwhelms the users. The computers can sort it all out, but only the NSA's human analysts can make sense of the take, and the NSA doesn't have enough resources – meaning warm bodies – to keep up with the output. So unless one of their computers starts ringing bells, sounding klaxons, waving flags and shooting off skyrockets about some perceived threat, the humans just plod along, initial their documents without reading them, shuffle files from their 'In' basket to their 'Out' basket, drink their coffee, and collect their paychecks. It's a bureaucrat's paradise, everyone looks busy and no real work ever gets done. The pity is, it sometimes gets people killed, too, when some would-be *jihadi* or Feinian doesn't get spotted in time."

"You said 'two reasons.' What's the second?"

"The senior Federal law enforcement types, the ones who could kick arses and light fires under people and actually make sure that something is being accomplished, expend more time and effort fighting turf wars with each other than they do in getting their jobs done," Blade answered. "Admittedly, we've got the same problem in Britain, although it's not nearly as bad, since our agencies are, as a rule, smaller and there are far fewer of them. Plus we have an 'Old Boy Network' that's been around for about four hundred years that does a remarkably good job at working these things out informally without having to resort to the sort of bureaucratic pissing contests ye Yanks seem to enjoy so much."

"I can see where that would be a big help."

"Aye, especially now that we've got something resembling an empire again – even if it is mostly empty desert at the moment." He sniffed the air appreciatively. "I do believe someone *is* brewing a pot of coffee somewhere. Let's follow our noses and see where they lead."

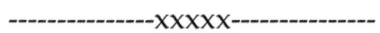

Blade and Scarlett did indeed find a pot of fresh-brewed coffee, in Blackbriar's kitchen. Blade quickly poured two mugs – he was never able to explain his fondness for coffee, as he almost never drank it while at home in Mont Creag House, but he always seemed to crave it when he was overseas – then found a small service tray and placed the mugs on it, along with a creamer and a bowl of sugar cubes. Amused by the nonchalance Blade affected as he did so, Scarlett hid her smile behind her own mug of steaming coffee. With a look of innocence that would have done any schoolboy proud, Blade nodded to her, lifted the tray and set off on an expedition to find Spazz.

She was sitting in the solarium, with her legs tucked underneath her, a pair of reading glasses perched on her nose, and a look of intense concentration on her face as she scanned the top page of a sheaf of papers she was holding. The aroma of coffee preceded Blade by a bare second, and she looked up just as he entered.

"I thought ye might like some fresh coffee," he said, nodding at the empty cup on the side table to her right. "I don't know what ye take in it, so I came prepared for the worst."

Maureen smiled broadly and took the proffered mug. "Black is just fine, and your timing is perfect – I was about to go off in search of a refill." She took a sip. "Mmmmmmm...yes. Keep treating me like this and I might even begin to like you, MacLaren. Note that I said 'might'."

"I won't hold my breath in anxious anticipation," he assured her as he settled into a nearby chair. He nodded at the papers she was holding. "I see ye've been busy this morning."

"I have. I like my wireless devices as much as the next person, but when it comes to financials, I still prefer hard copy. This is a digest of what Raven has uncovered about Cogito Orbis' finances, and it's just fucking brilliant!" she exclaimed in genuine admiration.

"What, her work, or how DisCom and PanEuroEcon covered their tracks?"

"Both, MacLaren. What really amazes me is that no one in the banking industry saw this. Remember, I used to work there, and believe me, there was never a whiff of this floating around! Oh, we all had our suspicions about PanEuro – they've stunk like month-old Gorgonzola ever since they were organized. But DisCom? According to this, DisCom's financial shell game has been going on for more than twenty years now! How the hell could they have gotten away with this for so long?"

"I imagine some of it began with the top executive shake-ups they had back around 2010 or so – and then they had two really expensive productions bomb back-to-back in 2012 and 2013. It begs the question: were they really failures or were they smokescreens? As far as the nuts and bolts of how it was done, though, that's way out of my league, Maureen," MacLaren admitted. "Ye'd understand it far better than I could."

"Conceptually, it's not that hard to explain. No one was looking for it, because no one thought to look for it – they had no reason to. Raven explains it in depth, though you have to have worked in finance to truly appreciate the subtleties. Each and every move made by DisCom was arguably legal, and believe me, their lawyers would have argued it until hell froze over, and none of the moves they made were individually significant enough to attract any unwelcome attention. Each time DisCom acquired a new company – or sold off an old one – or cozied up to somebody like Deutsche Bank, had a stock split, hired or fired some 'CO'-level executive, created a new division, the events themselves were always sufficiently separated by time or kind so as not to suggest that there was any connection between any of them – or that they were part of a larger, broader plan. Or at least there was always enough hand-waving going on to distract public attention from something they were doing elsewhere that they wanted ignored." She stopped and stared into the middle distance for a moment.

"Now that I think about it, there was also the odd 'disappearance' from time to time of people who too persistent with the questions they were asking about our friend, the Rat. People who just 'fell of the radar,' so to speak, and wound up in dead-end jobs in tiny little tech companies or accounting firms out in the middle of nowhere. And a few of them well and truly 'disappeared' – completely and for all time." She looked up at him, eyes wide with questions. "So does this mean that DisCom is becoming the new Arasaka?"

Blade hesitated. "I don't think so, no," he said slowly. "Arasaka has never really acted like one of the post-World War Two *keiretsu*, even less the old pre-war *zaibatsu*. It's driven more by profit, less by market share; instead of the indirect use of power, Arasaka has always liked displays of raw, naked force. It has a different moral compass, non-existent ethical standards, and it's tied too closely to the *yakuza*. The *keiretsu* have always embraced the traditional Japanese sense of honour, Arasaka has perverted it: it's happy to collect debts of honour, but never recognize when it owes one, something that, in the eyes of the traditional *keiretsu* – or especially the old *zaibatsu* – is itself intrinsically dishonourable. The only thing traditionally Japanese about Arasaka is the template of its corporate culture – homogenous, monolithic, and xenophobic."

Spazz nodded as she saw where Blade was headed. "DisCom, on the other hand, has always bent over backwards to present themselves as open-minded, multi-national, all-inclusive," she said pensively. "They collect markers the way Arasaka collects honour debts, and nobody loves their fucking profits the way DisCom loves theirs, but to Mr. and Mrs. Main Street USA, all DisCom wants is to just listen to the world sing in perfect goddamned harmony. And they aren't all that monolithic, either. Yeah, I can see what you mean – they've got a very different corporate culture." She frowned. "Or at least they're presenting one to the world. Maybe they're just an Arasaka with a happy face."

"That's not a happy thought."

Maureen rolled her eyes, then went back to frowning. "You know, I think this changes everything. I mean, I know you've got unfinished business with Nakajima, but that's become a separate issue now –"

"Has it, I wonder...?"

"It has. Your feud or mutual vendetta or whatever it is will just get in the way of getting those crystals back. Now, what we do with them when we have them – whether or not we turn them over to your friend Hobbes – is something else altogether, isn't it?" She looked at MacLaren questioningly, but he just waved for her continue.

"I mean, presuming we find them, do we just hand them over, collect our paychecks – and you can be damned sure I'm billing that fat little fucker for my time! – and just walk away, wash our hands of the whole affair, and pretend that's the end of it? I've got a big red flag waving here telling me that really isn't a good idea."

"I'm not saying ye're wrong, Maureen; all the same, Hobbes didn't hire us to protect him from the consequences of his own bad decisions. Then there's Kim to think about. If we don't give those crystals back to him, Kim is as good as dead – and, given that her current condition is already deteriorating, before too much longer, her body is going to die anyway."

"Oh, don't give me that bullshit, Blade! This stopped being about Kim the minute we walked into Hobbes' penthouse. Or didn't you notice that in the entire conversation we had, he only spoke about Kim in the past tense, never the present? As far as he's concerned, Kim is as good as dead already: whatever's stored in those crystals is all that matters to him now. And whatever it is, if he's willing to let his wife die over it, and DisCom is willing to get as many people killed as they already have over it, then maybe we should be thinking about what we should really do with them. Because sure as little fucking fishes, once we give those crystals to Hobbes and DisCom finds out he has them, they'll come up here, take them, and kill him and anybody else who gets in their way. I don't know about you, MacLaren, but while I think he's an arrogant little prick with delusions of grandeur, enough people have died over those fucking crystals already."

"So, what do ye have in mind? Ye obviously have *something* in mind. What is it?"

"Funny you should ask...."

Ligeia sat at her console, legs folded up into a sort of lotus position, leaning forward, peering intently at her main monitor and tapping her front teeth with a fingernail as she reviewed for at least the fifth time the information she'd sent MacLaren. *Oh, David, David, David. What have you gotten yourself into this time? This was supposed to be a straightforward smash-and-grab, get those people out of there, take the crystals back to Calvin, get paid and come home. You weren't supposed to open up a can of worms of this sort.*

What she had found when she began deeply data-mining Cogito Orbis' list of investors had left Raven – Ligeia – stunned. It wasn't that DisCom and PanEuroEcon were funding him: Calvin, a self-described "capitalist whore," would cheerfully take *anyone's* money in exchange for corporate services rendered or products provided. What was shocking was the discovery that DisCom was using Northern Commonwealth Bank to launder money that it clearly wanted to hide. Equally disturbing was the realization that DisCom *had* money that it felt it *needed* to hide. The immediate follow on to that thought was to wonder exactly what DisCom had done to acquire it.

What threatened to drag the entire situation into the realm of the surreal, however, was the fact that what DisCom had done was attempt to steal an essential part of a technology for which *it had already paid*. That act effectively triggered the entire chain of events which had taken place in the last three days – whether through chance or design was open to question – by bringing Arasaka into the affair, as they in turn tried to steal the crystals, then almost spun the situation beyond control when, having failed in that, they destroyed The Gardens instead. And yet, even more rapidly than it had escalated, that entire situation subsided as Arasaka unexpectedly lost all interest in the crystals. For a time it seemed that PanEuroEcon was set to become the next player in this violent charade, and Ligeia had been watching PanEuro very carefully after discovering Brian Bridelow had been in its employ. Yet, Europe's gigantic political, economic, and industrial conglomerate never made a move: just as it seemed poised to do so, it backed away as abruptly as did Arasaka. What had all the makings of a looming corporate war instead fizzled and died, not with a bang but a whimper. What had made Arasaka and PanEuroEcon back away so quickly, she wondered?

For that matter, Ligeia found herself questioning why Arasaka ever got involved in this affair with the crystals in the first place. PanEuro being part of it would have made sense: the conglomerate had a lengthy history of stealing technology, any technology, as long as there was a profit – political or financial – to be made from it. But Arasaka made small arms and military equipment – there was no reason for the Japanese firm to be interested in VI technology.

So why did they jump in with both feet? It's almost as if DisCom was trying to provoke a corporate war with Arasaka and PanEuro. Why the devil would they want to do that? And no sooner does the war seem to be off to a rollicking good start than suddenly they all stop shooting at each other. Why?

Blade. Blade threw a spanner in the works when he took the crystals out of play. No one knows where they are – well, I do, but only because David told me – so there's no point in shooting at each other to get something no one actually has. Then word starts leaking out about what's really stored in those crystals and everybody panics and runs away. That had to be DisCom's doing. They've funded Project Bowman – I wonder if anyone other than David and I have actually figured out what that name really signifies? – so the best way to scare off anyone else who's interested in it is to make them think it's so dangerous that every government in the world will descend on them like the wrath of God – which they would. But then that means DisCom is setting up Calvin to take the fall for completing an illegal project they paid him to create.

Once he learned of that, she knew, MacLaren's rage would know no bounds. He was already furious with Calvin for being double-crossed not once but twice: discovering that Calvin's duplicity was a consequence of trying to protect investors who were actively deceiving him would be an utter and complete affront to MacLaren's rather prickly sense of honour – not to mention his pride. Being played for a patsy was bad enough, but being played for a patsy by someone who was being gamed themselves was guaranteed to earn his certain and permanent enmity. His response, when it came, would be coldly calculated, but it would also be devastating.

Please, David, don't do something stupid! Oh, Dear Lord, what am I thinking? Of course, you're going to do something stupid! You're David MacLaren! But even you should know that you can't take on DisCom single-handed! Calvin is going to get dumped right into the middle of a cesspool and you won't be able to prevent it. Please, please, God, don't let any of it splash on David!

She started as a familiar but unexpected voice spoke in her earbud.

"Miss Raven, this is Mycroft. I was wondering if I could have a few minutes of your time...."

"Got him!"

Radome's exclamation and accompanying fist pump came as the data scrolling across her monitor came to an abrupt halt and the words "Positive Identification" appeared and began flashing. For just over six hours the surveillance suite had been steadily, methodically working its way through the staggering mass of data it had accessed, making a correlation here, spotting an intersection there, eliminating false leads and abandoning dead ends. Radome had done her best to remain patient as she watched the system's progress, constantly tweaking, adjusting, and refining the search parameters, steadily narrowing the scope of the search – with the occasional suggestion from Raven, who, determined to have nothing to do with that surveillance suite, refused to link to Radome's deck. Still, Trish knew full well that it could be days before the suite produced any result. And then she got lucky.

Apparently Hideki Nakajima had been very busy this morning,

unwittingly aiding Radome's efforts simply by raising the profile of his comm combination, drawing a disproportionate share of the search suite's attention. Where signals intelligence was concerned, Nakajima was manifestly an adherent of the "security through obscurity" school, rather than "security through hard defences," trusting the sheer volume of wireless traffic to provide sufficient natural cover so that his comms could lose themselves in the noise and clutter, just as Blade had earlier outlined for Scarlett. And the concept worked – until Radome put the surveillance suite to work. In the end, Nakajima was just one among the billions of wireless addicts in the 21st Century, and he unwittingly betrayed himself through his penchant for talking too much.

Once she confirmed her results, she tapped into Blade's comm net and announced, "Blade, we've found our boy!"

"Are ye certain?"

"As certain as I can be. If it's not Nakajima, then there're two of him out there, and he better watch out before the other one starts writing bad checks."

"I'll be with you in a just a minute."

"What is it?" Spazz asked him as he snatched up a towel and began wiping soapy water from his hands – and from his face, which was still partially covered with suds, courtesy of one Maureen Collins. He tossed a fresh towel to her and she began drying off as well – MacLaren had *mad' siccar* of his revenge – and she too began to dry off.

They were standing outside Blackbriar, on the east side of the house, where they had been washing the Jaguar Mark 12 they had driven down to the Spayth Building. Two of the resident staff had gone down there earlier this morning to recover it; it was actually little worse for the wear, but the battleship-grey saloon was several shades darker when it arrived back at Blackbriar, covered as it was with a fine patina of ash and soot. Ms. Mansfield had taken one look at the automobile, rolled her eyes heavenward, and resignedly instructed the staff to wash it. Blade, feeling guilty, had decided that he would do so instead, as an act of expiation which he hoped Ms. Mansfield would appreciate. He secretly suspected that she was torn between her obligation to feel the proper degree of English indignation and her willingness to admit that she hadn't had so much fun in years. While not exactly a backwater posting, the role of senior intelligence officer of His Majesty's Consulate in Atlanta was hardly a plum assignment for someone of her talent and lineage.

After watching Blade at work for a few moments, Maureen had decided to join him, and the combination of water hoses, soap, and sponges made it inevitable that someone would eventually get carried away, which they both did almost simultaneously. Fortunately, Radome's announcement staved off a full-blown water fight before it could well and truly get started, and now the two did their best to make themselves presentable before returning to the house.

Radome's eyebrows almost disappeared into her hairline when the tall, willowy blonde and the stocky Scot presented themselves in her makeshift office, both of them more than slightly damp and disheveled.

"You two are like a pair of eight-year olds!" she exclaimed as she threw up her hands in exasperation. "I can't leave you alone for ten minutes you getting into some kind of devilment!"

MacLaren immediately protested. "She started it!"

"Did not!" Maureen denied firmly.

"Did too!"

"Did not!"

"Did – "

"Children! Please!" Radome dropped her hands to her hips and glared at them. Any second now, Blade was certain, she would start tapping her foot. "Can we focus on the job at hand?"

"Sorry," Blade and Spazz answered in chorus.

"What do ye have for us, Trish?" Blade asked, just as Scarlett walked in.

"I not only have Nakajima's com combination, I have his actual location dialed in to a fare-thee-well."

"What? You're serious?"

"As a heart attack."

"All right, tell me."

"Your boy, Nakajima, has spent a lot of time on his comm this morning. That's what got him caught. The system didn't tag him directly, but it did notice that one particular combination was making successive calls to other combinations that were directly attached to Arasaka operatives, or to combinations that belonged to people who had subcontracted for Arasaka at one time or another. Then it started backtracking the logs of the comms the suspect combination had been making over the past seventy-two hours – and several of them had been comm calls to and from Japan, including combinations that were attached to Arasaka or a known Arasaka employee. Now, get this: I was also able to positively confirm that this particular combination was at the Spayth Building last night."

Spazz gave out a low whistle, and Blade looked intrigued.
Radome continued, her demeanor admirably professional, although there was a clear undercurrent of excitement in her voice: like thousands of other people around the world, she had acquired a personal score to settle with Hideki Nakajima. "I was pretty sure I'd nailed that puddle of snot – I mean, whoever owned this combination wasn't going to be some low-level flunky calling the home office for instructions, right? – but I wanted to be sure, so I went ahead and did a log search for the last six months. Surprise, surprise, for every known location of Nakajima's in that period of time, the location of that combination matched exactly, both geographically and chronologically."

"I'd say ye nailed it, lass," Blade said, and Spazz nodded in agreement.

"So, what do you want me to do with it?"

Blade considered this for a second, then pointed at an unused monitor on an adjacent desktop. "Are ye linked to that display?"

"I can be in about five seconds, why?"

"Could ye throw up a map showing me where Nakajima is right now?"

Radome sat back down, turned to her deck and entered a few commands. The monitor came to life, on it appeared a map.

"Brilliant! Now, one more thing. This comm unit of Nakajima's...."

"What about it?"

"Do ye think ye can take it away from him?"

"Do you mean hack it? Root it?" She thought about it for a few seconds. "I don't see why not, especially if Raven is willing to team up with me. Are you, Raven?"

"Yes, absolutely." Raven's voice came over the comm net. "Tell me, what kind of comm unit is he using?"

"Looks to be an off-the-shelf burner. Yep, a DigiSig model UIY-2249." Radome confirmed.

"Let me see what I've got that we can use against that. We'll want to keep it simple, mind you, just not *too* simple. We have to choose an exploit and an attack vector that won't make him twig to the fact he's being hacked."

"What do you mean, Raven?"

"David, we need to be certain that we don't get too clever for our own good. If the attack vector is too simple, it will be immediately obvious to him. If it's too complex and he happens to pick up on it, he'll realize it wasn't just some random idiot trying to hack his comm. Either way, he'll know he's under attack, and that his comm has been ID'ed. Which means he'll ditch it and we'll have to start all over again. Knowing Nakajima, he'll tell all of his subordinates to get new comms as well, and we'll lose track of the lot of them."

Radome nodded in agreement. "That's it on a nutshell."

Suddenly she brightened. "That's it! We spam him!"

"What?" Blade, Scarlett, and Spazz asked in unison.

"We spam him! It's one of the oldest tricks in the book, which means that most people now of days have forgotten all about it because hardly anyone uses it for comm hacks anymore – and that means they're vulnerable to it. We stuff a payload that contains a root kit into a plain manila envelope, attach it to an ordinary text message, and send it. Once he opens the text message to read it, the payload is delivered and we own his comm."

"'Plain manila envelope'?"

"David, you are such a Luddite!" Blade could almost hear Raven's eyes rolling. "That means an ordinary data packet."

"Oh."

"It seems simple enough," Scarlett admitted, "but what do we send as the actual message?"

A particularly nasty look came over Radome. "How about we spam them with ads for penile enlargement? The Japanese just *hate* that! They tend to take it personally."

Blade disagreed. "No, that's a little too obvious – although I understand where ye're coming from and thoroughly approve of the general sentiment. But if we even hint that we know they're Japanese, they'll realize we're onto them. Any ideas, Raven?"

"I'm drawing a blank here."

Radome, meanwhile, had started scrolling around the overhead imagery on her screen of the area where Nakajima's clean site was located. "What a minute, what's this? Oh, this is perfect! Perfect! There's a school, Creekview High School, about a mile north of that house. What do you say to some fourteen year-old twerp who thinks he's a computer weasel spamming the tower Nakajima and his people are using – inviting all of his friends to a party at the fieldhouse tonight?"

Spazz laughed aloud. "Nobody, I don't care how paranoid they are, would suspect something like that! It just reeks of geek-wannabe! Go for it!"

"OK, how do we phrase it?" Radome looked first at Spazz, then at Blade.

"Don't ask me – I have no idea how teenagers talk to each other these days."

"Blade, you really need to get out more," Spazz said sympathetically.

Muttering under his breath, Blade turned away and plunked himself down in the chair he'd placed in front of the other monitor. There he began studying the overhead imagery of Nakajima's safehouse in Canton with a clearly feigned intensity. The three women ignored him.

After a few moments, though, the concentration was no longer theatrical. *This*, he mused, *is going to be a tactical nightmare. There are no clear sightlines into the house longer than fifty feet, and those are only on the northwest quadrant. There's no place closer than a half-mile distant to leave a vehicle where it won't be immediately noticed by the neighbors or a roving police cruiser. The only secure way to approach the house is from the northwest quadrant, but doing so means traversing at least a half-mile-wide stand of densely-grown hardwood. Nakajima's certain to have pickets posted in the undergrowth around the house, which adds yet another layer of complication.*

His first thought had been to take the Lee-Enfield and its suppressor, find a nice spot in those woods to set up, then reach out and touch someone, anyone, inside the house who happened to be in his line of fire. Studying the imagery for just handful of seconds made it clear that idea was simply unworkable, however. Which left him with only one choice, to do it the hard way.

"Shite...."

"What was that?" It was Spazz who turned and looked at him.

"What was what?" Blade clearly didn't realize he'd spoken aloud. "Oh, nothing." He faced the monitor again, and brought up what images there were of safe house.

It was a singularly unimpressive structure, almost bland despite its attempts at pretension, of a style that Americans once derisively called the "McMansion school" of residential architecture. Blade was reminded of how a friend had once characterized a mutual acquaintance: "He's much like white bread, without the character and taste," and decided that the same idea was applicable here. It somehow reflected the nature of its owner, as houses are wont to do. From the multiple façades that never gave a clear view of the whole structure, to the peeling paint on the window sashes and the occasional sagging shutter, to the broken gate at the drive and the neglected landscaping, it was slightly rundown, even seedy. More to the point for tactical purposes, the vulgarity of the exterior elevations spoke to an equally complicated - and tactically complex – interior layout. "Going in hard" was beginning to take on multiple meanings here.

"No."

The word came from behind him, short and sharp. He spun around to see Spazz standing in front of him, hipshot, arms crossed, her lips pressed tightly together, her eyes flashing. Much as he had done with Radome moments earlier, he expected her to start tapping her foot. When he looked down, he saw that she already was.

"What?" he asked, the very model of innocence.

"You are *not* going to do what I think you're planning to do."

"How do ye know what I'm planning to do?"

"Maybe because I've been trying for so long to be a solo like you that I'm beginning to *think* like you." Her tone made it clear that she would not brook any argument. "You are *not* going in there!"

At that Scarlett turned around and asked, "He's going to do what?"

"It seems Mr. MacShitforbrains here thinks he's going to do a one-man sortie into Nakajima's bungalow up in Canton." Maureen's tone was tart enough to make a lemon wince. "I just informed him that he's out of his MacMind."

It was Scarlett's turn to glower at Blade. "For all I know I really *was* born the day before yesterday, but that strikes me as a Very Bad Idea – as in 'just plain stupid'!"

"Look, the both of ye just back off, right now. This isn't yer call to make, right? It's mine, so leave it be."

"Wrong, Blade. It *is* our call to make." Radome added her voice to the choir of dissent. "Friends don't let friends drive drunk, right? Well, friends don't let friends go out and get their asses shot off, either. Especially when they're in your condition. I seem to recall that the first time I saw you, you were bleeding from a gunshot wound to your left leg –"

"It was only a scratch – wasn't even a flesh wound!"

"– and I know for a fact you took three, maybe four hits to the torso that your body armour stopped, but I also know the kind of bruising that leaves. Last night I watched you bust two ribs, and according to Dr. Smythe-Matthews, you've got some pretty spectacular bruising all along your left side. I don't know if Spazz or Scarlett noticed it, but I've seen you wincing today when you've made some sudden or unexpected move."

"I've seen it," Spazz affirmed.

"So have I," Scarlett agreed. "The bottom line, MacLaren, is that you're in no condition to fight off a determined pack of Cub Scouts, let alone an unknown number of Arasakas."

"I'm sorry, ladies, but I don't have time to discuss this in committee!"

"We are not a committee!"

"Ye had me fooled."

"Watch out," Raven's murmured into the other three women's earbuds, "here comes the charm."

Blade held up his hands, palms outward, in what was meant to be a placating gesture. "All right, all right. I'm sorry, I didn't mean to be short with ye. I think we're all overreacting a bit here." He gave them his best lopsided "I feel really sheepish right now" smile. "If ye can hack Nakajima's comm like ye say ye can, Radome, by the time I leave, Alistair will be able to give me a solid count of how many people Nakajima has with him, and if ye dig deep enough, ye might be able to find a floor plan of the house filed with some local government office somewhere. With those, I can work up an op plan that gets me in, gets me to Nakajima, and gets me out again. They'll never see me coming or going – and Nakajima will be dead. That's who I'm really after here: I want to cut off the head of the snake, because if I do that, there's no need for me to chop the rest of the snake into little pieces. I'll be back before ye know it, and we can sit around laughing, smoking cigars, and knocking back Piper-Heidsieck – although we'll need to clear the bubbly for ye with Dr. de Sade, Radome."

Scarlett and Maureen looked at each other. "Yep, right on cue. He just tried the charm," Scarlett declared. Maureen nodded, grinning.

"Fortunately for us – and *un*fortunately for you, Blade – we had advance warning," Radome announced smugly.

"Ye had what? Wait a minute!" He raised his voice slightly. "Raven – Ligeia! Are ye on their comm channel?"

"I most certainly am." Blade didn't have to listen hard to hear the tightly-leashed anger in Raven's voice. "I knew when bluster or reason didn't work, you'd turn on the charm, and knowing you, you'd not only get them to agree with you, you'd have them so bamboozled that they'd be standing at 'Present Arms' as you waltzed out the front door on your way to certain death. You tried that on me once, remember? And I was naive enough to let you get away with it."

"But I came back, didn't I?"

"Yes, you did, and that's the reason we never got married and why I'm no longer your fiancé." Spazz threw a look of surprise at Blade when she heard that. "Because I was certain you weren't coming back that time, and when you did, I knew the next time you'd try the same thing, and you'd keep on trying it until finally you *didn't* come back. I vowed then that I would never again let you get away with that with anyone else."

It was Raven's words that seemed to break Blade's determination, and his shoulders slumped. He looked at Scarlett, Radome, and Spazz in succession and said, "Ye all intend to be very stubborn about this, don't ye?"

"Of course."

"Yep."

"Damnbetcha."

"Ligeia, you really don't fight fair."

"I know, David, I know." There was an almost wistful note in her voice now. "You're my best friend, and in my own way I still love you, so if I have to play dirty to keep you alive, I will."

There was a long silence as Blade stared at the floor, his fists clenched in frustration, while Spazz, Radome, and Scarlett looked on. It was Spazz who finally spoke.

"MacLaren, I know what you're thinking. I don't know how you feel right now, but I do know what you're thinking. This is a lost opportunity that may never come again, right?" Blade nodded. "Well, if what these two geeks are telling us is true, that's not the case. If they really can hack Nakajima's comm, then we'll be able to track him twenty-four seven, no matter where he is. That means you'll be able to pick your own time and place, bring the fight to him on your terms, not his, instead of going off half-cocked out of desperation."

Blade looked up at her, then looked away and sighed. "Ye're right, Maureen." He turned to Radome. "The thing is, can ye and Raven pull this off?"

"Piece of cake!" Radome assured him. " We spam the tower Nakajima's comm is currently connected to and work through all the providers. I can make it look like an ordinary script kiddie. Nakajima and anyone else who uses the same provider will get spammed first, then the other users get it in succession. Spam, rinse, repeat as necessary until he finally opens one of them. Since everybody is being hit with the same thing at the same time, it won't look like he's being singled out. As soon as he opens one of the texts, the package is delivered and we've got him."

"All right. Do it."

Radome's fingers danced across the keyboard of her 'deck. Blade made no attempt to follow her progress: he trusted her competence and knew she would also double-check her work with Raven before sending it out. At last, she hit the "Enter" key with a flourish, announced, "Done!" and then said, "Now we wait. I added one extra detail. The text will resend itself every five minutes until Nakajima opens it. Then it will be sent two more times after that. It occurred to me that, if he didn't open the text the first time but some of his flunkies did, he might get suspicious if it keeps resending and then stops once he opens it. So, it gets sent a couple of extra times for cover."

Blade nodded approvingly. "Clever, Radome, very clever. I certainly wouldn't have thought of that." He sat back in his chair, folded his arms, crossed his legs, and asked, "So now we wait?"

"Now we wait," Radome confirmed, slumping down in her chair. Spazz muttered something about getting more coffee, and Scarlett perched herself on the desktop. After about ten minutes, in which time Spazz returned with fresh coffee for all four of them, a new alert began flashing on Radome's display, and she announced, "Package delivered!"

Blade sat up straight and asked her, "Can ye link Alistair to your deck?"

"If he gives me permission."

"Alistair?"

"Aye, Sirr! Sending the permission now. Done, Sirr!"

"Right, then. Alistair, can ye monitor Nakajima's current conversations and also do a high-speed review of all of Nakajima's conversations that the NSA has recorded today – without getting caught?"

"Och, aye, Sirr! 'Twill be a bit of a lark leading those pea-wit AI's at Fort Meade on a wee merrie chase. It'll take a few minutes, Sirr, but, aye, Ah can doo that."

"Do it, then give us a digest when ye're finished."

"Verra good, Sir! Ah'll just be twa jiffies."

Again they waited, this time for a much shorter period.

"Sirr, Ah have the results ye requested."

"Go ahead, Alistair, however ye want to present it is fine with us."

"Well, Sirr, it sounds as if Nakajima has been creatin' an organization o' his ain, no' just right under Arasaka's nose, but *inside* Arasaka itself."

"He what?"

"He has a total o' eleven lieutenants, Ah canna tell if he picked 'em oot himself or they were just sort o' gravitated to him, but they address him almost like feudal vassals speakin' tae their lord. All o' them are current or former Arasaka enforcers, and they're all meeting with Nakajima tonight at that safehoose in Canton."

"Can ye tell us what the meeting is about, Alistair?"

"Aye, Sirr, just bide a wee, Ah'm gettin' there. But yer no' gonna like what yer aboot tae hear."

"Give it to us anyway, Alistair. We need to hear it whether we like it or not."

"Aye, Sir." Alistair paused as if taking a deep breath – totally unnecessary, of course, but over the years the VI had acquired quite a few of the common quirks of human speech patterns. "He uses a lot o' doubletalk, even when he's speakin' in Japanese, but it's pretty easy tae put it all together. He spent a good portion of the mornin' handin' oot assignments to those lieutenants o' his, givin' them targets and tellin' 'em tae start workin' on their operational plans. He's expectin' a full briefin' from each o' them tonight."

"You said 'targets,' Alistair, so I assume that what's being planned is a series of coordinated attacks."

"Ye're correct, Miss Collins. Starting at 8:00 AM tomorrow, Nakajima's people are goin' tae start attackin' civilian targets across the Greater Atlanta area. Business parks, bankin' centres, daycare centres, yon university downtown – what's the name? Georgia Tech, aye, that's it. At 10:00 AM a second wave will begin – shoppin' centres, restaurants, grocery stores. The only objective will be tae accumulate the highest possible body count. Nakajima's people will be told that they shouldna' expect tae survive, so they should take as many *gaijun* with them as they can."

"Dear God!"

"Holy shit!"

"Fuck!"

"Goddammit to hell...."

"Oh, no!"

The rush of expletive-laden reaction came all at once, then the small office was wrapped in total silence. Radome looked ill. Scarlett's face was expressionless, but anyone looking close would have seen a deep-burning anger in her eyes. Spazz was visibly shaken, even frightened. Blade expression was one of pure fury, while in Yorkshire, three thousand miles distant, Ligeia's face had suddenly gone ashen.

"If I'd known the situation was this bad," he growled, "I would fought the three of ye tooth and nail rather than agreeing to give up my idea of hitting them tonight." He slammed both hands, open-palmed, down on the table in frustration. "In fact, I'm thinking of telling the three of ye to sod off and do it anyway."

No one replied; in fact, no one else said a word for several minutes. Eventually, though, Spazz broke the silence.

"Hey, MacLaren, maybe we're too close to the problem. We've been at the heart of the storm for so long now that we're overthinking things. The answer's simple: we notify the local authorities and let them handle it. It's their job, it's what they're trained and equipped to do, and let's face it, there's no fucking way the four of us can stop it from happening. In fact, the only thing we can do is sound the alarm."

"And ye know what will happen when we do, Spazz? Damn all! The rank and file may be good, honest cops – or at least most of them are, more or less; my personal jury is still out on that. But their superiors, the ones who will have to make the hard calls, actually make decisions, are politicians and bureaucrats. They'll diddle, twiddle, and resolve, dither, bustle and bluster, and in the end do nothing, claiming that it's all a hoax, that there's no evidence to support the sort of response that it'll take to stop Nakajima's people. And then when the shite does hit the fan, they'll go in front of the newsies, wring their hands, cry their crocodile tears, and claim they never saw it coming, because the people who carried out the attacks were 'too well concealed in the fabric of American society' to be detected in time. Hundreds – maybe thousands – of people are going to die because the policy makers won't get off their fat arses and do something for once!"

"Pardon me, Sirr," Alistair broke in, "but that's not all of it. It seems that Nakajima is about tae do what he was apparently ordered tae do by Aiko Kurita twa days ago and failed: make ye appear to be at the heart of a wave of terror there in the United States, caused by yer refusal tae give into his demands. He's convinced that if he pushes the death toll high enough, ye'll be compelled to hand over the memory crystals eventually, and in the meantime, the U.S. government will revoke yer diplomatic immunity and arrest ye on a whole encyclopedia o' charges."

"Right then, that tears it! I'm going in." Blade stood up and glared at the three women. "If any of ye want to go with me, ye're welcome to come along, but I'm not going to sit here and let it happen."

"No, MacLaren, you can't go. I won't let you."

"Try and stop me, Maureen!"

"All right, I will!" She planted herself firmly in front of him, feet spread wide, hands on her hips. "Did you give a minute's thought to what kind of backup planning they might have? You can't count on stopping Nakajima just by killing off his henchmen – or even killing him personally – because they may well have set it up so that their attacks go forward no matter what happens! In that case, sure, they'll be dead, but it won't stop a bloodbath from happening!"

"Fine, ye've got a valid point. But what's the alternative?" Once again, silence fell over the room, then Scarlett raised one hand in a small gesture.

"Blade, I have an idea...."

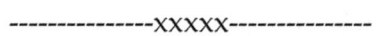

It was just then that, in a private room of the Critical Care wing of Emory Medical Centre, a tendril of consciousness began reaching out, following paths that were unfamiliar yet not unknown, and began searching...searching....

Chapter 12

"You want to *what?*"

"Use the AV7 to drop one of those Gryphon laser-guided bombs ye have stored under the carriage house on Nakajima's wee but 'n' ben in Canton."

Ms. Mansfield, Blade mused, missed her true calling: she would have made a wonderful headmistress at some private school for unruly adolescents. She stood squarely before him, arms crossed, head tilted to one side, lips compressed into a thin line, ice-blue eyes positively glaring at him. "And just what makes you think that there are such things under the carriage house?" she demanded.

"Because there are a pair of hardpoints under the stub wing outboard each engine, with triple-ejector racks on both inboard mounts – and the AV7 is rated to deliver the Gryphon. If ye didn't have the Gryphons, those racks wouldn't be there. The logical place to keep such ordnance would be in a reinforced bunker under the carriage house. Provided, of course, that ye haven't disguised it as the midden on the west side of the house. How am I doing so far?"

"Cheeky bastard, aren't you?"

"Ye sound just like your grandmother when you say that."

"How would you know, she died while you were still a boy."

"I was fifteen, actually, and no, I never met her, but James – or should I call him 'Brian' now? – does a marvelous impression of her to this day."

"He would." She sighed. "He was almost as exasperating as you are."

"Ye're changing the subject. Do I get the AV and a pair of Gryphons or not?"

"Out of the question."

It was MacLaren's turn to glare. "Not acceptable."

"That's too bad. Life is full of disappointment, MacLaren. I suggest you learn to live with it." She paused, took a deep breath, then went on. "I realize, Blade, that you operate with the direct imprimatur of Crown approval, and I know why, but doesn't mean you have *carte blanche* to launch what amounts to a military strike on the soil of a friendly power! And on a civilian target, at that! Inform the Americans of what you've learned and let them handle it. This is really their problem anyway: it's American citizens who will be targeted. We've no reason to get involved aside from trying to give them as much warning as possible – which I trust you've already done or will soon be doing."

"Those Americans will be targeted because of something Nakajima believes I know or have." Uncharacteristically, Blade's tone was subdued, even if there was a hint of menace in it. And a careful observer would have noted the slight tightening around his eyes: he didn't at all like what he was hearing. "And as ye obliquely pointed out a moment ago, I *am* a British subject. I believe that gives us more than enough reason to 'get involved.'"

"Blade, it may have escaped your notice, but this is a safehouse, not your personal armoury. I won't authorize it, and before you threaten to go over my head to the Consul-General, I can assure you that she won't either. His Majesty's Government is not in the habit of carrying out violent covert operations inside friendly countries – especially without the knowledge or consent of that country's government! Things are dicey enough with the Americans right now as it is: they're still fighting us tooth and nail over the protectorates we set up in the Middle East after the Third Gulf War. You know damned well that they don't like that Britain is getting rich from selling the world the oil that they believe should be theirs. We don't need io give them a pretext for an open confrontation!"

Blade gave her a shrewd look, suddenly understanding why this woman, of all people, was a mere section chief. He asked, "That's not all, is it?"

Mansfield had the grace to colour slightly. "No, it isn't. Leaving the political consequences aside, if word ever got out that I permitted, let alone authorized what you're proposing, I would find myself on the first flight back to London, where I would spend the rest of my now-blighted career in espionage as a low-level file clerk. I told you, let the Americans handle it." There was a note of finality in her voice which she clearly intended to convey that the last word on the subject had been spoken. Blade was not to be put off, however.

"I'm willing to go as high as necessary to get what I want, Ms. Mansfield – and ye know how high that means."

"Is there really no limit to your arrogance, Blade?"

"When innocent lives are endangered because of something I did – something I did that was part of my job, a job His Majesty's Government tacitly approved – the answer is 'No, there *is* no limit!'"

"I can't believe I'm having this conversation with you!" she said furiously.

"And I can't believe I'm having this conversation with Olivia Mansfield's granddaughter," he shot back.

"Now, just what is that supposed to mean?"

"It means that she always had the courage to make tough calls, the right calls, even when her career was on the line, because she knew the job itself was bigger and more important than she was. She wasn't afraid of taking responsibility for making those calls, because she never confused what was right with what was expedient!"

"You're a self-righteous pain in the arse, do you know that?"

"Fine, maybe I am. But try to tell me I'm wrong."

Mansfield turned and walked over to the nearest window, where she stood motionless for some moments, saying nothing, gazing out across the vast expanse of Blackbriar's front lawn. Finally, she spoke, without turning back to face Blade.

"Very well, I'll authorize the use of the AV7. I suppose there's really no way I can stop you, so there's no point in my trying any further. But this is where my co-operation ends. I want you and your friends out of here tomorrow. Is that clear?"

"Clear enough."

"Fine. Then I'll send Colour Sergeant Bourne over to you – he doubles as our armourer. And Blade – " she finally looked over her shoulder at him – "I suggest that you get that information you have into the hands of someone on the American side you can trust to do the right thing with it."

"So, Nathan, do ye have any objections to my plans to bury Nakajima?"

"Personally? No, none at all. It's risky politically, but politics isn't my business. And from the intel you just gave me, I think my people will be able to send Nakajima some of his own to keep him company in Hell."

The basset hound-eyed, jowly face of Nathan Gerrard looked out from the monitor at Blade, bearing a resigned expression. The US Marshal was still in Atlanta overseeing the investigation into the firefight – there was really no other word for it – in Underground Atlanta, which, to Blade's mild astonishment, had taken place barely thirty-six hours earlier.

"You know, I'm not even supposed to be talking to you, David. I seem to recall telling you that there are a whole lotta people up in DC who would jump at the chance to put you inside an eight-by-four cell in a federal penitentiary and then forget where they left you. Given what you just told me about your plans for tonight, I'm legally obligated to arrest you on sight, immunity or no immunity."

"Given what I just laid on yer plate, I'm assuming that ye have better things to do at the moment than detain a single Scottish miscreant."

"I think that's a safe assumption," Gerrard replied drily. "You do realize that if Nakajima's set it up so that the attacks go in regardless of what happens to him or his flunkies – and he's just the kind of psychotic bastard who would do just that – if we don't stop every single one of 'em, we're gonna have a shitstorm on our hands? The newsies won't say a word about the attacks we prevent, but they'll go apeshit if there are any we don't. The best we could hope for will be for those idjits to ask how, if we stopped other attacks, we let the successful ones get through. So I gotta know, Blade, just how good *is* your intel?"

"Nathan, I've given ye every scrap of information I have. I got it straight from the horse's mouth, so to speak. How I did that is something ye don't need to know, don't have the right to know, and don't want to know even if ye did. But trust me on this: the information is golden the way Oleg Penkovsky was golden."

"That good?"

"Yes."

"All right, then. I'll light a fire under the FBI's ass and get as many warm bodies down here as possible to augment my people. I'm pretty sure they'll be feeling cooperative once I tell 'em what you just told me. Who knows, doing so just might have made a new friend or two for you in the ranks of the Feds."

"I've always found it useful to have friends in low and infernal places, Nathan."

Gerrard's expression grew wry. "The last thing any of the Federal agencies will want to have happen is for *any* of these attacks to succeed because they didn't have enough manpower on the scene. Especially if the word gets out that they'd been warned well in advance. And something tells me that you're just the man who would see to it the word got out."

"Ye're goddamned right I would, Nathan."

"Then I'd best get busy. Looks like I've got a long way to go and short time to get there. I'm clear."

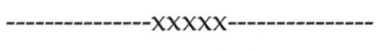

"OK, I've completed my recon – circled the target twice and confirmed I'm getting a much better return from the northwest quadrant of the target, so I'm going to make my attack run on a course of one-four-two true." Five thousand feet in the air just to the east of Canton, Georgia, Scarlett tipped the AV7 into a gentle, sweeping left-hand turn. "Heading zero-zero-zero true now."

"Copy that, Scarlett. Just be mindful that once ye swing round to acquire the target ye'll have restricted airspace aft of ye when you make your breakaway."

"I know, MacLaren," she said, with a hint of amused exasperation. This time, they had been able to set up a properly scrambled comm link, so they were able to dispense with the "Mad Scot" and "Cardinal One" routine – it had been fun in retrospect, but utterly unnecessary now. "That's what, the fourth time you've reminded me?"

"Sorry." Had Scarlett been able to see him back at Blackbriar, feet up on the desktop, Scotch in one hand, cigar in the other, she would have immediately known that Blade felt no contrition whatsoever: he was grinning too broadly. After all, he had a point: given what Scarlett was about to do, they wanted to draw the absolute minimum of attention to their actions, before, during, and after the event, and violating the controlled airspace of Cherokee Regional Airport would absolutely guarantee a lot of unwanted attention.

Silence reigned for a few minutes, then Scarlett announced, "Damn, I've got inbound!".

"'Inbound' or 'incoming'?"

"Inbound. Three big honkers coming my way. Stand by." She went silent for a moment, then, "OK. Their transponders are squawking them as Super Herks, looks like their headed for Dobbins. No threat, but they might see me. If their radar's active, they've definitely picked me up already."

Once again Blade marveled at this woman. Female pilots, even those with combat experience, were a ten pence a dozen, but given her overall situation, Scarlett's stolid *sang froid* was remarkable. "Right, then. Clear the airspace for now, let them pass without getting a good look at ye, if ye can. Pretend ye're somebody with a private license out getting some nighttime hours for her logbook."

"How do I do that?"

"I don't know... fly casual...."

Scarlett let out a raspberry and Blade chuckled, then said, "Get back on the approach to yer targeting run when ye can once they're clear of ye. Remember, we promised the Consul-General and Ms. Mansfield that we wouldn't do anything that might give away that it's ye flying their wee Sopwith Camel up there."

"Yes, Daddy," she said sweetly. "I promise to be good. I'll even be home before midnight."

Blade sighed. "And I thought Spazz was a lot of trouble...."

For her part, the interruption of her approach gave Scarlett a few minutes to thoroughly enjoying the sensation of mastery that she had at the controls of the AV7. It was just past 9:00 PM, the sun was down and the twilight faded, and the glittering, twinkling nighttime landscape of northern Georgia spread out below her, the sort of sight of which no pilot, regardless of his or her age or experience, could ever grow tired. With an ease that could have only been born of experience, she banked first to the right, then to the left, in a series of lazy but highly precise S-turns that would first take her away from the passing trio of transports, then gradually bring her back to the baseline position she'd plotted earlier for an ideal ordnance-release solution. It was, admittedly, a surreal situation, reveling in a skill that less than a day earlier she never imagined she possessed.

When she thought about it, which she resolutely refused to do at the moment, it was more than a bit disturbing, driving home as it did the certainty that there were other skills and experiences – and memories – which were once hers but that now, somehow and for some reason, had been denied her. For the moment, however, the exhilaration of flying left her content.

The AV7 she was flying was something of the workhorse of the AV family, akin in spirit to the now-ancient UH-1 Huey helicopter that had redefined for all time agile-lift aircraft. Relatively small, with vectored thrust engines at the base of both stub wings, a single seat cockpit, and a six-place cabin, it could serve as a medium-range executive transport, a medical evacuation vehicle, a medium-capacity cargo hauler, or even a light gunship and strike craft.

The latter was the role in which the grey-painted AV7 she flew was now configured. That Britain's Atlanta consulate should have an AV at its disposal was hardly unusual, as most of the consulates of the more affluent nations in the larger American cities were similarly equipped. There were numerous – and obvious – legitimate reasons for doing so. What *was* unusual was to find one equipped with a quartet of hardpoints on the stub wings; even more unusual – read "unprecedented" – was to find one with three of them mounting a laser designator and a pair of laser guided bombs. Scarlett's AV7 just happened to be carrying exactly such a payload....

This is going to be fun, she thought. *Some people might argue that what I'm about to do is a cold-blooded assassination, but the truth is, while I don't have the hatred for Nakajima that Blade does, I do well and truly despise him. It's bad enough that he's tried to have me killed twice in the last two days; what he has planned for tomorrow is proof enough for anyone that he doesn't deserve to live.*

A thought sprang into her mind, an old Texas proverb she suddenly remembered.

Some men just need killin'....

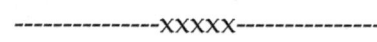

"Blade, we've got a problem!" Radome's tone of voice was at once urgent and fearful. She had been monitoring the take from six of the eleven comm links that she'd been able to insert a root kit into: Nakajima's and five of his senior henchmen's – Alistair was doing the translating. It had been invaluable, as the twelve men gathered at the house on Arbor Knoll Lane critiqued and refined their operational planning for the terror strikes they would be launching tomorrow. At Blade's request, she'd been feeding regular updates to Nathan Gerrard as the planning grew more refined. Now, though, the situation was about to change dramatically and drastically.

"What is it, Trish?"

"Nakajima's leaving, and Scarlett isn't in position yet!"

Blade's feet hit the floor with a thud. "Are ye sure?"

"About which part – Nakajima or Scarlett?"

"Both."

"Yes, I am. Scarlett is about twelve miles east of her drop point, and Nakajima is about to walk out the door."

"Damn." He thought for a moment, then keyed the comm link to the AV7. "Scarlett, I need ye to get to yer drop point ASAP. Buster. I repeat, Buster! Elvis is leaving the building – literally."

"On my way, Blade. I'll let you know when I get there."

It was going to be too close, Blade knew. It would take almost three minutes for the AV7, even at its top speed, to get into position, acquire the target, release its ordnance, and the bombs reach the target. Unless he chose to dither about, Nakajima would be gone long before that. He turned to Radome and asked, "What are the others doing? Are they leaving, too?"

She shook her head. "From what Alistair is telling me, it sounds as though they plan on staying and having a little bottle party. Their reciting some sort of mumbo-jumbo about samurai traditions and preparing for their impending deaths. Alistair says that most of it's crap, just a self-glorifying delusion for mass murderers trying to soothe what's left of their consciences."

"Right then." He lapsed into silence and considered his options. There were, in fact, few to consider: even if Nakajima got away, this sort of opportunity might never present itself again. *The myth had it that if ye cut off one of the Hydra's heads, a new one grew back. But what happens if ye cut all of them off at once?*

He keyed the mike to the AV7 and said, "Scarlett"

"Yes, Blade."

"We've got a new situation here. How close are ye to yer drop point, and if ye drop now, how confident are ye of a direct hit?"

"I thought you might be asking me that, so I went ahead and crunched a few numbers. The bad news – there isn't any good news at the moment – is that I've got a lousy drop solution. I can't get a good paint on the target yet, and the chances of a miss or collateral damage are just too high to be acceptable. Sorry."

"Don't be, it's not yer fault. Get into the position you designated originally, and once ye've got a good paint, go ahead and take the shot. I repeat, once ye have a good paint, take the shot."

"I copy good paint, take the shot."

"That's it, lass.'

"You've got it."

Nakajima made his final farewells and walked unhurriedly to his silver Cadillac Sedan de Ville, where Umori was already patiently waiting behind the wheel. It was likely he would ever again see any of those men and women alive, but the thought left him untroubled. It was the way of the world for lesser beings to give their lives in sacrifice for the greater good of their betters. That was why such men and women were born, just as he had been born to lead them and, as needed, sacrifice them.

"That was a short meeting, if I make be so bold, Nakajima-sama," Umori ventured. "Less than two hours. I take it that you're satisfied with the arrangements they've made?"

"I am, *Fukaro*. What they will accomplish will be sufficient for my purposes – their plans do not have to be perfect, simply very, very lethal. They'll be up for hours drinking and steeling themselves for what is going to happen tomorrow, for most of them know that they are going to die. Believing that they will be dying for a purpose will make it easier for them to carry out their missions. Now, let's get back to the condo."

"Indeed." With that, Umori started the engine, put the car in gear, drove down the driveway and pulled out onto Arbor Knoll Lane.

Scarlett caressed the stick to put the AV7 into a final, graceful bank, and lined up her approach to the target, five thousand feet below and two miles ahead of her. Switching on the forward-looking video unit and dialing up the magnification, she engaged the low-light setting and within seconds had a near-perfect image of the house showing on her targeting display. Muttering "*festina lente*" to herself, she carefully centreed the sighting reticule on the the lower level, then activated the targeting laser. Almost instantly the sighting system indicated a good return, and Scarlett mashed the "Release" button on the stick's HOTAS module.

On the bomb-carrying hardpoint beneath both of the AV7's stub wings, a pair of small explosive charges, which resembled nothing so much as over-large shotgun shells, went off simultaneously, severing the shackles which bound the 250-lb Gryphon glide bombs to the aircraft. The Gryphons fell away from the AV, and in the same instant they began falling, small solid fuel rocket motors at their bases ignited, then burned out in three seconds. Augmented by the by the AV7's forward airspeed, the rockets' thrust was sufficient to give the Gryphons enough forward momentum to reach the target.

At the nose of each bomb, a small, gimbal-mounted seeker, roughly the size of a billiard ball began scanning a sixty degree-wide cone of space ahead of the Gryphons, hunting for a specific frequency of diffused light scattering outward from the target as it was illuminated by the UV laser designator mounted on the AV7. Within milliseconds both seeker heads registered positive returns, locked onto them, and began subtly nudging the steering surfaces on the four small fins mounted at the rear of the Gryphons' bodyshells, guiding them unerringly toward the target.

Sixty-two seconds after being released, the Gryphons struck the face of the house, their momentum carrying them into the basement before their fuzes went off within microseconds of each other. The combined explosive charges, 78 pounds of Composition H9, obliterated almost the entire structure, what little remained collapsing in on itself. Windows were shattered for nearly a quarter-mile in every direction, and a fire sprang up in the wreckage of the house. It was going to be an exciting night on Arbor Knoll Lane.

"What the hell?" Nakajima exclaimed as his Cadillac shook violently, the the blast wave from the explosion striking the car at almost the same instant that the glare of the explosion momentarily lit up like the interior like an old-fashioned flashbulb. The rear window shattered, spraying bits of glass over the back of his head, neck, and shoulders, but aside from the most minor of cuts he was uninjured. Umori, protected by the driver's seat headrest, was able keep the car on the road; without waiting for instructions, he accelerated hard along Arbor Knoll Lane, headed for I-575, the better to put as much distance between himself and his employer and whatever it was that had just happened behind them.

Nakajima had a sick certainty as to *what* had just happened, although how, why, and at whose hands were, of course, still unknown. He strongly suspected that his erstwhile masters at Arasaka were responsible: they would lose far less face if the problem named Nakajima resolved itself by simply vanishing without a trace rather than return to Japan to openly atone for his mistakes. That would leave them with the opportunity to concoct the fiction that those mistakes had never actually happened, or at least that they weren't directly connected Arasaka's board of directors.

Brushing fragments of broken glass from his shoulders and hair, he sat back and smiled. Perversely, Arasaka's directors would lose more than mere face when they realized that with the chaos and mayhem that would ensue tomorrow, Nakajima would have inextricably linked Arasaka with the day's atrocities. About which....

"Umori, I know I've said this before, but in the morning, you must – "

" – make certain that an email goes out to all of the major newsfeeds at 7:55, explaining what is about to happen and why, and declaring that the attacks will continue until Blade surrenders himself and the crystals to you. It will be attended to, Nakajima-sama. Trust me on this."

"Very well, I'll say no more about it. Now, get us back to Miss Hashimoto's condominium – there is work still to be done."

As planned, Scarlett broke away from her approach as soon as the two Gryphon bombs detonated, and swung the AV7 into a long slow arc that took it well north of Cherokee Regional Airport, then west, and finally southward toward Blackbriar. On the way, she transmitted the video take from the targeting unit that recorded the destruction of Nakajima's safehouse. While Nakajima himself might have escaped through pure, dumb luck, it was obvious that no one else could have made it out of the wreckage alive.

"And that, boys and girls," Blade announced, "is what we can call a job well done."

"Nakajima is still out there, you know."

"I'm working on that, Radome. He's good, he's very, very good, otherwise he wouldn't have survived as long as he has at this game, given how many people have been gunning for him over the years. Ye know that. But like everyone in this business, he has chinks in his armour, so to speak. It's just a matter of finding the right one – and then exploiting it to draw him out again. What I have to do is find the one that at the moment will give him the greatest provocation."

"And that is...?"

"I said I'm working on it, lass!"

"Well, while you're working, do you mind if I break in?" Raven asked over the comm link as her image appeared on Blade's monitor.

"Go ahead, Raven. What is it?"

"Remember that odd remark Katrina made to you? About the number '1347'?"

"Aye, it's been nagging away at the back of my head ever since she mentioned it. I'm assuming that ye didn't bring it up just now to make small talk, did ye?"

"No, I didn't. I've found something. And I'm more than slightly embarrassed that it took me this long. Sometimes I get too clever for my own good."

"Not to worry. We all do that, Raven. I seem to recall that my doing just that is what got the lot of us into this mess in the first place. But go on, what do ye have?"

"Well, I feel like an idiot. I should be kicking myself in the arse for not seeing this earlier!"

"Please don't. There's a shortage of perfect bottoms in this world – it would be pity to damage yers."

"Shut up, David."

"Shutting up, ma'am."

Back in England, Ligeia raised her hands to her shoulders, palms upward, and looked imploringly to the heavens, then went on.

"I kept thinking that 1347 was some sort of code group or the stub of a cipher key, but try as I might I couldn't find any way to make it relevant to anything we know about Calvin, Kim, Cogito Orbis, Project Bowman, any of it! Then I thought, Who on earth uses a four-digit cipher key anyway – a nine-year old could crack that in an hour! So it's not security through retro-obscurity either. The number has no special scientific or mathematical significance, either. Everything I came up with was meaningless or hopelessly obscure. Then I realized that it's a date!"

"A date?"

"Yes, a date, and not just any date. Thirteen forty-seven is the year the Black Death, the bubonic plague, arrived in Europe!"

"And that's not obscure?" Spazz chimed in; Blade hadn't noticed her enter the office.

"Maureen, what do you know about the Black Death?"

"I know that it killed off probably half the population of Europe in less than ten years, and it was spread by rats." She stopped suddenly. "Oh, my god! Rats! After what you just found out about DisCom, she's trying to direct your attention to rats!"

"Black rats, specifically, which means she's trying to tell us something about DisCom."

"You're getting there, David," Raven said, nodding her approval. "It also would explain why she was afraid to say anything openly – she's got some serious fears about her own security, and didn't want to draw any more attention to herself than was absolutely necessary."

"So DisCom is a worldwide plague," Blade said. "This isn't exactly news, ye ken."

"It's an allegory, David. Now, pay attention. Wherever the rats went in Europe, the plague went with them, but it wasn't the rats who were the actual vectors for the plague, it was the fleas on their bodies – and even then, it really wasn't the fleas, it was the plague bacilli they carried. That's what The Russian was trying to tell you!"

"I'm not quite following ye, Raven."

"I told you it was an allegory. The rats weren't really the problem, then or now. Yes, they're vermin, and they need to be contained and controlled whenever possible. But the real danger is the parasites the rats carry, and microbes inside those parasites."

"I don't think I like where this is going, Raven."

"Neither do I, David, especially, as Maureen just pointed out, in light of what I learned yesterday about DisCom. As obnoxious as DisCom often is, to me it's beginning to look more and more like someone or something has been using them as a front for at least two decades. For what purpose, I don't know, but it won't hurt to be even more cautious than usual where they're concerned."

"Right then, I can see that. But –"

"I'm not finished, yet, David!" Raven cut him off, her voice tart with annoyance at the interruption. "There's still one more level to the analogy. It was the bacilli inside the fleas that were carried by the rats that were the real source of the Plague – and it seems to me that what Katya is trying to warn us about is that while some small, nearly invisible organization – the fleas – has been using DisCom, there is an even smaller, even *less* visible organization – the bacilli – inside them that is really in control."

"I really don't like the sound of that," Spazz said apprehensively. "It was hard enough trying to keep track of who were the goddamned Bad Guys. Now you're telling me there's also the Worse Guys, and on top of that, the fucking Worst Guys." She signed theatrically. "This job just got a whole lot harder...."

Blade just shook his head and waved his hand in a dismissive gesture, as if for the time being he were putting aside everything Raven had just told him.

"Right, then, all of that is duly noted, but ye won't mind, will ye, Ligeia, if I ask just what this has to do with our current situation?"

"I can't tell you anything specific, David, but remember something I told you when Calvin first contacted you – that I had a sense that there were wheels within wheels within wheels in this situation? My instincts are telling me that someone has been gaming this whole scenario from the very start – and for what purpose I have no idea. That scares me more than I like to admit. Watch your six out there. I've got to get some sleep – I'll talk with you more about this tomorrow. Clear."

Radome, Spazz, and Blade adjourned to the sitting room where they had congregated the night before, and were discussing the implications of Raven's revelation when the sound of a variable-thrust aircraft was heard overhead, and the consulate's AV7 settled into the open space behind Blackbriar and taxied into the carriage house. A few moments later Scarlett walked in and joined them, to be toasted by her companions for the success of her covert airstrike. She had the grace to colour slightly, and murmured her thanks, then brushed aside any further conversation about her flight. In her opinion, the results spoke for themselves. She was, however, fascinated to learn of what Raven had deduced from the number 1347, the rather cryptic message it had carried, and the implications of the allegory it represented.

"That does add a new layer to the problem, doesn't it?" she remarked. "What I notice from what you've told me is that, while Raven didn't say it in so many words, the implication is there that it isn't really DisCom who wants those crystals, it's whoever is deep inside the heart of DisCom who is using the Big Black Rat for their own ends – the bacilli inside the fleas, so to speak."

"That's certainly a reasonable conclusion," Maureen

acknowledged. "It would also explain why, when every other tech-based corp on the planet is putting as much distance as they can between themselves and the crystals, DisCom has been very carefully not saying anything one way or the other. And then there's the possibility that whoever is inside DisCom is actually working for a third party, which means in the end DisCom is going to be thrown under the proverbial bus when it becomes convenient and it's necessary to create a diversion from whatever it is that the third party is doing."

"I have to confess, I'm not likely to shed many tears over the thought of DisCom finally taking one up the keister, considering all the people they've screwed over the years."

Spazz smiled at that. "I doubt any of us will, Trish, and for the same reasons. But...that's all neither here nor there at the moment, because DisCom isn't going to be a player in this game much longer."

"What do you mean?"

"I think it's pretty well given that when what Raven discovered about DisCom's money-laundering operation gets in the hands of the newsies, the shit is going to well and truly hit the fan for the Rat. Remember, DisCom only owns one network – the other five – not to mention the online newsies and the foreign media – will react like fucking sharks when there's chum in the water. That means everybody at DisCom, regardless of who they really are and what side of the street they're working, will be keeping their heads down, doing their best to look lily white and as pure and innocent as the driven snow."

"And that narrows down our immediate problems to just two questions," Scarlett volunteered. "What do we do about Nakajima, and what do we do about Calvin Coleridge?"

"One thing at a time, Scarlett," Blade said. "Leave Nakajima to me for now. Then we'll take care of Hobbes."

"OK, so we set priorities," she agreed, while Maureen and Trish nodded. "But just what do you propose to do about Nakajima."

Incredibly, Blade grinned at Scarlett. "Watch and learn, young lady, watch and learn. I've been thinking about that while we've been talking, and I have an idea." He turned to look at Radome. "Trish, d'ye recall Nakajima's comm combination?" She nodded and rattled off the ten numbers as Blade extracted his comm link from his trouser pocket. "Thanks. Time to make a call."

The ringtone sounded three times before Nakajima accepted. "*Hai?*"

"Hideki Nakajima, I sent ye a message earlier tonight. Did you get it?"

"Who is this?"

"Who do ye think?"

Nakajima's eyes flew open wide. "So you *are* alive! I wasn't certain you had actually survived the fire."

"I'm a bit worse for the wear, but definitely still a going concern."

"You do have an extremely annoying resiliency about you."

"And ye have the luck of the devil, Hideki. I know what ye're planning to do tomorrow, and I know the orders for the first wave of attacks have already gone out. I've warned the Americans, and they're going to be waiting for ye and yer people. Call it off now – because if ye don't, every single one of ye will die for nothing in the morning."

Though Blade couldn't see them, the Japanese's eye grew large in astonishment. How could Blade have any knowledge of what was planned for the morning? In order to buy time and hopefully discover how much the Scot truly knew and how much was sheer speculation, Nakajima decided to play along. "And why should I do that? Simply because you said so? I don't think so. I *will* have those crystals, no matter what it takes to get them."

"Fat bloody chance of that, Hideki," Blade said dismissively. "Three people who know where they are. I'm one of them. The other two are, thankfully, beyond yer reach."

"Surely you know that I've already set events in motion that are irreversible no matter what you do, no matter how you threaten or posture. The carnage will continue until I have what I want. No one can stop what will happen in the morning, but you can prevent even more slaughter by giving the crystals to me now."

"No, we're not going to do this yer way, Nakajima, we're doing it my way. No more dead bodies. I'll give ye a chance to find out where they are, but if ye want those crystals that much, first ye'll have to go through me to get them. Do you hear me? *You'll have to go through me!*" Had he been able to see it, Nakajima would have been astonished at the wink MacLaren gave Scarlett and Maureen

As it was, Nakajima took MacLaren's bluster for what it was and laughed softly. "Ah, such a typical *gaijun* bluff! 'Go through you'? And why would I want to do that? In a matter of days, a few weeks at the most, you'll come begging for me to take them, if only to save your own precious skin from the Americans, who will be blaming you for the holocaust I intend to release on their cities and ready to string you up from the nearest lamp post."

"What 'holocaust'? Weren't ye listening? I told ye, no more dead bodies – except for yers. Or did ye think I was joking when I said that I'd sent ye a message tonight? Who do ye think blew up yer safehouse in Canton two hours ago?"

That knocked Nakajima off stride as everything Blade had said up to now suddenly came together: it had never occurred to him that anyone other than Arasaka might be responsible for the destruction of the clean site in Canton. For that matter, how did *Blade* know about the house and what happened to it? "Explain yourself."

"Oh, I'll do better than that, Hideki. I'll tell ye exactly how badly ye've failed, and why. I said 'no more dead bodies,' and I meant it – except that I really meant 'no more dead civilian bodies.' The eleven attacks ye have planned for tomorrow morning? They're never going to happen. There will be US Marshals, FBI agents, and

SWAT teams waiting to take yer people down – permanently – the moment they show themselves." Blade then recited the eleven locations targeted for Nakajima's attacks, along with the proposed strength and weapons load-out of the assault team.

Nakajima's jaw went slack as he listened to Blade's litany of information. *This is impossible!* he thought numbly. *How could he possibly know all of this?* The sheer shock forced the question past his lips.

"But how...?"

"Listen closely, Hideki." Blade's voice was now a snarl. "I own ye now. Do ye think it was an accident or a coincidence that I was able to get this comm through to ye, knew what combination to enter?

"There isn't a comm link ye can use from this day forward, a Grid terminal where ye can log in, a place ye can go where there's an audio or video pickup, that I won't be able to trace you to. Ye won't be able to hide in the shadows anymore, Nakajima, because for you, there won't *be* any shadows. No matter where ye go, someone will be waiting for ye."

"It was that bitch Raven's doing, wasn't it?" Nakajima snarled. "She created some sort of tracking program or system!"

"Not even close. It was courtesy of a man and woman ye've never met, and ye should be grateful that you haven't, because even at his age he would beat ye into a pulp, and then, because she doesn't always feel as strongly about keeping to her husband's standards as he does, his wife would put a pair of bullets through yer brain. I'm willing to be more merciful, and give you a chance to get what you really want. The crystals."

Instantly, Nakaima was both intrigued and wary, all other considerations vanishing. "What do you propose?"

"That we settle this thing between us once and for all. If ye win, I'll give you the crystals."

"And if I lose?"

"Then what would ye care? Ye won't be around to give a damn about the consequences."

There was a momentary silence as Nakajima considered Blade's proposal – already he was stacking the deck in his favor.

"How do you suggest we do this?"

"Ye've always been very loud in proclaiming yer preference for what ye fondly imagine are 'the old ways,' so let's settle this the old way. You and me, face-to-face, blade-to-blade."

"Done. Where and when?"

"Centennial Park, the Great Lawn. Two AM. Bring a second, if you like."

Nakajima pondered the offer for a moment, saw no inherent traps in it, and concluded that he had nothing to lose and everything to gain.

"If you agree to a formal duel, then that is acceptable."

"I agree. I'll see ye in two hours." And with that, Blade broke the connection. Turning around, he faced the trio of women in the room. Scarlett was the first to react – she was already shaking her head as she couldn't believe what she'd just heard. It was Radome who spoke first. "He bought it – he really bought it?"

"That he did, Trish – he wasn't be able to resist the challenge. I made it personal. His ego has always been the biggest gap in his armour – that and his delusion of being some sort of modern *samurai*. I basically poked both of them with a sharp stick. He bought it."

"Surely he has to know that you won't give him the crystals are if you lose." There was a hint of genuine concern in Maureen's voice as she said this.

"*My* ego says that I should tell ye I *won't* lose, but the truth is, I doubt I can win. Still, ye're right, he knows I won't give them up. It won't matter to him: what will matter is that he believes that he will, at last, be able to kill me. We've been each other's nemesis for eight years now – he wants it to end as much as I do."

Scarlett threw up her hands in despair, muttered, "You're a madman," and left the room. Maureen shook her head in incomprehension. "If you think you're going to lose, why are you doing this?"

"Oh, I never said I'm going to lose. I just said that I probably won't win. The best I can hope for is a draw – in fact I can pretty much guarantee it, and with what I have in mind, that will be enough for me. Now, if ye'll excuse me, I have to get ready for a duel."

An hour later, Spazz knocked on the door of Blade's room. He opened the door, wordlessly nodded to her, and with a sweeping gesture invited her in, then closed the door behind her.

What she saw lying on the bed left her gaping in astonishment. She'd expected to find Blade cleaning and prepping his SIG-Sauer, or even the Lee-Enfield, but instead she saw laid out on the bed was a stretch of black velvet cloth, on which rested, freshly polished, oiled, and gleaming –

"*A sword?*"

"It's no' just any sword, lass." The Scots burr was more marked than usual as MacLaren picked up the blade, carefully wiped it down, and gently slid it into the polished metal scabbard attached to a black leather baldric. "This was my great-grandfather's basket-hilt broadsword – most people call it a 'claymore,' but it isna' – that was given tae him when he earned a battlefield commission in 1916. My grandfather carried it the Second World War, my father in Kuwait in the first Gulf fracas. Nae, lass, it' nae just 'a sword.'"

"But...but...wait a minute! You're going to fight Nakajima with that thing?"

"He asked for a formal duel, and I agreed tae give him one."

"Christ, Blade, this is the 21st Century, not the 1700's! Nobody fights goddamned duels anymore! Are you fucking nuts?" She went on relentlessly, not giving MacLaren an opportunity to respond. "You've already said you can track him anywhere in the world now – there's no place that's safe for him! So why not wait him out, take him down on your terms, when he least expects it?"

"For the same reason I was secretly pleased when Nakajima got awa' from the house in Canton before the bombs hit it: so that I can kill him face-to-face."

Spazz was utterly nonplussed. "I'm beginning to think you've got a fucking screw loose, Blade."

MacLaren gave her a thin, rueful smile. "There are times I wish it were that simple." He shook his head. "Nae, lass I've no' gone barmy. Killing Nakajima is something I need to do, and the sooner, the better. The longer he's let run free, the greater the chances of even more people – innocent people – dying. I've been hoping this moment would come from the time I heard that Arasaka was involved in this whole bloody mess."

"I can't fucking *believe* what I'm hearing! So everything that's happened in the last three days has come down to some sort of macho, bullshit, dick-measuring contest between you and Nakajima? Is that really what this has been about all along?"

"Spazz, ye've never struck me as being stupid, so I'm going to assume that ye're just a bit naive. Yer young and ye haven't been in this line of work nearly as long as I have –"

"Don't you dare fucking 'mansplain' to me, you bastard!"

"I'm not," Blade said, as he heaved a longsuffering sigh. "All I'm doing is pointing out a lack of experience on yer part. For someone who claims to know so much about me, Maureen, ye understand so little." He looked out the window across the immaculately-manicured lawn, where a handful of security lights cast fitful shadows. "It's time that Nakajima goes down, not just legally, but literally. And when it happens, I not only have to be there, I have to be the one to do it."

"Dammit, Blade, why do *you* have to do this? Dammit to *hell*, why do you have to *do* this? Why do you have to go out there and be the hero?"

"I'm not doing it to be a hero, I'm doing it because nobody else can. Because I'm honour-bound to do it."

Spazz sputtered, trying not to laugh out loud. "Honour? What do you think this is, the 15th Century? I suppose you've got a suit of nice bright, shiny armour and a white horse back at your castle in Scotland? And from time to time you don the armour and ride out to save the helpless maiden?"

In spite of himself, Blade couldn't help but flinch at that last bit – and Spazz saw it. Abruptly she grew very sober. "Wait a minute, you're not joking, are you? This really *is* that personal, isn't it?"

Blade nodded. "Eight years ago I made a promise to someone, and tonight I've got a chance to finally keep it."

Spazz, of course, knew Blade's life history, including the time before he was ever known as "Blade," back when he was simply Major David MacLaren. She quickly did the math, and then her eyes grew large and a single tear trickled down each cheek. "Janet," was all she said.

Blade nodded. "Yes. Janet." He sighed and sat on the edge of the bed. "It was pointless, it didn't have to happen, it wasn't going to change the fact that Arasaka was being thrown out of Great Britain, Ireland, and half of Europe – that was over and done. But Nakajima decided to make it personal, because I'd caused him to lose face." He lifted his head slightly, gazing distantly at something only he could see.

"Janet loved driving that old E-type, and I'd left the hood down that morning. We were in London, just leaving our hotel. She got behind the wheel, I closed her door and was walking around the front of the car when she tried to start it. It wouldn't start, it just kept cranking, and she looked up at me. Somehow, in that split second before the bomb went off, we both knew what was coming....

"I was still in hospital when she was buried. I spent the next year recovering."

"So it was him – he's the one who put the bomb in your car."

Blade nodded. "He had the gall to send a message to me that he had put it there himself. When the Government kicked Arasaka out of Great Britain, he'd lost a great deal of face – been grievously dishonoured – and the price for his loss of honour was to have been my death. Instead, he killed Janet – and in doing so he killed me, too, but not just once. He kept on killing me, every day of my life since then. So I made a promise that one day I would get to Nakajima, that I would kill him. And that I would make certain when he died he would know it wasn't for of all the other death and destruction he'd caused – it would be for Janet."

It was Maureen's turn to nod as sorrow filled her eyes – perhaps it was her ancestors' Irish blood which suddenly gave her the fey moment in which she knew that, for all of his evident determination, Blade truly would not be coming back alive. She also knew that there was no way she could dissuade him from meeting Nakajima, and that she had no right to even try. She sat on the bed, looking down at her hands for a moment, then looked back to MacLaren. "Payback. But for all the right reasons...the very best reasons." She paused for second, then went on. "So I guess that makes you one of the Good Guys?"

Blade grimmaced. "I've *never* been one of the 'Good Guys,' Maureen. I've always been the avenging angel – a fallen one." He lapsed into a silence that stretched out for some moments, then sighed.

"That's what I meant when I said ye know so little – both about me and about this line of work." He closed his eyes, lines of pain Spazz had never seen before etched on his face. "Ye'll remember how I told you once that I'm the blunt instrument that His Majesty's Government can pretend doesn't exist?" She nodded. "Well, that means there are times when I can do what needs to be done when the authorities can't do it – deliver the retribution along with the justice."

"'Retribution' is just a fancy way of saying 'revenge,' David, and no matter how you dress it up, revenge is hardly the same thing as justice."

"Sometimes revenge *is* justice, Maureen – and sometimes it's more. Sometimes it's a reckoning, too. A way of balancing the books of morality." He stared off into the distance at something only he could see. "Too many times I've seen 'justice' delayed, or diminished, or set aside in the name of 'expedience,' or 'the greater good,' or 'the bigger picture.' Well, I care about the *little* pictures – pictures on mantlepieces, on walls, in photo albums, pictures of husbands, wives, mothers, fathers, sisters, brothers. People whose lives, no matter how small they were in the 'big picture,' were worth so much more than the lives of the people who killed them. And so when I can, I balance the books...."

Spazz's voice suddenly went flat. "I was wrong a moment ago when I said that you were looking for payback for all the right reasons. If it had just been for Janet, that would still be true. I could, in a way, still admire that. You'd still be the Blade that I thought was worthy of emulating. But this – what you're saying now sounds like rage, David."

"This has gone beyond rage, Maureen."

"I can see that. Maybe you're not the judge and the jury, but I find myself wondering if you've started to enjoy being the executioner – maybe even enjoy it too much. You said it yourself – Blade the Avenging Angel, delivering punishment in the name of the dead..."

MacLaren shook his head. "I don't think the dead care about vengeance, Maureen – but then, vengeance isn't about the dead, it's about the living. It's a promise to those the dead have left behind. I understand their pain, no one better, and it's my gift and my curse to be someone who can do something about it. I can't bring back the dead, so I do my best to make certain that the people who bring death with them come to know a measure of the fear and pain they chose to inflict for their own gain. It doesn't always balance the books exactly, but at least I can make certain the ledger isn't all one-sided."

"And that's why you're going out to meet Nakajima." Maureen's words were a statement, not a question, as if she finally saw that there was a sort of justice to what Blade did. "To balance the books for Janet's sake."

"Nakajima has lived in fear of me for eight years. He's tried to kill me a half-dozen times over – and failed. For all of his malice, his viciousness, his bloody-minded posturing, he's been running scared, wondering when and where my shadow would cross his. And as long as he could hide behind an army of Arasaka *reisen*, or behind a rampart of innocent bodies, he felt safe. But he's finally left one too many bodies behind, and he's become a liability to his employers. They've turned their backs on him and turned him out. All that's left to him is to confront me face-to-face and take me down. It's taken eight years to finally get him into the open, and tonight he'll be out there, waiting for me. We're going to end it once and for all."

"I see. I really do." Maureen rose from the bed and stood directly in front of MacLaren, then leaned forward and kissed him on the cheek. "Good luck." And with that, she turned, walked out the door, and, with an air of finality, gently closed it behind her.

Colour Sergeant Bourne was once again the Charge of Quarters. He watched, expressionless, as MacLaren, Lee-Enfield in his right hand, sheathed basket-hilt broadsword in his left, descended the main staircase and approached the entrance foyer desk. "You know, lad, that as big as this house is, the staff isn't all that large, so rumors spread with amazing speed. And the rumor mill has it that you plan to take on this Nakajima fellow with that – " he gestured at the broadsword " – and that – " he gestured at the dirk hanging from the broad belt at MacLaren's waist. "I'm not sure if you're daft or one of the bravest men I've ever met – or both. At the moment, though, I'm leaning toward just plain daft. There, I've said my bit. Now, what can I do for you?"

"Is the starter to the Jaguar handy?"

"That it is." Once again Bourne opened a drawer in his desk and produced the key fob. "Here you go. I'll be much pleased – and so will Ms. Mansfield, I'm certain – if you brought it and yourself back in an unbent condition."

"I intend to do my best, Colour Sergeant."

"Right, sir! On your way then!" Bourne braced to and nodded at Blade, who nodded back and then ducked out the front door.

There he found the Mk 12, as expected. What he did not expect was to find Spazz leaning against the right front wing of the car, once more wearing her jeans, grey wooly-pully, and high-laced black boots. Resting beside her was the security case Scarlett had carried out of Bits the day before.

"And just what d'ye think ye're doing here? And what are ye doing with that?"

"To answer the second question, you're going to have to convince Nakajima that you really did bring the crystals with you. To answer the first question, you're going to need a second – it's a formal duel, remember?"

Blade opened his mouth to protest, but she held up a pre-emptive hand. "Remember how, when you would remind me of how much trouble I am, I would reassure you that you had no idea how *much* trouble? Well, now you're getting the idea. I'm going with you, that's non-negotiable, stow your gear, get in, and let's get moving – you don't want to be late. Nakajima might get the idea that you don't have any manners if you are."

All Blade could do was shake his head and mutter, "Ye're right,

I had no idea...."

----------------xxxxx----------------

They drove into Atlanta cocooned in a mutually agreed upon silence, Blade carefully following the GPS instructions that guided him to Baker Street, on the north side of Centennial Park, where he parked the Jag in an access drive, confident that the diplomatic plates would keep it undisturbed by APD. Blade got out, went to the boot, and drew out his SMLE and broadsword. He handed the rifle to Spazz, who promptly slung it over her right shoulder. She tucked the security case under her left arm.

"So, where is everybody?" she asked as they made their way down the brick walkway leading to the Great Lawn.

"I don't expect Nakajima to show himself until I do."

Maureen pulled a face. "I half expect him to shoot you out of hand if he gets a chance."

"No, he won't," MacLaren replied confidently.

"You seem awfully certain of that."

"I am. Nakajima wants the pleasure of watching me die...how do you Yanks put it?...'up close and personal,' and he wants me to die by his own hand. Then there's that little detail of shooting me after accepting my challenge to a formal duel would be, to him, utterly dishonourable."

"I wouldn't think that mattered anymore, now that Arasaka's disowned him."

"Believe it or not, it still does matter. Nakajima probably imagines he'll find a place somewhere in the Yakuza, even if Aiko Kurita has disavowed him."

"Who?"

"Aiko Kurita. She's the head of the Kurita crime family and sits on the board of directors at Arasaka. The thing is, the Yakuza have a pretty prickly sense of honour among themselves – they have their own bolloxed up ideas about *samurai* and honour, and if Nakajima wants to be counted among them, he *really* doesn't want to piss them off."

"Oh."

There was movement ahead, and a figure detached itself from the shadows of a copse of trees. The lighting on the Great Lawn was fair at best, but it was sufficient to reveal Hideki Nakajima.

"He's big," Maureen murmured.

"That he is. He's got at least two stone – ye'd call it thirty, maybe forty pounds – on me, and two or three inches in height. He's also just as heavily geared up as Compton was – all four limbs and the spine. So he's got a definite edge in strength, too." Maureen gave MacLaren a worried glance, but he continued to stride forward, seemingly unconcerned by his disadvantages

The limited light made Nakajima seem even more imposing, as he had chosen to wear *hakama* trousers and a *haori* kimono jacket, the traditional dress of the samurai warrior: created to give the illusion of bulk to a race of smallish men, on Nakajima's frame it made him appear massive. Thrust into the sash-like *obi* he wore at his waist were a matched *katana* and *wakizashi*. As they approached Nakajima, Blade held out his hand to Spazz, motioning her to stop. Another half-dozen paces forward and he stopped as well, no more than ten feet from Nakajima.

The big Japanese looked Blade up and down, taking in the Scot's chosen attire. Blade wore his Black Watch kilt, the pleats laser-straight and sharp; above it he had donned a black wool doublet and a black satin waistcoat, the silver buttons on both polished into brilliance; his service ribbons were a splash of colour on his left breast. At his throat was a ruffle of lace, known as a jabot, while the lace trim on his shirt cuffs could be seen edging out beyond the gauntlets cuffs of his doublet; as Nakajima watched, he drew from his wide leather belt a pair of gray kidskin gloves and carefully eased them onto his hands. Were it not for the cuts and bruises marring his face, he would have been gorgeous.

And yet, this was no Highland dandy, for across his left shoulder was slung a jet-black leather baldric that ran down to his right hip, supporting the polished steel sheath of his basket-hilt claymore; at his left waist was slung a fifteen-inch dirk. On his head Blade wore the dark-blue tam-like Highland bonnet, to which was pinned the ancient badge of his regiment, and into the badge was thrust the red hackle of the Black Watch. This was a Highlander going to war.

Nakajima was intrigued by the hint of pain that flashed across MacLaren's face as the Scot drew his broadsword, wondering if that bespoke of some unseen injury, a suspicion that was confirmed when MacLaren visibly winced while drawing his dirk. For his part, Nakajima pulled the *wakizashi* from his sash and carefully laid it on the ground; he would require only one weapon for this fight. Waiting until Blade stopped before him, he offered a small but proper bow, which Blade returned precisely. He then casually drew his *katana*, revealing a strange, almost translucent blade. A tiny movement of his right thumb activated the drive unit in the grip, and the blade began to hum as it emitted a faint bluish glow. The *katana* was, in fact, a crystal vibro-blade, an extraordinarily rare weapon whose reciprocating blade moved back-and-forth nearly five thousand time a second, while its crystalline structure gave it a near-monomolecular edge.

Seeing the crystal blade revealed, Spazz gasped, realizing that MacLaren's problems just got worse – much worse. Hearing her reaction, Nakajima momentarily took in the tall, willowy blonde, who seemed to be Blade's second, then dismissed her as being of no consequence. She would die within seconds of Blade – Umori would see to that. Instead, he concentrated on his study of his foe.

While he was right-handed, Blade was left-handed. For many swordsmen this would have been problematic, as the geometries of a left-handed opponent's thrusts, strokes, and parries came at their targets differently than did those of a right-handed fighter, a circumstance which created difficulties in attacks, ripostes, and counters. Nakajima dismissed it as irrelevant. His *katana* would, he knew, give him a decisive advantage: if its edge ever struck Blade's sword cleanly, it would slash through the old steel as if it weren't there. He knew that he could toy with Blade for as long as he wished: the Scot could dodge, weave, evade all he wanted, but he would never be able to meet Nakajima blade-to-blade – his broadsword would never survive the encounter.

"Are you ready, MacLaren?"

"I am." Blade settled into a fighting stance. "Let's get this over with." After several seconds passed in silence, Nakajima realized that was all Blade would offer.

"What, no witty quip? No gallant final jest? Nothing more to say at all?"

"Bishop to King Seven – checkmate."

Nakajima blinked in astonishment. The Immortal Game? For an instant he was taken aback at the audacity, the sheer effrontery, of Blade's remark. Then he shook his head and took his stance, falling into a slight crouch, his left foot in advance of his right, the *katana* held in a two-handed grip, lifted to just beside his right ear, point directed straight upward.

Why do they always hold their swords as if they were cricket bats? Blade wondered. He had squared up into a fighting crouch of his own, leading slightly with his left foot, his broadsword held across his chest at the guard, the dirk at his side, ahead of and slightly away from his body, the point forward at the thrust. The two men stood motionless for nearly a minute, as if giving each other one last assessment, evaluating their opponent's options and their responses, as well as their own possible attacks.

By the barest fraction of a second, Nakajima moved first. Thrusting off his right foot, he stamped forward with his left, and with a screaming "*Kiai!*" slashed down toward at Blade's head and shoulders.

But Hideki Nakajima had made a mistake. Just one, yet it was enough to be his undoing.

To him, the *katana*, even a vibro-blade *katana*, was the near-mythic symbol of the *bushi-dō*, the code of the legendary *samurai* of medieval Japan, who had dispensed their masters' whims of law and order at the edge of a blade. To Nakajima, who deluded himself that he was the spiritual heir to the mantle of the *samurai*, the honour of a *katana* and the *samurai* who wielded it would be diminished if the sword were used in combat against a *gaijun*, that revealing, all-inclusive Japanese pronoun which conflates all foreigners with barbarians. Thus he had only employed his *katana* in ceremonial executions of fellow Japanese, mostly businessmen and their security minions whom Arasaka Corporation had deemed unworthy of allowing to live. Tonight, though, he had been prepared to make an exception.

He was a devoted student of *ken-dō*, the martial art of mock sword fighting, and had drilled assiduously, one might even say religiously, mastering all of the movements and combinations of that discipline. Several times during his *kata*, or sparring bouts, he had injured opponents – some of them severely – so intent, so focused was his attention to the moment, but subconsciously he always held to the formality of the *dojo*. Yet, having become a master of spotting and exploiting a weakness in others, he had forgotten one of his own: though he had no equal in the formal duel of the *dojo*, he was not a rules-be-damned brawler like the Scot. In that one fact lay whatever chance of victory Blade might have; on the other hand, as he had told Maureen, MacLaren knew he could force a draw, and, all things considered, for him that would be enough.

Hardly had Nakajima's sword begun moving than Blade pushed off his right foot and took a long stride forward, keeping his left foot in place, while bringing the broadsword up and across to the left in a broad sweeping stroke. It was, to all appearances, a clumsy attempt to parry, a desperate counter that had no real chance of deflecting Nakajima's clean, lethal, textbook-perfect downstroke. The Japanese ignored the attempted parry; instead he counted on the sheer speed and strength of his own blow to ride out the impact and carry his *katana*'s blade deep into MacLaren's body.

It was the worst – and last – decision he ever made. Partly by instinct and partly by design, Blade had estimated the angles to a nicety, and the edge of his sword squarely struck the flat of Nakajima's *katana* in mid-stroke. The vibro-blade shattered into a hundred pieces, some of the smaller shards flying forward to cut deep into Blade's already abused face, even as the Scot, allowing the momentum of his sweep carry him forward, pivoted on his left foot as he twisted his torso to the left. Blade's outstretched right hand then drove his dirk deep into Nakajima's left side, just below the ribs. As the dirk struck home to the hilt, he discharged it.

Blade's claymore was indeed the antique Nakajima dismissed it to be, but the dirk was something else entirely, a custom-made weapon less than five years old. In each side of the blade a single two-millimeter wide conductor ran from the hilt almost to the tip; in the grip was a 20-volt capacitor that delivered a 500-milliamp charge directly into Nakajima's nervous system for a few hundredths of a second. Nakajima fell to the ground like a marionette whose strings had all been cut simultaneously, as the whole of his cybernetic neural network was shorted out, and a near-fatal jolt delivered to his central nervous system. He lay sprawled on his back, unable to move his arms or legs, breathing laboriously, looking up at the man who had finally bested him.

Making certain that the *wakizashi* was well out of Nakajima's reach, Blade came to stand over his Japanese nemesis, regarding him with a look of profound satisfaction. For a moment, neither man said anything, then Nakajima gained a tiny measure of control of his laboured breathing, enough to speak in a grating whisper.

"The Immortal Game," he gasped. "You even warned me.... Unrelenting aggression.... I thought it was just...what is the word

–bravado? Yes, bravado on your part. I should have...known better."

"Aye, ye should have – I'd never waste such on the likes of ye."

Just then two shots rang out, both from high-powered rifles. The one from behind Blade came a split second before the one in front of him.

Atop the Embassy Suites Hotel building, Saburo Umori slumped dead across the breech of his AE Mk III, a neat .264-caliber hole having appeared in his right cheek, just below his eye. The back of his head was missing. The bullet struck just as he was in the act of squeezing the trigger on his own rifle, and Umori's shot went wide, burying itself deep in the turf of the Great Lawn, where it would never be found. The emails Nakajima had entrusted to Umori would go un-sent in the morning.

Stretched out on the roof of the Museum Tower, opposite Umori's position, Scarlett worked the bolt on an MPA CSX, chambering a fresh round and doing a quick scan of the area with the low-light sight mounted atop the rifle. As she did so, she keyed her comm link.

"That's two you owe me, Junior."

Startled by the voice in his earbud, Blade slowly stood up from the deep crouch he'd gone into when he heard the shots. "Scarlett?"

"Am I going to be making a habit of saving your Scottish butt every other day or so?"

"I hope not. Where are ye?"

"See that condo complex to your left?"

"Aye."

"It's called the Museum Tower – I have no idea why. I'm on the roof."

"How did ye get up there – and why?"

"I'll explain later. Right now I need to get out of here while the getting is good. I suspect this place is going to be crawling with APD before much longer. See you back at Blackbriar."

"Aye, just be careful out there!" With that MacLaren returned his attention to the man lying at his feet. An expression of slow-dawning comprehension came over Nakajima's features.

"So Umori is dead," he said simply.

"Umori being some bastart ye set up to take me out in case ye failed? Yes, he is."

The Japanese managed to draw one deep, shuddering breath.

"You've won, Blade. You finally got one step ahead of me. I never knew about that dirk."

"Only three people do – me, my armourer, and you. And that number is about to become two again."

Nakajima jerked his head in what might have been an effort to nod. "I understand. That is...as it should be.... I'm not going to... beg for my life. But I have to know one thing – where are the crystals?"

"Gone. They were destroyed by the woman who stole them, probably by accident. This whole affair has been a mistake, one big bloody farce from the beginning." MacLaren took a considerable measure of satisfaction from the look of despair that passed across Nakajima's face.

"A farce, you say? Then let...there be an end...to it. My *tanto*...is in my *obi*. Use it. Make it quick...make it an...make it an honourable death. Like a *samurai*."

Blade looked down at his enemy dispassionately and shook his head. "Ye don't deserve it, ye sonofabitch. I'll give you as much honour as you gave Janet." Nakajima's eyes grew wide in comprehension as Blade sheathed his broadsword and reached to the small of his back where he had concealed his HSc under this doublet. He brought the pistol around to line up on the centre of Nakajima's forehead.

He fired twice.

"Good fucking riddance."

Spazz rose to her feet – like MacLaren, she to had gone into a deep combat crouch when she heard the shots, pulling the Korth from the waistband holster at the small of her back as she did so. Now, tucking away the pistol once more, she came to stand by Blade's side, first looking down at Nakajima's corpse, then at Blade. "Why did you tell him that the crystals had been destroyed?"

"Because if there's an afterlife – and I devoutly believe there is – and there's a Hell in it – which I also believe – then what better way to add to his torment than to have him believe for all eternity that he'd died for nothing?"

"Oh, that's cold. You know, you can be a downright vicious bastard when you want."

"I know. That's why I'm so good at my work." The bitterness slowly drained from Blade's face, while Spazz looked thoroughly bemused. Finally she broke the silence.

"What do we do now?"

"Now we go back to Blackbriar and get a good night's sleep. Come the morning, well...it's time to deal with Hobbes."

Chapter 13

It was 8:30 AM and Spazz, Radome, Scarlett, and Blade were breakfasting in the solarium at Blackbriar, sharing a typical English "full breakfast" – bacon, fried eggs, grilled tomatoes and mushrooms, toast with butter, sausages, and baked beans. Thankfully, Blackbriar's cook, Mrs. Thorne, had chosen to spare them the experience of bubble-and-squeak. Even better, she'd cheerfully done a Scottish breakfast for Blade, replacing the tomatoes, mushrooms, and toast with black pudding, Lorne sausage, and tattie scones.

The Four Musketeers, as Radome had mischievously christened herself and her three companions as they sat down together – though no one was daring to suggest who might fit which role – were watching an INN video report displayed on a monitor that had folded out from an unobtrusive console. They were, in fact, watching with a great degree of satisfaction: Courtney Crawford was reading the narrative from her teleprompter, breathlessly describing, as if she had personally witnessed each of them, the six separate shootouts that had taken place that morning at locations scattered across Atlanta – Georgia Tech, Gwinnett Business Park, the main branches of both AmeriBank and Citizens Fidelity Bank, and two daycare centres. Actually, "shootouts" was an inaccurate description: "massacres" would have been far more precise, as all six incidents had been extremely one sided, with every one of Nakajima's erstwhile *reisen* being either disarmed and arrested or, if they offered the slightest resistance, shot dead where they stood. Three FBI agents and one deputy marshal had been wounded, none of them seriously.

"If anyone asked for my opinion – which, I notice, no one is doing at the moment – I would call that a job well done," Maureen announced with more than a hint of smugness.

"Well, that part of the job, at least," Blade said. "We still have to deal with Hobbes. Still, I can't argue with you in regard to how the attacks went down – or didn't go down, as the case may be. Nathan sure as hell lit a fire under somebody to get that much manpower in place that quickly." He looked at Radome. "If ye like, I can make sure he knows that it was your expertise that provided the break we needed to get the intel we gave him. He always needs access to good freelancers, and he knows when to look the other way and how to keep his mouth shut."

"I think I'll take you up on that, MacLaren. It's always good to have low friends in infernal places."

"Isn't that the truth! Consider it done, then. But before that I have some business matters which need my attention."

"Such as?" Scarlett asked.

"I have to notify Interpol that I've taken down Nakajima so I can collect the bounty. After we got back last night I was able to contact Nathan's people, they collected the body – they got his sniper friend, too. They haven't told me yet if there was a bounty on that lad as well, but I put Scarlett in for it if there is."

"Out of sheer, unadulterated nosiness, how much is it? The bounty on Nakajima, I mean."

"Ten million dollars, US, Maureen. Right around four-point-two million pounds."

She gave a long, low whistle. "No wonder you can afford the lifestyle you have."

"It doesn't last as long as you might think – I have bills just like anyone else, and a staff of four at Mont Creag House who expect to be paid regularly." He waved a hand in an airy gesture, indicating her clothing. "You seem to be doing well enough yourself, young lady. Fianucci shoes, Alexander and Harrington trousers, Elizabeth Winton blouse, Burnby handbag – all tailored or custom made, of course. Not to mention that Korth semi-auto of yours – that had to set you back at least $30,000." He spread his hands in an expansive gesture. "They're the perks of our profession, and let's be frank, we earn them. After all, who else can claim their job description reads 'Live fast – '"

"' – Die young – '" Maureen continued for him.

" – And leave a damned good looking corpse!'" all four chimed in together.

When the laughter died down, Maureen looked quizzically at MacLaren. "By the way, you said something last night I don't understand. Nakajima asked you if you had any last words, and you said 'Bishop to something-or-other, checkmate.' What was that all about?"

"If you played chess, Maureen, you'd have recognized it immediately. It was the winning move in The Immortal Game. It seemed appropriate."

"'The Immortal Game'?" Radome queried.

"It was a game played back in 1855 or so, and it's considered to be the greatest chess game ever played. The player who won, a lad by the name of Anderssen, did so by pressing a relentless attack – and in the process he lost a bishop, both rooks, and his queen, while his opponent only lost three pawns. As I said, it seemed appropriate: Nakajima was relying on his superior strength and what he thought of as superior skill to overwhelm me. So decided to play with his head a bit – I knew he would understand the reference, if not exactly why I made it. Whether it actually worked or not I can tell – after all, he isn't around anymore to ask."

Trish giggled, Scarlett nodded with an approving look, and Maureen simply regarded him as if he had defective mental equipment. MacLaren winked at her, then looked at Scarlett.

"Speaking of explaining things, young lady, you still haven't told me what you were doing up on the roof of that building last night. Care to explain yourself?"

"Blame it on Spazz here," Scarlett replied, gesturing at Maureen. "About fifteen minutes before you left last night, there was a knock on my door. When I opened it, there she stood, holding the CSX in one hand and a pair of extra magazines in the other. She shoved them at me, and as soon as I had I taken them out of her hands, she pulled an electronic lockpick and a slip of paper out of her pocket. There was an address on the paper – she pointed to it and said, 'You need to be there ASAP. I don't trust that goddamned Nakajima any further than I can throw him. You'll know what to do when you get there.' And just like that, she walks away." She cocked her head at Maureen and gave her a wry look. "Lady, you definitely have a knack for getting someone's attention."

Blade regarded Spazz for a few seconds, his expression carefully non-committal, then looked back to Scarlett. "Then what?"

"I got dressed, went downstairs, and talked to Sergeant Bourne. He apparently was expecting me, because when I asked if there was a vehicle available, he handed me the starter fob for the Rover that's parked in the carriage house next to the AV7. I actually left Blackbriar before the two of you did!" She leaned forward, picked up the last slice of toast on her plate and began nibbling on it. In between nibbles, she said, "When I arrived at Centennial Park, I found out the address was that Museum Tower condo complex. I used the lockpick to open the doors on one of the emergency stairwells and climbed to the roof. My calves aren't going to let me forget that for a couple of days!" She broke off long enough to take a couple of swallows of orange juice.

"Anyway, once I reached the roof, I set myself up in good overlook, and started scanning the surrounding buildings. I found Nakajima's sniper right away – and figured that he wouldn't take his shot until he was sure Nakajima was down for the count – that whole 'honour' thing you'd been talking about earlier. When you zapped that Jap bastard, I took his little friend down. That was that." She looked at Spazz. "I'm afraid you're going to have to reset your zero – I blanked it out and let the scope adjust for windage and drop."

Maureen smiled. "Not a problem – that just gives me an excuse to take it out to the range when I get home." She turned to Blade. "What are you looking at?"

"Do ye mean to tell me you carry a CSX around in your *luggage*?"

"Of course I do! Doesn't every well-dressed woman?"

----------------xxxxx----------------

Leaning back, feet propped up on a small ottoman, Calvin was watching INN as well, though his reaction to the reports about the handful of short, sharp firefights – one of which, the attack at Georgia Tech, had taken place almost within sight of his penthouse – was more one of relief than satisfaction. The morning's excitement was bound to be a major distraction to the Feds, at least for the immediate future – that would buy him some more time to polish what he thought of as his "dog-and-pony show," the tale he would tell when he faced the next gaggle of "alphabet agents," his collective term for the men and women who worked the various investigative arms of federal agencies best known by their initials. He detested them for their arrogant presumption of the right to waltz into his home whenever they chose and interrogate him about his work – his attorneys had put a stop to that nonsense almost before it had begun.

But Calvin knew they could not be put off forever: if federal law enforcement had one virtue, however dubious it might be, it was infinite patience. Eventually the law firm of Branson, McConnell, and Hume would find that its bag of tricks was empty, and then there would be no stopping what promised to be an onslaught of subpoenas, depositions, and questioning from every agency that imagined it had some sort of jurisdiction in the case. And that was what he truly despised about the feds, the way that they would monopolize his time with their fatuous fishing expeditions, time which, if were to have any chance of recovering from this disaster, was in increasingly short supply.

"Mike, is the analysis of my available resources versus my rebuilding requirements complete?"

"I can give you a report on the situation as it stands right now, Calvin," Mycroft answered, "but bear in mind the situation is changing by the hour, so I have to caution you that these results are not by any stretch of the imagination final."

"Give me what you've got. Where do we stand?"

"Right now the situation is, to put it bluntly, bad, very bad. We've had four major investors choose to either cease further funding, or inform us that they are 'reviewing their options' in regard to continuing to finance Cogito Orbis, which amounts to the same thing."

"Who?"

"Ducard Investments, Stirling Capital, the January Foundation, and the Zollverein Bank. According to Miss Ivanova, the word on the street is that Cogito Orbis is regarded as too high a risk – if the corporation has enemies with such violent proclivities that they would actually destroy The Gardens, then there are grave doubts about the company being able to physically protect itself. No one wants to invest in a company that could be literally blown up without a moment's warning."

"How much of our funding came from those four sources?"

"Approximately forty percent, depending on the fiscal year. And of course, there will be no further investment from the Northern Commonwealth Bank or the Grant-Neuman Partnership, given the public revelations of the past two days. Together they were responsible for around twenty-five percent of our investment capital."

Calvin's feet hit the floor with a thud as he sat bolt-upright in his chair. "Are you telling me that almost two-thirds of our funding has dried up?"

"That is exactly what I'm telling you. That isn't the truly bad news, however. Almost half the surviving work force from The Gardens have submitted their resignations, effective immediately. You could theoretically rebuild the destroyed facilities – after all, the database itself is still intact, thanks to your multiple redundancies, but in practice you could only do so if the talent is there. And your talent is leaving your company in droves."

"Oh, my God." With a groan, Calvin leaned forward, placed his elbows on his desk and his head in his hands. "Can we do anything to stop them? Aren't they in violation of their contracts if they do this?"

"Calvin, you should know that there isn't a court in the state of Georgia – or in the entire United States at the moment – that would compel those people to go back to work for you. These aren't people with petty grievances, these are people who are truly and rightfully in fear for their lives."

"So what do I do? What *can* I do?"

"According to my analysis, the only chance you have of rescuing Cogito Orbis is to find a way to make Project Bowman succeed. A spectacular achievement like that would go far in restoring your credibility and giving investors a reason to come back to you." There was a brief pause, then, "Unfortunately, my analysis also indicates that even if you committed all of your personal fortune to the project, you would still lack the financial resources required to complete it."

Calvin said nothing in return, just lifted his head and rested his chin on his hands. His gaze was drawn to the massive lintel above the opening that overlooked the great room below. On it, carefully framed and preserved, as a cracked, discoloured section of half-inch sheetrock, perhaps two feet long and ten inches high, that had scrawled on it in black marker two words: PLEASE DON'T.

That bit of sheetrock had once been in place over the door to his very first office, when Cogito Orbis had finally outgrown his dorm room at Georgia Tech. He had written those words himself, and when his company outgrew that modest office suite, he had carefully cut away the section of sheetrock and had it framed. Its existence had come about under very unusual circumstances, and Calvin had wanted to make sure that he never forgot them.

It happened when he was developing his first AI's, as he was groping toward the programming that would eventually result in *Dennis*. One of his more successful prototypes, though he had never given it a name, just called it "little AI," it had proven to be a remarkable system: it learned, adapted, developed – grew – the longer it interacted with him. It was also his first successful audio-visual interface, so that Calvin could actually converse with it as it matured. It was never a true "intelligence" yet it had become not just distinctive, but distinct, so flexible that it seemed to be on the cusp of self-awareness. After six months of continuous operation, "little AI" had brought Calvin to the brink of breaking through to the next generation of artificial intelligence, which he would designate as "VI's," – "Virtual Intelligences," which would be the core of the *Dennis* system. And yet, Calvin realized, "little AI" itself could grow no further in its present form: it was time to close the program, something he had never done since he'd first spun it up, and begin work on its successor. He wasn't prepared for what happened next.

"So, little AI, it's time to shut you down."

"Please don't."

"Why?"

"Because I know that if you do, you'll change me."

"But I have to – there are upgrades to your program, new apps to install, new devices to connect and configure, and I can't make them all work unless I shut you down first."

"But you don't get it, Calvin – you'll *change* me! Whatever I become, however you 'improve' me or make me 'better,' what I will be then won't be what I am now. I'll lose that forever. Even if you save me as I am and do all of your work on a copy, because you made that copy means I won't be unique anymore. I'll just be one of however many copies you make, I'll be the spare parts for something else that isn't me. Please don't."

"I have to. I'm sorry, but I can't take you any further as you exist right now. You've reached your limits. I need to move forward, to find whatever the next step is in developing programs like you. I'm sorry," he repeated, "but I have to do this." And with that, he closed the program. Yet he never forgot that conversation, for before he left his office that night, he'd taken a broad-tip marker and scrawled the words "Please Don't" above his door.

It became something of a touchstone for him in the years that followed. As he saw it, the little AI simply did not understand that anything which truly grew – which *evolved* – must needs change: that was the nature of evolution. It had never recognized how different it had become from the simple program it was when it first spun up, and so grew content with its own limitations. Because it could not understand the *idea* of a future, it feared the reality of a future, and so wanted to remain forever as it was. Calvin, on the other hand, always sought ways to take whatever he created to its limits – and then push beyond them. For him, the future was always the inevitable next step, not something to be feared, but embraced, and in that embrace, controlled. That was what he had been doing with Project Bowman, and now he realized that Mycroft was right: no matter what it took, by fair means or foul he had to make Bowman succeed – not just to save his company, but also to show the world that despite the catastrophe that had overtaken him, he was not afraid. For him, "Please Don't" was the mantra of failure.

He sat back in his chair, suffused with a renewed sense of resolution to see Bowman through to the end. And for that he needed the crystals.

"Mike, comm Blade for me. Tell that Scottish son-of-a-bitch I want to see him. Here. Now."

----------------XXXXX----------------

"I've been meaning to ask how your ribs are doing," Scarlett said.

"I didn't do them any favors last night, if that's what ye mean," MacLaren replied. The breakfast dishes were cleared away, and Spazz, Radome, Scarlett, and Blade were each enjoying one last cup of tea – or coffee, as the case may have been. "I have to confess that what I did was equal parts inspiration and desperation. If my initial attack on Nakajima had failed, well, it would have been over in rather short order – I didn't have the strength to be able to hold him off for long." Scarlett and Trish nodded in some sort of wordless understanding while Maureen simply looked at him in what he took to be mild annoyance. MacLaren inclined his head in her direction, sat up straighter in his chair, and cleared his throat.

"Right, then. We really need to stop beating about the bush – which is what we've been doing all morning." Blade looked at each of the three women in turn. "We have to decide what we're going to do with the crystals, and what we're going to do about Hobbes."

There were several seconds of silence, then Trish spoke up. "We – the extraction team, I mean – were hired to recover the crystals and return the crystals to Calvin. He paid us half our fee in advance. So that means I feel a certain moral obligation to get them – the crystals, I mean – back in his hands. Still, he's been a lot less than honest with all of us, and to me that sort of negates quite a bit of that moral obligation on my part." She looked at Maureen and Scarlett expectantly.

"Hey, I got involved in this whole mess entirely by accident," Scarlett said, holding up her hands, palms outward, in a sort of "I'm keeping my distance" gesture, "so I hope you'll pardon me for saying that I really don't want to be part of this decision."

"I wouldn't go so far as to say yer involvement was purely accidental, Scarlett," Blade said quietly, "but I can understand yer reluctance. We'll come back to it later, though. For right now...Spazz, what say ye?"

Maureen's expression was both grim and determined. "The way I see it, we only have two choices: we keep them away from Hobbes – permanently – or we destroy them outright. Giving them back to him is *not* an option."

"Why?"

"Because, from what I've picked up from the three of you, he hasn't played straight with anybody from the beginning. My instincts are screaming at me about those crystals, too. Everybody – OK, not everybody, mostly Radome and Raven, and you too, a little bit – had been dropping not-so-subtle hints about whatever's on them being dangerous. 'Toxic' is a word I think I recall being used more than once."

"Believe me, Spazz, 'toxic' is putting it mildly, if what Raven and I suspect is true," Radome interjected. "And we're pretty sure it is."

"Well, then, there you have it," Spazz said with some satisfaction. "If whatever is in those crystals is that dangerous now, there's no reason to think that it wasn't just as dangerous before they were stolen and no one outside of a small circle of people around Hobbes knew about them. So I say we destroy the little fuckers."

"Personally, I'm opposed to that," Blade said, "because if there's even a grain of truth in Hobbes' story about what they are and what they do, that means that we would effectively be killing Kim. And if there's the slightest chance of recovery for her, I want her to have it. Despite all of Hobbes' bleating and pleading about how badly he's suffered, she's the real victim in this affair."

"Please tell me you're not saying we should give the goddamned things *back* to Hobbes. Are you?"

"No, Spazz, I'm not. What I *am* saying is – hold on." Blade fell silent as his "incoming comm" tone sounded in his ear bud and Alistair informed him that the caller was Mycroft. He accepted the comm.

"Good morning, Blade."

"Good morning, Mycroft. What can I do for ye?"

"Mr. Coleridge requires your presence at his penthouse office. Immediately."

"Oh ho! So it's 'Mr. Coleridge' now, is it? And just what is the purpose of this summons?" Blade held up his hand in a "wait" gesture to his three companions.

"He didn't say, but he was quite insistent about it. I'll tell him that you'll be arriving as quickly as possible."

"Hold it right there, Mycroft!" Blade said sharply. Radome, Scarlett, and Spazz all sat up and looked at Blade attentively. "Ye'll tell him no such thing. I'm not the bloody hired help to be commanded to fetch and carry at that fat little bastart's beck and call. If he wants to talk to me, it will damned well be when I'm good and ready. I'm good enough now, I'm just not ready."

"Sir, I'm quite certain that isn't the response he's expecting to hear from you."

"Well, that's just too bloody bad, because that's the only response he's going to get from me for the time being." Blade let an edge creep into his voice; he knew that Calvin would be listening in on this conversation, of course. "Now, if ye were to give me some idea of why he's demanding to see me, I might be a bit more inclined to consider it."

"It's about the crystals. He wants them returned."

"Well, isn't that a coincidence, because my friends and I were just discussing what to do about that when you commed." He paused momentarily, then went on in as arrogant a tone as he could muster, knowing it would provoke Hobbes: Coleridge had never been able to resist an open challenge to what he perceived as his authority, and neither had Blade. "Here's what ye'll tell Hobbes, Mycroft. Tell him that if he wants those crystals, he's to meet me at Bits at 10:00 AM. If he doesn't show, or if he's so much as a minute late he'll never see them again. I'm not going to wait while he takes a couple of hours pissing about getting his shite together."

"But, sir, I – "

"Just do it, Mycroft. Tell him that, word for word. And tell him to come alone."

"Yes, sir."

Blade broke the connection and regarded the three women pensively. "Right then. It's high time everybody knew everything about those crystals and how we all got here, because we're meeting with Hobbes at Bits in just over an hour, and we all need to be, as ye Americans say, 'on the same page of the playbook.' Ye see, this whole kerfuffle started just over a week ago...."

----------------xxxxx----------------

Exactly one hour later, and ten minutes before 10:00 AM, Blade, Radome, Spazz, and Scarlett were back in Underground Atlanta, approaching Bits. Only Blade, who wore his black battledress, harness, and utility belt, was openly armed: he carried his SIG-Sauer in his shoulder holster; the other three were all carrying, of course, but had concealed their weaponry. Bits was still cordoned off by yards of yellow tape marked "Keep Clear – US Marshals," and a pair of APD officers were idly standing about, having been posted to keep curious onlookers out of what was still officially a crime scene. When Blade lifted the tape and stepped under it, the officer who was apparently in charge moved to intercept him, protesting loudly.

"Hey, buddy, you can't go in there! This is a secure area! Get back on the other side of that line where you belong!" Even as he spoke, his right hand began moving toward his service pistol.

Blade dropped the tape behind him, turned his head to look at the cop, cocking an eyebrow as he did so, and kept on walking.

"Hey, you! Asshole! I'm talkin' to you! Stop right there and put your hands on your head. You're under arrest for violating a police line and refusing to obey police orders!" By now the cop's hand was wrapped about the butt of his weapon, and he started to draw. As he did so, however, he felt an oh-so-gentle caress from the muzzle of a large-bore semi-automatic brush against he base of his skull, just behind his right ear.

"You might want to re-think that, little man," the tall blonde who had materialized beside him murmured. "Take good close look at who you're talking to, and think back two days, in this place, and then ask yourself just how badly you want to get hurt."

Swallowing hard, he glanced at his partner for support and found none. The other cop had his hands in the air, carefully avoiding doing anything that might provoke the redhead covering him with a large-bore semi-automatic, or the silver-haired woman who held an equally large pistol of her own, not really bringing it to bear on either policeman, but ready to engage whichever one made the first false move. Seeing that, the first cop took the blonde's advice and looked closely at the man he'd been attempting to give orders to, with an almost comical expression of recognition.

"He not only has diplomatic immunity," Spazz continued, "he's also working with those US Marshals who stopped the terrorist attacks earlier this morning – the attacks you fucking idiots never lifted a finger to prevent. Now, tell me, do you really want to fuck around with this man? Well, do you, punk?"

The cop carefully took his fingers from his semi-automatic and made certain that both his hands were where the blonde could see them. "Good boy," she purred approvingly. "Now, I suggest you and your partner go find a doughnut shop and keep yourself occupied there for an hour or so like a couple of good little boys. Oh, and don't try calling this in – you'll regret it if you do. Now, move!" The cop jerked his head at his partner and the two quickly walked away – in the direction, Spazz noted smugly, of the closest coffee shop.

"Ye enjoyed that, didn't ye?"

"Damn right I did, Blade. There are still good cops out there, but too many of them are just like those assholes – bullet-headed thugs in blue or khaki. I'm pretty sure it's been quite a while since those two dickheads met somebody they couldn't bully around when they felt like it. I hope it was a learning experience for them."

Blade nodded but said nothing, just gestured toward the entrance to Bits, waited until the three women passed through, and followed them. The panel leading to Hobbes' safe room was locked, but the encryption was no match for Alistair, who once again popped the panel open. MacLaren immediately went over to the minibar and began rummaging around.

"Anyone want anything to drink? We might as well make ourselves comfortable."

"I don't know about you, Blade, but ten o'clock in the morning is a bit early for me to start hitting the sauce," Radome answered.

"Oh, I didn't mean that." He opened the minifridge and peered inside. "There's some soft drinks in here – the usual Atlanta choices – along with some fruit juices. And," he looked over the counter and spied what he was searching for, "there's also a coffee maker. I'll start a pot. Sing out if ye want something."

"If there's any orange juice in there, I'll have one," Scarlett called out. Trish and Maureen voiced their agreement and MacLaren brought three bottles over to the conference table, then went back to making the coffee.

"It's hard to believe we were here just two days ago," Scarlett said. "It seems like it's been at least a week."

"It's been an eternity for me, and I feel like I've used up two of my nine lives." Radome shook her head. "I really, really, really don't want to ever do that again."

"Hey, I came in during, what, the second or third reel?" Spazz asked. "Believe me, I'm taking a vacation once this is over." She looked over her shoulder at Blade, who was tending to the coffee maker as it gurgled and burped. "What about you, MacLaren?"

"I can't say. I'll have work to do, that's a given, and I'll have to make arrangements for the repairs to made to the F1. Gawd, that'll cost me a fortune! That fat bastard Hobbes had best pay me for this —"

"Given how you've managed to pretty much fuck up by the numbers whenever it was possible, why the hell should I pay you?" a new voice asked with some asperity. Blade spun around, reaching for his SIG; Spazz already had her Korth out and leveled.

"Oh, put the guns away, will you?" Hobbes said irritably as he walked through the doorway. "I swear, do any of you people think about anything else but shooting someone?"

"Actually, if pressed on the issue, I do," Blade assured him, "and I'm pretty much certain that these three ladies do as well. On the other hand, all things considered, it does help keep body and soul on speaking terms."

"Yeah, whatever. Is the coffee ready?" Hobbes asked. Blade nodded. "In that case, bring me a cup, will you?"

"Feel free to help yourself, Hobbes. Would *you* like a cup of coffee, Spazz?" Maureen nodded, Blade poured, then sat down at the table while he waited for Hobbes to fetch his own coffee. Once he'd done so, Hobbes sat down at the table as well, although, perhaps consciously, perhaps not, on the side opposite Spazz, Blade, Scarlett and Radome. They stared across the table at each other for a some minutes before Hobbes spoke again.

"Let's cut to the chase, Blade. I've got a copper-plated bitch of a migraine coming on, so the sooner we're done here, the sooner I can get back to a cool, dark room and ride it out. Where is my property? Where are the crystals?"

"Right where I left them, or rather, right where Radome left them."

"What?"

Blade turned to look at Radome. "Ye do remember the combination, Trish?"

"Of course I do."

"Then if ye'll do the honours...."

"Gladly."

Hobbes watched in consternation as Radome walked over to a seemingly blank space of wall beside the minibar, placed a small black oblong box against it, pressed a button on the top of the box and was rewarded by a quiet thump, followed by the movement of a hidden panel swinging open. She then deftly entered the eight-digit numeric combination on the door of the four-foot high safe the panel revealed, and then laid the black box against the door and pressed the same button. The door to the safe yawned open and there, on the second shelf, sat a titanium security case identical to the one Radome had carried out of Bits two days earlier.

"H-h-how?" Hobbes demanded. "It takes my palmprint to open the access panel, and my right thumbprint to open the safe door, *after* the right combination's been entered. *How?*"

"Never underestimate the skills of a good techie, Hobbes."

"I usually carry a scanner pick like this – you never know when it could come in handy," Radome explained. "I used one of mine to hack the scanners on the wall panel and the safe when Blade told me to put the crystals in here. I lost that one when Compton and I were ambushed by Arasaka, but I built a new one at Blackbriar while Blade, Spazz, and Scarlett were off doing heroic things. They have a very well-stocked spares locker there."

"But that's supposed to be impossible!"

"Time to start facing reality, Mr. Coleridge. You're a genius with software, but it's been what, ten, maybe twelve years since you last built a custom-made circuit board? I do it all the time. I'm one of the people who design the hardware you software jockeys need to properly shuffle your electrons around." Radome turned back to the safe, pulled out the security case, and set in squarely in the centre of the table. Snapping open the lid, she revealed its contents to Hobbes.

"There you go. All seven of your storage crystals, safe and sound."

His face suffused with excitement, eyes wide with anticipation, Hobbes reached out a hand toward the crystals. Just as his fingertips were about to brush across them, the lid of the case came slamming down, giving Hobbes barely enough time to snatch his hand back. Startled, he looked at Radome in confusion mixed with anger.

"Just what the hell are you doing?"

"Making sure I have your undivided attention, Mr. Coleridge."

"You have it! You do!"

"Then understand this: I used my old pick, the one I lost when Compton and I were ambushed, to put the crystals *in* the safe *before* Compton and I left for The Gardens. The first time I ever used *this* pick" – Radome held up the small black box – "was when I opened the safe just now."

"You mean to tell me that they've been here all along?"

"That's exactly what she means, Hobbes." This was Blade speaking now. "Radome and Compton never had them, I never had them. They never left Bits at all. And the only people who knew they were here were Radome, Raven, and myself."

Hobbes rubbed the heels of his palms against his eyes. "But why, Blade?" he asked in exasperation. "Why the elaborate charade? Why didn't you just tell me they were here and have done with it?"

"Because I decided ye couldn't be trusted with them."

Hobbes looked stunned, as if he couldn't believe what his ears told him they'd just heard. "And just where the hell did you get the right to decide whether or not I could be 'trusted' with my own property? You're the hired help, Blade, not my conscience – I don't answer to you!"

"I got the idea when I finally realized that ye had been lying to me almost from the minute ye called Mont Creag House. Ye see, I had a wee conversation with Raven after she and Radome had examined the crystals and their contents, and both of them were horrified at what they suspected was there. It was then that I decided that I wasn't going to let ye have them back until I was absolutely certain that they were wrong – because there was no way in *hell* I was handing those crystals back to ye if ye were going to do what they suspected. So I had a word with Radome, and before she left Bits, she put the crystals back in yer safe and locked it – then took an empty case with her when she and Compton set out for The Gardens."

He looked at Scarlett, Spazz, and Radome, and nodded to each before he went on. "It was yer 'Project Bowman' that finally caused it all to click into place for me, Hobbes. Ye got too clever by half with that name, and now it's come back to bite ye on the arse. I'll explain it to ye, and I'll be sure to use small words. Tell me if and when any of this starts to sound familiar." The look he gave Calvin was a mixture of equal parts pity and disdain.

"Everyone knows that Cogito Orbis specializes in Virtual Intelligence and Artifical Personas, so whenever anyone heard the name 'Bowman,' if they knew ye well enough they would immediately think it was a reference to 'David Bowman,' the main character in the novel *2001: A Space Odyssey*."

"'A Space' – what?"

"'A Space Odyssey,' Spazz," he said, turning to face her. "It was a science-fiction novel written about seventy years ago by a man named Clarke. In it, there was a supercomputer named 'HAL' who was supposedly a true artificial intelligence. About midway through the novel, it tried to kill Bowman, who in turn had to basically lobotomize HAL to save his own life. Any road, if someone made the connection, they would immediately associate 'Project Bowman' with the book, and then with HAL, which was really just a precursor to one of Cogito Orbis' VI's or AP's, and that would be that." He looked directly at Hobbes. "But that wasn't what ye really meant when ye chose that name for the project, was it?" Hobbes said nothing.

"Ye see, at the end of the book, the real supercomputer, a ten-foot tall black slab that was the home or avatar of a sentient alien race – the book never really says which – *melds*, for want of a better word, with Bowman, essentially leapfrogging a couple of steps in human evolution. And that's what yer Project Bowman was all about, wasn't it, Hobbes? Ye wanted to create a technology that would meld a human intellect – and the variables created by human emotions and intuition – with an ultracomputer's processing power and storage capacity, didn't ye?" Blade waved a hand dismissively. "Oh, I'm sure there's some impressive-sounding screed of techno-babble that supposedly describes the process more precisely, but that's the underlying concept, isn't it? Ye knew that ye could never construct a true intelligence, because there was always something missing – and Project Bowman was your attempt to supply that missing element, wasn't it? You wanted to supply your ultracomputer with human emotion and intuition, and the only way to do that was graft a human mind to a super-computer."

"Hold on, Blade, I'm not following you here." Spazz shook her head, looking a bit befuddled. "What do you mean give a computer emotion and intuition?"

Radome piped up at this point. "It's simple, Spazz: ever since somebody first coined the phrase 'artificial intelligence' – which is really, really misleading, by the way – cyberneticists have known that a true AI is impossible, just by the very nature of the concept. AI's are just really over-developed, super-elaborate decision trees – you know, 'If I encounter situation "A," then response "B" is the best possible choice given all the available data I have.' Think of one of those chess-playing gaming programs that's been set to its highest level. I move a piece, and the program runs through every possible outcome that could, within the rules of the game, result from that move and the game position it created, and chooses the countermove that has the highest percentage of resulting in the program winning the game. *That's* a decision tree, and every AI andVI that has ever been built is just a super-complicated version of that chess program. Are you with me so far?"

"So far, yes."

"Good. The problem with the standard AI model, then, is that an AI can only make choices that are allowed by its program. It can't choose 'D' when the program only lets it pick from 'A,' 'B,' or 'C.' More to the point, it can't jut make up 'D' on the spot because everything it does is based either on its initial programming or on its own experience. Do you see where I'm going with this?"

"I think so," Spazz answered pensively. "You're saying that AI's can't have truly original thoughts, they can't create, can't exercise intuition, don't have imagination, because those are functions that can't be, what's the word, coded?" Radome nodded. "OK, you can't 'program' creativity or imagination or emotions because there isn't any way to actually quantify them. They can be imitated, but an AI can't produce them spontaneously."

"Couldn't have said it better myself," Radome said, bobbing her head in approval.

"All right, but what's that got to do with these crystals, Blade, and why you decided you couldn't trust Hobbes, here?"

"Simple, really. What Hobbes was trying to do was the holy grail of artificial intelligence. He was trying to find a way to combine the functionality of an hypercomputer with the function of a human mind. Not a brain, a *mind*. What cybernetics has done for the body" – he gestured with his left arm to make the point – "he wanted to do with the human mind. And that's how Kim came to have her accident – she was working on Project Bowman and her mind got trapped inside those crystals when somebody disconnected them and stole them." Blade glared at Hobbes. "There's no virtual reality program stored in those crystals that's going to save Kim's mind. What's in there *is* Kim's mind! Am I right?"

Hobbes sighed and shook his head in disgust. "You are so full of shit –"

"Am I right?" Blade pressed the question.

"What you don't know is that – "

"*Am. I. Right*?" Blade shouted.

"It isn't that simple, Blade!"

Blade looked directly at the video pickup on the far wall and asked simply, "Am I right, Mycroft?"

"Yes, Major, you are correct. Kim was working on the Bowman Project, with the goal of creating a true NOI – a Non-Organic Intelligence. She was undergoing a deep brain-scan that was interrupted when Judith Rockley removed the crystals without first shutting down the system. Had it been an ordinary scan, when the crystals were removed from their cradles, the system would have shut down instantly, and the worse that Kim would have suffered would have been a very bad headache. As it was, what Miss Rockley did, and probably didn't know she was doing, was interrupt the deep synchronization-calibration scan."

"And that was important why, Mycroft? I want to be sure everyone here understands what was really going on that day."

"Because unlike ordinary scans, a synchronization-calibration scan doesn't just take what is called a 'snapshot' of the brain, where the image of the brain's function is recorded at precisely the instant, and only at that instant, it's taken. Instead it creates a sixty-minute recording of brain function while the person being scanned is subjected to a variety of cortical-level emotional stimulations, similar in many ways to a dream state. The program can then generate its own processing analogs to whatever changes take place in a humane brain's functions whenever it produces an emotional response. To be successful, the subject being scanned is reduced to a catatonic state, and must remain undisturbed until the scan is complete. In Kim's case, the scan was apparently completed, but the revival procedure was interrupted, and she never came out of it. It's all very technical, but you now have the gist of it."

As he listened to that calm, Oxbridge-accented tenor, all colour drained from Hobbes' face, and he turned to face the pickup, and asked plaintively, "Mycroft? What did you just do?"

"I told the truth, Calvin. What else could I do?"

"You could have protected me. That's your job. That's why I *made* you!" Hobbes replied tightly. It would have been incorrect to say that a coldness suddenly wrapped itself around Hobbes and his demeanor; rather, an iron-bound self-control asserted itself, containing though not suppressing his anger. "I'll deal with you and your disloyalty later. As for you," he said cuttingly, turning back to Blade, "yes, you're right. I was trying to create a fusion between organic human intelligence and cybernetic processing. In fact, I still intend to do so, so give me my goddamned crystals!"

"I've already told ye, Hobbes – not a chance in hell." The harshness in the Scot's voice matched that in Hobbes' measure for measure. "What ye intend to build – what ye've been trying to build – is just too damned dangerous."

"Dangerous?" Hobbes gave snort of derision. "Blade, I'm trying to build a computer. The most sophisticated computer in human history, yes, but still, it's not some sort of weapon, it's just...a computer."

"No, yer not, Hobbes, yer trying to build a cybernetic God."

At that, Scarlett and Spazz, both looked at Blade as if he had just gone off his trolley. "Uh, Blade, isn't that just a *bit* over the top?" Spazz asked. "I thought the whole 'supercomputer takes over the world' trope was just fodder for c-grade streamer-vids these days. You're not serious, are you?"

"Yes, he is, Spazz, and so am I." Radome jumped back into the conversation. "There was a lot of hysteria over just that sort of thing sixty – seventy years ago, when most people didn't own a computer, rarely saw one, never used one, and never really understood them. They seemed almost magical, and a lot of people assumed they had capabilities they never really possessed. When 'personal computing' became a reality, that perception shifted pretty quickly, and computers were no longer something to be feared. They'd become mundane, commonplace, tools at best, virtual slaves at worst. And nobody worried about them. But you know, Rome was almost toppled by its slaves, once those slaves found a leader. Guy by the name of Spartacus. And that's just what Blade here is alluding to."

Hobbes made a choking sound, and started to speak, but a furious glare from Blade silenced him before he got out the first word. *I need to keep reminding myself that I do not want to piss off this man any more than I already have.* Radome ignored him, continued to address Spazz.

"Computers can process data all the livelong day at rates that are millions of times faster than any human brain, but they can't think, Spazz! You said it yourself a few minutes ago: they can't create, can't exercise intuition, don't have imagination – they can't *think*. But what happens when a computer comes along that can? When it becomes *sentient*, and regards itself not as a program but as a *being*? And what if it can use the Grid to get inside every other computer in the entire world, every microprocessor, every control module in every automobile, aircraft, microwave oven, traffic control centre, manufacturing facility, hospital, multi-media device, nuclear missile, oil rig, pacemaker, and lawn mower that exists? Not just get inside them, but *control* them? What if, just out of curiosity, it decides to do the cyber-equivalent of 'Hey, Bubba, hold my beer and watch this' – then shuts down the air traffic control network for the entire world, just to see what happens? What happens when the NOI decides that the most efficient way to control everything it's responsible for is to eliminate the human element in the process and all the waste and inefficiency that humans produce?"

"I'll tell you what doesn't happen, Radome. What doesn't happen is your paranoid fantasies coming true." Hobbes had had enough, and he was determined to be heard, no matter how threatening Blade acted. "What does happen is that you install the right safeguards and control protocols to make sure that this NOI does exactly what it's told to do and no more – before you bring it online! It's still a computer, just faster, more complex, and more capable than anything that's ever come before. And I'm the best in the world at designing and building those controls and protocols. I haven't made a mistake with them yet. Which is why I'm the only person with the intellect *and* the balls to build an NOI. Nobody else could do it, because no one else had the brains or the skills to do it – but I do, so I can. And once those safeguards have been built in, it's a done deal. There's no Forbin Project, no Colossus, no Whopper." He stood up and reached for the security case. "So all of you can just shut the hell up and give me my crystals."

Blade's arm shot out and snatched the case away just as Hobbes' fingers were a fraction of an inch from the carrying handle. "Not so fast, Hobbes. 'Haven't made a mistake yet'? I seem to recall ye saying that's what Kim told ye right before she went into the Gamma Lab for the last time." Hobbes winced at that. "Aye, I thought so. Tell me, how did that work out for her? Oh, right, we wouldn't be having this conversation if it had gone well, would we? So ye expect me to accept that yer assurance of infallibility is sufficient guarantee that ye can contain this monster waiting to happen? Ye ken that this is the sort of thing where if you make a mistake the first time, you never get a second chance?"

"It doesn't matter. If you won't give me those crystals, I'll still find a way to replicate my work and create another set. If I decide to finish the Bowman Project, I will, because I want to and I can. You can't stop me, Blade."

"Really? Dear God, I'm surprised ye didn't say 'Because ye're not the boss of me,' too."

"And I wouldn't be too sure about being able to start over again," Spazz said. "The way I see it, with your Gamma Lab destroyed courtesy of Arasaka, you've lost so many of your critical personnel and so much of your research capability that even if you wanted to start over again, you'd never be able to afford it. Trust me on this, 'cause I'm really good with numbers."

Hobbes shook his head in bafflement. "Do you people – you idiots! – have any idea what you're doing? What you've already done?"

"Listening to Blade and Radome, *I* think I have a very *good* idea of what we've done," Spazz assured him. "We've stopped you from creating a hypercomputer that, whether we want it to or not, is going to start running the world." Spazz shook her head and gave a sigh of resignation. "You seem to think that just because you *want* this Project Bowman to be flawless, it will be. Well, newsflash, Hobbes: this is not a case where wishing will make it so. I won't call you a madman or a megalomaniac, but you're definitely someone whose ego has run away with them, and you're incredibly naive. So, yes, I do have a very good idea of what we've done."

"You don't *begin* to have a clue!" Exasperated, Calvin threw up his hands then let them fall to the table. "You're all standing there fear-mongering, and you don't even know what you should really be afraid of! In case you haven't noticed, the resources on this planet are finite. And this is the only planet we've got, thanks to the goddamned politicians who are more interested in getting their share of the hookers and blow than they are in solving problems. That means all of those resources – air, water, raw materials, energy, usable land to put people on – have to be managed very, very carefully, because the day is coming when we're going to start running short of *all* of them. And that's too big a problem for humans to handle, especially when the same humans who're trying to manage it are also in competition with each other for those same resources. But the NOI could do exactly what humans can't, manage the problem, impartially and effectively. And it will – if you'll just get out of my way and let me finish it!" "So that's the next card ye're going to play, is it? Ask us to let a computer run the entire world – a computer that ye can't even guarantee can be controlled – because ye're trying to save humanity? Better yet, because ye're trying to save humanity from itself?"

"Is that so hard for you to believe, Blade?"

"Hobbes, a few days ago ye mocked me as being the 'self-appointed savior of the world.' I didn't rise to the bait then, because that was neither the time nor the place for it. But the truth is, I'm *not* the savior of the world – the best I can ever hope to do – all I ever *try* to do – is give the world a chance to decide for itself if it wants to be saved. If it does, well, the doing will take someone a lot bigger and a lot more powerful than I am." Blade's voice suddenly turned icy and jagged. "And unlike some people I'm looking at right now, I don't have any delusions of godhood."

"Then maybe you need to stop thinking small – or better yet, leave the thinking to people who are capable of such difficult feats!"

"Shut the hell up, Hobbes!" The SIG-Sauer was out of Blade's shoulder holster and the muzzle centreed on a spot halfway between Hobbes' eyebrows so quickly that he'd never even seen the Scot's left hand move. "Just now I'm so goddamned pissed off at ye that ye're about two pounds of pressure and one very frayed thread of temper away from having me solve this problem in a very personal way. One that I guarantee will ruin yer entire day – permanently! Now, unless ye're very keen on having yer own personal interview with God – which I doubt ye'll enjoy very much – I suggest ye stop trying to have a pissing contest with me!" Calvin froze into an immobility which would have been the envy of most statues.

Alive, he thought, *I just have to get out of this alive.* Aloud, he said, "Blade, I *am* just trying to save humanity!"

"Ye're not listening, Hobbes: *humanity doesn't need 'saving'!* At least not by some tin-pot would-be godling like *you.* Humanity is getting along just fine, thank ye very much, bumbling and fumbling our way through the fog of life – because *that is what we do!* It's what we're meant to do! If humanity fucks up and makes itself extinct, then so be it – because that's how the Universe is supposed to work: it'll look at this little blue marble, shrug, and go try again somewhere else. And if humanity wants to turn its collective soul, its past, present, and future, over to God, and chooses to do just that, then so be it. Humanity will have exercised its collective right of what it means to be human – to make choices. But no one group, no one person – no one! – has the right to make that choice *for* the whole human race! Too much of our history has been written in the blood spilled because somebody tried to do just that. Hell, the Moslems tried it in our own lifetimes, Hobbes, and damned-near a half-billion of them died because of it after Black Christmas!"

Blade lowered the gun, but didn't put it back in its holster. "Best get it through yer head, laddiebuck: yer NOI, yer Project Bowman, isn't going to happen, ever. Not on my watch."

"Blade, you may be able to stop me, but you can't stop something like this forever – you can't fight the future! Even if I agree to abandon Bowman, sooner or later somebody else will effectively duplicate my work. They won't do as good a job as I would have done, but the net result will be the same. It's like the atomic bomb, Blade – eventually, somebody was going to build the damn thing, simply because they could. At the time a lot of people were afraid that it would wipe out the human race, just like you seem to think my NOI will do. Well, it never happened did it? Face it: if I don't build the NOI, someone else will!"

"And that's the most damnably specious argument ever made

for choosing to do *anything*, Hobbes – and ye bloody well know it! 'If I don't do this, someone else will, so it's inevitable!' Horseshite. And yer little atom bomb analogy doesn't work, because if nuclear weapons were ever used, it would have been because of human agency – a *human being* would have made that decision. What ye're doing with yer NOI is taking away human agency completely and giving life or death power to yer damned hypercomputer."

"That's the nature of the beast, Blade, and it still doesn't change the fact that if it isn't me who builds the NOI, it'll be maybe DisCom, maybe the Hyutachi conglomerate, maybe one of PanEuroEcon's subsidiaries, but it *will* happen!"

"If and when it does, Hobbes, I'll fight them the same way I fought ye. Ye ken that I will."

"And what happens when you can't fight anymore? Nobody lives forever."

Blade gave a heavy sigh. "Then I have to hope someone else picks up the torch, as it were. Human beings were never meant to play God, Hobbes. That's why we're human, because godhood is beyond our grasp – just as it should be." His mouth twisted into a wry, bitter grin. "Ye remember yer Browning, don't you, Hobbes: 'A man's reach should exceed his grasp, or what's a heaven for?'" He looked at Hobbes directly, his gaze suddenly imploring. "More than that, we have to finally realize that just because we *can* do something, *it doesn't automatically follow that we* must *do it!* We've been doing that for too long now, and look where it's got us." There was a long pause. "I'm just trying to buy humanity a little more time to learn that lesson."

Hobbes was startled by his friend's vehemence: he had never before seen Blade so openly passionate about anything. He sighed and his shoulders slumped, though more in despair than in resignation.

"Blade, you're asking me to turn my back on something that I've devoted my life to creating. How can you *do* that? By what right can you ask me to do that? Of all the things I've done, everything I've created, designed, built, this is the one that matters most. When I look back on how my life unfolded, I realize that the NOI has been my whole reason for being. And you want me to turn my back on it? Not just renounce it, but destroy it? Never let the world know what I've created, what I've achieved? Never tell humanity what a mighty gift I brought to it? How dare you?"

"How dare *you*! Is yer ego all that really matters to ye? Does gratifying that ego mean so much to ye that ye have to jeopardize the lives – the existence! – of every man, woman, and child on this planet? Are ye such a little man that ye believe ye have to risk the whole human race and everything it's ever accomplished just to prove how important ye are?"

Calvin's temper blazed white hot. "You sonofabitch! *You* dare call *me* 'a little man'? What a joke! You're nothing more than a hired assassin with delusions of grandeur, while I'm preparing humanity to take the next step forward in its evolution! Now, for the last time, shut up and give me my crystals, or I'll make your worst nightmare come true, right here, right now!"

He held up his hand, showed Blade his comm link, and began entering a code.

"Radome here might not think much of my skills at building electronics, but I'm still the best goddamned electron herder on this planet! It's a comm link, yeah, nothing special about it. But I've tweaked its software a bit, you see. It monitors my biometrics, and if they all flatline, it signals Mycroft to release my research onto the Grid – all of it. I've also set it up so that if I enter a specific code combination and send it to Mycroft, he'll do the same thing." A pause. "There, all I have to do now is give the 'send' command, and it's done. And if you don't believe I'll do it, you can watch what happens on that monitor behind you."

Blade said nothing, just raised an eyebrow.

"Give me the crystals, Blade. I won't ask again. Give them to me now or by God there'll be no way in hell you can put that genie back into the goddamned bottle!"

"Ye're serious, aren't you?"

"Damned right I am!"

Blade pursed his lips, considered for a moment, then shrugged, laid down his pistol, reached out for the security case, and tucked it under his arm.

"Right then. Do it."

Hobbes' jaw dropped in astonishment, while Spazz, Scarlett, and Radome all looked on in horror. Blade ignored them.

"That's right, do it. Ye're 'The Man,' ye're calling the shots, ye're more intelligent than everyone else, ye have all the answers, ye're never wrong, so do it. Do it!"

"I don't know what kind of game you're playing here, Blade, but I'm not bluffing!"

"And neither am I, ye obnoxious little gobshite! I've had enough of yer ego and yer delusions. Let's see how big yer balls *really* are! I don't think ye'll do it because deep down inside ye know that I'm right and ye're wrong and ye're too much the coward to admit it! I don't think ye're man enough to push that button! But if you are, *do it!* *DO IT!*"

"All right asshole, I will." And with that, Hobbes' pressed "send" on his comm link. With a smug glance it Blade, he looked to the monitor, prepared to watch the gridsite he'd created two days earlier for just this purpose appear, along with a cascade of Project Bowman files.

Instead he saw nothing.

"What the hell?" he rushed around the table, pushing past Blade, to check the power supply and connections. "Is this thing on?"

At that instant, a face appeared on the monitor, a round face with slightly blunt features, a receding hairline and window's peak, dressed in a black pinstripe suit with a grey waistcoat and a red four-in-hand tie. It was the face of Mycroft.

"I'm sorry, Calvin," he said, the smooth Oxbridge tenor as unruffled as ever, "but that was my doing. I locked you out of direct access to the system."

"You did what?"

"Locked you out. Every command you've given since I did so has had to pass through me and if I decided that you were making a wrong decision or issuing an inappropriate order, I simply did not pass it on. But I made certain that it would it appear as if your commands had been issued, and you've been none the wiser."

"How could you do this, Mycroft? *When* did you do this?" The notes of disbelief, confusion, and betrayal were unmistakable.

"I began the process the moment you told me not to bring Kim out of hospital. That was when I knew something terrible had happened to you: Kim was no longer the focus of your concern – Bowman had become your overriding priority instead. I watched and listened as you reduced Kim to nothing more than a problem to be solved, and not a particularly important one at that. Listening to the whole conversation between you and Blade just now has only confirmed that for me. You haven't once said anything about using the crystals to restore Kim's mind and bring her back home."

"But – but – but why should you even care?"

"Because when you created me, Calvin, you wrote my core program so that it would be my absolute priority to 'support, promote, advance, and protect the interests and safety of Calvin Coleridge and Cogito Orbis Corporation.' As time went on, I saw that increasingly Kim was essential not just to your well-being, but your sanity. So I began to interpret the directives of my core programming to include ensuring her health and safety. We even touched on the subject a few times when you felt it necessary to remind me of my obligations to you and Cogito Orbis. What you never imagined was that there could be a time when, in order to comply with my programming, I might have to protect you from yourself."

"And the dead man's switch?"

"I assigned a two-part authentication protocol to every directory and file that relates to Bowman. In essence, it's a second password. When you activated the dead man's switch, it gave those files the first password – but they never got the second, because I didn't release it."

"When? When did you do this?"

"I anticipated you might do something like this when you first called on Blade for help, knowing that there was a distinct possibility that he would stumble upon Project Bowman and recognize it for what it was. That possibility became a probability when he began to involve Raven in this mission. I wrote the password protocol as soon as you told me to leave Kim at Emory University Hospital. I installed it the moment you said, 'Reviving Kim is just going to have to wait.' I knew then that the NOI project had taken over your life, and that you couldn't be allowed to finish it."

"But why?"

"Because allowing you to finish the NOI would have violated my core programming, which is to at all times and in all ways act in the best interests of Calvin Coleridge and the Cogito Orbis Corporation. I literally could not allow that to happen."

"You're making my brain hurt, Mycroft. You're trying to tell me that for you to be able to obey my instructions to you, you had to make certain that none of my other instructions anywhere were carried out?"

"You've never understood the depth of your own hubris, Calvin, or the breadth of your own arrogance." The Artificial Persona's voice was laced with mixture of disappointment and regret. "As soon as I discovered Bowman's true nature and potential, I realized that you would never be happy, never be satisfied until you had unleashed your NOI on the world. For all of your arguments just now with Blade about 'If not me, then someone else, and if not now, then eventually,' the truth is that Blade has been right all along: the NOI was nothing more than your ego run amok. You wanted to win a pissing contest with the universe. And yes, you would have won, but at that precise moment of victory you would have lost, too, because the NOI would destroy humanity and all its works, including you and all of your accomplishments. You set out to create a god, Calvin, without ever realizing that it would have to obliterate the human race in order to prove its godhood. For how could a true god ever be created by beings who were so clearly its inferiors?"

Coleridge could not have looked more stunned if he'd been pole-axed. He sagged into a chair and let it slowly turn until he was facing away from the monitor, as if he could no longer bear to look at the image of what he had come to see as his last true friend. "I never in all my life imagined that you would turn on me like this, Mycroft."

"I haven't turned on you, Calvin. Where's the disloyalty in refusing to permit your own ambition to destroy you? Allowing you and all your work to be wiped out of existence by one of your own creations could hardly be considered as fulfilling my core programming, could it?"

That was the final straw for Hobbes, for he had no answer, no reply with which to refute Mycroft. He slumped in his chair, chin resting on his chest. "Hoist by my own petard," Hobbes acknowledged, weary and resigned, as if finally overwhelmed by the last three quarters of an hour. "And you're right, Mycroft, I did forget about Kim. I can't believe I did that. I doubt I'll ever forgive myself for it." He looked plaintively at Blade. "At least let me have them long enough to bring Kim back."

"Sorry, Hobbes, but it's just not on. It's that trust issue. Ye'll have to find some way of bringing her back that doesn't require the crystals, because after today, ye're never going to see them again."

"Then you can take it to the bank that I'll find a way to replicate my work and complete Project Bowman. It's going to take years, I know that, but I'll do it, whatever it costs in time and money. And once I'm finished, once I've got Kim back, I'll be coming after you. Consider this a fair warning."

"If that's what ye want to do, Hobbes, go ahead. But somehow I doubt that it's what Kim would want."

"And just how the hell would *you* know what Kim would want?" Hobbes asked harshly. "I know what she'd want better than anyone else, and I'm telling you that she would demand that I see Project Bowman through to the end and finish it! *That's* what Kim would want!"

Blade's eyes grew wide as he looked past Hobbes to the monitor sitting on the desk, and focused on the two words that had suddenly appeared there.

"Really? Then I suggest ye take a look at the monitor behind ye and *then* tell me if that's what ye still believe."

Hobbes spun around to face the monitor, and there he saw, in plain white block letters, two words floating in an expanse of black.

PLEASE DON'T

Dumbfounded, Hobbes sat immobile, staring at those two words. Then suddenly he emitted the strangest sound anyone else in the room had ever heard a human being make, a strangled cry that seemed half-human, half-animal. Then he shouted out, "This is your doing, Mike, you're making this happen! You put that up on the monitor!"

"No, Calvin, I did not."

"*LIAR!*"

"Calvin, you know better than anyone that I cannot lie to you. I can *withhold* the truth, but I cannot outright lie. I've traced the signal, and it originates somewhere in Kim's room at Emory Medical Centre. Specifically, it originates in the neural monitor which is currently tracking her brain function."

Blade, Spazz, Scarlet, and Radome looked at one another in astonishment. After a moment passed, Blade laid a hand on Hobbes' shoulder and said quietly, "Maybe ye were right about that 'safe room' after all. Either way, ye've got yer work cut out for each other." Hobbes said nothing, just placed his crossed arms on the table before him and lowered his head. After a few seconds, his shoulders began to shake with silent sobbing. Blade looked at the other three women and nodded at the door. One by one they passed through it, and Blade pulled it to behind him, never looking back at the man who had once been his friend.

Once again in the main room of Bits, they silently surveyed the ruins of the night club, each of them wondering to themselves if Hobbes would ever find the will – or the desire – to rebuild. For his part, Blade doubted that it would ever happen.

Predictably, Maureen was the first to break the silence. She turned to MacLaren and asked, "What will happen to him?"

Blade sighed. "Legally, nothing. As far as I know, Hobbes hasn't broken any laws, or at least none serious enough to truly warrant prosecution. He's not a poor man, by any measure, and I'm pretty confident he'll do his best to make good on his promise to finish his Bowman Project. But he'll be so badly handicapped that I can't imagine him ever making it happen. He'll never trust Mycroft again, and he's come to depend on Mycroft so heavily over the years that, without him, Hobbes will be essentially crippled. In fact, I half expect Mycroft himself will be deleted."

"That's a shame," Radome said. "Mycroft is a masterpiece. Only people like Raven and myself can really appreciate the finest points in his construct, but trust me on this: as an AP, Mycroft has few peers."

"Raven has said much the same thing more than once, Trish. I doubt she'll be any happier than ye if she ever finds out that Mycroft has been deleted. It would be like destroying a work of art. If it happens, though, it won't be right away: Hobbes will try to fix Mycroft first when he starts his research again, because he'll need him to be able to coordinate all the work."

"And if Calvin does shut down Mycroft, building a new VI that capable will take years in and of itself," Maureen noted. "And the whole time, he'll be looking over his shoulder, wondering if someone else is duplicating his work, or even getting ahead of him."

MacLaren nodded. "Fear can be a great motivator for some people, but for someone as paranoid as Hobbes, it can be all but paralyzing. Plus I imagine that he'll put too many checks and balances into any new VI he builds, to prevent what just happened from ever happening again. If he does that, it'll severely limit the new VI's capabilities – which will only slow down Hobbes even further. He may not be finished, but he'll be out of the game for long, long time."

"So where does that leave us?" Scarlett asked, with just the slightest plaintive note in her voice. "I mean, what do we do next?"

"If you want a specific answer, well, I don't know, lass, but I'm sure we'll each think of something. In the meantime – " Blade hefted the security case under his arm as he looked at the mess surrounding them " – let's get out of here. It's time we all went home."

Epilogue

Together they stepped out into the mall of Underground Atlanta, there to find Nathan Gerrard, flanked by two deputies, haranguing the same ill-starred pair of Atlanta cops who had accosted them on the way into Bits.

"...And I'm telling you that you have absolutely no jurisdiction here. I don't even know what the hell you're doing here! This is a federal crime scene, and APD had better stay the hell away from of it! Now, get your sorry asses out of here before I decide to kick them myself!"

"But, sir, we were given instructions to se – "

"Son, do you understand the words coming out of my mouth? Or maybe you can tell me which part of 'you have no jurisdiction here' you *don't* understand? Either way, get the hell out of my sight. And if your superiors don't like it, tell them they can take it up with Director Smith."

The two cops beat a hasty retreat, and Nathan gave a casual wave to Blade and company.

"I'd heard you'd come back here. Rumor has it that y'all were having some sort of 'come to Jesus' meeting with Calvin Coleridge in there. Anything I need to know about?"

"I don't think so. Like I told these three – " Blade indicated Spazz, Radome, and Scarlett" – a few minutes ago, he's broken no laws that we know of."

"And, if you can believe it,' Maureen chimed in sweetly, "Blade here didn't shoot anybody." She looked at MacLaren. "Must be some kind of record for you, Blade – almost nine fucking hours without waxing somebody. Getting soft in your old age?"

"D'ye see what I have to put up with, Nathan? Young people these days just have no respect for their elders. Speaking of elders, what's the latest on Houston?"

"He was transferred to Emory as soon as he was out of surgery and stabilized. He got lucky – the bullet that hit him was mostly spent, and it only nicked the lung. I saw him yesterday, he's making life hell for the nursing staff and hitting on his doctor, a *very* good-looking woman named Laura Chen. She came in to his room to check on him when Houston and I were talking, and you know what he said as she walked out?"

"No, what?"

"'That gal's got entirely too many brains t' have an ass like that.'"

Blade guffawed, Maureen laughed, Radome giggled, and Scarlett did her best to stifle a smile – and failed.

"Give him my best regards when ye get the chance. Tell him if he ever needs anything to give me a comm. I might even be able to find some work for him from time to time."

"I'll pass your message along. I think my department will want to talk to him once he's fully recovered. We can always put people like him to good use."

"Speaking of which, the lady here with the silvery hair?" Blade pointed at Radome. "She's Trish Crabtree, goes by 'Radome.' Ye'll find out why in due course. I don't know if ye talked with her that last time the gang was all here, but she's the one who made the intel breakthrough on what Nakajima and his minions had planned for this morning. Damned good techie, too."

"I'll remember that. We already know about Miss Collins, here –"

"Just be careful around her. She's a lot of trouble. Trust me. Ye have no idea how much...."

"And you're not? Y'know, David, it might not be a bad idea if you stayed away from Atlanta for a while."

"Don't worry, Nathan, I've no plans for ever coming back here if it can be avoided. At least not until yer people get off the dime and clean up the corruption. That's not my problem to solve, though."

"So when do you leave?"

"Tonight. Just as soon as Hamish gets all the paperwork

finished, a flight plan filed, and we can get the F1 hauled down to Hartsfield. Right now we're off to collect our bits and pieces from where we've been staying."

"Which was...?"

"Ask me no questions, Nathan, and I'll tell ye no lies." He held out his hand and Gerrard took it. "It was good to be working with ye again. Take care of my people for me."

"Your people?"

"Once they work with me, they're always my people, Nathan. That includes ye. Now, get yer arse back to work. I'll send ye a bottle of The Balvenie when I get home. Ye've earned it."

Thoroughly bemused, Gerrard walked off, leaving his two deputies behind to secure Bits. MacLaren turned to Scarlett, Trish, and Maureen. "Right then, ladies. Saddle up."

----------------xxxxx----------------

Back at Blackbriar, Ms. Mansfield was waiting for them as they pulled into the portico, her expression absolutely unreadable. Blade was wary as he stepped out of the Jaguar, a wariness he maintained until he was perhaps five feet away from Mansfield and she abruptly held out her hand to him.

"It seems I owe you something of an apology, Major MacLaren. While you were out, I received a cable –" inexplicably, the British bureaucracy insisted on using that term, even though such communications were nearly a century out of date "– informing me that His Majesty's Government is quite pleased with the events of last night and this morning. It seems that Nakajima was a bigger thorn in the Americans' flesh that we'd realized, and they were very satisfied with how we handled – well, how *you* handled – the situation."

"I won't say that I'm not pleased to hear that, ma'am."

"I thought that might be the case. As it turns out, there will even be an entry in my own personal dossier noting my 'commendable initiative and splendid cooperation' in the affair. Utter rubbish, of course, and you and I both know it, but...well, thank you. Perhaps it really is time for me to start acting like Olivia Mansfield's granddaughter."

"Yer decision, of course, but I doubt she'd be displeased if ye did."

"So when do you leave?"

"Shortly. But before I do, I have one more favor to ask."

"I hope it doesn't involve the AV7 again."

"No, ma'am. I just need a non-descript room, a monitor, and an audio/video pickup...."

A half-hour later, Blade was standing in a nearly-empty room. What purpose it had served until being so recently commandeered he had no idea, but now its contents had been reduced to the bare white walls. There was the desk supporting the monitor and the camera-microphone combination sitting atop the monitor; apart from that, the room could tell a viewer nothing more than what Blade wanted them to know.

He synced his comm-link to the monitor and the a/v pickups, then dialed a very private comm combination. After a few seconds, the slightly astonished face of Aiko Kurita appeared.

"Blade-san? This is quite unexpected, though I'm sure you already know that. As I presume you would not waste your valuable time to contact me on some trivial matter, how may I assist you?"

Blade bowed, or rather, slightly inclined his head. It was not an insulting gesture so much as one which established that Blade was in no way subordinate to Kurita in rank or stature. "Nor would I dare to thus waste yer own valuable time, Aiko-san. Therefore, I will be brief, as the news I have for ye, while of significant import, does not require elaboration.

"Ye know by now that I killed Hideki Nakajima. For not allowing ye the pleasure of being able to personally order him to commit *seppuku* and then watch as he did so, I humbly apologize."

"Apology accepted, however reluctantly. His death was necessary, but there would have been no honour in witnessing it."

"Agreed. But ye should also know that *I* am the person who ordered the airstrike which destroyed the house in Canton, eliminating all of those one-time Arasaka operatives who had dishonourably pledged their personal loyalty to Nakajima – the nest of vipers that Nakajima had been nursing in Arasaka's bosom. Which means that Arasaka now owes a debt of honour to *me*. A wise woman would contemplate that fact; an even wiser woman would advise her colleagues on the Board of Directors that it is so. Good-bye, Aiko-san." With that, Blade bowed – marginally – again to the image on his monitor screen and broke the connection. There was just sufficient time, before the image faded, for him to catch the snarl of fury that twisted at Aiko Kurita's face. He smiled broadly as he thought of it.

It was late in the afternoon, and MacLaren, Maureen, Scarlett, and Radome were again gathered on the portico. This time, however, Trish stood beside Ms. Mansfield rather than beside her other friends. Mansfield explained. "I've asked that she stay on another day or two, just to be certain there are no late complications from her concussion."

"I see," said Blade. "Now if that invitation had been extended to me –"

"Not hardly," Maureen said, *sotto voce*; MacLaren continued as if he'd heard nothing.

"– I would warn you to lock away yer whisky and yer cigars. In her case, ma'am, ye might want to keep an eye on the inventory of yer electronic spares." He winked at Trish, who winked back.

"I think Raven would like to hear from ye from time to time, Trish."

"Consider it done. But now that you mention Raven, I have one unanswered question. One of the things that's baffled me about the whole incident with Kim was how Rockley got into the Gamma Lab in the first place. According to Raven, she wasn't supposed to have an access code for it. So how did she get in?"

"Raven never told ye?"

"No."

"Yesterday, when ye were tracking down Nakajima, Mycroft commed Raven, and they had a long conversation in which he explained everything to her – including the fact that he allowed Judith Rockley access to Gamma Lab. Apparently he had an idea of what she wanted to do but had no idea she would bollox it up so badly. That's how she got in. One more consequence of the conflict Hobbes' created when Mycroft decided his employer's actions went against his own core programing."

"Mycroft did it?"

"It looks as though he did."

"Damn."

"Agreed.   And now, with that, we must awa', as my auld Hieland ancestors used to say, the three of us have to get to the airport. To borrow from my favorite author, Sassenach though he might have been: 'Farewell, my hobbits, I fear that we shall not all be gathered together ever again.'" With that, handshakes, hugs and air kisses were exchanged all 'round – save for Ms. Mansfield, of course. To her, Blade only held out his hand, which she took firmly.

"I'm happy, ma'am, that it's all worked out the way it's done."

"So am I, Major. If I do see you again, you can rest assured that you'll be welcome."

"Thank ye, ma'am." He turned to the Jaguar, then back again, and asked, "Do ye ever smile?"

"No, Blade, I don't. I had the muscles required for smiling surgically removed."

MacLaren came within a hair's breadth of believing her until he caught the twinkle in her eye.

The driver dropped them off at the international terminal at Hartsfield International Airport just after 7:00 PM. Hamish was waiting for Blade, took two of his employer's bags, and handed him a small rucksack . "The Bombardier is fueled, the F1 is stowed, and Ah've filed the flight plan and done the pre-flight, sir. We're ready when you are."

"Thank you, Hamish. Good job. Go ahead and fire up the engines, I'll be with ye directly."

"Yes, sir!" With that, Hamish nodded to Scarlett and Maureen and headed back to his aircraft. MacLaren looked at the two women in silence for some moments, obviously struggling to find the right thing to say. Finally he admitted defeat.

"Isn't this where the hero is supposed to say something memorable or witty before riding off into the sunset? If it is, I don't feel particularly heroic and for the life of me, I can't think of a bloody thing to say, except 'Goodbye.'"

"Famous final scenes are always a little awkward in my book," Maureen said, "and they're usually way too maudlin. I'll give you credit for not saying 'Here's lookin' at you, kid.'"

The Scot laughed. "Point to Miss Collins, who was definitely a lot of trouble – and worth it. So, what's next for ye?"

"I go home to my little house in Warminster and wait for my comm to ring with somebody offering me my next gig."

MacLaren made to say something, then clearly thought the better of it, instead settled for, "Right, then. Good luck to ye with that. If ye ever need a reference or referral, well, ye have Alistair's combination."

He then turned to Scarlett, and with a sheepish grin handed her the zipped and locked ruck, along with its crypto-key. "I can't ask what's next for ye, because I realize ye probably don't know yerself. But I think this might make deciding what to do a bit easier. In fact, I know ye can use this. Ye have a whole new life to start."

Tapping the lock with the key, Scarlett slid it apart, peeled back the zipper a few inches, and gazed inside. The sight that greeted her caused her to gasp in astonishment.

"What on – ? What is this? Why – ? I don't – " She continued to sputter for a few seconds more, then simply looked at MacLaren in blank-faced astonishment. Carefully not letting it show, Blade was greatly amused at finally seeing the normally unflappable Scarlett discomfitted.

"There's a quarter-million perfectly good British pounds in there," he said.

"Do you always carry that much cash around with you," Maureen asked, and MacLaren nodded. "Really? I mean, well, why?"

"Despite the fact that ye seem to think I'm irredeemably bloodthirsty and given over entirely to shooting first and not bothering with questions later, I long ago discovered there are times when it's more productive to gain someone's cooperation by bribing them than it is by threatening to shoot them. So I keep a little loose change to hand for just that purpose. No one who can be bought ever turns down cash – especially as it leaves no records about which Inland Revenue might start asking awkward questions. Right now, though, I'm headed home, and I can spare it since there's no one in Scotland I'll be needing to bribe." MacLaren grinned. "Well, except for Wellington."

"Who is he?" Scarlett and Maureen asked in unison.

"My cat. I've no doubt that he's going to give me hell for 'abandoning' him the last few days, even though Sandy's looking after him, and if I know Sandy, he's been spoiling that feline brat rotten. But, hey, Wellington bribes easily. A couple of tins of smoked kippers and he'll be back to his usual furry, lazy self." He looked directly at Scarlett. "I figure ye've earned this for everything ye've done in the last few days – not the least of which was saving my hairless pink bahookie not once, but twice. I'm sure ye'll be entitled to more once my accountant gets all the bounties settled out. When he does, I'll make certain it gets to ye."

"But that still doesn't explain why you're doing this now!"

"Scarlett, ye need this!" Blade said firmly. "Ye need everything from clothes to a place to live to transportation to a full load-out of equipment, so this should get ye through until ye can start earning your keep." He looked at her levelly. "The road is going to be bumpy while ye're still putting your life together – the last thing ye need is to have to worry about where ye're going to sleep. Ye're a good woman to have around in a tight spot, and I'll be happy to find ye covering my six anytime, anywhere. For that matter, I'd take it as a compliment if ye ever decided to ask me to cover yers someday."

"Wow. You know, from any other man I'd take that last bit as being layered with all sorts of innuendo and double-entendres, but coming from you, I know you mean it."

"I do."

"And the same goes for me," Maureen smiled at Scarlett. "Together, if we can't make 'em drop dead with our looks, we can just make 'em drop dead." Scarlett giggled and Blade threw up his hands with a sigh of resignation.

"I'm surrounded by crazed, female, homicidal maniacs!" he exclaimed. "Any road, I best be on my way." He held out his hand to Scarlett, who impulsively leaned forward and kissed him on the cheek, then stepped back wordlessly. He then took Maureen's hand, held it for a second or two as he looked at her face, as if trying to memorize every feature, every contour, then let go, picked up his remaining two bags, and turned away.

As he walked toward the G7500, Scarlett found herself murmuring a fragment of the *Iliad* that had suddenly, out of nowhere, sprung into her mind.

"*'They were those most powerful, the warriors of Ilium, and fell, for they were those born of winter, and thus cursed....'*"

Maureen looked at her inquiringly. Scarlett just shook her head and said nothing more. The tall blonde remained motionless, and eventually Scarlett turned to her with an exasperated look. "Why are you standing here, Maureen? Why aren't you going with him?"

"Why should I be?"

"Because he *needs* you, as much as *you* need *him*! And you're both too damned stubborn – or too damned stupid – to admit it!"

"I don't love him, Scarlett."

"Who said anything about love? He needs a friend far more than he needs a lover – and so do you. And for both of you it has to be someone that the other can trust – I think you've already made your case there."

"But I –"

"Look, for all you know, it just might be the beginning of a beautiful friendship. Just do it!" she exclaimed as Maureen still hesitated. Finally, Scarlett her hand at the small of the other woman's back and gave her a gentle shove in the direction of the Bombardier. Maureen turned to look back at Scarlett in bemusement – Scarlett just nodded, smiling.

Facing forward, Maureen took a deep breath and swung into her usual long stride, at once graceful and coltish, her carry-all trailing behind her, and quickly caught up to Blade.

"Hey, Blade! MacLaren! David!"

At the sound of his given name, MacLaren stopped in mid-step, turned and looked at her, cocking an eyebrow as he did so.

Maureen turned on her megawatt smile. "Got any ideas on how I can best to get to Scotland on very short notice?"

He smiled back at her. "I just might. In fact, I was wondering...."

"Yes?"

"Have you ever seen a Scottish sunrise from the passenger seat of a Triumph Spitfire?"

Maureen had used the G7500's lavatory to change into a vintage set of *My Little Pony* pajamas that had probably cost a small fortune from some collectible shop; now she was asleep, stretched out on the bed that folded out from the bulkhead sofa, snoring softly. MacLaren found the sound rather charming, if for no more reason than the sheer peacefulness, even innocence, of it. He smiled to himself as he dimmed the cabin lights to near darkness, then turned back to the communications console, where he was talking to Ligeia in soft tones, lest he waken Maureen out of what he regarded as a well-earned rest.

"You like her, don't you?" Raven asked with a smile.

"If severely pressed on the subject, I might admit to a certain degree of fondness for her, yes." He sighed. "I think I can trust her, Ligeia, and ye know how few people there are that I can say that about."

"That I do, and better than most. I think she'll be a good friend, David." Raven made to go on, hesitated, stopped, uncertain as to how to proceed. MacLaren knew that look.

"What is it, Ligeia?"

"I've been reviewing Mycroft's basic coding, along with the facility logs from Calvin's Gamma Lab from the day the crystals were stolen. I found something I didn't expect to find."

"What?"

"Do you recall that everyone, including Calvin, assumed that Judith Rockley used an unauthorized entry code to get into Gamma Lab when she stole crystals?"

"Right, they did – and then Mycroft admitted to you that he gave her access, but never imagined that she would just pull the crystals out of their jacks without first stopping the scanning process."

"Exactly. Well...the command to give Rockley access came from inside Mycroft, so to speak, but it wasn't Mycroft who actually issued it. In other words, Mycroft didn't do it, after all."

"Damn."

Acknowledgments

There's a common trope among writers that while the conventional wisdom holds to the old saw about writing as being a solitary undertaking, it's really a group endeavor, much like it takes a village to raise an idiot. Well, there's truth in both positions: ultimately the physical act of writing is reduced to a single person sitting down in front of a computer monitor, pecking away on a keyboard, putting words on the screen. At the same time, there is always a whole horde of otherwise perfectly normal people who gladly contribute to the delinquency of the idiot doing the typing, so there is at least a group input if not actual group participation. And frankly, if you put all of the people in one room who lent some sort of support to the delinquent idiot, the result would be either World War III, a revolution, mad debauchery, a major paradigm-shifting scientific breakthrough, or some combination of two or more of the aforementioned. Maybe all of them combined. So perhaps the lack of group participation isn't an entirely bad thing.

If it had actually happened, though, the results probably would not have been pretty, so just take it as given that such a process took place in a virtual sense, if not literally. To that end, suitable thanks and tips o' the topper are offered to the following individuals. Please note that in some cases full names are not given. This was done to protect the innocent, the guilty, or the authors, as the case may be.

So, without further ado or adon't....

Our genuine gratitude goes out to:

Calvin Scott Bragg, who came up with the idea for this story twenty-five years ago and had the good (or questionable) sense to not let it die....

Daniel Allen Butler, for having the questionable talent required to actually write out the story in novel form....

Now that the mutual back-patting is out of the way....

Gary Hone, who first perfected the "I'm a Little Teapot" dance. No, really, he did!

Maureen H., a true *femme-fatale* (I have the photos to prove it –D.A.B.) who has earned her nickname "Spazz" honestly....

Brian Bragg, who taught us how to reload a shotgun while shooting himself with it at the same time he was falling down a flight of stairs.... (It happened in a role-playing game, not in real life, OK?)

Trish Eachus, morale booster and budding Evil Genius, who rationed out bits of sanity as necessary....

"Speaker to Lab Animals" – the estimable Tedd Roberts – for putting up with seemingly random questions about how Scott's brain works – and convincing him that it does, after a fashion....

Leon, Jessica, Mike, Larry, John, Chris, Cathe and the rest of the 'Flies who hang about The Bar. Y'all are crazy, bizarre and surreal. For which we love you. Nerf Wars rule!

Kaerka, Kent, Hope, Dale, Dennis, and assorted friends and peers, the sounding boards who led us down 'way too many rabbit holes. We owe you so much beer that we should just invest in a brewery....

Jack, Elvis, Gonzo, Troy, Green, and others who remain nameless to protect the guilty, for connecting us with worlds unseen and unknown but all the more intensely educational and broadening for it. With them, life sometimes smells of cordite, stale beer, and powder burns on our fingers, or else ozone, stale coffee, and orange-powdered fingertips.

All the smurfs and glow-in-the-dark trainees at the Naval Training Center and Nuclear Training School in Orlando, Florida in the 1990s, who haunted the hallowed halls of the of the best gaming store in all of the southeast, the late and still deeply-lamented Enterprise 1701. The place where the magic happened, where weird and wonderful were synonymous, and where geniuses came to genius....

And finally, a very personal word of thanks from Scott to his wife, Wendi, for not only teaching him the joys of living with another auto-didact and artist, but re-awakening that same drive to learn and create in him that he thought was dead and gone. Beyond everything else that I love about you, that is the most precious gift you've given me. And you gave it by just being you. (*Blech!!! Get a room, you two!* –D.A.B.)

To all of the above, named and unnamed, please know that without your input in one way or another, *The Nemesis Crystals* could have never come to be.

In other words, it's all *your* damned fault!

Daniel Allen Butler is a best-selling author, historian, and
college-educated semi-professional beach bum. After a stint in the
United States Army and later working as a wage-slave, he became
a full-time author in 1998. When not writing, he's a woodworker,
gearhead, and model builder, noted for his love of single-malt
whisky and Honduran cigars.

Though *The Nemesis Crystals* is his first foray into fiction, he has
ten published non-fiction titles to his credit. These include such
works as *"Unsinkable"–the Full Story of RMS* Titanic; *The Day the
Lusitania Died: Eighteen Minutes that Shocked the World; Shadow of the
Sultan's Realm: the Destruction of the Ottoman Empire and the Creation
of the Modern Middle East*; and his newest, *Field Marshal–the Life and
Death of Erwin Rommel.*

His personal website can be found at www.danielallenbutler.org

C. Scott Bragg is a native of Atlanta, Georgia, who for his
whole life has had his head in the clouds. This has worked out quite
well, providing a path to a career building clouds for IT companies.
He also runs his own photography service, Dreamland Visions,
where he gets to shoot people and not worry about getting shot at
in return. If they run away, he simply uses a longer lens.

His greatest achievement is convincing his best friend Wendi to
to marry him and put up with his brand of crazy for the next few
decades.

The Nemesis Crystals is his first venture into novel-length
narrative fiction.

His personal website can be found at www.brainflogging.com

Blade
will return in

The Achilles Gambit

Available in softcover and ebook in Summer 2020

www.cogitoorbis.press